W9-AFE-600

Date Due

OCT 10 1992			

BRODART, INC.   Cat. No. 23 233   Printed in U.S.A.

SARTOR RESARTUS:

THE LIFE AND OPINIONS

OF

HERR TEUFELSDRÖCKH

———

BY

THOMAS CARLYLE

———

Mein Vermächtniß, wie herrlich weit und breit!
Die Zeit ist mein Vermächtniß, mein Acker ist die Zeit

———

CHICAGO AND NEW YORK:

RAND, McNALLY & COMPANY

PUBLISHERS

TESTIMONIES OF AUTHORS.

I. Highest Class, Bookseller's Taster.

Taster to Bookseller.—" The Author of *Teufelsdröckh* is a person of talent; his work displays here and there some felicity of thought and expression, considerable fancy and knowledge: but whether or not it would take with the public seems doubtful. For a *jeu d'esprit* of that kind, it is too long; it would have suited better as an essay or article than as a volume. The Author has no great tact: his wit is frequently heavy ; and reminds one of the German Baron who took to leaping on tables, and answered that he was learning to be lively. *Is* the work a translation ? "

Bookseller to Editor.—" Allow me to say that such a writer requires only a little more tact to produce a popular as well as an able work. Directly on receiving your permission, I sent your *MS.* to a gentleman in the highest class of men of letters, and an accomplished German scholar ; I now enclose you his opinion, which you may rely upon it, is a just one ; and I have too high an opinion of your good sense to ' &c. &c.—*MS.* (*penes nos*), *London, 17th September,* 1831.

II. Critic of the Sun.

" Fraser's Magazine exhibits the usual brilliancy, and also the " &c. " *Sartor Resartus* is what old Dennis used to call ' a heap of clotted nonsense,' mixed, however, here and there, with passages marked by thought and striking poetic vigour. But what does the writer mean by ' Baphometic fire-baptism ? ' Why cannot he lay aside his pedantry, and write so as to make himself generally intelligible ? We quote by way of curiosity a sentence from the *Sartor Resartus ;* which may be read either backwards or forwards, for it is equally intelligible either way. Indeed, by beginning at the tail, and so working up to the head, we think the reader will stand the fairest chance of getting at its meaning: ' The fire-baptised soul, long so scathed and thunder-riven, here feels its own freedom ; which feeling is its Baphometic baptism: the citadel of its whole kingdom it has thus gained by assault, and will keep inexpugnable ; outwards from which the remaining dominions, not indeed without hard battering, will doubtless by degrees be conquered and pacificated.' Here is a "—, . . ,—*Sun Newspaper 1st April,* 1834.

III. North American Reviewer.

. . . . "After a careful survey of the whole ground, our belief is that no such persons as Professor Teufelsdröckh or Counseller Heuschrecke ever existed ; that the six Paper-bags, with their China-ink inscriptions and multifarious contents, are a mere figment of the brain · that the 'present Editor' is the only person who has ever written upon the Philosophy of Clothes ; and that the *Sartor Resartus* is the only taeatise that has yet appeared upon that subject ;—in short, that the whole account of the origin of the work before us,—which the supposed Editor relates with so much gravity, and of which we have given a brief abstract, is, in plain English, a *hum.*

"Without troubling our readers at any great length with our reasons for entertaining these suspicions, we may remark, that the absence of all other information on the subject, except what is contained in the work, is itself a fact of a most significant character.   The whole German press, as well as the particular one where the work purports to have been printed, seems to be under the control of *Stillschweigen and Cognie.*, —Silence and Company. If the Clothes-Philosophy and its Author are making so great a sensation throughout Germany as is pretended, how happens it that the only notice we have of the fact is contained in a few numbers of a monthy Magazine, published at London ? How happens it that no intelligence about the matter has come out directly to this country ? We pique ourselves here in New England upon knowing at least as much of what is going on in the literary way in the old Dutch Mother-land as our brethren of the fast-anchored Isle ; but thus far we have no tidings whatever of the 'extensive close-printed close-meditated volume,' which forms the subject of this pretended commentary. Again, we would respectfully inquire of the 'present Editor' upon what part of the map of Germany are we to look for the city of *Weissnichtwo*, —'Know-not-where,' at which place the work is supposed to have been printed and the Author to have resided. It has been our fortune to visit several portions of the German territory, and to examine pretty carefully, at different times and for various purposes, maps of the whole ; but we have no recollection of any such place. We suspect that the city of *Know-not-where* might be called, with at least as much propriety, *Nobody-knows-where*, and is to be found in the kingdom of *Nowhere*. Again, the village of *Entepfuhl*,—'Duck-pond,' where the supposed Author of the work is said to have passed his youth, and that of *Hinterschlag*, where he had his education, are equally foreign to our geography.   Duck-ponds enough there undoubtedly are in almost every village in Germany, as the traveller in that country knows too well to his cost, but any particular village denominated Duck-pond is to us altogether *terra incognita.* The names of the personages are not less singu lar than those of the places. Who can refrain from a smile at the yok-ing together of such a pair of appellatives as Diogenes Teufelsdröckh ? The supposed bearer of this strange title is represented as admitting in his pretended autobiography, that 'he had searched to no purpose through all the Heralds' books in and without the German empire, and through all manner of Subscribers'-lists, Militia-rolls, and other Name-catalogues,' but had nowhere been able to find 'the name Teufels-dröckh, except as appended to his own person.' We can readily believe this, and we doubt very much whether any Christian parent would think of condemning a son to carry through life the burden of so un-pleasant a title. That of Counsellor Heuschrecke,—Grasshopper, though not offensive, looks much more like a piece of fancy-work than a 'fair business transaction.' The same may be said of *Blumine,*—Flower Goddess, the heroine of the fable, and so of the rest.

"In short, our private opinion is, as we have remarked, that the whole story of a correspondence with Germany, a university of Nobody-knows-where, a Professor of Things in General, a Counsellor Grasshop-per, a Flower-Goddess Blumine, and so forth, has about as much foun-dation in truth, as the late entertaining account of Sir John Herschel's discoveries in the moon. Fictions of this kind are, however, not un-common, and ought not, perhaps, to be condemned with too much se-verity ; but we are not sure that we can exercise the same indulgence in regard to the attempt which seems to be made to mislead the public as to the substance of the work before us, and its pretended German original. Both purport, as we have seen, to be upon the subject of Clothes, or dress. *Clothes, their Origin and Influence,* is the title of the supposed German treatise of Professor Teufelsdröckh, and the rather odd name of *Sartor Resartus,*—the Tailor Patched,—which the present Editor has affixed to his pretended commentary, seems to look the same way. But though there is a good deal of remark throughout the work in a half-serious, half-comic style upon dress, it seems to be in reality a treatise upon the great science of Things in General, which Teufels-dröckh is supposed to have professed at the university of Nobody-knows where. Now, without intending to adopt a too rigid standard of morals, we own that we doubt a little the propriety of offering to the public a treatise on Things in General, under the name and in the form of an Essay on Dress. For ourselves, advanced as we unfortunately are in the journey of life, far beyond the period when dress is practically a matter of interest, we have no hesitation in saying that the real subject of the work is to us more attractive than the ostensible one. But this is probably not the case with the mass of readers. To the younger por-tion of the community, which constitutes every where the very great majority, the subject of dress is one of intense and paramount impor-tance. An author who treats it appeals like the poet, to the young men and maidens—*virginibus puerisque,*—and calls upon them by all the motives which habitually operate most strongly upon their feelings to buy his book. When, after opening their purses for this purpose, they have carried home the work in triumph, expecting to find in it some particular instruction in regard to the tying of their neckcloths, or the cut of their corsets, and meet with nothing better than a dissertation on Things in General, they will,—to use the mildest term,—not be in very good humour. If the last improvements in legislation, which we have made in this country, should have found their way to England, the author we think would stand some chance of being *Lynched.* Whether his object in this piece of *supercherie* be merely pecuniary profit, or whether he takes a malicious pleasure in quizzing the Dandies, we shall not undertake to say. In the latter part of the work, he devotes a separate chapter to this class of persons, from the tenour of which we should be disposed to conclude that he would consider any mode of divesting them of their property very much in the nature of a spoiling of the Egyptians.

"The only thing about the work, tending to prove that it is what it purports to be, a commentary on a real German treatise, is the style, which is a sort of Babylonish dialect, not destitute, it is true, of richness, vigour, and at times a sort of singular felicity of expression, but very strongly tinged throughout with the peculiar idiom of the German language. This quality in the style, however, may be a mere result of a great familiarity with German literature, and we cannot, therefore, look upon it as in itself decisive, still less as outweighing so much evidence of an opposite character."—*North American Review, No.* 89, *October,* 1835.

IV. New-England Editors.

"The Editors have been induced, by the expressed desire of many persons, to collect the following sheets out of the ephemeral pamphlets *
in which they first appeared, under the conviction that they contain in themselves the assurance of a longer date.

"The Editors have no expectation that this little Work will have a sudden and general popularity. They will not undertake, as there is no need, to justify the gay costume in which the Author delights to dress his thoughts, or the German idioms with which he has sportively sprinkled his pages. It is his humour to advance the gravest speculations upon the gravest topics in a quaint and burlesque style. If his masquerade offend any of his audience, to that degree that they will not hear what he has to say, it may chance to draw others to listen to his wisdom ; and what work of imagination can hope to please all ? But we will venture to remark that the distaste excited by these peculiarities in some readers is greatest at first, and is soon forgotten ; and that

* " Fraser's (London) Magazine, 1833-4."

the foreign dress and aspect of the Work are quite superficial, and cover a genuine Saxon heart. We believe, no book has been published for many years, written in a more sincere style of idiomatic English, or which discovers an equal mastery over all the riches of the language. The Author makes ample amends for the occasional eccentricity of his genius, not only by frequent bursts of pure splendour, but by the wit and sense which never fail him.

" But what will chiefly commend the Book to the discerning reader is the manifest design of the work, which is, a Criticism upon the Spirit of the Age,—we had almost said, of the hour, in which we live ; exhibiting in the most just and novel light the present aspects of Religion, Politics, Literature, Arts, and Social Life. Under all his gaiety the Writer has an earnest meaning, and discovers an insight into the manifold wants and tendencies of human nature, which is very rare among our popular authors. The philanthropy and the purity of moral sentiment which inspire the work, will find their way to the heart of every lover of virtue."—*Preface to Sartor Resartus : Boston*, 1836, 1837.

SUNT, FUERUNT VEL FUERE.

London, 30*th June,* 1838.

CONTENTS.

BOOK I.

BOOK II.

BOOK III.

SARTOR RESARTUS.

BOOK I.

CHAPTER I.

PRELIMINARY.

Considering our present advanced state of culture, and how the Torch of Science has now been brandished and borne about, with more or less effect, for five thousand years and upwards ; how, in these times especially, not only the Torch still burns, and perhaps more fiercely than ever, but innumerable Rust-lights, and Sulphur-matches, kindled thereat, are also glancing in every direction, so that not the smallest cranny or doghole in Nature or Art can remain unilluminated, —it might strike the reflective mind with some surprise that hitherto little or nothing of a fundamental character, whether in the way of Philosophy or History, has been written on the subject of Clothes.

Our Theory of Gravitation is as good as perfect : Lagrange, it is well known, has proved that the Planetary System, on this scheme, will endure for ever ; Laplace, still more cunningly, even guesses that it could not have been made on any other scheme. Whereby, at least, our nautical Logbooks can be better kept ; and water-transport of all kinds has grown more commodious. Of Geology and Geognosy we know enough : what with the labours of our Werners and Huttons, what with the ardent genius of their disciples, it has come about that now, to many a Royal Society, the Creation of a World is little more mysterious than the cooking of a Dumpling ; concerning which last, indeed, there have been minds to whom the question, *How the Apples were got in* presented difficulties. Why mention our disquisitions on the Social Contract, on the Standard of Taste, on the Migrations of the Herring? Then, have we not a Doctrine of Rent, a Theory of Value; Philosophies of Language, of History, of Pottery, of Apparitions, of Intoxicating Liquors? Man's whole life and environment have been laid open and elucidated; scarcely a fragment or fibre of his Soul, Body, and Possessions, but has been probed, dissected, distilled, desiccated, and scientifically decomposed: our spiritual Faculties, of which it appears there are not a few, have their Stewarts, Cousins, Royer Collards: every cellular, vascular, muscular Tissue glories in its Lawrences, Majendies, Bichâts.

How, then, comes it, may the reflective mind repeat, that the grand Tissue of all Tissues, the only real Tissue, should have been quite overlooked by Science,—the vestural Tissue, namely, of woollen or other cloth; which Man's Soul wears as its outmost wrappage and overall; wherein his whole other Tissues are included and screened, his whole Faculties work, his whole Self lives, moves, and has its being? For if, now and then, some straggling broken-winged thinker has cast an owl's glance into this obscure region, the most have soared over it altogether heedless; regarding Clothes as a property, not an accident, as quite natural and spontaneous, like the leaves of trees, like the plumage of birds. In all speculations they have tacitly figured man as a *Clothed Animal;* whereas he is by nature a *Naked Animal;* and only in certain circumstances, by purpose and device, masks himself in Clothes. Shakspeare says, we are creatures that look before and after: the more surprising that we do not look round a little, and see what is passing under our very eyes.

But here, as in so many other cases, Germany, learned, indefatigable, deep-thinking Germany comes to our aid. It is, after all, a blessing that, in these revolutionary times there should be one country where abstract Thought can still take shelter; that while the din and frenzy of Catholic Emancipations, and Rotten Boroughs, and Revolts of Paris, deafen every French and every English ear, the German can stand peaceful on his scientific watch-tower; and, to the raging, struggling multitude here and elsewhere, solemnly, from hour to hour, with preparatory blast of cowhorn, emit his *Höret ihr Herren und lasset's Euch sagen ;* in other words, tell the Universe, which so often forgets that fact, what o'clock it really is.   Not unfrequently the Germans have been blamed for an unprofitable diligence ; as if they struck into devious courses, where nothing was to be had but the toil of a rough journey ; as if, forsaking the gold-mines of Finance, and that political slaughter of fat oxen whereby a man himself grows fat, they were apt to run goose-hunting into regions of bilberries and crowberries, and be swallowed up at last in remote peat-bogs. Of that unwise science, which, as our Humorist expresses it,

> 'By geometric scale
> Doth take the size of pots of ale ; '

still more, of that altogether misdirected industry, which is seen vigorously enough thrashing mere straw, there can nothing defensive be said.   In so far as the Germans are chargeable with such, let them take the consequence.   Nevertheless be it remarked, that even a Russian steppe has tumuli and gold ornaments ; also many a scene that looks desert and rock-bound from the distance, will unfold itself, when visited, into rare valleys.   Nay, in any case, would Criticism erect not only finger-posts and turnpikes, but spiked gates and impassible barriers, for the mind of man?   It is written, 'Many shall run to and fro, and knowledge shall be increased.' Surely the plain rule is, Let each considerate person have his way, and see what it will lead to.   For not this man and that man, but all men make up mankind, and their united tasks the task of mankind.   How often have we seen some such adventurous, and perhaps much-censured wanderer light on some outlying, neglected, yet vitally momentous province ; the hidden treasures of which he first discovered, and kept proclaiming till the general eye and effort were directed thither, and the conquest was completed ;—thereby, in these his seemingly so aimless rambles, planting new standards, founding new habitable colonies, in the immeasurable circumambient realm of Nothingness and Night?   Wise man

was he who counselled that Speculation should have free
course, and look fearlessly towards all the thirty-two points
of the compass, whithersoever and howsoever it listed.

Perhaps it is proof of the stinted condition in which pure
Science, especially pure moral Science, languishes among us
English ; and how our mercantile greatness, and invaluable
Constitution, impressing a political or other immediately practical tendency on all English culture and endeavour, cramps
the free flight of Thought,—that this, not Philosophy of
Clothes, but recognition even that we have no such Philosophy, stands here for the first time published in our language.
What English intellect could have chosen such a topic, or by
chance stumbled on it ? But for that same unshackled, and
even sequestered condition of the German Learned, which
permits and induces them to fish in all manner of waters,
with all manner of nets, it seems probable enough, this ab-
struse Inquiry might, in spite of the results it leads to, have
continued dormant for indefinite periods. The Editor of
these sheets, though otherwise boasting himself a man of
confirmed speculative habits, and perhaps discursive enough, is
free to confess, that never, till these last months, did the
above very plain considerations, on our total want of a Philosophy of Clothes, occur to him ; and then, by quite foreign
suggestion. By the arrival, namely, of a new Book from Professor Teufelsdröckh of Weissnichtwo ; treating expressly of
this subject ; and in a style which, whether understood or
not, could not even by the blindest be overlooked. In the
present Editor's way of thought, this remarkable Treatise,
with its Doctrines, whether as judicially acceded to, or judicially denied, has not remained without effect.

' *Die Kleider, ihr Werden und Wirken* (Clothes, their Origin
'and Influence) : *von Diog. Teufelsdröckh, J. U. D. etc. Still-*
' *schweigen und Co$^{gnie.}$ Weissnichtwo,* 1831.

' Here,' says the *Weissnichtwo'sche Anzeiger,* ' comes a Vol-
' ume of that extensive, close-printed, close-meditated sort,
' which be it spoken with pride, is seen only in Germany,
' perhaps only in Weissnichtwo. Issuing from the hitherto
' irreproachable Firm of Stillschweigen and Company, with

'every external furtherance, it is of such internal quality as
' to set Neglect at defiance.' * * * * 'A work,' concludes
the well nigh enthusiastic Reviewer, 'interesting alike to the
' antiquary, the historian, and the philosophic thinker ; a mas-
' terpiece of boldness, lynx-eyed acuteness, and rugged inde-
' pendent Germanism and Philanthropy (*derben Kerndeutsch-*
' *heit und Menschenliebe*) ; which will not, assuredly, pass
' current without opposition in high places ; but must and
' will exalt the almost new name of Teufelsdröckh to the first
' rank of Philosophy, in our German Temple of Honour.'

Mindful of old friendship, the distinguished Professor, in
this the first blaze of his fame, which however does not dazzle
him, sends hither a Presentation-copy of his Book ; with compliments and encomiums which modesty forbids the present
Editor to rehearse ; yet without indicated wish or hope of
any kind, except what may be implied in the concluding
phrase : *Möchte es* (this remarkable Treatise) *auch im Brittis-
chen Boden gedeihen !*

CHAPTER II.

EDITORIAL DIFFICULTIES.

If for a speculative man, 'whose seedfield,' in the sublime
words of the Poet, 'is Time,' no conquest is important but
that of new ideas, then might the arrival of Professor Teufelsdröckh's Book be marked with chalk in the Editor's calendar.
It is indeed an 'extensive Volume,' of boundless, almost formless contents, a very Sea of thought ; neither calm nor clear,
if you will ; yet wherein the toughest pearl-diver may dive
to his utmost depth, and return not only with sea-wreck but
with true orients.

Directly on the first perusal, almost on the first deliberate
inspection, it became apparent that here a quite new Branch
of Philosophy, leading to as yet undescried ulterior results,
was disclosed ; farther, what seemed scarcely less interesting,
a quite new human Individuality, an almost unexampled personal character, that, namely, of Professor Teufelsdröckh the
Discloser. Of both which novelties, as far as might be pos-

sible, we resolved to master the significance. But as man is emphatically a Proselytising creature, no sooner was such mastery even fairly attempted, than the new question arose : How might this acquired good be imparted to others, perhaps in equal need thereof ; how could the Philosophy of Clothes, and the Author of such Philosophy, be brought home, in any measure, to the business and bosoms of our own English nation ? For if new-got gold is said to burn the pockets till it be cast forth into circulation, much more may new Truth.

Here, however, difficulties occurred. The first thought naturally was to publish Article after Article on this remarkable Volume, in such widely-circulating Critical Journals as the Editor might stand connected with, or by money or love procure access to. But, on the other hand, was it not clear that such matter as must here be revealed and treated of might endanger the Circulation of any Journal extant ? If, indeed, the whole parties of the State could have been abolished, Whig, Tory, and Radical, embracing in discrepant union ; and the whole Journals of the Nation could have been jumbled into one Journal, and the Philosophy of Clothes poured forth in incessant torrents therefrom, the attempt had seemed possible. But, alas, what vehicle of that sort have we, except *Fraser's Magazine?* A vehicle all strewed (figuratively speaking) with the maddest Waterloo-Crackers, exploding distractively and destructively, wheresoever the mystified passenger stands or sits ; nay, in any case, understood to be, of late years, a vehicle full to overflowing, and inexorably shut ! Besides, to state the Philosophy of Clothes without the Philosopher, the ideas of Teufelsdröckh without something of his personality, was it not to insure both of entire misapprehension? Now for Biography, had it been otherwise admissible, there were no adequate documents, no hope of obtaining such, but rather, owing to circumstances, a special despair. Thus did the Editor see himself, for the while, shut out from all public utterance of these extraordinary Doctrines, and constrained to revolve them, not without disquietude, in the dark depths of his own mind.

So had it lasted for some months ; and now the Volume on Clothes, read and again read, was in several points becoming lucid and lucent ; the personality of its Author more and more surprising, but, in spite of all that memory and conjecture could do, more and more enigmatic ; whereby the old disquietude seemed fast settling into fixed discontent,—when altogether unexpectedly arrives a Letter from Herr Hofrath Heuschrecke, our Professor's chief friend and associate in Weissnichtwo, with whom we had not previously corresponded. The Hofrath, after much quite extraneous matter, began dilating largely on the ' agitation and attention ' which the Philosophy of Clothes was exciting in its own German Republic of Letters ; on the deep significance and tendency of his Friend's Volume ; and then, at length, with great circumlocution, hinted at the practicability of conveying ' some knowledge of it, and of him, to England, and through England to the distant West : ' a Work on Professor Teufelsdröckh ' were undoubtedly welcome to the *Family,* the *National,* or any other of those patriotic *Libraries,* at present ' the glory of British Literature ; ' might work revolutions in Thought ; and so forth ;—in conclusion, intimating not obscurely, that should the present Editor feel disposed to undertake a Biography of Teufelsdröckh, he, Hofrath Heuschrecke, had it in his power to furnish the requisite Documents.

As in some chemical mixture, that has stood long evaporating, but would not crystallise, instantly when the wire or other fixed substance is introduced, crystallisation commences, and rapidly proceeds till the whole is finished, so was it with the Editor's mind and this offer of Heuschrecke's. Form rose out of void solution and discontinuity ; like united itself with like in definite arrangement : and soon either in actual vision and possession, or in fixed reasonable hope, the image of the whole Enterprise had shaped itself, so to speak, into a solid mass. Cautiously yet courageously, through the twopenny post, application to the famed redoubtable OLIVER YORKE was now made : an interview, interviews with that singular man have taken place ; with more of assurance on our side, with less of satire (at least of open satire) on his, than we anticipated ;—for the rest, with such issue as is now visible. As to these same 'patriotic *Libraries*,' the Hofrath's counsel could only be viewed with silent amazement ; but with his offer of Documents we joyfully and almost instantaneously closed. Thus, too, in the sure expectation of these, we already see our task begun ; and this our *Sartor Resartus*, which is properly a 'Life and Opinions of Herr Teufelsdröckh,' hourly advancing.

Of our fitness for the Enterprise, to which we have such title and vocation, it were perhaps uninteresting to say more. Let the British reader study and enjoy, in simplicity of heart, what is here presented him, and with whatever metaphysical acumen, and talent for Meditation he is possessed of. Let him strive to keep a free, open sense ; cleared from the mists of Prejudice, above all from the paralysis of Cant ; and directed rather to the Book itself than to the Editor of the Book. Who or what such Editor may be, must remain conjectural, and even insignificant : * it is a voice publishing tidings of the Philosophy of Clothes ; undoubtedly a Spirit addressing Spirits : whoso hath ears let him hear.

On one other point the Editor thinks it needful to give warning : namely, that he is animated with a true though perhaps a feeble attachment to the Institutions of our Ancestors ; and minded to defend these, according to ability, at all hazards ; nay, it was partly with a view to such defence that he engaged in this undertaking. To stem, or if that be impossible, profitably to divert the current of Innovation, such a Volume as Teufelsdröckh's, if cunningly planted down, were no despicable pile, or floodgate, in the Logical wear.

For the rest, be it no wise apprehended, that any personal connexion of ours with Teufelsdröckh, Heuschrecke, or this Philosophy of Clothes, can pervert our judgment, or sway us to extenuate or exaggerate. Powerless, we venture to promise, are those private Compliments themselves. Grateful they may well be ; as generous illusions of friendship ; as fair me-

* With us even he still communicates in some sort of mask, or muffler, and, we have reason to think, under a feigned name !—O. Y.

mentos of bygone unions, of those nights and suppers of the Gods, when lapped in the symphonies and harmonies of Philosophic Eloquence, though with baser accompaniments, the present Editor revelled in that feast of reason, never since vouchsafed him in so full measure ! But what then ? *Amicus Plato, magis amica veritas;* Teufelsdröckh is our friend, Truth is our divinity. In our historical and critical capacity, we hope we are strangers to all the world ; have feud or favour with no one,—save indeed the Devil, with whom, as with the Prince of Lies and Darkness, we do at all times wage inter-necine war. This assurance, at an epoch when Puffery and Quackery have reached a height unexampled in the annals of mankind, and even English Editors, like Chinese Shopkeepers, must write on their door-lintels, *No cheating here,*—we thought it good to premise.

CHAPTER III.

REMINISCENCES.

To the Author's private circle the appearance of this singu-lar Work on Clothes must have occasioned little less surprise than it has to the rest of the world. For ourselves, at least, few things have been more unexpected. Professor Teufels-dröckh, at the period of our acquaintance with him, seemed to lead a quite still and self-contained life : a man devoted to the higher Philosophies, indeed ; yet more likely, if he pub-lished at all, to publish a Refutation of Hegel and Bardili, both of whom, strangely enough, he included under a common ban ; than to descend, as he has here done, into the angry noisy Forum, with an Argument that cannot but exasperate and divide. Not, that we can remember, was the Philosophy of Clothes once touched upon between us. If through the high, silent, meditative Transcendentalism of our Friend we detected any practical tendency whatever, it was at most Po-litical, and towards a certain prospective, and for the present quite speculative, Radicalism ; as indeed some correspondence, on his part, with Herr Oken of Jena was now and then suspected ; though his special contributions to the *Isis* could never be more than surmised at. But, at all events, nothing Moral, still less any thing Didactico-Religious, was looked for from him.

Well do we recollect the last words he spoke in our hearing; which indeed, with the Night they were uttered in, are to be for ever remembered. Lifting his huge tumbler of *Gukguk,** and for a moment lowering his tobacco-pipe, he stood up in full coffee-house (it was *Zum Grünen Ganse,* the largest in Weissnichtwo, where all the Virtuosity, and nearly all the Intellect, of the place assembled of an evening) ; and there, with low, soul-stirring tone, and the look truly of an angel, though whether of a white or of a black one might be dubious, proposed this toast : *Die Sache der Armen in Gottes und Teufels Namen* (The Cause of the Poor in Heaven's name and ——'s) ! One full shout, breaking the leaden silence ; then a gurgle of innumerable emptying bumpers, again followed by universal cheering, returned him loud acclaim. It was the finale of the night : resuming their pipes ; in the highest enthusiasm, amid volumes of tobacco-smoke ; triumphant, cloud-capt without and within, the assembly broke up, each to his thoughtful pillow. *Bleibt doch ein echter Spass-und Galgenvogel,* said several ; meaning thereby that, one day, he would probably be hanged for his democratic sentiments. *Wo steckt der Schalk ?* added they, looking round : but Teufelsdröckh had retired by private alleys, and the Compiler of these pages beheld him no more.

In such scenes has it been our lot to live with this Philosopher, such estimate to form of his purposes and powers. And yet, thou brave Teufelsdröckh, who could tell what lurked in thee? Under those thick locks of thine, so long and lank, overlapping roof-wise the gravest face we ever in this world saw, there dwelt a most busy brain. In thy eyes too, deep under their shaggy brows, and looking out so still and dreamy, have we not noticed gleams of an ethereal or else a diabolic fire, and half fancied that their stillness was but the rest of infinite motion, the *sleep* of a spinning top ? Thy

* Gukguk is unhappily only an academical—beer.

little figure, there as, in loose, ill-brushed, threadbare habiliments, thou sattest, amid litter and lumber, whole days, to
'think and smoke tobacco,' held in it a mighty heart. The
secrets of man's Life were laid open to thee ; thou sawest into
the mystery of the Universe, farther than another ; thou hadst
in petto thy remarkable Volume on Clothes. Nay, was there
not in that clear logically-founded Transcendentalism of
thine ; still more, in thy meek, silent, deepseated Sansculottism, combined with a true princely Courtesy of inward nature, the visible rudiments of such speculation ? But great
men are too often unknown, or what is worse, misknown.
Already, when we dreamed not of it, the warp of thy remarkable Volume lay on the loom ; and silently, mysterious shut-
tles were putting in the woof!

How the Hofrath Heuschrecke is to furnish biographical
data in this case, may be a curious question ; the answer of
which, however, is happily not our concern, but his. To us
it appeared, after repeated trial, that in Weissnichtwo, from
the archives or memories of the best-informed classes, no
Biography of Teufelsdröckh was to be gathered ; not so much
as a false one. He was a Stranger there, wafted thither by
what is called the course of circumstances ; concerning whose
parentage, birth-place, prospects, or pursuits, Curiosity had
indeed made inquiries, but satisfied herself with the most in-
distinct replies. For himself, he was a man so still and altogether unparticipating, that to question him even afar off on
such particulars was a thing of more than usual delicacy : besides, in his sly way, he had ever some quaint turn, not without
its satirical edge, wherewith to divert such intrusions, and deter
you from the like. Wits spoke of him secretly as if he were
a kind of Melchizedek, without father or mother of any kind ;
sometimes, with reference to his great historic and statistic
knowledge, and the vivid way he had of expressing himself
like an eye-witness of distant transactions and scenes, they
called him the *Ewige Jude*, Everlasting, or as we say, Wandering Jew.

To the most, indeed, he had become not so much a Man as
a Thing ; which Thing doubtless they were accustomed to

see, and with satisfaction ; but no more thought of accounting for than for the fabrication of their daily *Allgemeine Zeitung*, or the domestic habits of the Sun. Both were there and welcome ; the world enjoyed what good was in them, and thought no more of the matter. The man Teufelsdröckh passed and repassed, in his little circle, as one of those originals and nondescripts, more frequent in German Universities than elsewhere ; of whom, though you see them alive, and feel certain enough that they must have a History, no History seems to be discoverable ; or only such as men give of mountain rocks and antediluvian ruins : That they have been created by unknown agencies, are in a state of gradual decay, and for the present reflect light and resist pressure ; that is, are visible and tangible objects in this phantasm world, where so much other mystery is.

It was to be remarked that though, by title and diploma, *Professor der Allerley-Wissenschaft*, or as we should say in English, 'Professor of Things in General,' he had never delivered any Course ; perhaps never been incited thereto by any public furtherance or requisition. To all appearance, the enlightened Government of Weissnichtwo, in founding their New University, imagined they had done enough, if 'in times like ours,' as the half-official Program expressed it, 'when all 'things are, rapidly or slowly, resolving themselves into 'Chaos, a Professorship of this kind had been established ; 'whereby, as occasion called, the task of bodying somewhat 'forth again from such Chaos might be, even slightly, facili-'tated.' That actual Lectures should be held, and Public Classes for the 'Science of Things in General,' they doubtless considered premature ; on which ground too they had only established the Professorship, nowise endowed it; so that Teufelsdröckh, 'recommended by the highest Names,' had been promoted thereby to a Name merely.

Great, among the more enlightened classes, was the admiration of this new Professorship : how an enlightened Government had seen into the Want of the Age (*Zeitbedürfniss*) ; how at length, instead of Denial and Destruction, we were to have a science of Affirmation and Reconstruction ; and Germany and Weissnichtwo were where they should be, in the vanguard of the world. Considerable also was the wonder at the new Professor, dropt opportunely enough into the nascent University ; so able to lecture, should occasion call ; so ready to hold his peace for indefinite periods, should an enlightened Government consider that occasion did not call. But such admiration and such wonder, being followed by no act to keep them living, could last only nine days ; and long before our visit to that scene, had quite died away. The more cunning heads thought it was all an expiring clutch at popularity, on the part of a Minister, whom domestic embarrassments, court intrigues, old age, and dropsy soon afterwards finally drove from the helm.

As for Teufelsdröckh, except by his nightly appearances at the *Grünen Ganse*, Weissnichtwo saw little of him, felt little of him. Here, over his tumbler of Gukguk, he sat reading Journals ; sometimes contemplatively looking into the clouds of his tobacco-pipe, without other visible employment: always, from his mild ways, an agreeable phenomenon there ; more especially when he opened his lips for speech ; on which occasions the whole Coffee-house would hush itself into silence, as if sure to hear something noteworthy. Nay, perhaps to hear a whole series and river of the most memorable utterances ; such as, when once thawed, he would for hours indulge in, with fit audience : and the more memorable, as issuing from a head apparently not more interested in them, not more conscious of them, than is the sculptured stone head of some public Fountain, which through its brass mouth-tube emits water to the worthy and the unworthy ; careless whether it be for cooking victuals or quenching conflagrations ; indeed maintains the same earnest assiduous look, whether any water be flowing or not.

To the Editor of these sheets, as to a young enthusiastic Englishman, however unworthy, Teufelsdröckh opened himself perhaps more than to the most. Pity only that we could not then half guess his importance, and scrutinise him with due power of vision ! We enjoyed, what not three men in Weissnichtwo could boast of, a certain degree of access to the

Professor's private domicile. It was the attic floor of the highest house in the Wahngasse; and might truly be called the
pinnacle of Weissnichtwo, for it rose sheer up above the contiguous roofs, themselves rising from elevated ground. Moreover, with its windows, it looked towards all the four *Orte*, or
as the Scotch say, and we ought to say, *Airts*: the Sitting-
room itself commanded three; another came to view in the
Schlafgemach (Bed-room) at the opposite end; to say nothing
of the Kitchen, which offered two, as it were *duplicates*, and
shewing nothing new. So that it was in fact the speculum or
watch-tower of Teufelsdröckh; wherefrom, sitting at ease, he
might see the whole life-circulation of that considerable City;
the streets and lanes of which, with all their doing and driving (*Thun und Treiben*), were for the most part visible there.

"I look down into all that wasp-nest or bee-hive," have we
heard him say, "and witness their wax-laying and honey-mak-
"ing, and poison-brewing, and choking by sulphur. From
"the Palace esplanade, where music plays while Serene High-
"ness is pleased to eat his victuals, down the low lane, where
'in her door-sill the aged widow, knitting for a thin liveli-
"hood, sits to feel the afternoon sun, I see it all; for, except
"the Schlosskirche weathercock, no biped stands so high.
"Couriers arrive bestrapped and bebooted, bearing Joy and
"Sorrow bagged up in pouches of leather; there, topladen,
"and with four swift horses, rolls in the country Baron and
"his household; here, on timber leg, the lamed Soldier hops
"painfully along, begging alms: a thousand carriages, and
"wains, and cars, come tumbling in with Food, with young
"Rusticity, and other Raw Produce, inanimate or animate,
"and go tumbling out again with Produce manufactured.
"That living flood, pouring through these streets, of all quali-
"ties and ages, knowest thou whence it is coming, whither it
"is going? *Aus der Ewigkeit, zu der Ewigkeit hin:* From Eter-
"nity, onwards to Eternity! These are Apparitions: what
"else? Are they not Souls rendered visible; in Bodies, that
"took shape and will lose it, melting into air? Their solid
"pavement is a Picture of the Sense; they walk on the bosom
"of Nothing, blank Time is behind them and before them.

" Or fanciest thou, the red and yellow Clothes-screen yonder,
" with spurs on its heels, and feather in its crown, is but of
" To-day, without a Yesterday or a To-morrow ; and had not
" rather its Ancestor alive when Hengst and Horsa overran
" thy Island ? Friend, thou seest here a living link in that
" Tissue of History, which inweaves all Being : watch well, or
" it will be past thee, and seen no more."

" *Ach, mein Lieber !* " said he once, at midnight, when he
had returned from the Coffee-house in rather earnest talk, " it
" it a true sublimity to dwell here. These fringes of lamp-
" light, struggling up through smoke and thousand-fold ex-
" halation, some fathoms into the ancient reign of Night, what
" thinks Boötes of them, as he leads his Hunting Dogs over the
" Zenith, in their leash of sidereal fire ? That stifled hum of
" Midnight, when Traffic has lain down to rest ; and the
" chariot-wheels of Vanity, still rolling here and there through
" distant streets, are bearing her to Halls roofed in, and lighted
" to the due pitch for her ; and only Vice and Misery, to prowl
" or to moan like nightbirds, are abroad ; that hum, I say, like
" the stertorous, unquiet slumber of sick Life, is heard in
" Heaven ! Oh, under that hideous coverlet of vapours, and
" putrefactions, and unimaginable gases, what a Fermenting-
" vat lies simmering and hid ! The joyful and the sorrowful
" are there ; men are dying there, men are being born, men are
" praying,—on the other side of a brick partition, men are curs-
" ing ; and around them all is the vast, void Night. The proud
" Grandee still lingers in his perfumed saloons, or reposes
" within damask curtains ; Wretchedness cowers into truckle-
" beds, or shivers hunger-stricken into its lair of straw : in ob-
" scure cellars, *Rouge-et-Noir* languidly emits its voice-of-des-
" tiny to haggard hungry Villains ; while Councillors of State
" sit plotting, and playing their high chess-game, whereof the
" pawns are Men. The Lover whispers his mistress that the
" coach is ready ; and she, full of hope and fear glides down,
" to fly with him over the borders : the Thief, still more silent-
" ly, sets to his picklocks and crowbars, or lurks in wait till
" the watchmen first snore in their boxes. Gay mansions,
" with supper-rooms, and dancing-rooms, are full of light and

" music and high-swelling hearts ; but in the Condemned
" Cells, the pulse of life beats tremulous and faint, and blood-
" shot eyes look out through the darkness, which is around and
" within, for the light of a stern last morning. Six men are
" to be hanged on the morrow : comes no hammering from
" the *Rabenstein?*—their gallows must even now be o'building.
" Upwards of five hundred thousand two-legged animals
" without feathers lie round us, in horizontal position ; their
" heads all in nightcaps, and full of the foolishest dreams.
" Riot cries aloud, and staggers and swaggers in his rank dens
" of shame ; and the Mother, with streaming hair, kneels over
" her pallid dying infant, whose cracked lips only her tears now
" moisten.—All these heaped and huddled together, with
" nothing but a little carpentry and masonry between them :
" —crammed in, like salted fish, in their barrel ;—or welter
" ing, shall I say, like an Egyptian pitcher of tamed Vipers,
" each struggling to get its *head above* the other : *such* work
" goes on under that smoke-counterpane !—But I, *mein Wer-*
" *ther*, sit above it all ; I am alone with the Stars."

We looked in his face to see whether, in the utterance of
such extraordinary Night-thoughts, no feeling might be traced
there ; but with the light we had, which indeed was only a
single tallow-light, and far enough from the window, nothing
save that old calmness and fixedness was visible.

These were the Professor's talking seasons : most commonly
he spoke in mere monosyllables, or sat altogether silent and
smoked : while the visitor had liberty either to say what he
listed, receiving for answer an occasional grunt ; or to look
round for a space, and then take himself away. It was a
strange apartment ; full of books and tattered papers, and
miscellaneous shreds of all conceivable substances, ' united in
a common element of dust.' Books lay on tables, and below
tables ; here fluttered a sheet of manuscript, there a torn hand-
kerchief, or nightcap hastily thrown aside ; ink-bottles alter-
nated with bread-crusts, coffee-pots, tobacco-boxes, Periodical
Literature, and Blücher Boots. Old Leischen (Lisekin, 'Liza),
who was his bed-maker and stove-lighter, his washer and
wringer, cook, errand-maid, and general lion's-provider, and

for the rest a very orderly creature, had no sovereign authority in this last citadel of Teufelsdröckh ; only some once in
the month, she half-forcibly made her way thither, with broom
and duster, and (Teufelsdröckh hastily saving his manuscripts)
effected a partial clearance, a jail-delivery of such lumber as
was not Literary. These were her *Erdbebungen* (Earthquakes),
which Teufelsdröckh dreaded worse than the pestilence ; nevertheless, to such length he had been forced to comply. Glad
would he have been to sit here philosophising for ever, or till
the litter, by accumulation, drove him out of doors: but Leischen was his right-arm, and spoon, and necessary of life, and
would not be flatly gainsayed. We can still remember the
ancient woman : so silent that some thought her dumb ; deaf
also you would often have supposed her ; for Teufelsdröckh
and Teufelsdröckh only would she serve or give heed to ; and
with him she seemed to communicate chiefly by signs ; if it
were not rather by some secret divination that she guessed all
his wants, and supplied them. Assiduous old dame ! she
scoured, and sorted, and swept, in her kitchen, with the least
possible violence to the ear ; yet all was tight and right there:
hot and black came the coffee ever at the due moment ; and
the speechless Leischen herself looked out on you, from under
her clean white coif with its lappets, through her clean withered face and wrinkles, with a look of helpful intelligence,
almost of benevolence.

Few strangers, as above hinted, had admittance hither : the
only one we ever saw there, ourselves excepted, was the Hofrath Heuschrecke, already known, by name and expectation,
to the readers of these pages. To us, at that period, Herr
Heuschrecke seemed one of those purse-mouthed, crane-
necked, clean-brushed pacific individuals, perhaps sufficiently
distinguished in society by this fact, that, in dry weather or
in wet, 'they never appear without their umbrella.' Had we
not known with what 'little wisdom' the world is governed ;
and how, in Germany as elsewhere, the ninety and nine Public Men can for most part be but mute train-bearers to the
hundredth, perhaps but stalking-horses and willing or unwil-
ling dupes,—it might have seemed wonderful how Herr

Heuschrecke should be named a *Rath*, or Councillor, and
Counsellor, even in Weissnichtwo.   What counsel to any man,
or to any woman, could this particular Hofrath give ; in
whose loose, zigzag figure ; in whose thin visage, as it went
jerking to and fro, in minute incessant fluctuation,—you
traced rather confusion worse confounded ; at most, Timidity
and physical Cold?   Some indeed said withal, he was 'the
very Spirit of Love embodied ;' blue earnest eyes, full of sadness and kindness ; purse ever open, and so forth ; the whole
of which, we shall now hope for many reasons, was not quite
groundless.   Nevertheless friend Teufelsdröckh's outline,
who indeed handled the burin like few in these cases, was
probably the best : *Er hat Gemüth und Geist, hat wenigstens
gehabt, doch ohne Organ, ohne Schicksals-gunst ; ist gegenwär-
tig aber halb-zerrüttet, halb-erstarrt,* " He has heart and talent,
" at least has had such, yet without fit mode of utterance, or
" favour of Fortune ; and so is now half-cracked, half-con-
" gealed."—What the Hofrath shall think of this when he sees
it, readers may wonder : we, safe in the stronghold of Historical Fidelity, are careless.

The main point, doubtless, for us all, is his love of Teufelsdröckh, which indeed was also by far the most decisive feature of Heuschrecke himself.   We are enabled to assert that
he hung on the Professor with the fondness of a Boswell for
his Johnson.   And perhaps with the like return ; for Teufelsdröckh treated his gaunt admirer with little outward regard,
as some half-rational or altogether irrational friend, and at
best loved him out of gratitude and by habit.   On the other
hand, it was curious to observe with what reverent kindness,
and a sort of fatherly protection, our Hofrath, being the
elder, richer, and as he fondly imagined far more practically
influential of the two, looked and tended on his little Sage,
whom he seemed to consider as a living oracle.   Let but
Teufelsdröckh open his mouth, Heuschrecke's also unpuckered
itself into a free doorway, besides his being all eye and all
ear, so that nothing might be lost : and then, at every pause
in the harangue, he gurgled out his pursy chuckle of a
cough-laugh (for the machinery of laughter took some time

to get in motion, and seemed crank and slack), or else his twanging nasal *Bravo! Das glaub' ich ;* in either case, by way of heartiest approval. In short, if Teufelsdröckh was Dalai-Lama, of which, except perhaps in his self-seclusion, and god-like Indifference, there was no symptom, then might Heuschrecke pass for his chief Talapoin, to whom no dough-pill he could knead and publish was other than medicinal and sacred.

In such environment, social, domestic, and physical, did Teufelsdröckh, at the time of our acquaintance, and most likely does he still, live and meditate. Here, perched up in his high Wahngasse watch-tower, and often, in solitude, outwatching the Bear, it was that the indomitable Inquirer fought all his battles with Dulness and Darkness ; here, in all probability, that he wrote this surprising Volume on *Clothes.* Additional particulars : of his age, which was of that standing middle sort you could only guess at ; of his wide surtout ; the colour of his trousers, fashion of his broad-brimmed steeple-hat, and so forth, we might report, but do not. The Wisest truly is, in these times, the Greatest ; so that an enlightened curiosity, leaving Kings and such like to rest very much on their own basis, turns more and more to the Philosophic Class : nevertheless, what reader expects that, with all our writing and reporting Teufelsdröckh could be brought home to him, till once the Documents arrive ? His Life, Fortunes, and Bodily Presence, are as yet hidden from us, or matter only of faint conjecture. But, on the other hand, does not his Soul lie enclosed in this remarkable Volume, much more truly than Pedro Garcia's did in the buried Bag of Doubloons? To the soul of Diogenes Teufelsdröckh, to his opinions, namely, on the 'Origin and Influence of Clothes,' we for the present gladly return.

CHAPTER IV.

CHARACTERISTICS.

It were a piece of vain flattery to pretend that this Work on Clothes entirely contents us; that it is not, like all works of Genius, like the very Sun, which, though the highest published Creation, or work of Genius, has nevertheless black spots and troubled nebulosities amid its effulgence,—a mixture of insight, inspiration, with dulness, double-vision, and even utter blindness.

Without committing ourselves to those enthusiastic praises and prophesying of the *Weissnichtwo'sche Anzeiger*, we admitted that the Book had in a high degree excited us to self-activity, which is the best effect of any book; that it had even operated changes in our way of thought; nay, that it promised to prove, as it were, the opening of a new mine-shaft, wherein the whole world of Speculation might henceforth dig to unknown depths. More specially it may now be declared that Professor Teufelsdröckh's acquirements, patience of research, philosophic and even poetic vigour, are here made indisputably manifest; and unhappily no less his prolixity and tortuosity and manifold ineptitude; that, on the whole, as in opening new mine-shafts is not unreasonable, there is much rubbish in his Book, though likewise specimens of almost invaluable ore. A paramount popularity in England we cannot promise him. Apart from the choice of such a topic as Clothes, too often the manner of treating it betokens in the Author a rusticity and academic seclusion, unblamable, indeed inevitable in a German, but fatal to his success with our public.

Of good society Teufelsdröckh appears to have seen little, or has mostly forgotten what he saw. He speaks out with a strange plainness; calls many things by their mere dictionary-names. To him the Upholsterer is no Pontiff, neither is any Drawing room a Temple, were it never so begilt and overhung: 'a whole immensity of Brussels carpets, and pier 'glasses, and or-moulu,' as he himself expresses it, 'cannot 'hide from me that such Drawing room is simply a section of 'Infinite Space, where so many God-created Souls do for the 'time meet together.' To Teufelsdröckh the highest Duchess is respectable, is venerable ; but nowise for her pearl bracelets, and Malines laces : in his eyes, the star of a Lord is little less and little more than the broad button of Birmingham spelter in a Clown's smock ; 'each is an implement,' he says, 'in its 'kind ; a tag for *hooking-together;* and, for the rest, was dug 'from the earth, and hammered on a stithy before smith's 'fingers.' Thus does the Professor look in men's faces with a strange impartiality, a strange scientific freedom ; like a man unversed in the higher circles, like a man dropped thither from the Moon. Rightly considered, it is in this peculiarity, running through his whole system of thought, that all these short-comings, over-shootings, and multiform perversities, take rise : if indeed they have not a second source, also natural enough, in his Transcendental Philosophies, and humour of looking at all Matter and Material things as Spirit ; whereby truly his case were but the more hopeless, the more lamentable.

To the Thinkers of this nation, however, of which class it is firmly believed there are individuals yet extant, we can safely recommend the Work : nay, who knows but among the fashionable ranks too, if it be true, as Teufelsdröckh maintains, that 'within the most starched cravat there passes a 'windpipe and weasand, and under the thickliest embroidered 'waistcoat beats a heart,'—the force of that rapt earnestness may be felt, and here and there an arrow of the soul pierce through. In our wild Seer, shaggy, unkempt, like a Baptist living on locusts and wild honey, there is an untutored energy, a silent, as it were unconscious, strength, which, except in the higher walks of Literature, must be rare. Many a deep glance, and often with unspeakable precision, has he cast into mysterious Nature, and the still more mysterious Life of Man. Wonderful it is with what cutting words, now and then, he severs asunder the confusion ; sheers down, were it furlongs deep, into the true centre of the matter ; and there not only hits the nail on the head, but with crushing force smites it home, and buries it.—On the other hand, let us be free to admit, he is the most unequal writer breathing. Often after some such feat, he will play truant for long pages, and go dawdling and dreaming, and mumbling and maundering the merest commonplaces, as if he were asleep with eyes open, which indeed he is.

Of his boundless Learning, and how all reading and literature in most known tongues, from *Sanchoniathon* to *Dr. Lingard*, from your Oriental *Shasters*, and *Talmuds*, and *Korans*, with Cassini's *Siamese Tables*, and Laplace's *Mécanique Céleste* down to *Robinson Crusoe* and the *Belfast Town and Country Almanack*, are familiar to him,—we shall say nothing : for unexampled as it is with us, to the Germans such universality of study passes without wonder, as a thing commendable, indeed, but natural, indispensable, and there of course. A man that devotes his life to learning, shall he not be learned ?

In respect of style our Author manifests the same genial capability, marred too often by the same rudeness, inequality, and apparent want of intercourse with the higher classes. Occasionally, as above hinted, we find consummate vigor, a true inspiration ; his burning Thoughts step forth in fit burning Words, like so many full formed Minervas, issuing amid flame and splendor from Jove's head ; a rich, idiomatic diction, picturesque allusions, fiery poetic emphasis, or quaint tricksy turns ; all the graces and terrors of a wild Imagination, wedded to the clearest Intellect, alternate in beautiful vicissitude. Were it not that sheer sleeping and soporific passages ; circumlocutions, repetitions, touches even of pure doting jargon, so often intervene ! On the whole, Professor Teufelsdröckh is not a cultivated writer. Of his sentences perhaps not more than nine-tenths stand straight on their legs ; the remainder are in quite angular attitudes, buttressed up by props (of parentheses and dashes), and ever with this or the other tagrag hanging from them ; a few even sprawl out helplessly on all sides, quite broken-back and dismembered. Nevertheless, in almost his very worst moods, there lies in him a singular attraction. A wild tone pervades the whole utterance of the man, like his keynote and regulator; now screwing itself aloft as into the Song of Spirits, or else the shrill mockery of Fiends ; now sinking in cadences, not without melodious heartiness, though sometimes abrupt enough, into the common pitch, when we hear it only as a monotonous hum ; of which hum the true character is extremely difficult to fix. Up to this hour we have never fully satisfied ourselves whether it is a tone and hum of real Humour, which we reckon among the very highest qualities of genius, or some echo of mere Insanity and Inanity, which doubtless ranks below the very lowest.

Under a like difficulty, in spite even of our personal intercourse, do we still lie with regard to the Professor's moral feeling. Gleams of an ethereal Love burst forth from him, soft wailings of infinite Pity ; he could clasp the whole Universe into his bosom, and keep it warm ; it seems as if under that rude exterior there dwelt a very seraph. Then again he is so sly and still, so imperturbably saturnine ; shews such indifference, malign coolness towards all that men strive after ; and ever with some half-visible wrinkle of a bitter sardonic humour, if indeed it be not mere stolid callousness,—that you look on him almost with a shudder, as on some incarnate Mephistopheles, to whom this great terrestrial and celestial Round, after all, were but some huge foolish Whirligig, where kings and beggars, and angels and demons, and stars and street sweepings, were chaotically whirled, in which only children could take interest. His look, as we mentioned, is probably the gravest ever seen : yet it is not of that cast-iron gravity frequent enough among our own Chancery suitors ; but rather the gravity of as some silent, high-encircled mountain pool, perhaps the crater of an extinct volcano ; into whose black deeps you fear to gaze : those eyes, those lights that sparkle in it, may indeed be reflexes of the heavenly Stars, but perhaps also glances from the region of Nether Fire !

Certainly a most involved, self-secluded, altogether enigmatic nature, this of Teufelsdröckh ! Here, however, we gladly recall to mind that once we saw him *laugh ;* once only, perhaps it was the first and last time in his life ; but then such a peal of laughter, enough to have awakened the Seven Sleepers! It was of Jean Paul's doing: some single billow in that vast World-Mahlstrom of Humour, with its heaven-kissing coruscations, which is now, alas, all congealed in the frost of Death! The large-bodied Poet and the small, both large enough in soul, sat talking miscellaneously together, the present Editor being privileged to listen; and now Paul, in his serious way, was giving one of those inimitable ' Extra-harangues;' and, as it chanced, On the Proposal for a *Cast-metal King:* gradually a light kindled in our Professor's eyes and face, a beaming, mantling, loveliest light; through those murky features, a radiant ever-young Apollo looked; and he burst forth like the neighing of all Tattersall's,—tears streaming down his cheeks, pipe held aloft, foot clutched into the air,—loud, long-continuing, uncontrollable; a laugh not of the face and diaphragm only, but of the whole man from head to heel. The present Editor, who laughed indeed, yet with measure, began to fear all was not right: however, Teufelsdröckh composed himself, and sank into his old stillness; on his inscrutable countenance there was, if anything, a slight look of shame; and Richter himself could not rouse him again. Readers who have any tincture of Psychology know how much is to be inferred from this; and that no man who has once heartily and wholly laughed can be altogether irreclaimably bad. How much lies in Laughter: the cipher-key, wherewith we decipher the whole man! Some men wear an everlasting barren simper; in the smile of others lies a cold glitter as of ice: the fewest are able to laugh, what can be called laughing, but only sniff and titter and snigger from the throat outward; or at best, produce some whiffling husky cachinnation, as if they were laughing through wool: of none such comes good. The man who cannot laugh is not only fit for treasons, stratagems, and spoils; but his whole life is already a treason and a stratagem.

Considered as an author, Herr Teufelsdröckh has one scarcely pardonable fault, doubtless his worst: an almost total want of arrangement. In this remarkable Volume, it is true, his adherence to the mere course of Time produces, through the Narrative portions, a certain shew of outward method; but of true logical method and sequence there is too little. Apart from its multifarious sections and subdivisions, the Work naturally falls into two Parts; a Historical-Descriptive, and a Philosophical-Speculative: but falls, unhappily, by no firm line of demarcation; in that labyrinthic combination, each Part overlaps, and indents, and indeed runs quite through the other. Many sections are of a debatable rubric, or even quite nondescript and unnameable; whereby the Book not only loses in accessibility, but too often distresses us like some mad banquet, wherein all courses had been confounded, and fish and flesh, soup and solid, oyster-sauce, lettuces, Rhine-wine and French mustard, were hurled into one huge tureen or trough, and the hungry Public invited to help itself. To bring what order we can out of this Chaos shall be part of our endeavour.

CHAPTER V.

THE WORLD IN CLOTHES.

' As Montesquieu wrote a *Spirit of Laws,*' observes our Professor, ' so could I write a *Spirit of Clothes;* thus, with an ' *Esprit des Loix,* properly an *Esprit de Coutumes,* we should ' have an *Esprit de Costumes.* For neither in tailoring nor in ' legislating does man proceed by mere Accident, but the hand ' is ever guided on by mysterious operations of the mind. In ' all his Modes, and habilatory endeavours, an Architectural ' Idea will be found lurking; his Body and the Cloth are the ' site and materials whereon and whereby his beautified edi- ' fice, of a Person, is to be built. Whether he flows gracefully ' out in folded mantles, based on light sandals; tower up in ' high headgear, from amid peaks, spangles and bell-girdles; ' swell out in starch ruffs, buckram stuffings and monstrous ' tuberosities; or girth himself into separate sections, and ' front the world an Agglomeration of four limbs,—will depend ° on the nature of such Architectural Idea: whether Grecian, ' Gothic, Later-Gothic, or altogether Modern, and Parisian

'or Anglo-Dandical.   Again, what meaning lies in Colour!
'From the soberest drab to the high-flaming scarlet, spiritual
'idiosyncrasies unfold themselves in choice of Colour : if the
'Cut betoken Intellect and Talent, so does the Colour betoken
'Temper and Heart.   In all which, among nations as among
'individuals, there is an incessant, indubitable, though in-
'finitely complex working of Cause and Effect : every snip of
'the Scissors has been regulated and prescribed by ever-active
'Influences, which doubtless to Intelligences of a superior
'order are neither invisible nor illegible.

'For such superior Intelligences a Cause-and-Effect Philoso-
'phy of Clothes, as of Laws, were probably a comfortable
'winter-evening entertainment : nevertheless, for inferior In-
'telligences, like men, such Philosophies have always seemed
'to me uninstructive enough.   Nay, what is your Montesquieu
'himself but a clever infant spelling Letters from a hiero-
'glyphical prophetic Book, the lexicon of which lies in Eter-
'nity, in Heaven ?—Let any Cause-and-Effect Philosopher ex-
'plain, not why I wear such and such a Garment, obey such
'and such a Law ; but even why *I* am *here*, to wear and obey
'any thing !—Much, therefore, if not the whole, of that same
'*Spirit of Clothes* I shall suppress, as hypothetical, ineffectual,
'and even impertinent: naked Facts, and Deductions drawn
'therefrom in quite another than that omniscient style, are
'my humbler and proper province.'

Acting on which prudent restriction, Teufelsdröckh has
nevertheless contrived to take in a well-nigh boundless extent
of field ; at least, the boundaries too often lie quite beyond
our horizon.   Selection being indispensable, we shall here
glance over his First Part only in the most cursory manner.
This First Part is, no doubt, distinguished by ominvorous learning, and utmost patience and fairness : at the same time, in
its results and delineations, it is much more likely to interest
the Compilers of some *Library* of General, Entertaining, Useful, or even Useless Knowledge than the miscellaneous readers of these pages.   Was it this Part of the Book which
Heuschrecke had in view, when he recommended us to that
joint-stock vehicle of publication, 'at present the glory of

'British Literature?' If so, the Library Editors are welcome to dig in it for their own behoof.

To the First Chapter, which turns on Paradise and Fig-leaves, and leads us into interminable disquisitions of a mythological, metaphorical, cabalistico-sartorial and quite antediluvian cast, we shall content ourselves with giving an unconcerned approval. Still less have we to do with 'Lilis, 'Adam's first wife, whom, according to the Talmudists, he 'had before Eve, and who bore him, in that wedlock, the 'whole progeny of aerial, aquatic, and terrestrial Devils,'— very needlessly, we think. On this portion of the Work, with its profound glances into the *Adam-Kadmon*, or Primeval Element, here strangely brought into relation with the *Nifl* and *Muspel* (Darkness and Light) of the antique North, it may be enough to say that its correctness of deduction, and depth of Talmudic and Rabbinical lore have filled perhaps not the worst Hebraist in Britain with something like astonishment.

But quitting this twilight region, Teufelsdröckh hastens from the Tower of Babel, to follow the dispersion of Mankind over the whole habitable and habilable globe. Walking by the light of Oriental, Pelasgic, Scandinavian, Egyptian, Ota-heitean, Ancient and Modern researches of every conceivable kind, he strives to give us in compressed shape (as the Nürn-bergers give an *Orbis Pictus*) an *Orbis Vestitus;* or view of the costumes of all mankind, in all countries, in all times. It is here that to the Antiquarian, to the Historian, we can tri-umphantly say : Fall to! Here is Learning : an irregular Treasury, if you will ; but inexhaustible as the Hoard of King Nibelung, which twelve wagons in twelve days, at the rate of three journeys a day, could not carry off. Sheepskin cloaks and wampum belts ; phylacteries, stoles, albs ; chlamides, togas, Chinese silks, Afghaun shawls, trunk-hose, leather breeches, Celtic philibegs (though breeches, as the name *Gallia Braccata* indicates, are the more ancient), Hussar cloaks, Vandyke tippets, ruffs, fardingales, are brought vividly before us,—even the Kilmarnock nightcap is not forgotten. For most part too we must admit that the Learning, heterogene-ous as it is, and tumbled down quite pell-mell, is true concen-

trated and purified Learning, the drossy parts smelted out
and thrown aside.

Philosophical reflections intervene, and sometimes touching
pictures of human life. Of this sort the following has surprised us. The first purpose of clothes, as our Professor
imagines, was not warmth or decency, but ornament. 'Mis-
'erable indeed,' says he, 'was the condition of the Aboriginal
'Savage, glaring fiercely from under his fleece of hair, which
'with the beard reached down to his loins, and hung round
'him like a matted cloak ; the rest of his body sheeted in its
'thick natural fell. He loitered in the sunny glades of the
'forest, living on wild fruits ; or, as the ancient Caledonian,
'squatted himself in morasses, lurking for his bestial or
'human prey ; without implements, without arms, save the
'ball of heavy Flint, to which, that his sole possession and
'defence might not be lost, he had attached a long cord of
'plaited thongs ; thereby recovering as well as hurling it with
'deadly unerring skill. Nevertheless, the pains of Hunger
'and Revenge once satisfied, his next care was not Comfort
'but Decoration (*Putz*). Warmth he found in the toils of the
'chase ; or amid dry leaves in his hollow tree, in his bark
'shed, or natural grotto : but for Decoration he must have
'Clothes. Nay, among wild people, we find tattooing and
'painting even prior to Clothes. The first spiritual want of
'a barbarous man is Decoration, as indeed we still see among
'the barbarous classes in civilized countries.

'Reader, the heaven-inspired melodious Singer ; loftiest Se-
'rene Highness : nay thy own amber-locked, snow-and-rose-
'bloom Maiden, worthy to glide sylphlike almost on air, whom
'thou lovest, worshippest as a divine Presence, which, indeed,
'symbolically taken, she is—has descended, like thyself, from
'that same hair-mantled, flint-hurling Aboriginal Anthro-
'pophagus ! Out of the eater cometh forth meat ; out of the
'strong cometh forth sweetness. What changes are wrought,
'not by Time, yet in Time ! For not Mankind only, but all
'that Mankind does or beholds, is in continual growth, re-
'genesis and self-perfecting vitality. Cast forth thy Act, thy
'Word, into the ever-living, ever-working Universe : it is a

'seed-grain that cannot die ; unnoticed to-day (says one), it
'will be found flourishing as a Banyan-grove (perhaps, alas, as
'a Hemlock-forest !) after a thousand years.

'He who first shortened the labour of Copyists by device
'of *Movable Types* was disbanding hired Armies, and cashier-
'ing most Kings and Senates, and creating a whole new Dem-
'ocratic world ; he had invented the Art of Printing. The
'first ground handful of Nitre, Sulphur, and Charcoal drove
'Monk Schwartz's pestel through the ceiling ; what will the
'last do? Achieve the final undisputed prostration of Force
'under Thought, of Animal courage under Spiritual. A simple
'invention it was in the old-world Grazier,—sick of lugging
'his slow Ox about the country till he got it bartered for corn
'or oil,—to take a piece of Leather, and thereon scratch or
'stamp the mere Figure of an Ox (or *Pecus*) ; put it in his
'pocket, and call it *Pecunia*, Money. Yet hereby did Barter
'grow Sale, the Leather Money is now Golden and Paper, and
'all miracles have been out-miracled : for there are Rothschilds
'and English National Debts ; and whoso has sixpence is
'Sovereign (to the length of sixpence) over all men ; com-
'mands Cooks to feed him, Philosophers to teach him, Kings
'to mount guard over him,—to the length of sixpence.—
'Clothes too, which began in foolishest love of Ornament,
'what have they not become! Increased Security, and
'pleasurable Heat soon followed : but what of these ? Shame,
'divine Shame (*Schaam*, Modesty), as yet a stranger to the
'Anthropophagous bosom, arose there mysteriously under
'Clothes ; a mystic grove-encircled shrine for the Holy in
'man. Clothes gave us individuality, distinctions, social
'polity ; Clothes have made Men of us ; they are threatening
'to make Clothes-screens of us.

'But on the whole,' continues our eloquent Professor, 'Man
'is a Tool-using Animal (*Hanthierendes Thier*). Weak in him-
'self, and of small stature, he stands on a basis, at most for
'the flattest-soled, of some half square-foot, insecurely enough ;
'has to straddle out his legs, lest the very wind supplant him.
'Feeblest of bipeds ! Three quintals are a crushing load for
'him ; the Steer of the meadow tosses him aloft, like a waste

'rag. Nevertheless he can use Tools, can devise Tools : with
' these the granite mountain melts into light dust before him ;
' he kneads glowing iron, as if it were soft paste ; seas are his
' smooth high-way, winds and fire his unwearying steeds.   No-
' where do you find him without Tools ; without Tools he is
' nothing, with Tools he is all.'

Here may we not, for a moment, interrupt the stream of
Oratory with a remark that this Definition of the Tool-using
Animal, appears to us, of all that Animal-sort, considerably
the precisest and best?   Man is called a Laughing Animal :
but do not the apes also laugh, or attempt to do it ; and is the
manliest man the greatest and oftenest laugher?   Teufelsdröckh himself, as we said, laughed only once.   Still less do
we make of that other French Definition of the Cooking Animal ; which, indeed, for rigorous scientific purposes, is as
good as useless.   Can a Tartar be said to cook, when he only
readies his steak by riding on it ?   Again, what Cookery does
the Greenlander use, beyond stowing up his whale-blubber,
as a marmot in the like case, might do ?   Or how would Mon-
sieur Ude prosper among those Orinocco Indians who, according to Humboldt, lodge in crow-nests, on the branches of
trees ; and, for half the year, have no victuals but pipe-clay,
the whole country being under water ?   But on the other
hand, shew us the human being, of any period or climate, without his Tools : those very Caledonians, as we saw, had their
Flint-ball, and Thong to it, such as no brute has or can have.

'Man is a Tool-using animal,' concludes Teufelsdröckh in
his abrupt way ; ' of which truth Clothes are but one ex-
'ample : and surely if we consider the interval between the
' first wooden Dibble fashioned by man, and those Liverpool
' Steam-carriages, or the British House of Commons, we shall
' note what progress he has made.   He digs up certain black
' stones from the bosom of the Earth, and says to them, *Trans-*
' *port me and this luggage, at the rate of five-and-thirty miles an*
' *hour ;* and they do it : he collects, apparently by lot, six
' hundred and fifty-eight miscellaneous individuals, and says
' to them, *Make this nation toil for us, bleed for us, hunger, and*
' *sorrow, and sin for us ;* and they do it.'

CHAPTER VI.

APRONS.

One of the most unsatisfactory Sections in the whole Volume is that on *Aprons.* What though stout old Gao, the Persian Blacksmith, ' whose apron, now indeed hidden under jewels, ' because raised in revolt which proved successful, is still the ' royal standard of that country;' what though John Knox's Daughter, ' who threatened Sovereign Majesty that she would ' catch her husband's head in her Apron, rather than he ' should lie and be a bishop;' what though the Landgravine Elizabeth, with many other Apron worthies,—figure here? An idle wire-drawing spirit, sometimes even a tone of levity, approaching to conventional satire, is too clearly discernible. What, for example, are we to make of such sentences as the following?

'Aprons are Defences; against injury to cleanliness, to ' safety, to modesty, sometimes to roguery. From the thin ' slip of notched silk (as it were, the Emblem and beatified ' Ghost of an Apron), which some highest-bred housewife, ' sitting at Nürnberg Workboxes and Toyboxes, has gracefully ' fastened on ; to the thick-tanned hide, girt round him with ' thongs, wherein the Builder builds, and at evening sticks ' his trowel ; or to those jingling sheet-iron Aprons, wherein ' your otherwise half-naked Vulcans hammer and smelt in ' their smelt-furnace,—is there not range enough in the fashion ' and uses of this Vestment ? How much has been concealed, ' how much has been defended in Aprons ! Nay, rightly con- ' sidered, what is your whole Military and Police Establish- ' ment, charged at uncalculated millions, but a huge scarlet- ' coloured, iron-fastened Apron, wherein Society works ' (uneasily enough) ; guarding itself from some soil and ' stithy-sparks, in this Devil's-smithy (*Teufels-schmiede*) of a ' world ? But of all Aprons the most puzzling to me hitherto ' has been the Episcopal or Cassock. Wherein consists the ' usefulness of this Apron ? The Overseer (*Episcopus*) of Souls,

' I notice, has tucked-in the corner of it, as if his day's work
' was done : what does he shadow forth thereby ? ' &c. &c.

Or again, has it often been the lot of our readers to read
such stuff as we shall now quote?

'I consider those printed Paper Aprons, worn by the Pari-
' sian Cooks, as a new vent, though a slight one, for Typog·
'raphy ; therefore as an encouragement to modern Literature,
' and deserving of approval : nor is it without satisfaction that
' I hear of a celebrated London Firm having in view to intro-
' duce the same fashion, with important extensions, in England.'—We who are on the spot hear of no such thing ; and
indeed have reason to be thankful that hitherto there are
other vents for our Literature, exuberant as it is.—Teufelsdröckh continues : ' If such supply of printed Paper should
' rise so far as to choke up the highways and public thorough-
' fares, new means must of necessity be had recourse to. In
' a world existing by Industry, we grudge to employ fire as a
' destroying element, and not as a creating one. However,
'Heaven is omnipotent, and will find us an outlet. In the
' meanwhile, is it not beautiful to see five million quintals of
' Rags picked annually from the Laystall ; and annually, after
' being macerated, hot-pressed, printed on, and sold,—re-
' turned thither ; filling so many hungry mouths by the way ?
' Thus is the Laystall, especially with its Rags or Clothes-
' rubbish, the grand Electric Battery, and Fountain-of-motion,
' from which and to which the Social Activities (like vitreous
' and resinous Electricities) circulate, in larger or smaller
' circles, through the mighty, billowy, stormtost Chaos of Life,
' which they keep alive ! '—Such passages fill us, who love the
man, and partly esteem him, with a very mixed feeling.

Farther down we meet with this : ' The Journalists are now
' the true Kings and Clergy : henceforth Historians, unless
' they are fools, must write not of Bourbon Dynasties, and
' Tudors and Hapsburgs ; but of Stamped Broad-sheet Dy-
'nasties, and quite new successive Names, according as this
' or the other Able Editor, or Combination of Able Editors,
' gains the world's ear. Of the British Newspaper Press,
'perhaps the most important of all, and wonderful enough in

'its secret constitution and procedure, a valuable descriptive
'History already exists, in that language, under the title of
'*Satan's Invisible World Displayed* ; which, however, by search
'in all the Weissnichtwo Libraries, I have not yet succeeded
'in procuring (*vermöchte nicht aufzutreiben*).'

Thus does the good Homer not only nod, but snore. Thus
does Teufelsdröckh, wandering in regions where he had little
business, confound the old authentic Presbyterian Witch-
finder, with a new, spurious, imaginary Historian of the *Britt-
tische Journalistik* ; and so stumble on perhaps the most
egregious blunder in modern Literature !

CHAPTER VII.

MISCELLANEOUS-HISTORICAL.

Happier is our Professor, and more purely scientific and
historic, when he reaches the Middle Ages in Europe, and
down to the end of the Seventeenth Century ; the true era of
extravagance in costume. It is here that the Antiquary and
Student of Modes comes upon his richest harvest. Fantastic
garbs, beggaring all fancy of a Teniers or a Callot, succeed
each other, like monster devouring monster in a Dream. The
whole too in brief authentic strokes, and touched not seldom
with that breath of genius which makes even old raiment live.
Indeed, so learned, precise, graphical, and every way interesting have we found these Chapters, that it may be thrown out
as a pertinent question for parties concerned, Whether or not
a good English Translation thereof might henceforth be profitably incorporated with Mr. Merrick's valuable Work *On Ancient Armour ?* Take, by way of example, the following sketch ;
as authority for which Paulinus's *Zeitkurzende Lust* (ii. 678)
is, with seeming confidence, referred to :

'Did we behold the German fashionable dress of the Fif-
'teenth Century, we might smile ; as perhaps those bygone
'Germans, were they to rise again, and see our haberdashery,
'would cross themselves, and invoke the Virgin. But happily
'no bygone German, or man, rises again ; thus the Present

' is not needlessly trammelled with the Past ; and only grows
' out of it, like a Tree, whose roots are not intertangled with
' its branches, but lie peaceably under ground.   Nay it is very
' mournful, yet not useless, to see and know, how the Great-
' est and Dearest, in a short while, would find his place quite
' filled up here, and no room for him ; the very Napoleon, the
' very Byron, in some seven years, has become obsolete, and
' were now a foreigner to his Europe.   Thus is the Law of
' Progress secured ; and in Clothes, as in all other external
' things whatsoever, no fashion will continue.

   ' Of the military classes in those old times, whose buff belts,
' complicated chains and gorgets, huge churn-boots, and other
' riding and fighting gear have been bepainted in modern Ro-
' mance, till the whole has acquired somewhat of a sign-post
' character,—I shall here say nothing : the civil and pacific
' classes, less touched upon, are wonderful enough for us.

   ' Rich men, I find, have *Teusinke'* (a perhaps untranslateable
article) ; ' also a silver girdle, whereat hang little bells ; so that
' when a man walks it is with continual jingling.   Some few,
' of musical turn, have a whole chime of bells (*Glockenspiel*)
' fastened there ; which especially, in sudden whirls, and the
' other accidents of walking, has a grateful effect.   Observe
' too how fond they are of peaks, and Gothic-arch intersec-
' tions.   The male world wears peaked caps, an ell long, which
' hang bobbing over the side (*schief*) : their shoes are peaked
' in front, also to the length of an ell, and laced on the side
' with tags ; even the wooden shoes have their ell-long noses ;
' some also clap bells on the peak.   Further, according to my
' authority, the men have breeches without seat (*ohne Gesäss*) :
' these they fasten peakwise to their shirts ; and the long
' round doublet must overlap them.

   ' Rich maidens, again, flit abroad in gowns scolloped out be-
' hind and before, so that back and breast are almost bare.
' Wives of quality, on the other hand, have train-gowns four
' or five ells in length ; which trains there are boys to carry
' Brave Cleopatras, sailing in their silk-cloth Galley, with a
' Cupid for steersman !   Consider their welts, a handbreadth
' thick, which waver round them by way of hem ; the long

' flood of silver buttons, or rather silver shells, from throat to
' shoe, wherewith these same welt-gowns are buttoned.   The
' maidens have bound silver snoods about their hair, with
' gold spangles, and pendent flames (*Flammen*), that is, spark-
' ling hair-drops : but of their mother's headgear who shall
' speak ?   Neither in love of grace is comfort forgotten.   In
' winter weather you behold the whole fair creation (that can
' afford it) in long mantles, with skirts wide below, and, for
' hem, not one but two sufficient handbroad welts ; all ending
' atop in a thick well-starched Ruff, some twenty inches broad :
' these are their Ruff-mantles (*Kragenmäntel*).

   ' As yet among the womankind hoop-petticoats are not ;
' but the men have doublets of fustian, under which lie mul-
' tiple ruffs of cloth, pasted together with batter (*mit Teig*
' *zusammengekleistert*), which create protuberance enough.
' Thus do the two sexes vie with each other in the art of Deco-
' ration ; and as usual the stronger carries it.'

   Our Professor, whether he have Humour himself or not,
manifests a certain feeling of the Ludicrous, a sly observance
of it, which, could emotion of any kind be confidently pre-
dicated of so still a man, we might call a real love.   None of
those bell-girdles, bushel-breeches, cornuted shoes or other
the like phenomena, of which the History of Dress offers so
many, escape him ; more especially the mischances, or striking adventures, incident to the wearers of such, are noticed
with due fidelity.   Sir Walter Raleigh's fine mantle, which he
spread in the mud under Queen Elizabeth's feet, appears to
provoke little enthusiasm in him ; he merely asks, Whether at
that period the Maiden Queen ' was red-painted on the nose,
' and white-painted on the cheeks, as her tirewomen, when
' from spleen and wrinkles she would no longer look in any
glass, were wont to serve her ? '   We can answer that Sir
Walter knew well what he was doing, and had the Maiden
Queen been stuffed parchment died in verdigris, would have
done the same.

   Thus too, treating of those enormous habiliments, that were
not only slashed and galooned, but artificially swollen out on
the broader parts of the body, by introduction of Bran,—our

Professor fails not to comment on that luckless Courtier, who having seated himself on a chair with some projecting nail on it, and therefrom rising, to pay his *devoir* on the entrance of Majesty, instantaneously emitted several pecks of dry wheat-dust: and stood there diminished to a spindle, his galoons and slashes dangling sorrowful and flabby round him. Whereupon the Professor publishes this reflection:

' By what strange chances do we live in History ! Erostra-
' tus by a torch ; Milo by a bullock ; Henry Darnley, an un-
' fledged booby and bustard, by his limbs ; most Kings and
' Queens by being born under such and such a bed-tester ;
' Boileau Despreaux (according to Helvetius) by the peck of
' a turkey ; and this ill-starred individual by a rent in his
' breeches,—for no Memoirist of Kaiser Otto's Court omits
' him. Vain was the prayer of Themistocles for a talent of
' Forgetting : my Friends, yield cheerfully to Destiny, and
' read since it is written.'—Has Teufelsdröckh to be put in mind that, nearly related to the impossible talent of Forgetting, stands that talent of Silence, which even travelling Englishmen manifest ?

' The simplest costume,' observes our Professor, ' which I
' anywhere find alluded to in History, is that used as regimen-
' tal, by Bolivar's Cavalry, in the late Columbian wars. A
' square Blanket, twelve feet in diagonal, is provided (some
' were wont to cut off the corners, and make it circular) : in
' the centre a slit is effected eighteen inches long : through
' this the mother-naked Trooper introduces his head and
' neck ; and so rides shielded from all weather, and in battle
' from many strokes (for he rolls it about his left arm) ; and
' not only dressed, but harnessed and draperied.'

With which picture of a State of Nature, affecting by its singularity, and Old-Roman contempt of the superfluous, we shall quit this part of our subject.

CHAPTER VIII.

THE WORLD OUT OF CLOTHES.

If in the Descriptive-Historical Portion of this Volume, Teufelsdröckh, discussing merely the *Werden* (Origin and successive Improvement) of Clothes, has astonished many a reader, much more will he in the Speculative-Philosophical Portion, which treats of their *Wirken* or Influences. It is here that the present Editor first feels the pressure of his task; for here properly the higher and new Philosophy of Clothes commences: an untried, almost inconceivable region, or chaos; in venturing upon which, how difficult, yet how unspeakably important is it to know what course, of survey and conquest, is the true one; where the footing is firm substance and will bear us, where it is hollow, or mere cloud, and may engulf us! Teufelsdröckh undertakes no less than to expound the moral, political, even religious Influences of Clothes; he undertakes to make manifest, in its thousandfold bearings, this grand Proposition, that Man's earthly interests 'are all hooked and buttoned together, and held up, by Clothes.' He says in so many words, 'Society is founded upon Cloth;' and again, 'Society sails through the Infinitude 'on Cloth, as on a Faust's Mantle, or rather like the Sheet of 'clean and unclean beasts in the Apostle's Dream; and with- 'out such Sheet or Mantle, would sink to endless depths, or 'mount to inane limboes, and in either case be no more.'

By what chains, or indeed infinitely complected tissues, of Meditation this grand Theorem is here unfolded, and innumerable practical Corollaries are drawn therefrom, it were perhaps a mad ambition to attempt exhibiting. Our Professor's method is not, in any case, that of common school Logic, where the truths all stand in a row, each holding by the skirts of the other; but at best that of practical Reason, proceeding by large Intuition over whole systematic groups and kingdoms; whereby, we might say, a noble complexity, almost like that of Nature, reigns in his Philosophy, or spiritual Picture of Nature: a mighty maze, yet as faith whispers, not without a plan. Nay we complained above, that a certain ignoble complexity, what we must call mere confusion, was also discernible. Often, also, we have to exclaim : Would to Heaven those same Biographical Documents were come ! For it seems as if the demonstration lay much in the Author's individuality ; as if it were not Argument that had taught him, but Experience. At present it is only in local glimpses, and by significant fragments, picked often at wide enough intervals from the original Volume, and carefully collated, that we can hope to impart some outline or foreshadow of this Doctrine. Readers of any intelligence are once more invited to favour us with their most concentrated attention : let these, after intense consideration, and not till then, pronounce, Whether on the utmost verge of our actual horizon there is not a looming as of Land ; a promise of new Fortunate Islands, perhaps whole undiscovered Americas, for such as have canvass to sail thither?—As exordium to the whole, stand here the following long citation :

'With men of a speculative turn,' writes Teufelsdröckh, 'there come seasons, meditative, sweet, yet awful hours, when 'in wonder and fear you ask yourself that unanswerable question : Who am *I ;* the thing that can say "I" (*das Wesen* '*das sich* ICH *nennt*)? The world, with its loud trafficking, 'retires into the distance ; and through the paper-hangings, 'and stone-walls, and thick-plied tissues of Commerce and 'Polity, and all the living and lifeless integuments (of Society 'and a Body), wherewith your Existence sits surrounded,— 'the sight reaches forth into the void Deep, and you are alone 'with the Universe, and silently commune with it as one 'mysterious Presence with another.

'Who am I ; what is this ME? A voice, a Motion, an Ap-'pearance ;—some embodied, visualised Idea in the Eternal 'Mind ? *Cogito, ergo sum.* Alas, poor Cogitator, this takes 'us but a little way. Sure enough I am ; and lately was not : 'but Whence ? How ? Whereto ? The answer lies around, 'written in all colours and motions, uttered in all tones of 'jubilee and wail, in thousand-figured, thousand-voiced, har-

'monious Nature : but where is the cunning eye and ear to
'whom that God-written Apocalypse will yield articulate
'meaning ? We sit as in a boundless Phantasmagoria and
'Dream-grotto ; boundless, for the faintest star, the remotest
'century, lies not even nearer the verge thereof : sounds and
'many-coloured visions flit around our sense ; but Him, the
'Unslumbering, whose work both Dream and Dreamer are,
'we see not ; except in rare half-waking moments, suspect
'not. Creation, says one, lies before us, like a glorious Rain-
'bow ; but the Sun that made it lies behind us, hidden from
'us. Then, in that strange Dream, how we clutch at shadows
'as if they were substances ; and sleep deepest while fancy-
'ing ourselves most awake ! Which of your Philosophical
'Systems is other than a dream-theorem ; a net quotient,
'confidently given out, where divisor and dividend are both
'unknown ? What are all your national Wars, with their
'Moscow Retreats, and sanguinary hate-filled Revolutions,
'but the Somnambulism of uneasy Sleepers ? This Dream-
'ing, this Somnabulism is what we on Earth call Life ; where-
'in the most indeed undoubtingly wander, as if they knew
'right hand from left ; yet they only are wise who know that
'they know nothing.

' Pity that all Metaphysics had hitherto proved so inexpres-
'sibly unproductive ! The secret of Man's Being is still like
'the Sphinx's secret : a riddle that he cannot rede ; and for
'ignorance of which he suffers death, the worst death, a
'spiritual. What are your Axioms, and Categories, and
'Systems, and Aphorisms ? Words, words. High Air-castles
'are cunningly built of Words, the Words well bedded also in
'good Logic-mortar ; wherein, however, no Knowledge will
'come to lodge. *The whole is greater than the part :* how ex-
'ceedingly true ! *Nature abhors a vacuum :* how exceedingly
'false and calumnious ! Again, *Nothing can act but where it
'is :* with all my heart ; only WHERE is it ? Be not the slave
'of Words : is not the Distant, the Dead, while I love it, and
'long for it, and mourn for it, Here, in the genuine sense, as
'truly as the floor I stand on ? But that same WHERE, with
'its brother, WHEN, are from the first the master-colours of

4

'our Dream-grotto ; say rather, the Canvass (the warp **and**
'woof thereof) whereon all our Dreams and Life-visions **are**
'painted. Nevertheless, has not a deeper meditation taught
'certain of every climate and age, that the WHERE and WHEN,
'so mysteriously inseparable from all our thoughts, are but
'superficial terrestrial adhesions to thought ; that the Seer
'may discern them where they mount up out of the celestial
'EVERYWHERE and FOREVER : have not all nations conceived
'their God as Omnipresent and Eternal ; as existing in a
'universal HERE, an everlasting Now ? Think well, thou too
'wilt find that Space is but a mode of our human Sense, so
'likewise Time ; there *is* no Space and no Time : WE are—
'we know not what ;—light-sparkles floating in the æther of
'Deity !

'So that this so solid-seeming World, after all, were but an
'air-image, our ME the only reality : and Nature, with its
'thousand-fold production and destruction, but the reflex of
'our own inward Force, the " phantasy of our Dream ; " or
'what the Earth-Spirit in *Faust* names it, *the living visible*
'*Garment of God.*

> ' " In Being's floods, in Action's storm,
>   I walk and work, above, beneath,
>   Work and weave in endless motion !
>   Birth and Death,
>   An infinite ocean ;
>   A seizing and giving
>   The fire of the Living :
>   'Tis thus at the roaring Loom of Time I ply,
>   And weave for God the Garment thou seest Him by."

'Of twenty millions that have read and spouted this thunder.
'speech of the *Erdgeist*, are there yet twenty units of us that
'have learned the meaning thereof ?

'It was in some such mood, when wearied and foredone
'with these high speculations, that I first came upon the
'question of Clothes. Strange enough, it strikes me, is this
'same fact of there being Tailors and Tailored. The Horse I
'ride has his own whole fell : strip him of the girths and flaps
'and extraneous tags I have fastened round him, and the

'noble creature is his own sempster and weaver and spinner:
'nay his own bootmaker, jeweller, and man-milliner; he
'bounds free through the valleys, with a perennial rainproof
'court suit on his body; wherein warmth and easiness of fit
'have reached perfection; nay, the graces also have been con-
'sidered, and frills and fringes, with gay variety of colour,
'featly appended, and ever in the right place, are not want-
'ing. While I—good Heaven!—have thatched myself over
'with the dead fleeces of sheep, the bark of vegetables, the
'entrails of worms, the hides of oxen or seals, the felt of
'furred beasts; and walk abroad a moving Rag-screen, over-
'heaped with shreds and tatters raked from the Charnel-house
'of Nature, where they would have rotted, to rot on me more
'slowly! Day after day, I must thatch myself anew; day
'after day, this despicable thatch must lose some film of its
'thickness; some film of it, frayed away by tear and wear,
'must be brushed off into the Ashpit, into the Laystall; till
'by degrees the whole has been brushed thither, and I, the
'dust-making, patent Rag-grinder, get new material to grind
'down. O subter-brutish! vile! most vile! For have not I
'too a compact all-enclosing Skin, whiter or dingier? Am I
'a botched mass of tailors' and cobblers' shreds, then; or a
'tightly-articulated, homogeneous little Figure, automatic,
'nay alive?

'Strange enough how creatures of the human-kind shut
'their eyes to plainest facts; and by the mere inertia of Ob-
'livion and Stupidity, live at ease in the midst of Wonders
'and Terrors. But indeed man is, and was always, a block-
'head and dullard; much readier to feel and digest, than to
'think and consider. Prejudice, which he pretends to hate,
'is his absolute lawgiver; mere use-and-wont everywhere
'leads him by the nose: thus let but a Rising of the Sun,
'let but a Creation of the World happen *twice*, and it ceases
'to be marvellous, to be noteworthy, or noticeable. Perhaps
'not once in a lifetime does it occur to your ordinary biped,
'of any country or generation, be he gold-mantled Prince or
'russet-jerkined Peasant, that his Vestments and his Self are
'not one and indivisible; that *he* is naked, without vestments,

' till he buy or steal such, and by forethought sew and button
' them.

'For my own part, these considerations, of our Clothes-
'thatch, and how, reaching inwards even to our heart of
' hearts, it tailorises and demoralises us, fill me with a certain
' horror at myself, and mankind ; almost as one feels at those
'Dutch Cows, which, during the wet season, you see grazing
'deliberately with jackets and petticoats (of striped sacking),
' in the meadows of Gouda.   Nevertheless there is something
'great in the moment when a man first strips himself of ad-
'ventitious wrappages ; and sees indeed that he is naked,
'and, as Swift has it, "a forked straddling animal with bandy
'legs ;" yet also a Spirit, and unutterable Mystery of Mys-
'teries.'

CHAPTER IX.

ADAMITISM.

Let no courteous reader take offence at the opinions
broached in the conclusion of the last Chapter. The Editor
himself, on first glancing over that singular passage, was in-
clined to exclaim : What, have we got not only a Sansculot-
tist, but an enemy to Clothes in the abstract? A new
Adamite, in this century, which flatters itself that it is the
Nineteenth, and destructive both to Superstition and Enthusiasm ?

Consider, thou foolish Teufelsdröckh, what benefits unspeakable all ages and sexes derive from Clothes. For example, when thou thyself, a watery, pulpy, slobbery fresh-
man and new-comer in this Planet, sattest muling and puking
in thy nurse's arms; sucking thy coral, and looking forth into
the world in the blankest manner, what hadst thou been,
without thy blankets, and bibs, and other nameless hulls?
A terror to thyself and mankind ! Or hast thou forgotten the
day when thou first receivedst breeches, and thy long clothes
became short? The village where thou livedst was all ap-
prized of the fact ; and neighbour after neighbour kissed thy
pudding-cheek, and gave thee, as hansel, silver or copper

coins, on that the first gala-day of thy existence. Again, wert
not thou, at one period of life, a Buck, or Blood, or Macaroni,
or Incroyable, or Dandy, or by whatever name, according to
year and place, such phenomenon is distinguished? In that
one word lie included mysterious volumes. Nay, now when
the reign of folly is over, or altered, and thy clothes are not
for triumph but for defence, hast thou always worn them per-
force, and as a consequence of Man's Fall ; never rejoiced in
them as in a warm movable House, a Body round thy Body,
wherein that strange THEE of thine sat snug, defying all varia-
tions of Climate? Girt with thick double-milled kerseys ;
half buried under shawls and broadbrims, and overalls and
mudboots, thy very fingers cased in doeskin and mittens, thou
hast bestrode that 'Horse I ride ;' and, though it were in
wild winter, dashed through the world, glorying in it as if
thou wert its lord. In vain did the sleet beat round thy temples ; it lighted only on thy impenetrable, felted or woven,
case of wool. In vain did the winds howl,—forests sounding and creaking, deep calling unto deep,—and the storms
heap themselves together into one huge Arctic whirlpool ;
thou flewest through the middle thereof, striking fire from
the highway ; wild music hummed in thy ears, thou too
wert as a 'sailor of the air ;' the wreck of matter and the
crash of worlds was thy element and propitiously wafting tide.
Without Clothes, without bit or saddle, what hadst thou been ;
what had thy fleet quadruped been ?—Nature is good, but she
is not the best; here truly was the victory of Art over Nature.
A thunderbolt indeed might have pierced thee ; all short of
this thou couldst defy.

Or, cries the courteous reader, has your Teufelsdröckh forgotten what he said lately about 'Aboriginal Savages,' and
their 'condition miserable indeed ?' Would he have all this
unsaid ; and us betake ourselves again to the 'matted cloak,'
and go sheeted in a 'thick natural fell ?'

Nowise, courteous reader! The Professor knows full well
what he is saying ; and both thou and we, in our haste, do
him wrong. If Clothes, in these times, 'so tailorise and de-
moralise us,' have they no redeeming value ; can they not be

altered to serve better; must they of necessity be thrown to
the dogs? The truth is, Teufelsdröckh, though a Sansculot-
tist, is no Adamite: and much perhaps as he might wish to
go forth before this degenerate age, 'as a Sign,' would nowise
wish to do it, as those old Adamites did, in a state of Nakedness. The utility of Clothes is altogether apparent to him:
nay perhaps he has an insight into their more recondite, and
almost mystic qualities, what we might call the omnipotent
virtue of Clothes, such as was never before vouchsafed to any
man. For example:

'You see two individuals,' he writes, 'one dressed in fine
'Red, the other in coarse threadbare Blue: Red says to Blue,
'"Be hanged and anatomised;" Blue hears with a shudder,
'and (O wonder of wonders!) marches sorrowfully to the gal-
'lows; is there noosed up, vibrates his hour, and the sur-
'geons dissect him, and fit his bones into a skeleton for medi-
'cal purposes. How is this; or what make ye of your *Nothing
'can act but where it is?* Red has no physical hold of Blue, no
'*clutch* of him, is nowise in *contact* with him: neither are
'those ministering Sheriffs and Lord Lieutenants and Hang-
'men and Tipstaves so related to commanding Red, that he
'can tug them hither and thither; but each stands distinct
'within his own skin. Nevertheless, as it is spoken, so it is
'done: the articulated Word sets all hands in Action; and
'Rope and Improved-drop perform their work.

'Thinking reader, the reason seems to me twofold: First,
'that *Man is a Spirit*, and bound by invisible bonds to *All
'Men:* Secondly, that *he wears Clothes*, which are the visible
'emblems of that fact. Has not your Red hanging-individual
'a horsehair wig, squirrel-skins, and a plush gown; whereby
'all mortals know that he is a JUDGE?—Society, which the
'more I think of it astonishes me the more, is founded upon
'Cloth.

'Often in my atrabiliar moods, when I read of pompous
'ceremonials, Frankfort Coronations, Royal Drawing-rooms,
'Levees, Couchees; and how the ushers and macers and pur-
'suivants are all in waiting; how Duke this is presented by
'Archduke that, and Colonel A by General B, and innumera-

'ble Bishops, Admirals, and miscellaneous Functionaries, are
' advancing gallantly to the Anointed Presence ; and I strive,
' in my remote privacy, to form a clear picture of that solem-
' nity,—on a sudden, as by some enchanter's wand, the—shall
' I speak it ?—the Clothes fly off the whole dramatic corps ;
' and Dukes, Grandees, Bishops, Generals, Anointed Presence
' itself, every mother's son of them, stand straddling there,
' not a shirt on them ; and I know not whether to laugh or
' weep. This physical or psychical infirmity, in which perhaps
' I am not singular, I have, after hesitation, thought right to
' publish, for the solace of those afflicted with the like.'

Would to Heaven, say we, thou hadst thought right to keep
it secret ! Who is there now that can read the five columns of
Presentations in his Morning Newspaper without a shudder ?
Hypochondriac men, and all men are to a certain extent hypochondriac, should be more gently treated. With what readiness our fancy, in this shattered state of the nerves, follows
out the consequences which Teufelsdröckh, with a devilish
coolness, goes on to draw :

' What would Majesty do, could such an accident befall in
' reality ; should the buttons all simultaneously start, and the
' solid wool evaporate, in very Deed, as here in Dream ? *Ach*
' *Gott!* How each skulks into the nearest hiding-place ; their
' high State Tragedy (*Haupt-und Staats-Action*) becomes a
' Pickleherring Farce to weep at, which is the worst kind of
' Farce ; *the tables* (according to Horace), and with them, the
' whole fabric of Government, Legislation, Property, Police,
' and Civilized Society, *are dissolved*, in wails, and howls.'

Lives the man that can figure a naked Duke of Windlestraw
addressing a naked House of Lords ? Imagination, choked as
in mephitic air, recoils on itself, and will not forward with
the picture. The Woolsack, the Ministerial, the Opposition
Benches—*infandum ! infandum !* And yet why is the thing
impossible ? Was not every soul, or rather everybody, of these
Guardians of our Liberties, naked, or nearly so, last night ;
' a forked Radish with a head fantastically carved ? And why
might he not, did our stern Fate so order it, walk out to St.
Stephen's, as well as into bed, in that no-fashion ; and there,

with other similar Radishes, hold a Bed of Justice? 'Solace of those afflicted with the like!' Unhappy Teufelsdröckh, had man ever such a 'physical or psychical infirmity' before? And now how many, perhaps, may thy unparalleled confession (which we, even to the sounder British world, and goaded on by Critical and Biographical duty, grudge to re-impart) incurably infect therewith! Art thou the malignest of Sansculottists, or only the maddest?

'It will remain to be examined,' adds the inexorable Teufelsdröckh, 'in how far the SCARECROW, as a Clothed Person, is not 'also entitled to benefit of clergy, and English trial by jury: 'nay perhaps, considering his high function (for is not he too 'a defender of Property, and Sovereign armed with the *terrors* 'of the Law?), to a certain royal Immunity and Inviolability; 'which, however, misers and the meaner class of persons are 'not always voluntarily disposed to grant him.' * *

* * 'O my friends, we are (in Yorick Sterne's words) but 'as "turkeys driven, with a stick and red clout, to the market;" 'or if some drivers, as they do in Norfolk, take a dried bladder 'and put peas in it, the rattle thereof terrifies the boldest!'

CHAPTER X.

PURE REASON.

It must now be apparent enough that our Professor, as above hinted, is a speculative Radical, and of the very darkest tinge; acknowledging, for most part, in the solemnities and paraphernalia of civilised Life, which we make so much of, nothing but so many Cloth-rags, turkey-poles, and 'bladders with dried peas.' To linger among such speculations, longer than mere Science requires, a discerning public can have no wish. For our purposes the simple fact that such a *Naked World* is possible, nay actually exists (under the Clothed one), will be sufficient. Much, therefore, we omit about 'Kings wrestling naked on the green with Carmen,' and the Kings being thrown: 'dissect them with scalpels,' says Teufelsdröckh; 'the same viscera, tissues, livers, lights, and other

'Life-tackle are there : examine their spiritual mechanism;
'the same great Need, great Greed, and little Faculty ; nay
'ten to one but the Carman, who understands draught-cattle,
'the rimming of wheels, something of the laws of unstable
'and stable equilibrium, with other branches of wagon-sci-
'ence, and has actually put forth his hand and operated on
'Nature, is the more cunningly gifted of the two. Whence,
'then, their so unspeakable difference ? From Clothes.'
Much also we shall omit about confusion of Ranks, and Joan
and My Lady, and how it would be every where 'Hail fellow
well met,' and Chaos were come again: all which to any one
that has once fairly pictured out the grand mother-idea, *Society in a state of Nakedness*, will spontaneously suggest itself.
Should some sceptical individual still entertain doubts whether
in a world without Clothes, the smallest Politeness, Polity, or
even Police, could exist, let him turn to the original Volume,
and view there the boundless Serbonian Bogs of Sansculottism, stretching sour and pestilential : over which we have
lightly flown ; where not only whole armies but whole nations
might sink ! If indeed the following argument, in its brief
riveting emphasis, be not of itself incontrovertible and final :

'Are we Opossums ; have we natural Pouches, like the
'Kangaroo ? Or how, without Clothes, could we possess the
'master-organ, soul's-seat, and true pineal gland of the Body
'Social : I mean, a Purse ?'

Nevertheless it is impossible to hate Professor Teufelsdröckh ; at worst, one knows not whether to hate or to love
him. For though in looking at the fair tapestry of human
Life, with its royal and even sacred figures, he dwells not on
the obverse alone, but here chiefly on the reverse ; and indeed turns out the rough seams, tatters, and manifold thrums
of that unsightly wrong-side, with an almost diabolic patience
and indifference, which must have sunk him in the estimation
of most readers,—there is that within which unspeakably
distinguishes him from all other past and present Sansculottists. The grand unparalleled peculiarity of Teufelsdröckh
is, that with all this Descendentalism, he combines a Transcendentalism, no less superlative ; whereby if on the one hand

he degrade man below most animals, except those jacketed Gouda Cows, he, on the other, exalts him beyond the visible Heavens, almost to an equality with the gods.

'To the eye of vulgar Logic,' says he, 'what is man? An 'omnivorous Biped that wears Breeches. To the eye of Pure 'Reason what is he? A soul, a Spirit, and divine Apparition. 'Round his mysterious ME, there lies, under all those wool-'rags, a Garment of Flesh (or of Senses), contextured in the 'Loom of Heaven; whereby he is revealed to his like, and 'dwells with them in UNION and DIVISION; and sees and fash-'ions for himself a Universe, with azure Starry Spaces, and 'long Thousands of Years. Deep-hidden is he under that 'strange Garment; amid Sounds and Colours and Forms, as 'it were, swathed in, and inextricably overshrouded: yet it 'is skywoven, and worthy of a God. Stands he not thereby 'in the centre of Immensities, in the conflux of Eternities? 'He feels; power has been given him to know, to believe; 'nay does not the spirit of Love, free in its celestial primeval 'brightness, even here, though but for moments look through? 'Well said Saint Chrysostom, with his lips of gold, "the true 'SHEKINAH is Man:" where else is the GOD'S-PRESENCE mani-'fested not to our eyes only, but to our hearts, as in our fel-'low man?'

In such passages, unhappily too rare, the high Platonic Mysticism of our Author, which is perhaps the fundamental element of his nature, bursts forth, as it were, in full flood; and, through all the vapour and tarnish of what is often so perverse, so mean in his exterior and environment, we seem to look into a whole inward Sea of Light and Love;—though, alas, the grim coppery clouds soon roll together again, and hide it from view.

Such tendency to Mysticism is everywhere traceable in this man; and indeed, to attentive readers, must have been long ago apparent. Nothing that he sees but has more than a common meaning, but has two meanings: thus, if in the highest Imperial Sceptre and Charlemagne-Mantle, as well as in the poorest Ox-goad and Gipsy-Blanket, he finds Prose, Decay, Contemptibility; there is in each sort Poetry also,

and a reverend Worth. For Matter, were it never so despicable, is Spirit, the manifestation of Spirit : were it never so
honourable, can it be more ? The thing Visible, nay the
thing Imagined, the thing in any way conceived as Visible,
what is it but a Garment, a Clothing of the higher, celestial
Invisible, 'unimaginable, formless, dark with excess of bright ? '
Under which point of view the following passage, so strange
in purport, so strange in phrase, seems characteristic enough :

'The beginning of all Wisdom is to look fixedly on Clothes,
' or even with armed eyesight, till they become *transparent.*
' "The Philosopher," says the wisest of this age, "must sta-
'tion himself in the middle :" how true ! The Philosopher
'is he to whom the Highest has descended, and the Lowest
'has mounted up ; who is the equal and kindly brother of
'all.

'Shall we tremble before clothwebs and cobwebs, whether
' woven in Arkwright looms, or by the silent Arachnes that
'weave unrestingly in our Imagination ? Or, on the other
'hand, what is there that we cannot love ; since all was cre-
'ated by God ?

'Happy he who can look through the Clothes of a Man
'(the woollen, and fleshly, and official Bank-paper, and State-
'paper Clothes), into the Man himself ; and discern, it may
'be, in this or the other Dread Potentate, a more or less in-
'competent Digestive-apparatus ; yet also an inscrutable ven-
'erable Mystery, in the meanest Tinker that sees with eyes !'

For the rest, as is natural to a man of this kind, he deals
much in the feeling of Wonder ; insists on the necessity and
high worth of universal Wonder ; which he holds to be the
only reasonable temper for the denizen of so singular a Planet
as ours. 'Wonder,' says he, 'is the basis of Worship : the
' reign of wonder is perennial, indestructible in Man ; only at
' certain stages (as the present), it is, for some short season,
'a reign *in partibus infidelium.*' That progress of Science,
which is to destroy Wonder, and in its stead substitute Men-
suration and Numeration, finds small favour with Teufelsdröckh, much as he otherwise venerates these two latter
processes.

'Shall your Science,' exclaims he, 'proceed in the small
'chink lighted, or even oil-lighted, underground workshop of
'Logic alone; and man's mind become an Arithmetical Mill,
'whereof Memory is the Hopper, and mere Tables of Sines
'and Tangents, Codification, and Treatises of what you call
'Political Economy, are the Meal? And what is that Science,
'which the scientific head alone, were it screwed off, and (like
the Doctor's in the Arabian Tale) set in a basin, to keep it
'alive, could persecute without shadow of a heart,—but one
'other of the mechanical and menial handicrafts, for which
'the Scientific Head (having a Soul in it) is too noble an or-
'gan? I mean that Thought without Reverence is barren,
'perhaps poisonous; at best, dies like cookery with the day
'that called it forth; does not live, like sowing, in successive
'tilths and wider-spreading harvests, bringing food and plen-
'teous increase to all Time.'

In such wise does Teufelsdröckh deal hits, harder or softer,
according to ability; yet ever, as we would fain persuade
ourselves, with charitable intent. Above all, that class of
'Logic-choppers, and treble-pipe Scoffers, and professed Ene-
'mies to Wonder; who, in these days, so numerously patrol
'as night-constables about the Mechanics' Institute of Science,
'and cackle, like true Old-Roman geese and goslings round
'their Capitol, on any alarm, or on none; nay who often, as
'illuminated Sceptics walk abroad into peaceable society, in
'full daylight, with rattle and lantern, and insist on guiding
'you and guarding you therewith, though the Sun is shining,
'and the street populous with mere justice-loving men:' that
whole class is inexpressibly wearisome to him. Hear with
what uncommon animation he perorates:

'The man who cannot wonder, who does not habitually
'wonder (and worship), were he President of innumerable
'Royal Societies, and carried the whole *Mécanique Céleste* and
'*Hegel's Philosophy*, and the epitome of all Laboratories and
'Observatories with their results, in his single head,—is but
'a Pair of Spectacles behind which there is no Eye. Let
'those who have Eyes look through him, then he may be
'useful.

'Thou wilt have no Mystery and Mysticism ; wilt walk
'through thy world by the sunshine of what thou callest
'Truth, or even by the hand-lamp of what I call Attorney-
'Logic ; and "explain" all, "account" for all, or believe
'nothing of it ? Nay, thou wilt attempt laughter ; whoso
'recognizes the unfathomable, all-pervading domain of Mys-
'tery, which is everywhere under our feet and among our
'hands ; to whom the Universe is an Oracle and Temple, as
'well as a Kitchen and Cattle-stall,—he shall be a delirious
'Mystic ; to him thou, with sniffing charity, wilt protrusively
'proffer thy hand-lamp, and shriek, as one injured, when he
'kicks his foot through it?—*Armer Teufel!* Doth not thy
'cow calve, doth not thy bull gender? Thou thyself, wert
'thou not born, wilt thou not die ? "Explain" me all this,
'or do one of two things : Retire into private places with thy
'foolish cackle ; or, what were better, give it up, and weep,
'not that the reign of wonder is done, and God's world all
'disembellished and prosaic, but that thou hitherto art a
'Dilettante and sandblind Pedant.'

CHAPTER XI.

PROSPECTIVE.

The Philosophy of Clothes is now to all readers, as we pre-
dicated it would do, unfolding itself into new boundless ex-
pansions, of a cloudcapt, almost chimerical aspect, yet not
without azure loomings in the far distance, and streaks as of
an Elysian brightness ; the highly questionable purport and
promise of which it is becoming more and more important for
us to ascertain. Is that a real Elysian brightness, cries many
a timid wayfarer, or the reflex of Pandemonian lava ? Is it of
a truth leading us into beatific Asphodel meadows, or the
yellow-burning marl of a Hell-on-Earth ?

Our Professor, like other Mystics, whether delirious or inspired, gives an Editor enough to do. Ever higher and dizzier
are the heights he leads us to ; more piercing, all-compre-
hending, all-confounding are his views and glances. For example, this of Nature being not an Aggregate but a Whole :

'Well sang the Hebrew Psalmist: "If I take the wings of
'the morning and dwell in the uttermost parts of the universe,
'God is there." Thou too, O cultivated reader, who too prob-
'ably art no Psalmist, but a Prosaist, knowing GOD only by
'tradition, knowest thou any corner of the world where at
'least FORCE is not? The drop which thou shakest from thy
'wet hand, rests not where it falls, but to-morrow thou findest
'it swept away; already, on the wings of the Northwind, it is
'nearing the Tropic of Cancer. How came it to evaporate,
'and not lie motionless? Thinkest thou there is aught
'motionless; without Force and utterly dead?

'As I rode through the Schwarzwald, I said to myself:
'That little fire which glows star-like across the dark-growing
'(*nachtende*) moor, where the sooty smith bends over his anvil,
'and thou hopest to replace thy lost horse-shoe,—is it a de-
'tached, separated speck, cut off from the whole Universe; or
'indissolubly joined to the whole? Thou fool, that smithy-
'fire was (primarily) kindled at the Sun; is fed by air that
'circulates from before Noah's Deluge, from beyond the Dog-
'star; therein, with Iron Force, and Coal Force, and the far
'stranger Force of Man, are cunning affinities and battles and
'victories of Force brought about: it is a little ganglion, or
'nervous centre, in the great vital system of Immensity. Call
'it, if thou wilt, an unconscious Altar, kindled on the bosom of
'the All; whose iron sacrifice, whose iron smoke and influ-
'ence reach quite through the All; whose Dingy Priest, not
'by word, yet by brain and sinew, preaches forth the mystery
'of Force; nay preaches forth (exoterically enough) one little
'textlet from the Gospel of Freedom, the Gospel of Man's
'Force, commanding, and one day to be all-commanding.

'Detached, separated! I say there is no such separation:
'nothing hitherto was ever stranded, cast aside; but all,
'were it only a withered leaf, works together with all; is
'borne forward on the bottomless, shoreless flood of Action,
'and lives through perpetual metamorphoses. The withered
'leaf is not dead and lost, there are Forces in it and around
'it, though working in inverse order; else how could it *rot?*
'Despise not the rag from which man makes Paper, or the

' litter from which the Earth makes Corn. Rightly viewed
' no meanest object is insignificant ; all objects are as windows,
' through which the philosophic eye looks into Infinitude
' itself.'

Again, leaving that wondrous Schwarzwald Smithy-Altar,
what vacant, high-sailing air-ships are these, and whither will
they sail with us?

' All visible things are Emblems ; what thou seest is not
' there on its own account ; strictly taken, is not there at all :
' Matter exists only spiritually, and to represent some Idea,
' and *body* it forth.   Hence Clothes, as despicable as we think
' them, are so unspeakably significant.   Clothes, from the
' King's mantle downwards, are Emblematic, not of want only,
' but of a manifold cunning Victory over Want.   On the other
' hand, all Emblematic things are properly Clothes, thought-
' woven or hand-woven : must not the Imagination weave Gar-
' ments, visible Bodies, wherein the else invisible creations
' and inspirations of our Reason are, like Spirits, revealed, and
' first become all-powerful ;—the rather if, as we often see,
' the Hand too aid her, and (by wool Clothes or otherwise) re-
' veal such even to the outward eye ?

' Men are properly said to be clothed with Authority,
' clothed with Beauty, with Curses, and the like.   Nay, if
' you consider it, what is Man himself, and his whole ter-
' restrial Life, but an Emblem ; a Clothing or visible Gar-
' ment for that divine ME of his, cast hither, like a light-
' particle, down from Heaven ?   Thus is he said also to be
' clothed with a Body.

' Language is called the Garment of Thought : however,
' it should rather be, Language is the Flesh-Garment, the
' Body, of Thought.   I said that Imagination wove this
' Flesh-Garment ; and does she not?   Metaphors are her
' stuff : examine Language ; what, if you except some few
' primitive elements (of natural sound), what is it all but
' Metaphors, recognised as such, or no longer recognised :
' still fluid and florid, or now solid-grown and colourless?
' If those same primitive elements are the osseous fixtures
' in the Flesh-Garment, Language,—then are Metaphors its

'muscles and tissues and living integuments. An unmeta-
'phorical style you shall in vain seek for : is not your very
'*Attention* a *Stretching-to?* The difference lies here : some
'styles are lean, adust, wiry, the muscle itself seems osseous;
'some are even quite pallid, hunger-bitten, and dead-look-
'ing; while others again glow in the flush of health and
'vigorous self-growth, sometimes (as in my own case) not
'without an apoplectic tendency. Moreover, there are sham
'Metaphors, which overhanging that same Thought's-Body
'(best naked), and deceptively bedizening, or bolstering it
'out, may be called its false stuffings, superfluous show-
'cloaks (*Putz-Mäntel*), and tawdry woolen rags ; whereof he
'that runs and reads may gather whole hampers,—and burn
'them.'

Than which paragraph on Metaphors did the reader ever
chance to see a more surprisingly metaphorical? However,
that is not our chief grievance ; the Professor continues :

'Why multiply instances? It is written, the Heavens and
'the Earth shall fade away like a Vesture ; which indeed
'they are : the Time-vesture of the External. Whatsoever
'sensibly exists, whatsoever represents Spirit to Spirit, is
'properly a Clothing, a suit of Raiment, put on for a season,
'and to be laid off. Thus in this one pregnant subject of
'CLOTHES, rightly understood, is included all that men have
'thought, dreamed, done and been : the whole External Uni-
'verse and what it holds is but Clothing ; and the essence
'of all Science lies in the PHILOSOPHY OF CLOTHES.'

Towards these dim infinitely-expanded regions, close-bor-
dering on the impalpable Inane, it is not without apprehension, and perpetual difficulties, that the Editor sees himself
journeying and struggling. Till lately a cheerful daystar of
hope hung before him, in the expected Aid of Hofrath
Heuschrecke ; which daystar, however, melts now, not into
the red of morning, but into a vague, gray half-light, uncertain whether dawn of day or dusk of utter darkness. For
the last week, these so-called Biographical Documents are
in his hand. By the kindness of a Scottish Hamburg Mer-
chant, whose name, known to the whole mercantile world,

he must not mention; but whose honourable courtesy, now and often before spontaneously manifested to him, a mere literary stranger, he cannot soon forget,—the bulky Weissnichtwo Packet, with all its Customhouse seals, foreign hieroglyphs, and miscellaneous tokens of Travel, arrived here, in perfect safety, and free of cost. The reader shall now fancy with what hot haste it was broken up, with what breathless expectation glanced over; and, alas, with what unquiet disappointment it has, since then, been often thrown down, and again taken up.

Hofrath Heuschrecke, in a too long-winded Letter, full of compliments, Weissnichtwo politics, dinners, dining repartees, and other ephemeral trivialities, proceeds to remind us of what we knew well already: that however it may be with Metaphysics, and other abstract Science originating in the Head (*Verstand*) alone, no Life Philosophy (*Lebensphilosophie*), such as this of Clothes pretends to be, which originates equally in the Character (*Gemüth*), and equally speaks thereto, can attain its significance till the Character itself is known and seen; 'till the Author's View of the 'World (*Weltansicht*), and how he actively and passively came 'by such view, are clear: in short till a Biography of him 'has been philosophico-poetically written, and philosophico- 'poetically read.' 'Nay,' adds he, 'were the speculative 'scientific Truth even known, you still, in this inquiring age, 'ask yourself, Whence came it, and Why, and How?—and 'rest not, till, if no better may be, Fancy have shaped out 'an answer; and either in the authentic lineaments of Fact, 'or the forged ones of Fiction, a complete picture and Genet- 'ical History of the Man and his spiritual Endeavour lies 'before you. But why,' says the Hofrath, and indeed say we, 'do I dilate on the uses of our Teufelsdröckh's Biog- 'raphy? The great Herr Minister von Goethe has pene- 'tratingly remarked that "Man is properly the *only* object 'that interests man:" thus I too have noted, that in Weiss- 'nichtwo our whole conversation is little or nothing else 'but Biography or Autobiography; ever humano-anecdotical '(*menschlich-anecdotisch*). Biography is by nature the most

5

'universally profitable, universally pleasant of all things
'especially Biography of distinguished individuals.

'By this time, *mein Verehrtester* (my Most Esteemed),' continues he, with an eloquence which, unless the words be pur-
loined from Teufelsdröckh, or some trick of his, as we suspect, is well nigh unaccountable, 'by this time you are fairly
'plunged (*vertieft*) in that mighty forest of Clothes-Philosophy;
'and looking round, as all readers do, with astonishment
'enough. Such portions and passages as you have already
'mastered, and brought to paper, could not but awaken a
'strange curiosity touching the mind they issued from; the
'perhaps unparalleled psychical mechanism, which manufac-
'tured such matter, and emitted it to the light of day. Had
'Teufelsdröckh also a father and mother; did he, at one
'time, wear drivel-bibs, and live on spoon-meat? Did he
'ever, in rapture and tears, clasp a friend's bosom to his;
'looks he also wistfully into the long burial-aisle of the Past,
'where only winds, and their low harsh moan, give inarticu-
'late answer? Has he fought duels;—good Heaven! how
'did he comport himself when in Love? By what singular
'stair-steps, in short, and subterranean passages, and sloughs
'of Despair, and steep Pisgah hills, has he reached this won-
'derful prophetic Hebron (a true Old-Clothes Jewry) where
'he now dwells?

'To all these natural questions the voice of Public History
'is as yet silent. Certain only that he has been, and is, a
'Pilgrim, and Traveller from a far Country; more or less
'footsore and travel-soiled; has parted with road-companions;
'fallen among thieves, been poisoned by bad cookery, blistered
'with bugbites; nevertheless, at every stage (for they have
'let him pass), has had the Bill to discharge. But the whole
'particulars of his Route, his Weather-observations, the pic-
'turesque Sketches he took, though all regularly jotted down
'(in indelible sympathetic-ink by an invisible interior Pen-
'man), are these nowhere forthcoming? Perhaps quite lost:
'one other leaf of that mighty Volume (of human Memory)
'left to fly abroad, unprinted, unpublished, unbound up, as
'waste paper; and rot, the sport of rainy winds?

'No, *verehrtester Herr Herausgeber*, in no wise ! I here, by 'the unexampled favour you stand in with our Sage, send not 'a Biography only, but an Autobiography : at least the ma-'terials for such ; wherefrom, if I misreckon not, your per-'spicacity will draw fullest insight : and so the whole Philos-'ophy and Philosopher of Clothes will stand clear to the 'wondering eyes of England, nay thence, through America, 'through Hindostan, and the antipodal New Holland, finally 'conquer (*einnehmen*) great part of this terrestrial Planet !'

And now let the sympathising reader judge of our feeling when, in place of this same Autobiography with 'fullest insight,' we find—Six considerable PAPER BAGS, carefully sealed, and marked successively, in gilt China-ink, with the symbols of the Six southern Zodiacal Signs, beginning at Libra ; in the inside of which sealed Bags lie miscellaneous masses of Sheets, and oftener Shreds and Snips, written in Professor Teufelsdröckh's scarce legible *cursiv-schrift ;* and treating of all imaginable things under the Zodiac and above it, but of his own personal history only at rare intervals and then in the most enigmatic manner !

Whole fascicles there are, wherein the Professor, or, as he here speaking in the third person calls himself, ' the Wanderer,' is not once named. Then again, amidst what seems to be a Metaphysico-theological Disquisition, ' Detached Thoughts on the Steamengine,' or, ' The continued Possibility of Prophecy,' we shall meet with some quite private, not unimportant Biographical fact. On certain sheets stand Dreams, authentic or not, while the circumjacent waking Actions are omitted. Anecdotes, oftenest without date of place or time, fly loosely on separate slips, like Sibylline leaves. Interspersed also are long purely Autobiographical delineations ; yet without connexion, without recognisable coherence ; so unimportant, so superfluously minute, they almost remind us of 'P.P. Clerk of this Parish.' Thus does famine of intelligence alternate with waste. Selection, order appears to be unknown to the Professor. In all Bags the same imbroglio ; only perhaps in the Bag *Capricorn*, and those near it, the confusion a little worse confounded. Close by a rather eloquent Oration, ' On receiving the Doctor's Hat,' lie wash-bills marked *bezahlt* (settled). His Travels are indicated by the Street-Advertisements of the various cities he has visited ; of which Street-Advertisements, in most living tongues, here is perhaps the completest collection extant.

So that if the Clothes-Volume itself was too like a Chaos, we have now instead of the solar Luminary that should still it, the airy Limbo which by intermixture will further vola-tilise and discompose it! As we shall perhaps see it our duty ultimately to deposit these Six Paper-Bags in the British Museum, farther description, and all vituperation of them, may be spared. Biography or autobiography of Teufels-dröckh there is, clearly enough, none to be gleaned here : at most some sketchy, shadowy fugitive likeness of him may, by unheard-of-efforts, partly of intellect, partly of imagination, on the side of Editor and of Reader, rise up between them. Only as a gaseous-chaotic Appendix to that aqueous-chaotic Volume can the contents of the Six Bags hover round us, and portions thereof be incorporated with our delineation of it.

Daily and nightly does the Editor sit (with green specta-cles) deciphering these unimaginable Documents from their perplexed *cursiv-schrift ;* collating them with the almost equally unimaginable Volume, which stands in legible print. Over such a universal medley of high and low, of hot, cold, moist and dry, is he here struggling (by union of like with like, which is Method) to build a firm Bridge for British travellers. Never perhaps since our first Bridge-builders, Sin and Death, built that stupendous Arch from Hell-gate to the Earth, did any Pontifex, or Pontiff, undertake such a task as the present Editor. For in this Arch too, leading, as we humbly presume, far otherwards than that grand primeval one, the materials are to be fished up from the weltering deep, and down from the simmering air, here one mass, there another, and cunningly cemented, while the elements boil be-neath ; nor is there any supernatural force to do it with ; but simply the Diligence and feeble thinking Faculty of an Eng-lish Editor, endeavouring to evolve printed Creation out of a German printed and written Chaos, wherein, as he shoots to and fro in it, gathering, clutching, piecing the Why to the far-distant Wherefore, his whole Faculty and Self are like to be swallowed up.

Patiently, under these incessant toils and agitations, does the Editor, dismissing all anger, see his otherwise robust health declining ; some fraction of his alloted natural sleep nightly leaving him, and little but an inflamed nervous-system to be looked for. What is the use of health, or of life, if not to do some work therewith ? And what work nobler than transplanting foreign Thought into the barren domestic soil ; except indeed planting Thought of your own, which the fewest are privileged to do ? Wild as it looks, this Philosophy of Clothes, can we ever reach its real meaning, promises to reveal new-coming Eras, the first dim rudiments and already budding germs of a nobler Era, in Universal History. Is not such a prize worth some striving ? Forward with us, courageous reader ; be it towards failure, or towards success ! The latter thou sharest with us, the former also is not all our own.

BOOK II.

CHAPTER I.

GENESIS.

In a psychological point of view, it is perhaps questionable whether from birth and genealogy, how closely scrutinised soever, much insight is to be gained. Nevertheless, as in every phenomenon the Beginning remains always the most notable moment; so, with regard to any great man, we rest not till, for our scientific profit or not, the whole circumstances of his first appearance in this planet, and what manner of Public Entry he made, are with utmost completeness rendered manifest. To the Genesis of our Clothes-Philosopher, then, be this First Chapter consecrated. Unhappily, indeed, he seems to be of quite obscure extraction; uncertain, we might almost say, whether of any: so that this Genesis of his can properly be nothing but an Exodus (or transit out of Invisibility into Visibility); whereof the preliminary portion is nowhere forthcoming.

'In the village of Entepfuhl,' thus writes he, in the Bag *Libra*, on various Papers, which we arrange with difficulty, ' dwelt Andreas Futteral and his wife ; childless, in still seclu- ' sion, and cheerful though now verging towards old age. ' Andreas had been grenadier Sergeant, and even regimental ' Schoolmaster under Frederick the Great ; but now, quitting ' the halbert and ferule for the spade and pruning-hook, cul- ' tivated a little orchard, on the produce of which, he Cincin- ' natus-like, lived not without dignity. Fruits, the peach, the ' apple, the grape, with other varieties came in their season ; ' all which Andreas knew how to sell: on evenings he smoked ' largely, or read (as beseemed a regimental Schoolmaster), ' and talked to neighbours that would listen about the Vic-

' tory of Rossbach ; and how Fritz the Only (*der Einzige*) had
' once with his own royal lips spoken to him, had been pleased
' to say, when Andreas as camp-sentinel demanded the pass-
' word, "*Schweig' Hund* (Peace hound) ! " before any of his
' staff-adjutants could answer. "*Das nenn' ich mir einen
' König,* There is what I call a King," would Andreas exclaim ;
' "but the smoke of Kunersdorf was still smarting his eyes."

' Gretchen, the housewife, won like Desdemona by the
' deeds rather than the looks of her now veteran Othello,
' lived not in altogether military subordination ; for, as An-
' dreas said, "the womankind will not drill (*wer kann die
' Weiberchen dressiren*) : " nevertheless she at heart loved him
' both for valour and wisdom ; to her a Prussian grenadier
' Sergeant and Regiment's Schoolmaster was little other than
' a Cicero and Cid : what you see, yet cannot see over, is as
' good as infinite. Nay, was not Andreas in very deed a man
' of order, courage, downrightness (*Geradheit*) ; that under-
' stood Büsching's Geography, had been in the victory of
' Rossbach, and left for dead in the camisade of Hochkirch ?
' The good Gretchen, for all her fretting, watched over him
' and hovered around him, as only a true house-mother can :
' assiduously she cooked and sewed and scoured for him ; so
' that not only his old regimental sword and grenadier-cap,
' but the whole habitation and environment, where on pegs
' of honour they hung, looked ever trim and gay ; a roomy
' painted Cottage, embowered in fruit-trees and forest-trees,
' evergreens and honeysuckles ; rising many-coloured from
' amid shaven grass-plots, flowers struggling in through the
' very windows; under its long projecting eaves nothing but
' garden-tools in methodic piles (to screen them from rain),
' and seats where, especially on summer nights, a King might
' have wished to sit and smoke, and call it his. Such a *Bauer-
' gut* (Copyhold) had Gretchen given her veteran ; whose
' sinewy arms, and long-disused gardening talent, had made
' it what you saw.

' Into this umbrageous Man's-nest, one meek yellow even-
' ing or dusk, when the Sun, hidden indeed from terrestrial
' Entepfuhl, did nevertheless journey visible and radiant along

' the celestial Balance (*Libra*), it was that a Stranger of rev-
' erend aspect entered; and with grave salutation, stood be-
' fore the two rather astonished housemates. He was close-
' muffled in a wide mantle; which without farther parley
' unfolding, he deposited therefrom what seemed some Basket,
' overhung with green Persian silk; saying only : *Ihr lieben*
' *Leute, hier bringe ein unschätzbares Verleihen ; nehmt es in aller*
' *Acht, sorgfältigst benützt es : mit hohem Lohn, oder wohl mit*
' *schweren Zinsen, wird's einst zurückgefordert.* "Good Chris-
' tian people, here lies for you an invaluable Loan; take all
' heed thereof, in all carefulness employ it: with high recom-
' pense, or else with heavy penalty, will it one day be required
' back." Uttering which singular words, in a clear, bell-like,
' forever memorable tone, the Stranger gracefully withdrew;
' and before Andreas or his wife, gazing in expectant wonder,
' had time to fashion either question or answer, was clean
' gone. Neither out of doors could aught of him be seen or
' heard; he had vanished in the thickets, in the dusk; the
' Orchard-gate stood quietly closed : the Stranger was gone
' once and always. So sudden had the whole transaction
' been, in the autumn stillness and twilight, so gentle, noise-
' less, that the Futterals could have fancied it all a trick of
' Imagination, or some visit from an authentic Spirit. Only
' that the green silk Basket, such as neither Imagination nor
' authentic Spirits are wont to carry, still stood visible and
' tangible on their little parlour-table. Towards this the as-
' tonished couple, now with lit candle, hastily turned their at-
' tention. Lifting the green veil, to see what invaluable it
' hid, they descried there amid down and rich white wrap-
' pages, no Pitt Diamond or Hapsburg Regalia, but in the
' softest sleep, a little red-coloured Infant! Beside it, lay a
' roll of gold Friedrichs the exact amount of which was never
' publicly known; also a *Taufschein* (baptismal certificate),
' wherein unfortunately nothing but the Name was decipher-
' able; other documents or indication none whatever.

'To wonder and conjecture was unavailing, then and always
'thenceforth. Nowhere in Entepfuhl, on the morrow or next
day, did tidings transpire of any such figure as the Stranger ;

'nor could the Traveller, who had passed through the neigh-
'bouring Town in coach-and-four, be connected with this
'Apparition, except in the way of gratuitous surmise. Mean-
'while, for Andreas and his wife, the grand practical problem
'was : What to do with this little sleeping red-coloured Infant?
'Amid amazements and curiosities, which had to die away
'without external satisfying, they resolved, as in such circum-
'stances charitable prudent people needs must, on nursing it,
'though with spoon-meat, into whiteness, and if possible into
'manhood. The Heavens smiled on their endeavour : thus
'has that same mysterious Individual ever since had a status
'for himself in this visible Universe, some modicum of victual
'and lodging and parade-ground ; and now expanded in bulk,
'faculty, and knowledge of good and evil, he, as HERR DIOGENES
'TEUFELSDRÖCKH, professes or is ready to profess, perhaps not
'altogether without effect, in the new University of Weiss-
'nichtwo, the new Science of Things in General.'

Our Philosopher declares here, as indeed we should think
he well might, that these facts, first communicated, by the
good Gretchen Futteral, in his twelfth year, 'produced on
'the boyish heart and fancy a quite indelible impression.
'Who this reverend Personage,' he says, 'that glided into the
'Orchard Cottage when the Sun was in Libra, and then, as
'on spirit's wings, glided out again, might be ? An inexpressi-
'ble desire, full of love and of sadness, has often since strug-
'gled within me to shape an answer. Ever, in my distresses
'and my loneliness, has Fantasy turned, full of longing(*sehn-*
'*suchtsvoll*), to that unknown Father, who perhaps far from
'me, perhaps near, either way invisible, might have taken me
'to his paternal bosom, there to lie screened from many a
'woe. Thou beloved Father, dost thou still, shut out from
'me only by thin penetrable curtains of earthly Space, wend
'to and fro among the crowd of the living ? Or art thou hid-
'den by those far thicker curtains of the Everlasting Night, or
'rather of the Everlasting Day, through which my mortal eye
'and outstretched arms need not strive to reach ? Alas ! I
'know not, and in vain vex myself to know. More than once,
'heart-deluded, have I taken for thee this and the other noble-

'looking Stranger ; and approached him wistfully, with infinite
'regard ; but he too had to repel me, he too was not thou.

'And yet, O Man born of Woman,' cries the Autobiographer,
with one of his sudden whirls, 'wherein is my case peculiar?
'Hadst thou, any more than I, a Father whom thou knowest?
'The Andreas and Gretchen, or the Adam and Eve, who led
'thee into Life, and for a time suckled and pap-fed thee there,
'whom thou namest Father and Mother; these were, like
'mine, but thy nursing-father and nursing-mother : thy true
'Beginning and Father is in Heaven, whom with the bodily
'eye thou shalt never behold, but only with the spiritual.'

' The little green veil,' adds he, among much similar moral-
ising, and embroiled discoursing, ' I yet keep ; still more in-
' separably the Name, Diogenes Teufelsdröckh. From the
' veil can nothing be inferred : a piece of now quite faded
' Persian silk, like thousands of others. On the name I have
' many times meditated and conjectured ; but neither in this
' lay there any clue. That it was my unknown Father's name
' I must hesitate to believe. To no purpose have I searched
' through all the Herald's Books, in and without the German
' Empire, and through all manner of Subscriber-Lists (*Pränu-*
' *meranten*), Militia-Rolls, and other Name-catalogues ; extra-
' ordinary names as we have in Germany, the name Teufels-
' dröckh, except as appended to my own person, nowhere occurs.
' Again what may the unchristian rather than Christian "Diog-
' enes" mean? Did that reverend Basket-bearer intend by
' such designation, to shadow forth my future destiny, or his
' own present malign humour? Perhaps the latter, perhaps
' both. Thou ill-starred Parent, who like an Ostrich hadst to
' leave thy ill-starred offspring to be hatched into self-sup-
' port by the mere sky-influences of Chance, can thy pilgrim-
' age have been a smooth one? Beset by Misfortune thou
' doubtless hast been ; or indeed by the worst figure of Mis-
' fortune, by Misconduct. Often have I fancied how, in thy
' hard life-battle, thou wert shot at and slung at, wounded,
' hand-fettered, hamstrung, browbeaten and bedevilled, by
' the Time-Spirit (*Zeitgeist*) in thyself and others, till the good
' soul first given thee was seared into grim rage ; and thou

'hadst nothing for it but to leave in me an indignant appeal
' to the Future, and living speaking Protest against the Devil,
' as that same Spirit not of the Time only, but of Time itself,
' is well named! Which Appeal and Protest, may I now
' modestly add, was not perhaps quite lost in air.

' For indeed as Walter Shandy often insisted, there is much,
' nay almost all, in Names. The Name is the earliest Gar-
' ment you wrap round the Earth-visiting ME; to which it
' thenceforth cleaves, more tenaciously (for there are Names
' that have lasted nigh thirty centuries) than the very skin.
' And now from without, what mystic influences does it not
' send inwards, even to the centre ; especially in those plastic
' first-times, when the whole soul is yet infantine, soft, and
' the invisible seed-grain will grow to be an all-overshadowing
' tree! Names? Could I unfold the influence of Names,
' which are the most important of all clothings, I were a second
' greater Trismegistus. Not only all common Speech, but Sci-
' ence, Poetry itself is no other, if thou consider it, than a
' right *Naming*. Adam's first task was giving names to natural
' Appearances : what is ours still but a continuation of the
' same ; be the appearances exotic-vegetable, organic, mechanic,
' stars, or starry movements (as in Science), or (as in Poetry)
' passions, virtues, calamities, God-attributes, Gods ?—In a
' very plain sense the Proverb says, *Call one a thief, and he will
' steal ;* in an almost similar sense, may we not perhaps say,
' *Call one Diogenes Teufelsdröckh, and he will open the Philos-
' ophy of Clothes.*'

' Meanwhile the incipient Diogenes, like others, all ignorant
' of his Why, his How or Whereabout, was opening his eyes
' to the kind Light ; sprawling out his ten fingers and toes ;
' listening, tasting, feeling ; in a word, by all his Five Senses,
' still more by his sixth Sense of Hunger, and a whole infini-
' tude of inward, spiritual, half-awakened Senses, endeavour-
' ing daily to acquire for himself some knowledge of this
' strange Universe where he had arrived, be his task therein
' what it might. Infinite was his progress ; thus in some
' fifteen months, he could perform the miracle of—Speech! To
breed a fresh Soul, is it not like brooding a fresh (celestial)

' Egg ; wherein as yet all is formless ; powerless ; yet by de-
' grees organic elements and fibres shoot through the watery
' albumen ; and out of vague Sensation, grows Thought, grows
' Fantasy and Force, and we have Philosophies, Dynasties,
' nay Poetries and Religions!

' Young Diogenes, or rather young Gneschen, for by such
' diminutive had they in their fondness named him, travelled
' forward to those high consummations, by quick yet easy
' stages. The Futterals, to avoid vain talk, and moreover
' keep the roll of gold Friedrichs safe, gave out that he was a
' grand-nephew ; the orphan of some sister's daughter, sud-
' denly deceased, in Andreas's distant Prussian birth-land ; of
' whom, as of her indigent sorrowing widower, little enough
' was known at Entepfuhl. Heedless of all which, the Nurse-
' ling took to his spoon-meat, and throve. I have heard him
' noted as a still infant, that kept his mind much to himself ;
' above all, that seldom or never cried. He already felt that
' time was precious ; that he had other work cut out for him
' than whimpering.'

Such, after utmost painful search and collation among these
miscellaneous Paper-masses, is all the notice we can gather of
Herr Teufelsdröckh's genealogy. More imperfect, more enigmatic it can seem to few readers than to us. The Professor,
in whom truly we more and more discern a certain satirical
turn, and deep under-currents of roguish whim, for the present stands pledged in honour, so we will not doubt him : but
seems it not conceivable that, by the ' good Gretchen Futteral,' or some other perhaps interested party, he has himself
been deceived ? Should these sheets, translated or not, ever
reach the Entepfuhl Circulating-Library, some cultivated native of that district might feel called to afford explanation.
Nay, since Books, like invisible scouts, permeate the whole
habitable globe, and Tombuctoo itself is not safe from British
Literature, may not some Copy find out even the mysterious
Basket-bearing stranger, who in a state of extreme senility perhaps still exists ; and gently force even him to disclose himself ; to claim openly a son, in whom any father may feel pride ?

CHAPTER II.

IDYLLIC.

'Happy season of Childhood!' exclaims Teufelsdröckh:
' Kind Nature, that art to all a bountiful mother; that visitest
' the poor man's hut with auroral radiance; and for thy
' Nurseling hast provided a soft swathing of Love and infinite
' Hope, wherein he waxes and slumbers, danced-round (*um-*
' *gäukelt*) by sweetest Dreams! If the paternal Cottage still
' shuts us in, its roof still screens us; with a Father we have
' as yet a prophet, priest and king, and an Obedience that
' makes us Free. The young spirit has awakened out of Eter-
' nity, and knows not what we mean by Time; as yet Time is
' no fast-hurrying stream, but a sportful sunlit ocean; years
' to the child are as ages: ah! the secret of Vicissitude, of
' that slower or quicker decay and ceaseless down-rushing of
' the universal World-fabric, from the granite mountain to the
' man or day-moth, is yet unknown; and in a motionless Uni-
' verse, we taste, what afterwards in this quick-whirling Uni-
' verse is forever denied us, the balm of Rest. Sleep on, thou
' fair Child, for thy long rough journey is at hand! A little
' while, and thou too shalt sleep no more, but thy very dreams
' shall be mimic battles; thou too, with old Arnauld, wilt have
' to say in stern patience: "Rest? Rest? Shall I not have
' all Eternity to rest in?" Celestial Nepenthe! though a
' Pyrrhus conquer empires, and an Alexander sack the world,
' he finds thee not; and thou hast once fallen gently, of thy
' own accord, on the eyelids, on the heart of every mother's
' child. For as yet, sleep and waking are one: the fair Life-
' garden rustles infinite around, and everywhere is dewy fra-
' grance, and the budding of Hope; which budding, if in
' youth, too frostnipt, it grows to flowers, will in manhood
' yield no fruit, but a prickly, bitter-rinded stone-fruit, of
' which the fewest can find the kernel.'

In such rose-coloured light does our Professor, as Poets are
wont, look back on his childhood; the historical details of

which (to say nothing of much other vague oratorical matter) he accordingly dwells on, with an almost wearisome minuteness. We hear of Entepfuhl standing 'in trustful derangement' among the woody slopes; the paternal Orchard flanking it as extreme outpost from below; the little Kuhbach gushing kindly by, among beech-rows, through river after river, into the Donau, into the Black Sea, into the Atmosphere and Universe; and how 'the brave old Linden,' stretching like a parasol of twenty ells in radius, overtopping all other rows and clumps, towered up from the central *Agora* and *Campus Martius* of the Village, like its Sacred Tree; and how the old man sat talking under its shadow (Gneschen often greedily listening), and the wearied labourers reclined, and the unwearied children sported, and the young men and maidens often danced to flute-music. 'Glorious summer twi-'lights,' cries Teufelsdröckh, 'when the Sun like a proud 'Conqueror and Imperial Taskmaster turned his back, with 'his gold purple emblazonry, and all his fire-clad bodyguard '(of Prismatic Colours); and the tired brickmakers of this 'clay Earth might steal a little frolic, and those few meek 'Stars would not tell of them!'

Then we have long details of the *Weinlesen* (Vintage), the Harvest-Home, Christmas, and so forth; with a whole cycle of the Entepfuhl Children's-games, differing apparently by mere superficial shades from those of other countries. Concerning all which, we shall here, for obvious reasons, say nothing. What cares the world for our as yet miniature Philosopher's achievements under that 'brave old Linden?' Or even where is the use of such practical reflections as the following? 'In all the sports of children, were it only in 'their wanton breakages and defacements, you shall discern 'a creative instinct (*schaffeden Trieb*): the Mankin feels that 'he is a born Man, that his vocation is to Work. The 'choicest present you can make him is a Tool; be it knife or 'pen-gun, for construction or for destruction; either way it 'is for Work, for Change. In gregarious sports of skill 'or strength, the Boy trains himself to Co-operation, for war 'or peace. as governor or governed: the little Maid again,

' provident of her domestic destiny, takes with preference to
' Dolls.'

Perhaps, however, we may give this anecdote, considering
who it is that relates it : ' My first short-clothes were of yel-
' low serge ; or rather, I should say, my first short cloth, for
' the vesture was one and indivisible, reaching from neck to
' ankle, a mere body with four limbs : of which fashion how
' little could I then divine the architectural, how much less
' the moral significance ! '

More graceful is the following little picture : ' On fine even-
' ings I was wont to carry forth my supper (bread-crumb
' boiled in milk), and eat it out of doors. On the coping of
' the Orchard wall, which I could reach by climbing, or still
' more easily if Father Andreas would set up the pruning-
' ladder, my porringer was placed : there, many a sunset,
' have I, looking at the distant western Mountains, consumed,
' not without relish, my evening meal. Those hues of gold
' and azure, that hush of World's expectation as Day died,
' were still a Hebrew Speech for me ; nevertheless I was look-
' ing at the fair illuminated Letters, and had an eye for their
' gilding.'

With ' the little one's friendship for cattle and poultry,' we
shall not much intermeddle. It may be that hereby he acquired a ' certain deeper sympathy with animated Nature ; '
but when, we would ask, saw any man, in a collection of Biographical Documents, such a piece as this : ' Impressive
' enough (*bedeutungsvoll*) was it to hear, in early morning, the
' Swineherd's horn ; and know that so many hungry happy
' quadrupeds were, on all sides, starting in hot haste to join
' him, for breakfast on the Heath. Or to see them, at even-
' tide, all marching in again, with short squeak, almost in
' military order ; and each, topographically correct, trotting
' off in succession to the right or left, through its own lane, to
' its own dwelling ; till old Kunz, at the Village-head, now
' left alone, blew his last blast, and retired for the night. We
' are wont to love the Hog chiefly in the form of Ham ; yet
' did not these bristly thick-skinned beings here manifest in-
' telligence, perhaps humour of character ; at any rate, a

' touching, trustful submissiveness to Man,—who were he but
a Swineherd, in darned gabardine, and leather breeches
' more resembling slate or discoloured tin breeches, is still
' the Hierarch of this lower world?'

It is maintained, by Helvetius and his set, that an infant of
genius is quite the same as any other infant, only that certain
surprisingly favourable influences accompany him through life,
especially through childhood, and expand him, while others lie
close-folded and continue dunces.   Herein, say they, consists
the whole difference between an inspired Prophet and a double-
barrelled Game-preserver : the inner man of the one has been
fostered into generous development ; that of the other, crushed
down perhaps by vigour of animal digestion, and the like, has
exuded and evaporated, or at best sleeps now irresuscitably
stagnant at the bottom of his stomach.   ' With which opinion,'
cries Teufelsdröckh, 'I should as soon agree as with this other,
' that an acorn might, by favourable or unfavourable influences
' of soil and climate, be nursed into a cabbage, or the cabbage-
' seed into an oak.

' Nevertheless,' continues he, ' I too acknowledge the all-but
' omnipotence of early culture and nurture : hereby we have
' either a doddered dwarf bush, or a high-towering, wide-shad-
' owing tree ; either a sick yellow cabbage, or an edible, lux-
' uriant green one.   Of a truth, it is the duty of all men, espe-
' cially of all philosophers, to note down with accuracy the char-
' acteristic circumstances of their Education, what furthered,
' what hindered, what in any way modified it : to which duty,
' now-a-days so pressing for many a German Autobiographer,
' I also zealously address myself.'—Thou rogue! Is it by short
clothes of yellow serge, and swineherd horns, that an infant of
genius is educated ?   And yet, as usual, it ever remains doubtful whether he is laughing in his sleeve at these Autobiographical times of ours, or writing from the abundance of his own
fond ineptitude.   For he continues : 'If among the ever-
' streaming currents of Sighs, Hearings, Feelings for Pain or
' Pleasure, whereby, as in a Magic Hall, young Gneschen went
' about environed, I might venture to select and specify, per-
' haps these following were also of the number :

6

'Doubtless, as childish sports call forth Intellect, Activity,
'so the young creature's Imagination was stirred up, and a
'Historical tendency given him by the narrative habits of Father
'Andreas ; who with his battle-reminiscences, and grey austere
'yet hearty patriarchal aspect, could not but appear another
'Ulysses and "Much-enduring Man." Eagerly I hung upon
'his tales, when listening neighbours enlivened the hearth :
'from these perils and these travels, wild and far almost as
'Hades itself, a dim world of Adventure expanded itself with-
'in me. Incalculable also was the knowledge I acquired in
'standing by the Old Men under the Linden-tree : the whole
'of Immensity was yet new to me ; and had not these reverend
'seniors, talkative enough, been employed in partial surveys
'thereof for nigh fourscore years ? With amazement I began
'to discover that Entepfuhl stood in the middle of a Country,
'of a World : that there was such a thing as History, as Biog-
'raphy ; to which I also, one day, by hand and tongue, might
'contribute.

'In a like sense worked the *Postwagen* (Stage-Coach), which,
'slow-rolling under its mountains of men and luggage, wended
'through our Village : northwards, truly in the dead of night ;
'yet southwards visibly at eventide. Not till my eighth year,
'did I reflect that this Postwagon could be other than some
'terrestrial Moon, rising and setting by mere Law of Nature,
'like the heavenly one ; that it came on made highways, from
'far cities towards far cities ; weaving them like a monstrous
'shuttle into closer and closer union. It was then that, in-
'dependently of Schiller's *Wilhelm Tell*, I made this not quite
'insignificant reflection (so true also in spiritual things) : *Any*
'*road, this simple Entepfuhl road, will lead you to the end of the*
'*World !*

'Why mention our Swallows, which, out of fair Africa as I
'learned, threading their way over seas and mountains, cor-
'porate cities and belligerent nations, yearly found themselves,
'with the month of May, snug-lodged in our Cottage Lobby ?
'the hospitable Father (for cleanliness' sake) had fixed a little
'bracket, plumb under their nest : there they built, and caught
'flies, and twittered, and bred ; and all, I chiefly, from the

' heart loved them. Bright, nimble creatures, who taught *you*
' the mason-craft; nay, stranger still, gave you a masonic in-
' corporation, almost social policy? For if, by ill chance, and
' when time pressed, your House fell, have I not seen five
' neighbourly Helpers appear next day; and swashing to and
' fro, with animated loud, long-drawn chirpings, and activ-
' ity almost super-hirundine, complete it again before night-
' fall?

'But undoubtedly the grand summary of Entepfuhl child's
' culture, where as in a funnel its manifold influences were con-
' centrated and simultaneously poured down on us, was the
' annual Cattle-fair. Here, assembling from all the four winds,
' came the elements of an unspeakable hurly-burly. Nut-
' brown maids and nutbrown men, all clear-washed, loud-
' laughing, bedizened and beribanded; who came for dancing,
' for treating, and if possible for happiness. Topbooted
'Graziers from the North; Swiss Brokers, Italian Drovers,
' also topbooted, from the South; these with their subalterns
' in leather jerkins, leather skull-caps, and long ox-goads;
' shouting in half-articulate speech, amid the inarticulate bark-
' ing and bellowing. Apart stood Potters from far Saxony,
' with their crockery in fair rows; Nürnberg Pedlars, in booths
' that to me seemed richer than Ormuz bazaars; Showmen
' from the Lago Maggiore; detachments of the *Wiener Schub*
' (Offscourings of Vienna) vociferously superintending games
' of chance. Ballad-singers brayed, Auctioneers grew hoarse;
' cheap New Wine (*heuriger*) flowed like water, still worse con-
' founding the confusion; and high over all, vaulted, in ground-
' and-lofty tumbling, a particoloured Merry Andrew, like the
' genius of the place and of Life itself.

'Thus encircled by the mystery of Existence; under the
' deep heavenly Firmament; waited on by the four golden
' Seasons with their vicissitudes of contribution, for even grim
' Winter brought its skating-matches and shooting-matches,
' its snow-storms and Christmas carols,—did the child sit and
' learn. These things were the Alphabet, whereby in after-

'time he was to syllable and partly read the grand Volume of
'the World: what matters it whether such Alphabet be in
'large gilt letters or in small ungilt ones, so you have an eye
'to read it? For Gneschen, eager to learn, the very act of
'looking thereon was a blessedness that gilded all: his ex-
'istence was a bright, soft element of Joy; out of which, as
'in Prospero's Island, wonder after wonder bodied itself forth,
'to teach by charming.

'Nevertheless, I were but a vain dreamer to say, that even
'then my felicity was perfect. I had, once for all, come down
'from Heaven into the Earth. Among the rainbow colours
'that glowed on my horizon, lay even in childhood a dark ring
'of Care, as yet no thicker than a thread, and often quite
'overshone; yet always it reappeared, nay ever waxing broad-
'er and broader; till in after-years it almost overshadowed
'my whole canopy, and threatened to engulf me in final
'night. It was the ring of Necessity, whereby we are all be-
'girt; happy he for whom a kind heavenly Sun brightens it
'into a ring of Duty, and plays round it with beautiful pris-
'matic diffractions; yet ever, as basis and as bourne for our
'whole being, it is there.

'For the first few years of our terrestrial Apprenticeship,
'we have not much work to do; but, boarded and lodged
'gratis, are set down mostly to look about us over the work-
'shop, and see others work, till we have understood the tools
'a little, and can handle this and that. If good Passivity
'alone, and not good Passivity and good Activity together,
'were the thing wanted, then was my early position favour-
'able beyond the most. In all that respects openness of Sense,
'affectionate Temper, ingenuous Curiosity, and the fostering
'of these, what more could I have wished? On the other
'side, however, things went not so well. My Active Power
'(*Thatkraft*) was unfavourably hemmed in; of which mis-
'fortune how many traces yet abide with me! In an orderly
'house, where the litter of children's sports is hateful enough,
'your training is too stoical; rather to bear and forbear than
'to make and do. I was forbid much: wishes in any measure
'bold I had to renounce; everywhere a strait bond of Obe-

' dience inflexibly held me down. Thus already Freewill
' often came in painful collision with Necessity ; so that my
' tears flowed, and at seasons the Child itself might taste that
' root of bitterness, wherewith the whole fruitage of our life
' is mingled and tempered.

' In which habituation to Obedience, truly, it was beyond
' measure safer to err by excess than by defect. Obedience
' is our universal duty and destiny ; wherein whoso will not
' bend must break : too early and too thoroughly we cannot
' be trained to know that Would, in this world of ours, is as
' mere zero to Should, and for most part as the smallest of
' fractions even to Shall. Hereby was laid for me the basis
' of worldly Discretion, nay, of Morality itself. Let me not
' quarrel with my upbringing ! It was rigorous, too frugal,
' compressively secluded, every way unscientific : yet in that
' very strictness and domestic solitude might there not lie the
' root of deeper earnestness, of the stem from which all noble
' fruit must grow ? Above all, how unskilful soever, it was
' loving, it was well-meant, honest ; whereby every deficiency
' was helped. My kind Mother, for as such I must ever love
' the good Gretchen, did me one altogether invaluable service :
' she taught me, less indeed by word than by act and daily
' reverent look and habitude, her own simple version of the
' Christian Faith. Andreas too attended Church ; yet more
' like a parade duty for which he in the other world expected
' pay with arrears,—as, I trust, he has received ; but my
' Mother, with a true woman's heart, and fine though uncul-
' tivated sense, was in the strictest acceptation Religious.
' How indestructibly the Good grows, and propagates itself,
' even among the weedy entanglements of Evil ! The highest
' whom I knew on Earth I here saw bowed down, with awe
' unspeakable, before a Higher in Heaven : such things, es-
' pecially in infancy, reach inwards to the very core of your
' being; mysteriously does a Holy of Holies build itself into
' visibility in the mysterious deeps ; and Reverence, the di-
' vinest in man, springs forth undying from its mean envelop-
' ment of Fear. Wouldst thou rather be a peasant's son that
' knew, were it never so rudely, there was a God in Heaven

' and in Man ; or a duke's son that only knew there were two
' and thirty quarters on the family-coach ? '

To which last question we must answer : Beware, O Teufelsdröckh, of spiritual pride !

CHAPTER III.

PEDAGOGY.

Hitherto we see young Gneschen, in his indivisible case of
yellow serge, borne forward mostly on the arms of kind Nature
alone ; seated, indeed, and much to his mind, in the terrestrial
workshop ; but (except his soft hazel eyes, which we doubt
not already gleamed with a still intelligence) called upon for
little voluntary movement there. Hitherto accordingly his
aspect is rather generic, that of an incipient Philosopher and
Poet in the abstract : perhaps it would puzzle Herr Heuschrecke himself to say wherein the Special Doctrine of Clothes
is as yet foreshadowed or betokened. For with Gneschen, as
with others, the Man may indeed stand pictured in the Boy
(at least all the pigments are there) ; yet only some half of the
Man stands in the Child, or young Boy, namely, his Passive
endowment, not his Active. The more impatient are we to
discover what figure he cuts in this latter capacity ; how when,
to use his own words, ' he understands the tools a little, and
can handle this or that,' he will proceed to handle it.

Here, however, may be the place to state that, in much of
our Philosopher's history, there is something of an almost Hindoo character : nay, perhaps in that so well fostered and every-
way excellent ' Passivity ' of his, which, with no free development of the antagonist Activity, distinguished his childhood,
we may detect the rudiments of much that, in after-days, and
still in these present days, astonishes the world. For the
shallow-sighted Teufelsdröckh is oftenest a man without Activity of any kind, a No-man ; for the deep-sighted, again, a man
with Activity almost superabundant, yet so spiritual, close-
hidden, enigmatic, that no mortal can foresee its explosions,
or even when it has exploded, so much as ascertain its signifi-

cance. A dangerous, difficult temper for the modern European ; above all, disadvantageous in the hero of a Biography !
Now as heretofore it will behove the Editor of these pages,
were it never so unsuccessfully, to do his endeavour.

Among the earliest tools of any complicacy which a man,
especially a man of letters, gets to handle, are his Class-books.
On this portion of his History, Teufelsdröckh looks down pro-
fessedly as indifferent. Reading he ' cannot remember ever
to have learned ;' so perhaps had it by nature. He says generally : ' Of the insignificant portion of my Education, which
' depended on Schools, there need almost no notice be taken.
' I learned what others learnt ; and kept it stored by in a cor-
' ner of my head, seeing as yet no manner of use in it. My
' Schoolmaster, a down-bent, brokenhearted, underfoot mar-
' tyr, as others of that guild are, did little for me, except dis-
' cover that he could do little : he, good soul, pronounced me
' a genius, fit for the learned professions ; and that I must be
' sent to the Gymnasium, and one day to the University.
' Meanwhile, what printed thing soever I could meet with I
' read. My very copper pocket-money I laid out on stall litera-
' ture ; which, as it accumulated, I with my own hands sewed
' into volumes. By this means was the young head furnished
' with a considerable miscellany of things and shadows of
' things : History in authentic fragments lay mingled with
' Fabulous chimeras, wherein also was reality ; and the whole
' not as dead stuff, but as living pabulum, tolerably nutritive
' for a mind not yet so peptic.'

That the Entepfuhl Schoolmaster judged well, we now
know. Indeed, already in the youthful Gneschen, with all his
outward stillness, there may have been manifest an inward
vivacity that promised much ; symptoms of a spirit singularly
open, thoughtful, almost poetical. Thus, to say nothing of
his Suppers on the Orchard-wall, and other phenomena of
that earlier period, have many readers of these pages stumbled,
in their twelfth year, on such reflections as the following ? 'It
' struck me much, as I sat by the Kuhbach, one silent noon-
' tide, and watched it flowing, gurgling, to think how this
' same streamlet had flowed and gurgled, through all changes

'of weather and of fortune, from beyond the earliest date of
'History. Yes, probably on the morning when Joshua forded
'Jordan; even as at the mid-day when Cæsar doubtless with
'difficulty, swam the Nile, yet kept his *Commentaries* dry,—
'this little Kuhbach, assiduous as Tiber, Eurotas or Siloa, was
'murmuring on across the wilderness, as yet unnamed, un-·
'seen; here, too, as in the Euphrates and the Ganges, is a
'vein or veinlet of the grand World-circulation of Waters,
'which, with its atmospheric arteries, has lasted and lasts
'simply with the World. Thou fool! Nature alone is an-
'tique, and the oldest Art a mushroom; that idle crag thou
'sittest on is six thousand years of age.' In which little
thought, as in a little fountain, may there not lie the beginning or those well-nigh unutterable meditations on the grandeur and mystery of TIME, and its relation to ETERNITY, which
play such a part in this Philosophy of Clothes?

Over his Gymnastic and Academic years the Professor by
no means lingers so lyrical and joyful as over his childhood.
Green sunny tracts there are still; but intersected by bitter
rivulets of tears, here and there stagnating into sour marshes
of discontent. 'With my first view of the Hinterschlag Gym-
'nasium,' writes he, 'my evil days began. Well do I still re-
'member the red sunny Whitsuntide morning, when trotting
'full of hope, by the side of Father Andreas, I entered the
'main street of the place, and saw its steeple clock (then
'striking Eight) and *Schuldthurm* (Jail), and the aproned or
'disaproned Burghers moving in to breakfast: a little dog,
'in mad terror, was rushing past; for some human imps had
'tied a tin kettle to its tail; thus did the agonised creature,
'loud jingling, career through the whole length of the
'Borough, and become notable enough. Fit emblem of many
'a Conquering Hero, to whom Fate (wedding Fantasy to
'Sense, as it often elsewhere does) has malignantly appended
'a tin kettle of Ambition, to chase him on; which, the faster
'he runs, urges him the faster, the more loudly and more
'foolishly! Fit emblem also of much that awaited myself, in
'that mischievous Den; as in the world, whereof it was a
'portion and epitome!

' Alas, the kind beech-rows of Entepfuhl were hidden in the
' distance : I was among strangers, harshly, at best indiffer-
' ently, disposed towards me ; the young heart felt, for the
' first time, quite orphaned and alone.' His schoolfellows, as
is usual, persecuted him : ' They were Boys,' he says, ' mostly
' rude Boys, and obeyed the impulse of rude Nature, which
' bids the deerherd fall upon any stricken hart, the duck-flock
' put to death any broken-winged brother or sister, and on all
' hands the strong tyrannise over the weak.' He admits that
though ' perhaps in an unusual degree morally courageous,'
he succeeded ill in battle, and would fain have avoided it ; a
result, as it would appear, owing less to his small personal
stature (for in passionate seasons, he was ' incredibly nimble '),
than to his ' virtuous principles : ' ' if it was disgraceful to be
' beaten,' says he, ' it was only a shade less disgraceful to have
' so much as fought ; thus was I drawn two ways at once, and
' in this important element of school-history, the war element,
' had little but sorrow.' On the whole, that same excellent
' Passivity,' so notable in Teufelsdröckh's childhood, is here
visibly enough again getting nourishment. ' He wept often ;
' indeed to such a degree that he was nicknamed *Der Wei-*
' *nende* (the Tearful), which epithet, till towards his thirteenth
' year, was indeed not quite unmerited. Only at rare inter-
' vals did the young soul burst forth into fire-eyed rage, and,
' with a Stormfulness (*Ungestüm*) under which the boldest
' quailed, assert that he too had Rights of Man, or at least of
' Mankin.' In all which, who does not discern a fine flower-
tree and cinnamon-tree (of genius) nigh choked among pump-
kins, reedgrass, and ignoble shrubs ; and forced, if it would
live, to struggle upwards only, and not outwards ; into a *height*
quite sickly, and disproportioned to its *breadth ?*

We find, moreover, that his Greek and Latin were ' mechanically ' taught ; Hebrew scarce even mechanically ; much else
which they call History, Cosmography, Philosophy, and so
forth, no better than not at all. So that, except inasmuch as
Nature was still busy ; and he himself ' went about, as was of
old his wont, among the Craftsmen's workshops, there learning many things ; ' and farther lighted on some small store of

curious reading, in Hans Wachtel the Cooper's house, where he lodged,—his time, it would appear, was utterly wasted. Which facts the Professor had not yet learned to look upon with any contentment. Indeed, throughout the whole of this Bag *Scorpio*, where we now are, and often in the following Bag, he shews himself unusually animated on the matter of Education, and not without some touch of what we might presume to be anger.

'My teachers,' says he, 'were hide-bound Pedants, without 'knowledge of man's nature or of boy's ; or of aught save 'their lexicons and quarterly account-books. Innumerable 'dead Vocables (no dead Language, for they themselves knew 'no Language) they crammed into us, and called it fostering 'the growth of mind. How can an inanimate, mechanical 'Gerund-grinder, the like of whom will, in a subsequent cen- 'tury, be manufactured at Nürnberg out of wood and leather, 'foster the growth of anything ; much more of Mind, which 'grows, not like a vegetable (by having its roots littered with 'etymological compost), but like a Spirit, by mysterious con- 'tact of Spirit ; Thought kindling itself at the fire of living 'Thought? How shall *he* give kindling, in whose own inward 'man there is no live coal, but all is burnt out to a dead 'grammatical cinder ? The Hinterschlag Professors knew 'Syntax enough ; and of the human soul thus much : that it 'had a faculty called Memory, and could be acted on through 'the muscular integument by appliance of birch rods.

'Alas, so is it everywhere, so will it ever be ; till the Hod- 'man is discharged, or reduced to Hodbearing ; and an Archi- 'tect is hired, and on all hands fitly encouraged ; till com- 'munities and individuals discover, not without surprise, that 'fashioning the souls of a generation by Knowledge can rank 'on a level with blowing their bodies to pieces by Gunpow- 'der ; that with Generals and Field-marshals for killing, there 'should be world-honoured Dignitaries, and were it possible, 'true God-ordained Priests, for teaching. But as yet, though 'the soldier wears openly, and even parades, his butchering- 'tool, nowhere, far as I have travelled, did the Schoolmaster 'make show of his instructing-tool : nay were he to walk

' abroad with birch girt on thigh, as if he therefrom expected
' honour, would there not, among the idler class, perhaps a
· certain levity be excited ? '

In the third year of this Gymnasic period, Father Andreas
seems to have died: the young Scholar, otherwise so maltreated, saw himself for the first time clad outwardly in sables,
and inwardly in quite inexpressible melancholy. 'The dark
' bottomless Abyss, that lies under our feet, had yawned open ;
' the pale kingdoms of Death, with all their innumerable silent
' nations and generations stood before him ; the inexorable
' word, NEVER! now first shewed its meaning. My Mother
' wept, and her sorrow got vent ; but in my heart there lay a
' whole lake of tears, pent up in silent desolation. Neverthe-
' less, the unworn Spirit is strong ; Life is so healthful that
' it even finds nourishment in Death : these stern experiences,
' planted down by Memory in my Imagination, rose there to
' a whole cypress-forest, sad but beautiful ; waving, with not
' unmelodious sighs, in dark luxuriance, in the hottest sun-
' shine, through long years of youth :—as in manhood also it
' does, and will do ; for I have now pitched my tent under a
' Cypress-tree ; the Tomb is now my inexpugnable Fortress,
' ever close by the gate of which I look upon the hostile arma-
' ments, and pains and penalties, of tyrannous Life placidly
' enough, and listen to its loudest threatenings with a still
' smile. O ye loved ones, that already sleep in the noiseless
' Bed of Rest, whom in life I could only weep for and never
' help ; and ye, who wide-scattered still toil lonely in the mon-
' ster-bearing Desert, dyeing the flinty ground with your blood,
' —yet a little while, and we shall all meet THERE, and our
' Mother's bosom will screen us all ; and Oppression's harness,
' and Sorrow's fire-whip, and all the Gehenna Bailiffs that
' patrol and inhabit ever-vexed Time, cannot thenceforth harm
' us any more ! '

Close by which rather beautiful apostrophe, lies a laboured
Character of the deceased Andreas Futteral ; of his natural
ability, his deserts in life (as Prussian Sergeant) ; with long
historical inquiries into the genealogy of the Futteral Family,
here traced back as far as Henry the Fowler : the whole of

which we pass over, not without astonishment. It only concerns us to add, that now was the time when Mother Gretchen revealed to her foster-son that he was not at all of this kindred; or indeed of any kindred, having come into historical existence in the way already known to us. 'Thus was I doubly orphaned,' says he; 'bereft not only of Possession, but even of Remembrance. Sorrow and Wonder, here suddenly united, could not but produce abandoned fruit. Such a disclosure, in such a season struck its roots through my whole nature; ever till the years of mature manhood, it mingled with my whole thoughts, was as the stem whereon all my day-dreams and night-dreams grew. A certain poetic elevation, yet also a corresponding civic depression, it naturally imparted: *I was like no other:* in which fixed-idea, leading sometimes to highest, and oftener to frightfulest results, may there not lie the first spring of Tendencies, which in my Life have become remarkable enough? As in birth, so in action, speculation, and social position, my fellows are perhaps not numerous.'

In the Bag *Sagittarius*, as we at length discover Teufelsdröckh has become a University man; though how, when, or of what quality, will nowhere disclose itself with the smallest certainty. Few things, in the way of confusion and capricious indistinctness, can now surprise our readers; not even the total want of dates, almost without parallel in a Biographical work. So enigmatic, so chaotic we have always found, and must always look to find, these scattered Leaves. In *Sagittarius*, however, Teufelsdröckh begins to shew himself even more than usually Sibylline; fragments of all sorts; scraps of regular Memoir, College Exercises, Programs, Professional Testimonials, Milkscores, torn Billets, sometimes to appearance of an amatory cast; all blown together as if by merest chance, henceforth bewilder the sane Historian. To combine any picture of these University, and the subsequent years; much more, to decipher therein any illustrative primordial elements of the Clothes-Philosophy, becomes such a problem as the reader may imagine.

So much we can see; darkly, as through the foliage of some

wavering thicket: a youth of no common endowment, who nas passed happily through Childhood, less happily yet still vigourously through Boyhood, now at length perfect in 'dead vocables,' and set down, as he hopes, by the living Fountain, there to superadd Ideas and Capabilities. From such Fountain he draws, diligently, thirstily, yet nowise with his whole heart, for the water nowise suits his palate ; discouragements, entanglements, aberrations are discoverable or supposable. Nor perhaps are even pecuniary distresses wanting ; for ' the good ' Gretchen, who in spite of advices from not disinterested rela-' tives has sent him hither, must after a time withdraw her ' willing but too feeble hand.' Nevertheless, in an atmosphere of Poverty and manifold Chagrin, the Humour of that young Soul, what character is in him, first decisively reveals itself ; and, like strong sunshine in weeping skies, gives out variety of colours, some of which are prismatic. Thus, with the aid of Time, and of what Time brings, has the stripling Diogenes Teufelsdröckh waxed into manly stature ; and into so questionable an aspect, that we ask with new eagerness How he specially came by it, and regret anew that there is no more explicit answer. Certain of the intelligible and partially significant fragments, which are few in number, shall be extracted from that Limbo of a Paper-bag, and presented with the usual preparation.

As if, in the Bag *Scorpio,* Teufelsdröckh had not already expectorated, his antipedagogic spleen ; as if, from the name *Sagittarius,* he had thought himself called upon to shoot arrows, we here again fall in with such matter as this : 'The ' University where I was educated still stands vivid enough in ' my remembrance, and I know its name well ; which name, ' however, I, from tenderness to existing interests and per-' sons, shall in no wise divulge. It is my painful duty to ' say that, out of England and Spain, ours was the worst of ' all hitherto discovered Universities. This is indeed a time ' when right Education is, as nearly as may be, impossible : ' however, in degrees of wrongness there is no limit: nay, I can conceive a worse system than that of the Nameless it-' self ; as poisoned victual may be worse than absolute hunger.

'It is written, When the blind lead the blind, both shall fall
'into the ditch ; wherefore, in such circumstances, may it
'not sometimes be safer, if both leader and led simply—sit
'still? Had you, anywhere in Crim Tartary, walled-in a
'square enclosure ; furnished it with a small, ill-chosen
'Library ; and then turned loose into it eleven hundred
'Christian striplings, to tumble about as they listed, from
'three to seven years : certain persons, under the title of
'Professors, being stationed at the gates, to declare aloud
'that it was a University, and exact considerable admission-
'fees,—you had, not indeed in mechanical structure, yet in
'spirit and result, some imperfect resemblance of our High
'Seminary. I say, imperfect ; for if our mechanical structure
'was quite other, so neither was our result altogether the
'same : unhappily, we were not in Crim Tartary, but in a
'corrupt European city, full of smoke and sin ; moreover, in
'the middle of a Public, which, without far costlier apparatus,
'than that of the Square Enclosure, and Declaration aloud,
'you could not be sure of gulling.

'Gullible, however, by fit apparatus, all Publics are ; and
'gulled, with the most surprising profit. Towards any thing
'like a *Statistics of Imposture*, indeed, little as yet has been
'done : with a strange indifference, our Economists, nigh
'buried under Tables for minor Branches of Industry, have
'altogether overlooked the grand all-overtopping Hypocrisy
'Branch ; as if our whole arts of Puffery, of Quackery,
'Priestcraft, Kingcraft, and the innumerable other crafts and
'mysteries of that genus, had not ranked in Productive In-
'dustry at all ! Can any one, for example, so much as say,
'What moneys, in Literature and Shoe-blacking, are realized
'by actual Instruction and actual jet Polish ; what by ficti-
'tious-persuasive Proclamation of such ; specifying, in dis-
'tinct items, the distributions, circulations, disbursements,
'incomings of said moneys, with the smallest approach to
'accuracy? But to ask, How far, in all the several infinitely
'complected departments of social business, in government,
'education, in manual, commercial, intellectual fabrication of
'every sort, man's Want is supplied by true Ware ; how far

' by the mere Appearance of true Ware :—in other words, To
' what extent, by what methods, with what effects, in various
' times and countries, Deception takes the place and wages of
' Performance ; here truly is an Inquiry big with results for
' the future time, but to which hitherto only the vaguest
' answer can be given. If for the present, in our Europe, we
' estimate the ratio of Ware to Appearance of Ware so high
' even as at One to a Hundred (which considering the Wages
' of a Pope, Russian Autocrat, English Game-Preserver, is
' probably not far from the mark),—what almost prodigious
' saving may there not be anticipated, as the *Statistics of Im-*
' *posture* advances, and so the manufacturing of Shams (that
' of Realities rising into clearer and clearer distinction there-
' from) gradually declines, and at length becomes all but
' wholly unnecessary !

' This for the coming golden ages. What I had to remark,
' for the present brazen one, is, that in several provinces, as
' in Education, Polity, Religion, where so much is wanted
' and indispensable, and so little can as yet be furnished,
' probably Imposture is of sanative, anodyne nature, and
' man's Gullibility not his worst blessing. Suppose your
' sinews of war quite broken ; I mean your military chest in-
' solvent, forage all but exhausted ; and that the whole army
' is about to mutiny, disband, and cut your and each other's
' throat,—then were it not well could you, as if by miracle,
' pay them in any sort of fairy-money, feed them on coagu-
' lated water, or mere imagination of meat ; whereby, till the
' real supply came up, they might be kept together, and quiet?
' Such perhaps was the aim of Nature, who does nothing with-
' out aim, in furnishing her favourite, Man, with this his so
' omnipotent or rather omnipatient Talent of being Gulled.

' How beautifully it works, with a little mechanism ; nay,
' almost makes mechanism for itself ! These Professors in
' the Nameless lived with ease, with safety, by a mere Repu-
' tation constructed in past times, and then too with no great
' effort by quite another class of persons. Which Reputation,
' like a strong brisk-going undershot-wheel, sunk into the
' general current, bade fair, with only a little annual repaint-

'ing on their part, to hold long together, and of its own ac-
'cord assiduously grind for them. Happy that it was so, for
'the Millers! They themselves needed not to work; their at-
'tempts at working, at what they called Educating, now when
'I look back on it, fill me with a certain mute admiration.

'Besides all this, we boasted ourselves a Rational Univer-
'sity; in the highest degree, hostile to Mysticism; thus was
'the young vacant mind furnished with much talk about
'Progress of the Species, Dark Ages, Prejudice, and the like;
'so that all were quickly enough blown out into a state of
'windy argumentativeness; whereby the better sort had soon
'to end in sick, impotent Scepticism; the worser sort ex-
'plode (crepiren) in finished Self-conceit, and to all spiritual
'intents become dead.—But this too is portion of mankind's
'lot. If our era is the Era of Unbelief why murmur under
'it; is there not a better coming, nay come? As in long-
'drawn Systole and longdrawn Diastole, must the period of
'Faith alternate with the period of Denial; must the vernal
'growth, the summer luxuriance of all Opinions, Spiritual
'Representations and Creations, be followed by, and again
'follow, the autumnal decay, the winter dissolution. For
'man lives in Time, has his whole earthly being, endeavour,
'and destiny shaped for him by Time: only in the transi-
'tory Time-Symbol is the ever-motionless Eternity we stand
'on made manifest. And yet, in such winter-seasons of De-
'nial, it is for the nobler-minded perhaps a comparative
'misery to have been born, and to be awake, and work; and
'for the duller a felicity, if like hibernating animals, safe-
'lodged in some Salamanca University, or Sybaris City, or
'other superstitious or voluptuous Castle of Indolence, they can
'slumber through, in stupid dreams, and only awaken when the
'loud-roaring hailstorms have all done their work, and to our
'prayers and martyrdoms the new Spring has been vouchsafed.'

That in the environment, here mysteriously enough shadowed forth, Teufelsdröckh must have felt ill at ease, cannot
be doubtful. 'The hungry young,' he says, 'looked up to
'their spiritual Nurses; and, for food, were bidden eat the
'east wind. What vain jargon of controversial Metaphysic,

' Etymology, and mechanical Manipulation falsely named
' Science, was current there, I indeed learned, better perhaps
' than the most. Among eleven hundred Christian youths,
' there will not be wanting some eleven eager to learn. By
' collision with such, a certain warmth, a certain polish was
' communicated; by instinct and happy accident, I took less
' to rioting (*renommiren*), than to thinking and reading, which
' latter also I was free to do. Nay from the chaos of that Li-
' brary, I succeeded in fishing up more books perhaps than
' had been known to the very keepers thereof. The founda-
' tion of a Literary Life was hereby laid: I learned, on my
' own strength, to read fluently in almost all cultivated lan-
' guages, on almost all subjects, and sciences; farther, as man
' is ever the prime object to man, already it was my favourite
' employment to read character in speculation, and from the
' Writing to construe the Writer. A certain groundplan of
' Human Nature and Life began to fashion itself in me; won-
' drous enough, now when I look back on it; for my whole
' Universe, physical and spiritual, was as yet a Machine!
' However, such a conscious, recognized groundplan, the tru-
' est I had, *was* beginning to be there, and by additional expe-
' riments, might be corrected and indefinitely extended.'

Thus from poverty does the strong educe nobler wealth;
thus in the destitution of the wild desert, does our young
Ishmael acquire for himself the highest of all possessions,
that of Self-help. Nevertheless a desert this was, waste, and
howling with savage monsters. Teufelsdröckh gives us long
details of his ' fever-paroxysms of Doubt;' his Inquiries concerning Miracles, and the Evidences of religious Faith; and
how ' in the silent night watches, still darker in his heart
' than over sky and earth, he has cast himself before the All-
' seeing, and with audible prayers, cried vehemently for Light,
' for deliverance from Death and the Grave. Not till after
' long years, and unspeakable agonies, did the believing heart
' surrender; sink into spell-bound sleep, under the nightmare,
' Unbelief; and, in this hag-ridden dream, mistake God's fair
' living world for a pallid, vacant Hades and extinct Pande-
' monium. But through such Purgatory pain,' continues he,

7

'it is appointed us to pass; first must the dead Letter of
'Religion, own itself dead, and drop piecemeal into dust, if
'the living Spirit of Religion, freed from this its charnel-house,
'is to arise on us, newborn of Heaven, and with new healing
'under its wings.'

To which Purgatory pains, seemingly severe enough, if we
add a liberal measure of Earthly distresses, want of practical
guidance, want of sympathy, want of money, want of hope ;
and all this in the fervid season of youth, so exaggerated in
imagining, so boundless in desires, yet here so poor in means,
—do we not see a strong incipient spirit oppressed and over-
loaded from without and from within ; the fire of genius
struggling up among fuel-wood of the greenest, and as yet
with more of bitter vapour than of clear flame.

From various fragments of Letters and other documentary
scraps, it is to be inferred that Teufelsdröckh, isolated, shy,
retiring as he was, had not altogether escaped notice : certain
established men are aware of his existence ; and, if stretching
out no helpful hand, have at least their eyes upon him. He
appears, though in dreary enough humour, to be addressing
himself to the Profession of Law ;—whereof, indeed, the
world has since seen him a public graduate. But omitting
these broken, unsatisfactory thrums of Economical relation,
let us present rather the following small thread of Moral relation ; and therewith, the reader for himself weaving it in
at the right place, conclude our dim arras picture of these
University years.

'Here also it was that I formed acquaintance with Herr
'Towgood, or, as it is perhaps better written, Herr Toughgut ;
'a young person of quality (*von Adel*), from the interior parts
'of England. He stood connected, by blood and hospitality,
'with the Counts von Zähdarm, in this quarter of Germany ;
'to which noble Family I likewise was, by his means, with all
'friendliness, brought near. Towgood had a fair talent, un-
'speakably ill-cultivated ; with considerable humour of char-
'acter : and, bating his total ignorance, for he knew nothing
'except Boxing and a little Grammar, shewed less of that
'aristocratic impassivity, and silent fury, than for most pat-

'belongs to Travellers of his nation. To him I owe my first
'practical knowledge of the English and their ways; perhaps
'also something of the partiality with which I have ever since
'regarded that singular people. Towgood was not without
'an eye, could he have come at any light. Invited doubtless
'by the presence of the Zähdarm Family, he had travelled
'hither, in the almost frantic hope of perfecting his studies;
'he, whose studies had as yet been those of infancy, hither to
'a University where so much as the notion of perfection, not
'to say the effort after it, no longer existed! Often we would
'condole over the hard destiny of the Young in this era: how,
'after all our toil, we were to be turned out into the world,
'with beards on our chins indeed, but with few other
'attributes of manhood; no existing thing that we were
'trained to Act on, nothing that we could so much as Believe.
'"How has our head on the outside a polished Hat," would
'Towgood exclaim, "and in the inside Vacancy, or a froth of
'Vocables and Attorney Logic! At a small cost men are
'educated to make leather into shoes; but at a great cost,
'what am I educated to make? By Heaven, Brother! what
'I have already eaten and worn, as I came thus far, would
'endow a considerable Hospital of Incurables."—"Man, in-
'deed," I would answer, "has a Digestive Faculty, which
'must be kept working, were it even partly by stealth. But
'as for our Miseducation, make not bad worse; waste not the
'time yet ours, in trampling on thistles because they have
'yielded us no figs. *Frisch zu Bruder!* Here are Books,
'and we have brains to read them; here is a whole Earth and a
'whole Heaven, and we have eyes to look on them: *Frisch zu!*"

'Often also our talk was gay; not without brilliancy, and
'even fire. We looked out on Life, with its strange scaffold-
'ing, where all at once harlequins dance, and men are be-
'headed and quartered: motley, not unterrific was the aspect;
'but we looked on it like brave youths. For myself, these were
'perhaps my most genial hours. Towards this young warm-
'hearted, strongheaded and wrongheaded Herr Towgood, I
'was even near experiencing the now obsolete sentiment of
'Friendship. Yes, foolish Heathen that I was, I felt that,

'under certain conditions, I could have loved this man, and 'taken him to my bosom, and been his brother once and al-'ways. By degrees, however, I understood the new time, and 'its wants. If man's *Soul* is indeed, as in the Finnish Lan-'guage, and Utilitarian Philosophy, a kind of *Stomach*, what 'else is the true meaning of Spiritual Union but an Eating 'together? Thus we, instead of Friends, are Dinner-guests ; 'and here as elsewhere have cast away chimeras.'

So ends, abruptly as is usual, and enigmatically, this little incipient romance. What henceforth becomes of the brave Herr Towgood, or Toughgut? He has dived under, in the Autobiographical Chaos, and swims we see not where. Does any reader ' in the interior parts of England ' know of such a man?

CHAPTER IV.

GETTING UNDER WAY.

'Thus nevertheless,' writes our Autobiographer, apparently as quitting College, ' was there realised Somewhat ; namely, I, ' Diogenes Teufelsdröckh : a visible Temporary Figure (*Zeit-'bild*), occupying some cubic feet of Space, and containing ' within it Forces both physical and spiritual ; hopes, passions, 'thoughts ; the whole wondrous furniture, in more or less ' perfection, belonging to that mystery, a Man. Capabilities ' there were in me to give battle, in some small degree, against ' the great Empire of Darkness : does not the very Ditcher ' and Delver, with his spade, extinguish many a thistle and ' puddle ; and so leave a little Order, where he found the op-' posite? Nay your very Daymoth has capabilities in this ' kind ; and ever organises something (into its own Body, if no ' otherwise), which was before Inorganic ; and of mute dead air ' makes living music, though only of the faintest, by humming.

' How much more, one whose capabilities are spiritual ; who 'has learned, or begun learning, the grand thaumaturgic art ' of Thought ! Thaumaturgic I name it ; for hitherto all 'Miracles have been wrought thereby, and henceforth in-'numerable will be wrought ; whereof we, even in these days,

'witness some. Of the Poet's and Prophet's inspired Message,
'and how it makes and unmakes whole worlds, I shall forbear
'mention; but cannot the dullest hear Steam-engines clank-
'ing around him? Has he not seen the Scottish Brassmith's
'IDEA (and this but a mechanical one) travelling on fire-wings
'round the Cape, and across two Oceans; and stronger than
'any other Enchanter's Familiar, on all hands unweariedly
'fetching and carrying: at home, not only weaving Cloth;
'but rapidly enough overturning the whole old system of
'Society; and, for Feudalism and Preservation of the Game,
'preparing us, by indirect but sure methods, Industrialism
'and the Government of the Wisest? Truly a Thinking Man
'is the worst enemy the Prince of Darkness can have; every
'time such a one announces himself, I doubt not, there runs
'a shudder through the Nether Empire; and new Emissaries
'are trained, with new tactics, to, if possible, entrap him, and
'hoodwink and handcuff him.

'With such high vocation had I too, as denizen of the Uni-
'verse, been called. Unhappy it is, however, that though born
'to the amplest Sovereignty, in this way, with no less than
'sovereign right of Peace and War against the Time-Prince
'(*Zeitfurst*), or Devil, and all his Dominions, your coronation-
'ceremony costs such trouble, your sceptre is so difficult to
'get at, or even to get eye on!'

By which last wiredrawn similitude, does Teufelsdröckh
mean no more than that young men find obstacles in what we
call 'getting under way?' 'Not what I Have,' continues he,
'but what I Do is my Kingdom. To each is given a certain
'inward Talent, a certain outward Environment of Fortune;
'to, each, by wisest combination of these two, a certain maxi-
'mum of Capability. But the hardest problem were ever this
'first: To find by study of yourself, and of the ground you
'stand on, what your combined inward and outward Capa-
'bility specially is. For, alas, our young soul is all budding
'with Capabilities, and we see not yet which is the main
'and true one. Always too the new man is in a new time,
'under new conditions; his course can be the *fac-simile* of no
'prior one, but is by its nature original. And then how sel-

'dom will the outward Capability fit the inward : though tal-
'ented wonderfully enough, we are poor, unfriendly, dyspep-
'tical, bashful ; nay what is worse than all, we are foolish.
'Thus, in a whole imbroglio of Capabilities, we go stupidly
'groping about, to grope which is ours, and often clutch the
'wrong one : in this mad work, must several years of our
'small term be spent, till the purblind Youth, by practice,
'acquire notions of distance, and become a seeing Man. Nay,
'many so spend their whole term, and in ever-new expecta-
'tion, ever-new disappointment, shift from enterprise to en-
'terprise, and from side to side : till at length, as exasperated
'striplings of threescore and ten, they shift into their last
'enterprise, that of getting buried.

'Such, since the most of us are too ophthalmic, would be
'the general fate ; were it not that one thing saves us : our
'Hunger. For on this ground, as the prompt nature of Hun-
'ger is well known, must a prompt choice be made : hence
'have we, with wise foresight, Indentures and Apprenticeships
'for our irrational young ; whereby, in due season, the vague
'universality of a Man shall find himself ready-moulded into
'a specific Craftsman ; and so thenceforth work, with much
'or with little waste of Capability as it may be ; yet not with
'the worst waste, that of time. Nay even in matters spiritual,
'since the spiritual artist too is born blind, and does not, like
'certain other creatures, receive sight in nine days, but far
'later, sometimes never,—is it not well that there should be
'what we call professions, or Bread-studies (*Brodtzwecke*),
'preappointed us? Here, circling like the gin-horse, for
'whom partial or total blindness is no evil, the Bread-artist
'can travel contentedly round and round, till fancying that it
'is forward and forward ; and realize much : for himself
'victual ; for the world an additional horse's power in the
'grand corn-mill or hemp-mill of Economic Society. For me
'too had such a leading-string been provided; only that it
'proved a neck-halter, and had nigh throttled me, till I broke
'it. Then, in the words of Ancient Pistol, did the World gen-
'erally become mine oyster, which I, by strength of cunning,
'was to open, as I would and could. Almost had I deceased

' (*fast wär ich umgekommen*), so obstinately did it continue
'shut.'

We see here, significantly foreshadowed, the spirit of much
that was to befall our Autobiographer ; the historical embodiment of which, as it painfully takes shape in his Life, lies
scattered, in dim disastrous details, through this Bag *Pisces*,
and those that follow. A young man of high talent, and
high though still temper, like a young mettled colt, ' breaks
off his neck-halter,' and bounds forth, from his peculiar manger, into the wide world ; which, alas, he finds all rigorously
fenced in. Richest clover-fields tempt his eye ; but to him
they are forbidden pasture : either pining in progressive star-
vation, he must stand ; or, in mad exasperation, must rush to
and fro, leaping against sheer stone walls, which he cannot
leap over, which only lacerate and lame him ; till at last, after
thousand attempts and endurances, he, as if by miracle, clears
his way : not indeed into luxuriant and luxurious clover, yet
into a certain bosky wilderness where existence is still possible, and Freedom though waited on by Scarcity is not without sweetness. In a word, Teufelsdröckh having thrown up
his legal Profession, finds himself without landmark of outward guidance ; whereby his previous want of decided Belief,
or inward guidance, is frightfully aggravated. Necessity
urges him on ; Time will not stop, neither can he, a Son of
Time ; wild passions without solacement, wild faculties without employment, ever vex and agitate him. He too must
enact that stern Monodrama, *No Object and no Rest ;* must
front its successive destinies, work through to its catastrophe, and deduce therefrom what moral he can.

Yet let us be just to him, let us admit that his 'neck-halter'
sat nowise easy on him ; that he was in some degree forced
to break it off. If we look at the young man's civic position,
in this Nameless Capital, as he emerges from its Nameless University, we can discern well that it was far from enviable. His
first Law-Examination he has come through triumphantly ;
and can even boast that the *Examen Rigorosum* need not have
frightened him : but though he is hereby ' an *Auscultator* of
respectability ' what avails it ? There is next to no employ-

ment to be had.   Neither, for a youth without connexions, is
the process of Expectation very hopeful in itself ; nor for one
of his disposition much cheered from without.   'My fellow
'Auscultators,' he says, 'were Auscultators : they dressed, and
'digested, and talked articulate words ; other vitality shewed
'they almost none. Small speculation in those eyes, that they
'did glare withal! Sense neither for the high nor for the deep,
'nor for aught human or divine, save only for the faintest
'scent of coming Preferment.'   In which words, indicating a
total estrangement on the part of Teufelsdröckh, may there
not also lurk traces of a bitterness as from wounded vanity?
Doubtless these prosaic Auscultators may have sniffed at him,
with his strange ways ; and tried to hate, and what was much
more impossible, to despise him.   Friendly communion, in
any case, there could not be : already has the young Teufelsdröckh left the other young geese ; and swims apart, though
as yet uncertain whether he himself is cygnet or gosling.

Perhaps too what little employment he had was performed
ill, at best unpleasantly.   'Great practical method and expert-
ness' he may brag of ; but is there not also great practical
pride, though deep-hidden, only the deeper-seated ?   So shy
a man can never have been popular.   We figure to ourselves,
how in those days he may have played strange freaks with his
Independence, and so forth : do not his own words betoken
as much?   'Like a very young person, I imagined it was
'with Work alone, and not also with Folly and Sin, in myself
'and others, that I have been appointed to struggle.'   Be this
as it may, his progress from the passive Auscultatorship, towards any active Assessorship, is evidently of the slowest.
By degrees, those same established men, once partially in-
clined to patronise him, seem to withdraw their countenance,
and give him up as 'a man of genius :' against which procedure he, in these Papers, loudly protests.   'As if,' says he,
'the higher did not presuppose the lower ; as if he who can
'fly into heaven, could not also walk post if he resolved on it!
'But the world is an old woman, and mistakes any gilt far-
'thing for a gold coin : whereby being often cheated she will
'thenceforth trust nothing but the common copper.'

How our winged sky-messenger, unaccepted as a terrestrial runner, contrived, in the meanwhile, to keep himself from flying skyward without return, is not too clear from these Documents. Good old Gretchen seems to have vanished from the scene, perhaps from the Earth; other Horn of Plenty, or even of Parsimony, nowhere flows for him ; so that 'the prompt nature of Hunger being well known,' we are not without our anxiety. From private Tuition, in never so many languages and sciences, the aid derivable is small ; neither, to use his own words, 'does the young Adventurer hitherto suspect 'in himself any literary gift ; but at best earns bread-and-'water wages, by his wide faculty of Translation. Neverthe-'less,' continues he, 'that I subsisted is clear, for you find me 'even now alive.' Which fact, however, except upon the principle of our true-hearted, kind old Proverb, that 'there is always life for a living one,' we must profess ourselves unable to explain.

Certain Landlords' Bills, and other economic Documents, bearing the mark of Settlement, indicate that he was not without money ; but, like an independent Hearth-holder, if not House-holder, paid his way. Here also occur, among many others, two little mutilated Notes, which perhaps throw light on his condition. The first has now no date, or writer's name, but a huge Blot ; and runs to this effect : 'The (*Inkblot*), tied 'down by previous promise, cannot, except by best wishes, 'forward the Herr Teufelsdröckh's views on the Assessorship 'in question ; and sees himself under the cruel necessity of 'forbearing, for the present, what were otherwise his duty 'and joy, to assist in opening the career for a man of genius, 'on whom far higher triumphs are yet waiting.' The other is on gilt paper ; and interests us like a sort of epistolary mummy now dead, yet which once lived and beneficently worked. We give it in the original : '*Herr Teufelsdröckh wird von der Frau* '*Gräfinn, auf Donnerstag, zum* Æsthetischen Thee, *schönstens* '*eingeladen.*'

Thus in answer to a cry for solid pudding, whereof there is the most urgent need, comes epigrammatically enough, the invitation to a wash of quite fluid *Æsthetic Tea !* How Teufelsdröckh, now at actual handgrips with Destiny herself, may have comported himself among these Musical and Literary Dilettanti of both sexes, like a hungry lion invited to a feast of chickenweed, we can only conjecture. Perhaps in expressive silence, and abstinence : otherwise if the lion, in such case, is to feast at all, it cannot be on the chickenweed, but only on the chickens. For the rest, as this Frau Gräfinn dates from the *Zähdarm House*, she can be no other than the Countess and mistress of the same ; whose intellectual tendencies, and good will to Teufelsdröckh, whether on the footing of Herr Towgood, or on his own footing, are hereby manifest. That some sort of relation, indeed, continued, for a time, to connect our Autobiographer, though perhaps feebly enough, with this noble House, we have elsewhere express evidence. Doubtless, if he expected patronage, it was in vain ; enough for him if he here obtained occasional glimpses of the great world, from which we at one time fancied him to have been always excluded. 'The Zähdarms,' says he, 'lived in the soft ' sumptuous garniture of Aristocracy ; whereto Literature and ' Art, attracted and attached from without, were to serve as ' the handsomest fringing. It was to the *Gnädigen Frau* (her ' Ladyship) that this latter improvement was due : assiduously ' she gathered, dexterously she fitted on, what fringing was to ' be had ; lace or cobweb, as the place yielded.' Was Teufelsdröckh also a fringe, of lace or cobweb ; or promising to be such ? ' With his *Excellenz* (the Count),' continues he, ' I have ' more than once had the honour to converse ; chiefly on gen-' eral affairs, and the aspect of the world, which he, though ' now past middle life, viewed in no unfavourable light ; find-' ing indeed, except the Outrooting of Journalism (*die auszu-' rottende Journalistik*), little to desiderate therein. On some ' points, as his *Excellenz* was not uncholeric, I found it more ' pleasant to keep silence. Besides, his occupation being that ' of Owning Land, there might be faculties enough, which, as ' superfluous for such use, were little developed in him.'

That to Teufelsdröckh the aspect of the world was nowise so faultless, and many things besides 'the Outrooting of Journalism,' might have seemed improvements, we can readily conjecture. With nothing but a barren Auscultatorship from without, and so many mutinous thoughts and wishes from within, his position was no easy one. 'The Universe,' he says, ' was as a mighty Sphinx-riddle, which I knew so little of, yet ' must rede, or be devoured. In red streaks of unspeakable ' grandeur, yet also in the blackness of darkness, was Life ' to my too-unfurnished Thought, unfolding itself. A strange ' contradiction lay in me ; and I as yet knew not the solution ' of it ; knew not that spiritual music can spring only from ' discords set in unison ; that but for Evil there were no Good, ' as victory is only possible by battle.'

'I have heard affirmed (surely in jest),' observes he else-' where, by not unphilanthropic persons, that it were a real ' increase of human happiness, could all young men from the ' age of nineteen be covered under barrels, or rendered other-' wise invisible ; and there left to follow their lawful studies ' and callings, till they emerged, sadder and wiser, at the age ' of twenty-five. With which suggestion, at least as considered ' in the light of a practical scheme, I need scarcely say that I ' nowise coincide. Nevertheless it is plausibly urged that, as ' young ladies (*Mädchen*) are, to mankind, precisely the most ' delightful in those years ; so young gentlemen (*Bübchen*) do ' then attain their maximum of detestability. Such gawks ' (*Gecken*) are they, and foolish peacocks, and yet with such a ' vulturous hunger for self-indulgence : so obstinate, obstreper-' ous, vain-glorious ; in all senses, so froward and so forward. ' No mortal's endeavour or attainment will, in the smallest, ' content the as yet unendeavouring, unattaining young gentle-' man ; but he could make it all infinitely better, were it wor-' thy of him. Life everywhere is the most manageable matter, ' simply as a question in the Rule of Three : multiply your ' second and third term together, divide the product by the ' first, and your quotient will be the answer,—which you are ' but an ass if you cannot come at. The booby has not yet ' found out, by any trial, that, do what one will, there is ever ' a cursed fraction, oftenest a decimal repeater, and no net ' integer quotient so much as to be thought of.'

In which passage does there not lie an implied confession that Teufelsdröckh himself, besides his outward obstructions,

had an inward, still greater, to contend with ; namely, a certain temporary, youthful, yet still afflictive derangement of
head ? Alas! on the former side alone, his case was hard
enough. 'It continues ever true,' says he, 'that Saturn, or
'Chronos, or what we call TIME, devours all his Children :
' only by incessant Running, by incessant Working, may you
' (for some threescore and ten years) escape him ; and you
' too he devours at last. Can any Sovereign, or Holy Alli-
' ance of Sovereigns, bid Time stand still ; even in thought,
' shake themselves free of Time ? Our whole terrestrial
' being is based on Time, and built of Time ; it is wholly a
' Movement, a Time-impulse ; Time is the author of it, the
' material of it. Hence also our Whole Duty, which is to
' move, to work,—in the right direction. Are not our Bodies
' and our Souls in continual movement, whether we will or
' not ; in a continual Waste, requiring a continual Repair ?
' Utmost satisfaction of our whole outward and inward Wants
' were but satisfaction for a space of Time ; thus, whatso we
' have done, is done, and for us annihilated, and ever must
' we go and do anew. O Time-Spirit, how hast thou envi-
' roned and imprisoned us, and sunk us so deep in thy troub-
' lous dim Time-Element, that, only in lucid moments, can
' so much as glimpses of our upper Azure Home be revealed
' to us ! Me, however, as a Son of Time, unhappier than
' some others, was Time threatening to eat quite prematurely ;
' for, strive as I might, there was no good Running, so ob-
' structed was the path, so gyved were the feet.' That is to
say, we presume, speaking in the dialect of this lower world,
that Teufelsdröckh's whole duty and necessity was, like other
men's, 'to work,—in the right direction,' and that no work
was to be had ; whereby he became wretched enough. As
was natural : with haggard Scarcity threatening him in the
distance ; and so vehement a soul languishing in restless in-
action, and forced thereby, like Sir Hudibras's sword by rust,

> To eat into itself, for lack
> Of something else to hew and hack !

But on the whole, that same 'excellent Passivity,' as it has
all along done, is here again vigourously flourishing ; in

which circumstance, may we not trace the beginnings of
much that now characterises our Professor ; and perhaps, in
faint rudiments, the origin of the Clothes-Philosophy itself ?
Already the attitude he has assumed towards the World is
too defensive ; not, as would have been desirable, a bold attitude of attack. ' So far hitherto,' he says, ' as I had mingled
' with mankind, I was notable, if for any thing, for a certain
' stillness of manner, which, as my friends often rebukingly
' declared, did but ill express the keen ardour of my feelings.
' I, in truth, regarded men with an excess both of love and of
' fear. The mystery of a Person, indeed, is ever divine, to
' him that has a sense for the Godlike. Often, notwithstand-
' ing, was I blamed, and by half-strangers hated, for my so-
' called Hardness (*Härte*), my Indifferentism towards men ;
' and the seemingly ironic tone I had adopted, as my favour-
' ite dialect in conversation. Alas, the panoply of Sarcasm
' was but as a buckram case, wherein I had striven to envelope
' myself ; that so my own poor Person might live safe there,
' and in all friendliness, being no longer exasperated by
' wounds. Sarcasm I now see to be, in general, the language
' of the Devil ; for which reason I have, long since, as good
' as renounced it. But how many individuals did I, in
' those days, provoke into some degree of hostility thereby !
' An ironic man, with his sly stillness, and ambuscading ways,
' more especially an ironic young man, from whom it is least
' expected, may be viewed as a pest to society. Have we not
' seen persons of weight and name, coming forward, with
' gentlest indifference, to tread such a one out of sight, as an
' insignificancy and worm, start ceiling-high (*balkenhoch*), and
' thence fall shattered and supine, to be borne home on shut-
' ters, not without indignation, when he proved electric and
' a torpedo ! '

Alas, how can a man with this devilishness of temper make
way for himself in Life ; where the first problem, as Teufelsdröckh too admits, is 'to unite yourself with some one, and
with somewhat (*sich anzuschliessen*) ?' Division, not union, is
written on most part of his procedure. Let us add too that,
in no great length of time, the only important connexion he

had ever succeeded in forming, his connexion with the Zähdarm Family, seems to have been paralysed, for all practical
uses, by the death of the 'not uncholeric' old Count. This
fact stands recorded, quite incidentally, in a certain *Discourse
on Epitaphs*, huddled into the present Bag, among so much
else ; of which Essay the learning and curious penetration are
more to be approved of than the spirit.   His grand principle
is, that lapidary inscriptions, of what sort soever, should be
Historical rather than Lyrical.   'By request of that worthy
Nobleman's survivors,' says he, 'I undertook to compose his
' Epitaph ; and not unmindful of my own rules, produced the
' following ; which, however, for an alleged defect of Latinity,
' a defect never yet fully visible to myself, still remains unen-
' graven ;'—wherein, we may predict, there is more than the
Latinity that will surprise an English reader :

HIC JACET

PHILIPPUS ZAEHDARM, COGNOMINE MAGNUS,

ZAEHDARMI COMES

EX IMPERII CONCILIO,

VELLERIS AUREI, PERISCELIDIS, NECNON VULTURIS NIGRI
EQUES.

QUI DUM SUB LUNA AGEBAT,

QUINQUIES MILLE PERDRICES

PLUMBO CONFECIT :

VARII CIBI

CENTUMPONDIA MILLIES CENTENA MILLIA,

PER SE, PERQUE SERVOS QUADRUPEDES BIPEDESVE,

HAUD SINE TUMULTU DEVOLVENS,

IN STERCUS

PALAM CONVERTIT.

NUNC A LABORE REQUIESCENTEM
OPERA SEQUUNTUR.

SI MONUMENTUM QUÆRIS,
FIMETUM ADSPICE.

PRIMÙM IN ORBE DEJECIT [*sub dato*] ; POSTREMÙM [*sub dato*].

CHAPTER V.

ROMANCE.

'For long years,' writes Teufelsdröckh, 'had the poor He-
' brew, in this Egypt of an Auscultatorship, painfully toiled,
' baking bricks without stubble, before ever the question once
' struck him with entire force : For what?—*Beym Himmel!*
' For Food and Warmth! And are Food and Warmth no-
' where else, in the whole wide Universe, discoverable?—Come
' of it what might, I resolved to try.'

Thus then are we to see him in a new independent capacity,
though perhaps far from an improved one. Teufelsdröckh is
now a man without Profession. Quitting the common Fleet
of herring-busses and whalers, where indeed his leeward, lag-
gard condition was painful enough, he desperately steers off,
on a course of his own, by sextant and compass of his own.
Unhappy Teufelsdröckh! Though neither Fleet, nor Traffic,
nor Commodores pleased thee, still was it not *a Fleet*, sailing
in prescribed track, for fixed objects; above all, in combination, wherein, by mutual guidance, by all manner of loans
and borrowings, each could manifoldly aid the other? How
wilt thou sail in unknown seas; and for thyself find that
shorter North-west Passage to thy fair Spice-country of a Nowhere?—A solitary rover on such a voyage, with such nautical
tactics, will meet with adventures. Nay, as we forthwith discover, a certain Calypso-Island detains him at the very outset;
and as it were falsifies and oversets his whole reckoning.

'If in youth,' writes he once, 'the Universe is majestically
' unveiling, and everywhere Heaven revealing itself on Earth,
' nowhere to the Young Man does this Heaven on Earth so
' immediately reveal itself as in the Young Maiden. Strangely
' enough, in this strange life of ours, it has been so appointed.
' On the whole, as I have often said, a Person (*Personlichkeit*)
' is ever holy to us; a certain orthodox Anthropomorphism
' connects my *Me* with all *Thees* in bonds of Love: but it
' is in this approximation of the Like and Unlike, that such

' heavenly attraction, as between Negative and Positive, first
' burns out into a flame. Is the pitifulest mortal Person,
' think you, indifferent to us? Is it not rather our heartfelt
' wish to be made one with him; to unite him to us, by
' gratitude, by admiration, even by fear; or failing all these,
' unite ourselves to him? But how much more, in this case
' of the Like-Unlike! Here is conceded us the higher mystic
' possibility of such a union, the highest in our Earth; thus,
' in the conducting medium of Fantasy, flames forth that *fire-*
' development of the universal Spiritual Electricity, which, as
' unfolded between man and woman, we first emphatically
' denominate LOVE.

' In every well-conditioned stripling, as I conjecture, there
' already blooms a certain prospective Paradise, cheered by
' some fairest Eve; nor, in the stately vistas, and flowerage
' and foliage of that Garden, is a Tree of Knowledge, beautiful
' and awful in the midst thereof, wanting. Perhaps too the
' whole is but the lovelier, if Cherubim and a Flaming Sword
' divide it from all footsteps of men; and grant him, the im-
' aginative stripling, only the view, not the entrance. Happy
' season of virtuous youth, when Shame is still an impassable
' celestial barrier; and the sacred air-cities of Hope have not
' shrunk into the mean clay-hamlets of Reality; and man,
' by his nature, is yet infinite and free!

' As for our young Forlorn,' continues Teufelsdröckh, evidently meaning himself, ' in his secluded way of life, and with
' his glowing Fantasy, the more fiery that it burnt under cover,
' as in a reverberating furnace, his feeling towards the Queens
' of this Earth was, and indeed is, altogether unspeakable.
' A visible Divinity dwelt in them; to our young Friend all
' women were holy, were heavenly. As yet he but saw them
' flitting past, in their many-coloured angel-plumage; or hov-
' ering mute and inaccessible on the outskirts of *Æsthetic Tea:*
' all of air they were, all Soul and Form; so lovely, like mys-
' terious priestesses, in whose hand was the invisible Jacob's-
' ladder, whereby man might mount into very Heaven. That
' he, our poor Friend, should ever win for himself one of these
' Gracefuls (*Holden*) *Ach Gott!* how could he hope it; should

' he not have died under it? There was a certain delirious
' vertigo in the thought.

'Thus was the young man, if all sceptical of Demons and
'Angels such as the vulgar had once believed in, nevertheless
'not unvisited by hosts of true Sky-born, who visibly and
'audibly hovered round him whereso he went; and they had
'that religious worship in his thought, though as yet it was
'by their mere earthly and trivial name that he named them.
'But now, if on a soul so circumstanced, some actual Air-
'maiden, incorporated into tangibility and reality, should cast
'any electric glance of kind eyes, saying thereby, "Thou too
'"mayest love and be loved;" and so kindle him,—good
'Heaven, what a volcanic, earthquake-bringing, all-consuming
'fire were probably kindled!'

Such a fire, it afterwards appears, did actually burst forth,
with explosions more or less Vesuvian, in the inner man of
Herr Diogenes; as indeed how could it fail? A nature,
which, in his own figurative style, we might say, had now not a
little carbonised tinder, of Irritability; with so much nitre of
latent Passion, and sulphurous Humour enough; the whole
lying in such hot neighbourhood, close by 'a reverberating
furnace of Fantasy:' have we not here the components of
driest Gunpowder, ready, on occasion of the smallest spark,
to blaze up? Neither, in this our Life-element, are sparks
anywhere wanting. Without doubt, some Angel, whereof so
many hovered round, would one day, leaving 'the outskirts of
Æsthetic Tea,' flit nigher; and, by electric Promethean glance,
kindle no despicable firework. Happy, if it indeed proved a
Firework, and flamed off rocket-wise, in successive beautiful
bursts of splendour, each growing naturally from the other,
through the several stages of a happy Youthful Love; till the
whole were safely burnt out; and the young soul relieved,
with little damage! Happy, if it did not rather prove a Conflagration and mad Explosion; painfully lacerating the heart
itself; nay perhaps bursting the heart in pieces (which were
Death); or at best, bursting the thin walls of your 'reverberating furnace,' so that it rage thenceforth all unchecked
among the contiguous combustibles (which were Madness):

8

till of the so fair and manifold internal world of our Diogenes, there remained Nothing, or only the ' crater of an extinct volcano ! '

From multifarious Documents in this Bag *Capricornus*, and in the adjacent ones on both sides thereof, it becomes manifest that our Philosopher, as stoical and cynical as he now looks, was heartily and even franticly in Love ; here therefore may our old doubts whether his heart were of stone or of flesh give way. He loved once ; not wisely but too well. And once only : for as your Congreve needs a new case or wrappage for every new rocket, so each human heart can properly exhibit but one Love, if even one ; the 'First Love which is infinite ' can be followed by no second like unto it. In more recent years, accordingly, the Editor of these Sheets was led to regard Teufelsdröckh as a man not only who would never wed, but who would never even flirt ; whom the grand-climacteric itself, and *St. Martin's Summer* of incipient Dotage, would crown with no new myrtle garland. To the Professor, women are henceforth Pieces of Art ; of Celestial Art, indeed ; which celestial pieces he glories to survey in galleries, but has lost thought of purchasing.

Psychological readers are not without curiosity to see how Teufelsdröckh, in this for him unexampled predicament, de. means himself ; with what specialities of successive configura tion, splendour and colour, his Firework blazes off. Small, as usual, is the satisfaction that such can meet with here. From amid these confused masses of Eulogy and Elegy, with their mad Petrarchan and Werterean ware lying madly scattered among all sorts of quite extraneous matter, not so much as the fair one's name can be deciphered. For, without doubt, the title *Blumine*, whereby she is here designated, and which means simply Goddess of Flowers, must be fictitious. Was her real name Flora, then ? But what was her surname, or had she none ? Of what station in Life was she ; of what parentage, fortune, aspect ? Specially, by what Pre-established Harmony of occurrences did the Lover and the Loved meet one another in so wide a world ; how did they behave in such meeting ? To all which questions, not unessential in a Biographic work, mere Conjecture must for most part return answer. 'It was 'appointed,' says our Philosopher, 'that the high celestial 'orbit of Blumine should intersect the low sublunary one of 'our Forlorn ; that he, looking in her empyrean eyes, should 'fancy the upper Sphere of Light was come down into this 'nether sphere of Shadows ; and finding himself mistaken, 'make noise enough.'

We seem to gather that she was young, hazel-eyed, beautiful, and some one's Cousin ; highborn and of high spirits ; but unhappily dependent and insolvent ; living, perhaps, on the not too gracious bounty of monied relatives. But how came 'the Wanderer' into her circle ? Was it by the humid vehicle of *Æsthetic Tea*, or by the arid one of mere Business ? Was it on the hand of Herr Towgood ; or of the Gnädige Frau, who, as an ornamental Artist, might sometimes like to promote flirtation, especially for young cynical Nondescripts ? To all appearance, it was chiefly by Accident, and the grace of Nature.

'Thou fair Waldschloss,' writes our Autobiographer, 'what 'stranger ever saw thee, were it even an absolved Auscultator, 'officially bearing in his pocket the last *Relatio ex Actis* he 'would ever write ; but must have paused to wonder ! Noble 'Mansion ! There stoodest thou, in deep Mountain Amphi-'theatre, on umbrageous lawns, in thy serene solitude ; 'stately, massive, all of granite ; glittering in the western 'sunbeams, like a palace of El Doredo, overlaid with precious 'metal. Beautiful rose up, in wavy curvature, the slope of 'thy guardian Hills : of the greenest was their sward, em-'bossed with its dark-brown frets of crag, or spotted by some 'spreading solitary Tree and its shadow. To the unconscious 'Wayfarer thou wert also as an Ammon's Temple, in the 'Libyan Waste ; where, for joy and woe, the tablet of his Des-'tiny lay written. Well might he pause and gaze ; in that 'glance of his were prophecy and nameless forebodings.'

But now let us conjecture that the so presentient Auscultator has handed in his *Relatio ex Actis ;* been invited to a glass of Rhine-wine ; and so, instead of returning dispirited and athirst to his dusty Town-home, is ushered into the Gar-

denhouse, where sit the choicest party of dames and cavaliers;
if not engaged in Æsthetic Tea, yet in trustful evening conversation, and perhaps Musical Coffee, for we hear of 'harps
and pure voices making the stillness live.' Scarcely, it would
seem, is the Gardenhouse inferior in respectability to the
noble Mansion itself. 'Embowered amid rich foliage, rose-
' clusters, and the hues and odours of thousand flowers, here
' sat that brave company; in front, from the wide-opened
' doors, fair outlook over blossom and bush, over grove and
' velvet green, stretching, undulating onwards to the remote
' Mountain peaks : so bright, so mild, and everywhere the mel-
' ody of birds and happy creatures : it was all as if man had
' stolen a shelter from the Sun in the bosom-vesture of Sum-
' mer herself. How came it that the Wanderer advanced
' thither with such forecasting heart (ahndungsvoll), by the
' side of his gay host? Did he feel that to these soft influ-
' ences his hard bosom ought to be shut; that here, once
' more, Fate had it in view to try him ; to mock him, and see
' whether there were Humour in him ?

' Next moment he finds himself presented to the party ; and
' especially by name to—Blumine ! Peculiar among all dames
' and damosels, glanced Blumine, there in her modesty, like
' a star among earthly lights. Noblest maiden ! whom he
' bent to, in body and in soul ; yet scarcely dared look at, for
' the presence filled him with painful yet sweetest embarrass-
' ment.

'Blumine's was a name well known to him ; far and wide
' was the fair one heard of, for her gifts, her graces, her ca-
' prices : from all which vague colourings of Rumour, from
' the censures no less than from the praises, had our Friend
' painted for himself a certain imperious Queen of Hearts,
' and blooming warm Earth-angel, much more enchanting
' than your mere white Heaven-angels of women, in whose
' placid veins circulates too little naphtha-fire. Herself also
' he had seen in public places ; that light, yet so stately form ;
' those dark tresses, shading a face where smiles and sunlight
' played over earnest deeps : but all this he had seen only as
' a magic vision, for him inaccessible, almost without reality.

' Her sphere was too far from his ; how should she ever think
' of him ; O Heaven ! how should they so much as once meet
' together? And now that Rose-goddess sits in the same
' circle with him ; the light of *her* eyes has smiled on him, if
' he speak she will hear it ! Nay, who knows, since the
' heavenly Sun looks into lowest valleys, but Blumine herself,
' might have aforetime noted the so unnotable ; perhaps, from
' his very gainsayers, as he had from hers, gathered wonder,
' gathered favour for him ? Was the attraction, the agitation
' mutual, then ; pole and pole trembling towards contact,
' when once brought into neighbourhood ? Say rather, heart
' swelling in presence of the Queen of Hearts ; like the Sea
' swelling when once near its Moon ! With the Wanderer it
' was even so : as in heavenward gravitation, suddenly as at
' the touch of a Seraph's wand, his whole soul is roused from its
' deepest recesses ; and all that was painful, and that was bliss-
' ful there, dim images, vague feelings of a whole Past and a
' whole Future, are heaving in unquiet eddies within him.

' Often, in far less agitating scenes, had our still Friend
' shrunk forcibly together ; and shrouded up his tremours
' and flutterings, of what sort soever, in a safe cover of Silence,
' and perhaps of seeming Stolidity. How was it, then, that
' here, when trembling to the core of his heart, he did not
' sink into swoons, but rose into strength, into fearlessness
' and clearness? It was his guiding Genius (*Dämon*) that in-
' spired him ; he must go forth and meet his Destiny. Shew
' thyself now, whispered it, or be forever hid. Thus some-
' times it is even when your anxiety becomes transcendental,
' that the soul first feels herself able to transcend it ; that she
' rises above it, in fiery victory ; and, borne on new-found
' wings of victory, moves so calmly, even because so rapidly,
' so irresistably. Always must the Wanderer remember, with
' a certain satisfaction and surprise, how in this case he sat not
' silent, but struck adroitly into the stream of conversation ;
' which thenceforth, to speak with an apparent not a real
' vanity, he may say that he continued to lead. Surely, in
' those hours, a certain inspiration was imparted him, such in-
' spiration as is still possible in our late era. The self-secluded

'unfolds himself in noble thoughts, in free, glowing words;
'his soul is as one sea of light, the peculiar home of Truth
'and Intellect; wherein also Fantasy bodies forth form after
'form, radiant with all prismatic hues.'

It appears, in this otherwise so happy meeting, there talked
one 'Philistine;' who even now, to the general weariness, was
dominantly pouring forth Philistinism (*Philistriositäten*); little
witting what hero was here entering to demolish him! We
omit the series of Socratic, or other Diogenic utterances, not
unhappy in their way, whereby the monster, 'persuaded into
'silence,' seems soon after to have withdrawn for the night.
'Of which dialectic marauder,' writes our hero, 'the discom-
'fiture was visibly felt as a benefit by most: but what were all
'applauses to the glad smile, threatening every moment to
'become a laugh, wherewith Blumine herself repaid the vic-
'tor? He ventured to address her, she answered with atten-
'tion: nay, what if there were a slight tremour in that silver
'voice; what if the red glow of evening were hiding a tran-
'sient blush!

'The conversation took a higher tone, one fine thought
'called forth another: it was one of those rare seasons, when
'the soul expands with full freedom, and man feels himself
'brought near to man. Gaily in light, graceful abandonment,
'the friendly talk played round that circle; for the burden
'was rolled from every heart; the barriers of Ceremony, which
'are indeed the laws of polite living, had melted as into
'vapour; and the poor claims of *Me* and *Thee*, no longer
'parted by rigid fences, now flowed softly into one another;
'and Life lay all harmonious, many-tinted, like some fair
'royal champaign, the sovereign and owner of which were
'Love only. Such music springs from kind hearts, in a kind
'environment of place and time. And yet as the light grew
'more aërial on the mountain-tops, and the shadows fell
'longer over the valley, some faint tone of sadness may have
'breathed through the heart; and, in whispers more or less
'audible, reminded every one that as this bright day was draw-
'ing towards its close, so likewise must the Day of Man's Ex-
'istence decline into dust and darkness; and with all its sick

' toilings, and joyful and mournful noises, sink in the still
' Eternity.

'To our Friend the hours seemed moments; holy was he
' and happy: the words from those sweetest lips came over
' him like dew on thirsty grass; all better feelings in his soul
' seemed to whisper: It is good for us to be here. At part-
' ing, the Blumine's hand was in his: in the balmy twilight,
' with the kind stars above them, he spoke something of meet-
' ing again, which was not contradicted; he pressed gently
' those small soft fingers, and it seemed as if they were not
' hastily, not angrily withdrawn.'

Poor Teufelsdröckh! it is clear to demonstration thou art
smit: the Queen of Hearts would see a 'man of genius' also
sigh for her; and there, by art magic, in that preternatural
hour, has she bound and spell-bound thee. 'Love is not
' altogether a Delirium,' says he elsewhere, 'yet has it many
' points in common therewith. I call it rather a discerning of
' the Infinite in the Finite, of the Idea made Real; which dis-
' cerning again may be either true or false, either seraphic or
' demoniac, Inspiration or Insanity. But in the former case
' too, as in common Madness, it is Fantasy that superadds it-
' self to sight; on the so petty domain of the Actual plants its
' Archimedes-lever, whereby to move at will the infinite Spirit-
' ual. Fantasy I might call the true Heaven-gate and Hell-
' gate of man: his sensuous life is but the small temporary
' stage (*Zeitbühne*) whereon thick-streaming influences from
' both these far yet near regions meet visibly, and act tragedy
' and melodrama. Sense can support herself handsomely, in
' most countries, for some eighteenpence a day; but for Fan-
' tasy planets and solar-systems will not suffice. Witness your
' Pyrrhus conquering the world, yet drinking no better red
' wine than he had before.' Alas! witness also your Diogenes, flame-clad, scaling the upper Heaven, and verging towards Insanity, for prize of a high-souled Brunette, as if
the Earth held but one and not several of these!

He says that, in Town, they met again: 'day after day, like
' his heart's sun, the blooming Blumine shone on him. Ah!
' a little while ago, and he was yet in all darkness: him what

' Graceful (*Holde*) would ever love ?   Disbelieving all things,
' the poor youth had never learned to believe in himself.
' Withdrawn in proud timidity, within his own fastnesses :
' solitary from men, yet baited by night-spectres enough, he
' saw himself, with a sad indignation, constrained to renounce
' the fairest hopes of existence.   And now, O now !   " She
' " looks on thee," cried he ; " she the fairest, noblest ; do not
' " her dark eyes tell thee, thou art not despised?   The
' " Heaven's-Messenger !   All Heaven's blessings be hers ! "
' Thus did soft melodies flow through his heart ; tones of an
' infinite gratitude ; sweetest intimations that he also was a
' man, that for him also unutterable joys had been provided.

  'In free speech, earnest or gay, amid lambent glances,
' laughter, tears, and often with the inarticulate mystic speech
' of Music ; such was the element they now lived in ; in such
' a many-tinted, radiant Aurora, and by this fairest of Orient
' Light-bringers must our Friend be blandished, and the new
' Apocalypse of Nature unrolled to him.   Fairest Blumine !
' And, even as a Star, all Fire and humid Softness, a very
' Light-ray incarnate !   Was there so much as   fault, a a
' " caprice," he could have dispensed with ?   Was she not to
' him in very deed a morning-Star ; did not her presence
' bring with it airs from Heaven ?   As from Æolean Harps in
' the breath of dawn, as from the Memnon's Statue struck by
' the rosy finger of Aurora, unearthly music was around him,
' and lapped him into untried balmy Rest.   Pale Doubt fled
' away to the distance ; Life bloomed up with happiness and
' hope.   The Past, then, was all a haggard dream ; he had
' been in the Garden of Eden, then, and could not discern it !
' But lo now ! the black walls of his prison melt away ; the
' captive is alive, is free.   If he loved his Disenchantress ?
' *Ach Gott !*   His whole heart and soul and life were hers,
' but never had he named it Love : existence was all a Feel-
' ing, not yet shaped into a Thought.'

  Nevertheless, into a Thought, nay into an Action, it must
be shaped ; for neither Disenchanter nor Disenchantress, mere
'Children of Time,' can abide by feeling alone.   The Professor knows not, to this day, 'how in her soft, fervid bosom,

' the Lovely found determination, even on hest of Necessity,
' to cut asunder these so blissful bounds.' He even appears
surprised at the 'Duenna Cousin,' whoever she may have
been, 'in whose meagre, hunger-bitten philosophy, the re-
' ligion of young hearts was, from the first, faintly approved
' of.' We, even at such distance, can explain it without
necromancy. Let the Philosopher answer this one question :
What figure, at that period, was a Mrs. Teufelsdröckh likely
to make in polished society ? Could she have driven so much
as a brass-bound Gig, or even a simple ironspring one ?
Thou foolish 'absolved Auscultator,' before whom lies no
prospect of capital, will any yet known 'religion of young
hearts keep the human kitchen warm ?' Pshaw ! thy divine
Blumine, when she ' resigned herself to wed some richer,'
shews more philosophy though but ' a woman of genius,'
than thou, a pretended man.

Our readers have witnessed the origin of this Love-mania,
and with what royal splendour it waxes, and rises. Let no
one ask us to unfold the glories of its dominant state ; much
less the horrors of its almost instantaneous dissolution. How
from such inorganic masses, henceforth madder than ever, as
lie in these Bags, can even fragments of a living delineation
be organised? Besides, of what profit were it ? We view
with a lively pleasure, the gay silk Montgolfier start from the
ground, and shoot upwards, cleaving the liquid deeps, till it
dwindle to a luminous star : but what is there to look longer
on, when once, by natural elasticity, or accident of fire, it has
exploded ? A hapless air-navigator, plunging, amid torn
parachutes, sand-bags, and confused wreck, fast enough into
the jaws of the Devil ! Suffice it to know that Teufelsdröckh
rose into the highest regions of the Empyrean, by a natural
parabolic track, and returned thence in a quick perpendicular
one. For the rest, let any feeling reader, who has been unhappy enough to do the like, paint it out for himself : considering only that if he, for his perhaps comparatively insignificant mistress, underwent such agonies and frenzies, what
must Teufelsdröckh's have been, with a fire-heart, and for a
nonpareil Blumine ! We glance merely at the final scene :

'One morning, he found his Morning-star all dimmed and
' dusky-red ; the fair creature was silent, absent, she seemed
' to have been weeping. Alas, no longer a Morning-star, but
' a troublous skyey Portent, announcing that the Doomsday
' had dawned ! She said, in a tremulous voice, They were to
' meet no more.' The thunderstruck Air-sailor is not wanting
to himself in this dread hour : but what avails it ? We omit
the passionate expostulations, entreaties, indignations, since
all was vain, and not even an explanation was conceded him ;
and hasten to the catastrophe. ' "Farewell, then, Madam ! "
' said he, not without sternness, for his stung pride helped
' him. She put her hand in his, she looked in his face, tears
' started to her eyes : in wild audacity he clasped her to his
' bosom ; their lips were joined, their two souls, like two dew-
' drops, rushed into one,—for the first time, and for the last ! '
Thus was Teufelsdröckh made immortal by a kiss. And then ?
Why, then—' thick curtains of Night rushed over his soul, as
' rose the immeasurable Crash of Doom ; and through the
' ruins as of a shivered Universe was he falling, falling, to-
' wards the Abyss.'

CHAPTER VI.

SORROWS OF TEUFELSDRÖCKH.

We have long felt that, with a man like our Professor, matters must often be expected to take a course of their own ;
that in so multiplex, intricate a nature, there might be chan-
nels, both for admitting and emitting, such as the Psycholo-
gist had seldom noted ; in short, that on no grand occasion
and convulsion, neither in the joy-storm nor in the woe-storm,
could you predict his demeanour.

To our less philosophical readers, for example, it is now clear
that the so passionate Teufelsdröckh, precipitated through
'a shivered Universe' in this extraordinary way, has only one
of three things which he can next do: Establish himself in
Bedlam ; begin writing Satanic Poetry ; or blow out his
brains. In the progress towards any of which consummations, do not such readers anticipate extravagance enough ;

breast-beating, brow-beating (against walls), lion-bellowings
of blasphemy and the like, stampings, smitings, breakages of
furniture, if not arson itself?

Nowise so does Teufelsdröckh deport him. He quietly lifts
his *Pilgerstab* (Pilgrim-staff), 'old business being soon wound
up;' and begins a perambulation and circumambulation of
the terraqueous globe! Curious it is, indeed, how with such
vivacity of conception, such intensity of feeling; above all,
with these unconscionable habits of Exaggeration in speech,
he combines that wonderful stillness of his, that stoicism in
external procedure. Thus, if his sudden bereavement, in this
matter of the Flower-goddess, is talked of as a real Doomsday and Dissolution of Nature, in which light doubtless it
partly appeared to himself, his own nature is nowise dissolved
thereby ; but rather is compressed closer. For once, as we
might say, a Blumine by magic appliances has unlocked that
shut heart of his, and its hidden things rush out tumultuous,
boundless, like genii enfranchised from their glass phial : but
no sooner are your magic appliances withdrawn, than the
strange casket of a heart springs-to again ; and perhaps there
is now no key extant that will open it: for a Teufelsdröckh,
as we remarked, will not love a second time. Singular Diogenes ! No sooner has that heart-rending occurrence fairly
taken place, than he affects to regard it as a thing natural, of
which there is nothing more to be said. ' One highest hope,
' seemingly legible in the eyes of an Angel, had recalled him
' as out of Death-shadows into celestial life : but a gleam of
' Tophet passed over the face of his Angel ; he was rapt away
' in whirlwinds, and heard the laughter of Demons. It was
' a Calenture,' adds he, 'whereby the Youth saw green Para-
' dise-groves in the waste Ocean-waters : a lying vision, yet
' not wholly a lie, for *he* saw it.' But what things soever
passed in him, when he ceased to see it ; what ragings and
despairings soever Teufelsdröckh's soul was the scene of, he
has the goodness to conceal under a quite opaque cover of
Silence. We know it well ; the first mad paroxysm past, our
brave Gneschen collected his dismembered philosophies, and
buttoned himself together; he was meek, silent, or spoke of

the weather, and the Journals : only by a transient knitting
of those shaggy brows, by some deep flash of those eyes,
glancing one knew not whether with tear-dew or with fierce
fire,—might you have guessed what a Gehenna was within ;
that a whole Satanic School were spouting, though inaudibly,
there. To consume your own choler, as some chimneys consume their own smoke ; to keep a whole Satanic School
spouting, if it must spout, inaudibly, is a negative yet no
slight virtue, nor one of the commonest in these times.

Nevertheless, we will not take upon us to say, that in the
strange measure he fell upon, there was not a touch of latent
Insanity ; whereof indeed the actual condition of these Documents in *Capricornus* and *Aquarius* is no bad emblem. His
so unlimited Wanderings, toilsome enough, are without as-
signed or perhaps assignable aim ; internal Unrest seems his
sole guidance ; he wanders, wanders, as if that curse of the
Prophet had fallen on him, and he were ' made like unto a
wheel.' Doubtless, too, the chaotic nature of these Paperbags
aggravates our obscurity. Quite without note of preparation,
for example, we come upon the following slip : ' A peculiar
' feeling it is that will rise in the Traveller, when turning
' some hill-range in his desert road, he descries lying far below,
' embosomed among its groves and green natural bulwarks,
' and all diminished to a toybox, the fair Town, where so many
' souls, as it were seen and yet unseen, are driving their multi-
' farious traffic. Its white steeple is then truly a starward-
' pointing finger ; the canopy of blue smoke seems like a sort
' of Life-breath : for always, of its own unity, the soul gives
' unity to whatso it looks on with love ; thus does the little
' Dwellingplace of men, in itself a congeries of houses and
' huts, become for us an individual, almost a person. But
' what thousand other thoughts unite thereto, if the place has
' to ourselves been the arena of joyous or mournful experi-
' ences ; if perhaps the cradle we were rocked in still stands
' there, if our Loving ones still dwell there, if our Buried ones
' there slumber ! ' Does Teufelsdröckh, as the wounded eagle
is said to make for its own eyrie, and indeed military desert-
ers, and all hunted outcast creatures, turn as if by instinct in

the direction of their birth-land,—fly first, in this extremity, towards his native Entepfuhl; but reflecting that there no help awaits him, take but one wistful look from the distance, and then wend elsewhither?

Little happier seems to be his next flight: into the wilds of Nature; as if in her mother-bosom he would seek healing. So at least we incline to interpret the following Notice, separated from the former by some considerable space, wherein, however, is nothing note-worthy:

‘ Mountains were not new to him; but rarely are Mountains ‘ seen in such combined majesty and grace as here. The rocks ‘ are of that sort called Primitive by the mineralogists, which ‘ always arrange themselves in masses of a rugged, gigantic ‘ character; which ruggedness, however, is here tempered by ‘ a singular airiness of form, and softness of environment: in ‘ a climate favourable to vegetation, the gray cliff, itself cov- ‘ ered with lichens, shoots up through a garment of foliage or ‘ verdure; and white, bright cottages, tree-shaded, cluster ‘ round the everlasting granite. In fine vicissitude, Beauty ‘ alternates with Grandeur: you ride through stony hollows, ‘ along strait passes, traversed by torrents, overhung by ‘ high walls of rock; now winding amid broken shaggy ‘ chasms, and huge fragments; now suddenly emerging into ‘ some emerald valley, where the streamlet collects itself into ‘ a Lake, and man has again found a fair dwelling, and it seems as if Peace had established herself in the bosom of ‘ Strength.

‘ To Peace, however, in this vortex of existence, can the ‘ Son of Time not pretend: still less if some Spectre haunt ‘ him from the Past; and the Future is wholly a Stygian ‘ Darkness, spectre-bearing. Reasonably might the Wan- ‘derer exclaim to himself: Are not the gates of this world’s ‘ Happiness inexorably shut against thee; hast thou a hope ‘ that is not mad? Nevertheless, one may still murmur audi- ‘ bly, or in the original Greek if that suit better: “ Whoso ‘ can look on Death will start at no shadows.”

‘ From such meditations is the Wanderer’s attention called ‘ outwards; for now the Valley closes in abruptly, intersected

' by a huge mountain mass, the stony waterworn ascent of
' which is not to be accomplished on horseback.   Arrived
' aloft, he finds himself again lifted into the evening sunset
' light ; and cannot but pause, and gaze round him, some
' moments there.   An upland irregular expanse of wold,
' where valleys in complex branchings are suddenly or slowly
' arranging their descent towards every quarter of the sky.
' The mountain-ranges are beneath your feet, and folded to-
' gether : only the loftier summits look down here and there
' as on a second plain ; lakes also lie clear and earnest in their
' solitude.   No trace of man now visible ; unless indeed it
' were he who fashioned that little visible link of Highway,
' here, as would seem, scaling the inaccessible, to unite
' Province with Province.   But sunwards, lo you ! how it
' towers sheer up, a world of Mountains, the diadem and cen-
' tre of the mountain region !   A hundred and a hundred
' savage peaks, in the last light of Day ; all glowing, of gold
' and amethyst, like giant spirits of the wilderness ; there in
' their silence, in their solitude, even as on the night when
' Noah's Deluge first dried !   Beautiful, nay solemn, was the
' sudden aspect to our Wanderer.   He gazed over those stu-
' pendous masses with wonder, almost with longing desire ;
' never till this hour had he known Nature, that she was One,
' that she was his Mother and divine.   And as the ruddy
' glow was fading into clearness in the sky, and the Sun had
' now departed, a murmur of Eternity and Immensity, of
' Death and of Life, stole through his soul ; and he felt as if
' Death and Life were one, as if the Earth were not dead, as
' if the Spirit of the Earth had its throne in that splendour,
' and his own spirit were therewith holding communion.

   ' The spell was broken by a sound of carriage-wheels.
' Emerging from the hidden Northward, to sink soon into the
' hidden Southward, came a gay barouche-and-four : it was
' open ; servants and postilions wore wedding-favours : that
' happy pair, then, had found each other, it was their mar-
' riage evening !   Few moments brought them near : *Du*
' *Himmel !*   It was Herr Towgood and — — Blumine !   With
' slight unrecognising salutation they passed me ; plunged

'down amid the neighbouring thickets, onwards, to Heaven,
' and to England ; and I, in my friend Richter's words, *I re-*
' *mained alone, behind them, with the Night.*'

Were it not cruel in these circumstances, here might be
the place to insert an observation, gleaned long ago from the
great *Clothes-Volume,* where it stands with quite other intent :
' Some time before Small-pox was extirpated,' says the Professor, ' there came a new malady of the spiritual sort on
' Europe : I mean the epidemic, now endemical, of View-
' hunting. Poets of old date, being privileged with Senses,
' had also enjoyed external Nature ; but chiefly as we enjoy
' the crystal cup which holds good or bad liquor for us ; that
' is to say, in silence, or with slight incidental commentary :
' never, as I compute, till after the *Sorrows of Werter,* was
' there man found who would say : Come let us make a De-
' scription ! Having drunk the liquor, come let us eat the
' glass ! Of which endemic the Jenner is unhappily still to
' seek.' Too true !

We reckon it more important to remark that the Professor's
Wanderings, so far as his stoical and cynical envelopment admits us to clear insight, here first take their permanent character, fatuous or not. That Basilisk-glance of the Barouche-
and-four seems to have withered up what little remnant of a
purpose may have still lurked in him : Life has become wholly
a dark labyrinth ; wherein, through long years, our Friend,
flying from spectres, has to stumble about at random, and
naturally with more haste than progress.

Foolish were it in us to attempt following him, even from
afar, in this extraordinary world-pilgrimage of his ; the
simplest record of which, were clear record possible, would
fill volumes. Hopeless is the obscurity, unspeakable the confusion. He glides from country to country, from condition to
condition ; vanishing and re-appearing, no man can calculate
how or where. Through all quarters of the world he wanders, and apparently through all circles of society. If in any
scene, perhaps difficult to fix geographically, he settles for a
time, and forms connexions, be sure he will snap them
abruptly asunder. Let him sink out of sight as Private

Scholar (*Privatisirender*), living by the grace of God, in some
European capital, you may next find him as Hadjee in the
neighbourhood of Mecca. It is an inexplicable Phantasmagoria, capricious, quick-changing; as if our Traveller, instead
of limbs and highways, had transported himself by some
wishing carpet, or Fortunatus' Hat. The whole, too, imparted
emblematically, in dim multifarious tokens (as that collection
of Street-Advertisements); with only some touch of direct
historical notice sparingly interspersed: little light-islets in
the world of haze! So that, from this point, the Professor is
more of an enigma than ever. In figurative language, we
might say he becomes, not indeed a spirit, yet spiritualised,
vaporised. Fact unparalleled in Biography: The river of his
History, which we have traced from its tiniest fountains, and
hoped to see flow onward, with increasing current, into the
ocean, here dashes itself over that terrific Lover's Leap; and,
as a mad-foaming cataract, flies wholly into tumultuous clouds
of spray! Low down it indeed collects again into pools and
plashes; yet only at a great distance, and with difficulty, if at
all, into a general stream. To cast a glance into certain of
those pools and plashes, and trace whither they run, must, for
a chapter or two, form the limit of our endeavour.

For which end doubtless those direct historical Notices,
where they can be met with, are the best. Nevertheless, of
this sort too there occurs much, which, with our present light,
it were questionable to emit. Teufelsdröckh, vibrating everywhere between the highest and the lowest levels, comes into
contact with public History itself. For example, those con-
versations and relations with illustrious Persons, as Sultan
Mahmoud, the Emperor Napoleon, and others, are they not as
yet rather of a diplomatic character than of a biographic?
The Editor, appreciating the sacredness of crowned heads,
nay perhaps suspecting the possible trickeries of a Clothes-
Philosopher, will eschew this province for the present: a new
time may bring new insight and a different duty.

If we ask now, not indeed with what ulterior Purpose, for
there was none, yet with what immediate outlooks; at all
events, in what mood of mind, the Professor undertook and

prosecuted this world-pilgrimage,—the answer is more distinct than favourable. 'A nameless Unrest,' says he, 'urged me 'forward ; to which the outward motion was some momentary 'lying solace. Whither should I go? My Loadstars were 'blotted out ; in that canopy of grim fire shone no star. Yet 'forward must I; the ground burnt under me ; there was no 'rest for the sole of my foot. I was alone, alone ! Ever too the 'strong inward longing shaped Fantasms for itself : towards 'these, one after the other, must I fruitlessly wander. A feel-'ing I had that, for my fever-thirst, there was and must be 'somewhere a healing Fountain. To many fondly imagined 'Fountains, the Saints' Wells of these days, did I pilgrim ; to 'great Men, to great Cities, to great Events : but found there 'no healing. In strange countries, as in the well-known ; in 'savage deserts, as in the press of corrupt civilisation, it was 'ever the same : how could your Wanderer escape from—*his* '*own Shadow?* Nevertheless still Forward ! I felt as if in 'great haste ; to do I saw not what. From the depths of my 'own heart, it called to me, Forwards! The winds and the 'streams, and all Nature sounded to me, Forwards ! *Ach Gott,* 'I was even, once for all, a Son of Time.'

From which is it not clear that the internal Satanic School was still active enough? He says elsewhere ; 'The *Enchiri-*'*dion of Epictetus* I had ever with me, often as my sole ration-'al companion ; and regret to mention that the nourishment 'it yielded was trifling.' Thou foolish Teufelsdröckh ! How could it else ? Hadst thou not Greek enough to understand thus much : *The end of Man is an Action, and not a Thought,* though it were the noblest?

'How I lived ?' writes he once. 'Friend, hast thou con-'sidered the "rugged all-nourishing Earth," as Sophocles well 'names her ; how she feeds the sparrow on the house-top, 'much more her darling, man? While thou stirrest and livest, 'thou hast a probability of victual. My breakfast of tea has 'been cooked by a Tartar woman, with water of the Amur, 'who wiped her earthen-kettle with a horse-tail. I have 'roasted wild eggs in the sand of Sahara ; I have awakened in 'Paris *Estrapades* and Vienna *Malzleins,* with no prospect of

9

'breakfast beyond elemental liquid. That I had my living to
'seek saved me from Dying,—by suicide. In our busy Eu-
'rope, is there not an everlasting demand for Intellect, in the
'chemical, mechanical, political, religious, educational, com-
'mercial departments? In Pagan countries, cannot one write
'Fetishes? Living! Little knowest thou what alchemy is in
'an inventive Soul; how, as with its little finger, it can create
'provision enough for the body (of a Philosopher); and then,
'as with both hands, create quite other than provision;
'namely, spectres to torment itself withal.'

Poor Teufelsdröckh! Flying with Hunger always parallel
to him; and a whole Infernal Chase in his rear; so that the
countenance of Hunger is comparatively a friend's! Thus
must he, in the temper of ancient Cain, or of the modern
Wandering Jew, save only that he feels himself not guilty and
but suffering the pains of guilt,—wend to and fro with aimless
speed. Thus must he, over the whole surface of the Earth
(by foot-prints), write his *Sorrows of Teufelsdröckh;* even as
the great Goethe, in passionate words, had to write his
Sorrows of Werter, before the spirit freed herself, and he
could become a Man. Vain truly is the hope of your swift-
est Runner to escape 'from his own Shadow!' Nevertheless, in these sick days, when the Born of Heaven first descries himself (about the age of twenty) in a world such as
ours, richer than usual in two things, in Truths grown obsolete, and Trades grown obsolete,—what can the fool
think but that it is all a Den of Lies, wherein whoso will not
speak Lies and act Lies, must stand idle and despair?
Whereby it happens that, for your nobler minds, the publishing of some such Work of Art, in one or the other dialect, becomes almost a necessity. For what is it properly but an
Altercation with the Devil, before you begin honestly Fighting
him? Your Byron publishes his *Sorrows of Lord George,* in
verse and in prose, and copiously otherwise : your Bonaparte
represents his *Sorrows of Napoleon* Opera, in an all-too stupendous style; with music of cannon-volleys, and murder-
shrieks of a world; his stage-lights are the fires of Conflagration; his rhyme and recitative are the tramp of embattled

Hosts and the sound of falling Cities.—Happier is he who, like our Clothes-Philosopher, can write such matter, since it must be written, on the insensible Earth, with his shoe-soles only ; and also survive the writing thereof !

CHAPTER VII.

THE EVERLASTING NO.

Under the strange nebulous envelopment, wherein our Professor has now shrouded himself, no doubt but his spiritual nature is nevertheless progressive, and growing : for how can the 'Son of Time,' in any case, stand still ? We behold him, through those dim years, in a state of crisis, of transition : his mad Pilgrimings, and general solution into aimless Discontinuity, what is all this but a mad Fermentation ; wherefrom, the fiercer it is, the clearer product will one day evolve itself ?

Such transitions are ever full of pain : thus the Eagle when he moults is sickly ; and, to attain his new beak, must harshly dash off the old one upon rocks. What Stoicism soever our Wanderer, in his individual acts and motions, may effect, it is clear that there is a hot fever of anarchy and misery raving within ; coruscations of which flash out : as, indeed, how could there be other ? Have we not seen him disappointed, bemocked of Destiny, through long years ? All that the young heart might desire and pray for has been denied ; nay, as in the last worst instance, offered and then snatched away. Ever an 'excellent Passivity ; ' but of useful, reasonable Activity, essential to the former as Food to Hunger, nothing granted : till at length, in this wild Pilgrimage, he must forcibly seize for himself an Activity, though useless, unreasonable. Alas ! his cup of bitterness, which had been filling drop by drop, ever since the first 'ruddy morning' in the Hinterschlag Gymnasium, was at the very lip ; and then with that poison-drop, of the Towgood-and-Blumine business, it runs over, and even hisses over in a deluge of foam.

He himself says once, with more justness than originality : ' Man is, properly speaking, based upon Hope, he has no other

' possession but Hope ; this world of his is emphatically the
' Place of Hope.' What then was our Professor's possession ?
We see him, for the present, quite shut out from Hope ; looking not into the golden orient, but vaguely all around into a
dim copper firmament, pregnant with earthquake and tornado.

Alas, shut out from Hope, in a deeper sense than we yet
dream of! For as he wanders wearisomely through this world,
he has not lost all tidings of another and higher.   Full of religion, or at least of religiosity, as our Friend has since exhibited himself, he hides not that in those days, he was wholly
irreligious : ' Doubt had darkened into Unbelief,' says he ;
' shade after shade goes grimly over your soul, till you have
' the fixed, starless, Tartarean black.'   To such readers as have
reflected, what can be called reflecting, on man's life, and happily discovered, in contradiction to much Profit-and-Loss Philosophy, speculative and practical, that Soul is *not* synonymous
with Stomach ; who understand, therefore, in our Friend's
words, ' that, for man's well-being, Faith is properly the one
' thing needful ; how, with it, Martyrs, otherwise weak, can
' cheerfully endure the shame and the cross ; and without it,
' Worldlings puke up their sick existence, by suicide in the
' midst of luxury :' to such it will be clear that, for a pure
moral nature, the loss of his religious Belief was the loss of
every thing.   Unhappy young man ! All wounds, the crush of
long-continued Destitution, the stab of false Friendship, and of
false Love, all wounds in thy so genial heart, would have healed
again, had not its life-warmth been withdrawn. Well might he
exclaim, in his wild way : 'Is there no God, then ; but at best an
' absentee God, sitting idle, ever since the first Sabbath, at the
' outside of his Universe, and *see*ing it go ? Has the word
' Duty no meaning ; is what we call Duty no divine Messen-
' ger and Guide, but a false earthly Fantasm, made up of De-
' sire and Fear, of emanations from the Gallows and from
' Doctor Graham's Celestial-bed ?   Happiness of an approving
' Conscience !   Did not Paul of Tarsus, whom admiring men
' have since named Saint, feel that *he* was " the chief of sin-
' ners," and Nero of Rome, jocund in spirit (*wohlgemuth*),
' spend much of his time in fiddling? Foolish Word-monger,

and Motive-grinder, who in thy Logic-mill hast an earthly
' mechanism for the God-like itself, and wouldst fain grind
' me out Virtue from the husks of Pleasure,—I tell thee, Nay!
' To the unregenerate Prometheus Vinctus of a man, it is ever
' the bitterest aggravation of his wretchedness that he is con-
' scious of Virtue, that he feels himself the victim not of suf-
' fering only, but of injustice. What then? Is the heroic in-
' spiration we name Virtue but some Passion; some bubble of
' the blood, bubbling in the direction others *profit* by? I
' know not : only this I know, If what thou namest Happiness
' be our true aim, then are we all astray. With Stupidity and
' sound Digestion man may front much. But what, in these
' dull unimaginative days, are the terrors of Conscience to the
' diseases of the Liver! Not on Morality, but on Cookery let
' us build our stronghold : there brandishing our fryingpan,
' as censer, let us offer sweet incense to the Devil, and live at
' ease on the fat things *he* has provided for his Elect!'

Thus has the bewildered Wanderer to stand, as so many
have done, shouting question after question into the Sibyl-
cave of Destiny, and receive no Answer but an Echo. It is
all a grim Desert, this once fair world of his; wherein is
heard only the howling of wild beasts, or the shrieks of de-
spairing, hate-filled men; and no Pillar of Cloud by day, and
no Pillar of Fire by night, any longer guides the Pilgrim.
To such length has the spirit of Inquiry carried him. 'But
what boots it (*was thuts*)?' cries he ; 'it is but the common
' lot in this era. Not having come to spiritual majority prior
' to the *Siècle de Louis Quinze*, and not being born purely a
' Loghead (*Dummkopf*), thou hadst no other outlook. The
' whole world is, like thee, sold to Unbelief; their old Tem-
' ples of the Godhead, which for long have not been rain-
' proof, crumble down ; and men ask now : Where is the
' Godhead ; our eyes never saw him!'

Pitiful enough were it, for all these wild utterances, to call
our Diogenes wicked. Unprofitable servants as we all are,
perhaps at no era of his life was he more decisively the Servant of Goodness, the Servant of God, than even now when
doubting God's existence. 'One circumstance I note.' says

he : ' after all the nameless woe that Inquiry, which for me,
' what it is not always, was genuine Love of Truth, had
' wrought me, I nevertheless still loved Truth, and would
' bate no jot of my allegiance to her. "Truth!" I cried,
' "though the Heavens crush me for following her: no Falsehood! though a whole celestial Lubberland were the price
' of Apostacy." In conduct it was the same. Had a divine
' Messenger from the clouds, or miraculous Handwriting on
' the wall, convincingly proclaimed to me *This thou shalt do*,
' with what passionate readiness, as I often thought, would I
' have done it, had it been leaping into the infernal Fire !
' Thus, in spite of all Motive-grinders, and Mechanical Profit-
' and-Loss Philosophies, with the sick ophthalmia and hallu-
' cination they had brought on, was the Infinite nature of
' Duty still dimly present to me : living without God in the
' world, of God's light I was not utterly bereft; if my as yet
' sealed eyes, with their unspeakable longing, could nowhere
' see Him, nevertheless in my heart He was present, and His
' heaven-written Law still stood legible and sacred there.'

Meanwhile, under all these tribulations, and temporal and
spiritual destitutions, what must the Wanderer, in his silent
soul, have endured! 'The painfullest feeling,' writes he, 'is
' that of your own Feebleness (*Unkraft*) ; ever as the English
' Milton says, to be weak is the true misery. And yet of
' your Strength there is and can be no clear feeling, save by
' what you have prospered in, by what you have done. Be-
' tween vague wavering Capability and fixed indubitable Per-
' formance, what a difference! A certain inarticulate Self-
' consciousness dwells dimly in us ; which only our Works
' can render articulate and decisively discernible. Our Works
' are the mirror wherein the spirit first sees its natural linea-
' ments. Hence, too, the folly of that impossible Precept,
' *Know thyself* ; till it be translated into this partially possible
' one, *Know what thou canst work at*.

' But for me, so strangely unprosperous had I been, the
' net result of my Workings amounted as yet simply to—
' Nothing. How then could I believe in my Strength, when
' there was as yet no mirror to see it in? Ever did this agi-

' tating, yet, as I now perceive, quite frivolous question, re-
' main to me insoluble : Hast thou a certain Faculty, a certain
' Worth, such even as the most have not ; or art thou the
' completest Dullard of these modern times ? Alas ! the fear-
' ful Unbelief is unbelief in yourself ; and how could I believe?
' Had not my first, last Faith in myself, when even to me the
' Heavens seemed laid open, and I dared to love, been all-too
' cruelly belied ? The speculative Mystery of Life grew ever
' more mysterious to me ; neither in the practical Mystery
' had I made the slightest progress, but been everywhere
' buffeted, foiled, and contemptuously cast, out. A feeble
' unit in the middle of a threatening Infinitude, I seemed to
' have nothing given me but eyes, whereby to discern my
' own wretchedness. Invisible yet impenetrable walls, as of
' Enchantment, divided me from all living : was there, in the
' wide world, any true bosom I could press trustfully to mine?
' O Heaven, No, there was none ! I kept a lock upon my
' lips : why should I speak much with that shifting variety of
' so-called Friends, in whose withered, vain, and too hungry
' souls, Friendship was but an incredible tradition ? In such
' cases, your resource is to talk little, and that little mostly from
' the Newspapers. Now when I look back, it was a strange isola-
' tion I then lived in. The men and women around me, even
' speaking with me, were but Figures : I had, practically, for-
' gotten that they were alive, that they were not merely au-
' tomatic. In midst of their crowded streets, and assem-
' blages, I walked solitary ; and (except as it was my own
' heart, not another's, that I kept devouring) savage also, as
' the tiger in his jungle. Some comfort it would have been,
' could I, like a Faust, have fancied myself tempted and tor-
' mented of the Devil ; for a Hell, as I imagine, without Life,
' though only diabolic Life, were more frightful : but in our
' age of Downpulling and Disbelief, the very Devil has been
' pulled down, you cannot so much as believe in a Devil. To
' me the Universe was all void of Life, of Purpose, of Volition,
' even of Hostility : it was one huge, dead, immeasurable
' Steam-engine, rolling on, in its dead indifference, to grind
' me limb from limb. O the vast, gloomy, solitary Golgotha,

' and Mill of Death ! Why was the Living banished thither
' companionless, conscious ? Why if there is no Devil ; nay,
' unless the Devil is your God ? '

A prey incessantly to such corrosions, might not, moreover, as the worst aggravation to them, the iron constitution
even of a Teufelsdröckh threaten to fail ? We conjecture that
he has known sickness ; and, in spite of his locomotive habits,
perhaps sickness of the chronic sort. Hear this, for example :
' How beautiful to die of broken-heart, on Paper ! Quite
' another thing in Practice ; every window of your Feeling,
' even of your Intellect as it were, begrimed and mud-bespat-
' tered, so that no pure ray can enter ; a whole Drugshop in
' your inwards ; the foredone soul drowning slowly in quag-
' mires of Disgust ! '

Putting all which external and internal miseries together,
may we not find in the following sentences, quite in our Professor's still vein, significance enough? 'From Suicide a
' certain after-shine (*Nachschein*) of Christianity withheld me :
' perhaps also a certain indolence of character ; for, was not
' that a remedy I had at any time within reach ? Often, how-
' ever, was there a question present to me : Should some one
' now, at the turning of that corner, blow thee suddenly out
' of Space, into the other World, or other No-world, by pistol-
' shot,—how were it ? On which ground, too, I have often,
' in sea-storms and sieged cities and other death-scenes, ex-
' hibited an imperturbability, which passed, falsely enough, for
' courage.'

' So had it lasted,' concludes the Wanderer, 'so had it last-
' ed as in bitter protracted Death-agony, through long years.
' The heart within me, unvisited by any heavenly dewdrop,
' was smouldering in sulphurous, slow-consuming fire. Al-
' most since earliest memory I had shed no tear ; or once only
' when I, murmuring half-audibly, recited Faust's Deathsong,
' that wild *Selig der den er im Sieges-glanze findet* (Happy
' whom *he* finds in Battle's splendour), and thought that of
' this last Friend even I was not forsaken, that destiny itself
' could not doom me not to die. Having no hope, neither
' had I any definite fear, were it of Man or of Devil : nay, I often

' felt as if it might be solacing, could the Arch-Devil himself,
' though in Tartarean terrors, but rise to me, that I might tell
' him a little of my mind. And yet, strangely enough, I lived
' in a continual, indefinite, pining fear ; tremulous, pusillani-
' mous, apprehensive of I knew not what : it seemed as if all
' things in the Heavens above and the Earth beneath would
' hurt me ; as if the Heavens and the Earth were but bound-
' less jaws of a devouring monster, wherein I, palpitating,
' waited to be devoured.

' Full of such humour, and perhaps the miserablest man in
' the whole French Capital or Suburbs, was I, one sultry Dog-
' day, after much perambulation, toiling along the dirty little
' *Rue Saint-Thomas de l'Enfer*, among civic rubbish enough,
' in a close atmosphere, and over pavements hot as Nebuchad-
' nezzar's Furnace ; whereby doubtless my spirits were little
' cheered ; when, all at once, there rose a Thought in me, and
' I asked myself " What *art* thou afraid of ? Wherefore, like
' a coward, dost thou for ever pip and whimper, and go cow-
' ering and trembling ? Despicable biped ! what is the sum-
' total of the worst that lies before thee ? Death ? Well,
' Death ; and say the pangs of Tophet too, and all that the
' Devil and Man may, will, or can do against thee ! Hast thou
' not a heart ; canst thou not suffer whatso it be ; and, as a
' Child of Freedom, though outcast, trample Tophet itself
' under thy feet, while it consumes thee ? Let it come, then ;
' I will meet it and defy it ! " And as I so thought, there
' rushed like a stream of fire over my whole soul ; and I shook
' base Fear away from me for ever. I was strong, of unknown
' strength ; a spirit, almost a god. Ever from that time, the
' temper of my misery was changed : not Fear or whining
' Sorrow was it, but Indignation and grim fire-eyed Defiance.

' Thus had the Everlasting No (*das ewige Nein*) pealed
' authoritatively through all the recesses of my Being, of my
' Me ; and then was it that my whole Me stood up, in native
' God-created majesty, and with emphasis recorded its Protest.
' Such a Protest, the most important transaction in Life, may
' that same Indignation and Defiance, in a psychological point
' of view, be fitly called. The Everlasting No had said : " Be-

' hold, thou art fatherless, outcast, and the Universe is mine
' (the Devil's) ;" to which my whole ME now made answer:
' " *I* am not thine, but Free, and forever hate thee ! "

' It is from this hour that I incline to date my Spiritual
' New-birth, or Baphometic Fire-baptism ; perhaps I directly
' thereupon began to be a Man.'

CHAPTER VIII.

CENTRE OF INDIFFERENCE.

Though, after this ' Baphometic Fire-baptism' of his, our
Wanderer signifies that his Unrest was but increased ; as, indeed, 'Indignation and Defiance,' especially against things in
general, are not the most peaceable inmates ; yet can the Psy-
chologist surmise that it was no longer a quite hopeless Unrest ; that henceforth it had at least a fixed centre to revolve
round. For the fire-baptised soul, long so scathed and thunder-riven, here feels its own Freedom, which feeling is its
Baphometic Baptism : the citadel of its whole kingdom it has
thus gained by assault, and will keep inexpugnable ; outwards
from which the remaining dominions, not indeed without hard
battling, will doubtless by degrees be conquered and pacificated. Under another figure, we might say, if in that great
moment, in the *Rue Saint-Thomas de l'Enfer*, the old inward
Satanic School was not yet thrown out of doors, it received
peremptory judicial notice to quit ;—whereby, for the rest,
its howl-chantings, Ernulphus-cursings, and rebellious gnash-
ing of teeth, might, in the mean while, become only the more
tumultuous, and difficult to keep secret.

Accordingly, if we scrutinize these Pilgrimings well, there
is perhaps discernible henceforth a certain incipient method
in their madness. Not wholly as a Spectre does Teufelsdröckh
now storm through the world ; at worst as a spectre-fighting
Man, nay who will one day be a Spectre-queller. If pilgrim-
ing restlessly to so many 'Saints' Wells,' and ever without
quenching of his thirst, he nevertheless finds little secular
wells, whereby from time to time some alleviation is minis-

tered. In a word, he is now, if not ceasing, yet intermitting to 'eat his own heart;' and clutches round him outwardly on the NOT-ME for wholesomer food. Does not the following glimpse exhibit him in a much more natural state?

'Towns also and Cities, especially the ancient, I failed not
'to look upon with interest. How beautiful to see thereby,
'as through a long vista, into the remote Time; to have, as it
'were, an actual section of almost the earliest Past brought
'safe into the Present, and set before your eyes! There, in
'that old City, was a live ember of Culinary Fire put down,
'say only two thousand years ago; and there, burning more
'or less triumphantly, with such fuel as the region yielded, it
'has burnt, and still burns, and thou thyself seest the very
'smoke thereof. Ah! and the far more mysterious live ember
'of Vital Fire was then also put down there; and still miracu-
'lously burns and spreads; and the smoke and ashes thereof
'(in these Judgment-Halls and Churchyards), and its bellows-
'engines (in these Churches), thou still seest; and its flame,
'looking out from every kind countenance, and every hateful
'one, still warms thee or scorches thee.

'Of Man's Activity and Attainment the chief results are
'aeriform, mystic, and preserved in Tradition only: such are
'his Forms of Government, with the Authority they rest on;
'his Customs, or Fashions both of Cloth-Habits and of Soul-
'habits; much more his collective stock of Handicrafts, the
'whole Faculty he has required of manipulating Nature: all
'these things, as indispensable and priceless as they are, can-
'not in any way be fixed under lock and key, but must flit,
'spirit-like, on impalpable vehicles, from Father to Son; if
'you demand sight of them, they are nowhere to be met with.
'Visible Ploughmen and Hammermen there have been, ever
'from Cain and Tubalcain downwards: but where does your
'accumulated Agricultural, Metallurgic, and other Manufac-
'turing SKILL lie warehoused? It transmits itself on the at-
'mospheric air, on the sun's rays (by Hearing and by Vision);
'it is a thing aeriform, impalpable, of quite spiritual sort.
'In like manner, ask me not, Where are the LAWS; where is
'the GOVERNMENT? In vain wilt thou go to Schönbrunn, to

'Downing Street, to the Palais Bourbon : thou findest noth-
'ing there, but brick or stone houses, and some bundles of
'Papers tied with tape.   Where then is that same cunningly-
'devised almighty GOVERNMENT of theirs to be laid hands on?
'Every where, yet nowhere : seen only in its works, this too
'is a thing aeriform, invisible ; or if you will, mystic and
'miraculous.   So spiritual (*geistig*) is our whole daily Life :
'all that we do springs out of Mystery, Spirit, invisible Force ;
'only like a little Cloud-image, or Armida's Palace, air-built,
'does the Actual body itself forth from the great mystic
'Deep.

'Visible and tangible products of the Past, again, I reckon
'up to the extent of three : Cities, with their Cabinets and
'Arsenals ; then tilled Fields, to either or to both of which
'divisions Roads with their Bridges may belong ; and thirdly
'—— Books.   In which third truly, the last-invented, lies a
'worth far surpassing that of the two others.   Wondrous in-
'deed is the virtue of a true Book.   Not like a dead city of
'stones, yearly crumbling, yearly needing repair ; more like
'a tilled field, but then a spiritual field : like a spiritual tree,
'let me rather say, it stands from year to year, and from age
'to age (we have Books that already number some hundred-
'and-fifty human ages) ; and yearly comes its new produce of
'leaves (Commentaries, Deductions, Philosophical, Political
'Systems ; or were it only Sermons, Pamphlets, Journalistic
'Essays), every one of which is talismanic and thaumaturgic,
'for it can persuade men.   O thou who art able to write a
'Book, which once in the two centuries or oftener there is a
'man gifted to do, envy not him whom they name City-
'builder, and inexpressibly pity him whom they name Con-
'queror or City-burner !   Thou too art a Conqueror and Vic-
'tor ; but of the true sort, namely over the Devil : thou too
'hast built what will outlast all marble and metal, and be a
'wonder-bringing City of the Mind, a Temple and Seminary
'and Prophetic Mount, whereto all kindreds of the Earth will
'pilgrim.—Fool ! why journeyest thou wearisomely, in thy
'antiquarian fervour, to gaze on the stone pyramids of Geeza
'or the clay ones of Sacchara ?   These stand there, as I can

' tell thee, idle and inert, looking over the Desert, foolishly
' enough, for the last three thousand years : but canst thou
' not open thy Hebrew BIBLE, then, or even Luther's Version
' thereof ? '

No less satisfactory is his sudden appearance not in Battle,
yet on some Battle-field ; which, we soon gather, must be that
of Wagram : so that here, for once, is a certain approximation
to distinctness of date. Omitting much, let us impart what
follows :

' Horrible enough! A whole Marchfield strewed with shell-
' splinters, cannon-shot, ruined tumbrils, and dead men and
' horses ; stragglers still remaining not so much as buried.
' And those red mould heaps : ay, there lie the Shells of Men,
' out of which all the Life and Virtue has been blown ; and
' now are they swept together, and crammed down out of
' sight, like blown Egg-shells !—Did Nature, when she bade
' the Donau bring down his mould cargoes from the Carin-
' thian and Carpathian Heights, and spread them out here
' into the softest, richest level,—intend thee, O Marchfield,
' for a corn-bearing Nursery, whereon her children might be
' nursed ; or for a Cockpit, wherein they might the more com-
' modiously be throttled and tattered ? Were thy three broad
' highways, meeting here from the ends of Europe, made for
' Ammunition-wagons then ? Were thy Wagrams and Still-
' frieds but so many ready-built Casemates, wherein the house
' of Hapsburg might batter with artillery, and with artillery
' be battered ? König Ottokar, amid yonder hillocks, dies
' under Rodolf's truncheon ; here Kaiser Franz falls a-swoon
' under Napoleon's : within which five centuries, to omit the
' others, how has thy breast, fair Plain, been defaced and de-
' filed! The greensward is torn up and trampled down ;
' man's fond care of it, his fruit-trees, hedge-rows, and pleas-
' ant dwellings, blown away with gunpowder; and the kind
' seedfield lies a desolate, hideous Place of Sculls.—Neverthe-
' less, Nature is at work ; neither shall these Powder-Devil-
' kins with their utmost devilry gainsay her : but all that gore
' and carnage will be shrouded in, absorbed into manure ;
' and next year the Marchfield will be green, nay, greener.

' Thrifty unwearied Nature, ever out of our great waste educ-
' ing some little profit of thy own,—how dost thou, from the
' very carcass of the Killer, bring Life for the Living.

' What, speaking in quite unofficial language, is the net
' purport and upshot of war? To my own knowledge, for
' example, there dwell and toil, in the British village of Dum-
' drudge, usually some five hundred souls. From these, by
' certain "Natural Enemies" of the French, there are succes-
' sively selected, during the French war, say thirty able-bodied
' men : Dumdrudge, at her own expense, has suckled and
' nursed them ; she has, not without difficulty and sorrow, fed
' them up to manhood, and even trained them up to crafts, so
' that one can weave, another build, another hammer, and the
' weakest can stand under thirty stone avoirdupois. Never-
' theless, amid much weeping and swearing, they are selected ;
' all dressed in red ; and shipped away, at the public charges,
' some two thousand miles, or say only to the south of Spain ;
' and fed there till wanted. And now to that same spot in the
' south of Spain, are thirty similar French artisans, from a
' French Dumdrudge, in like manner wending : till at length,
' after infinite effort, the two parties come into actual juxta-
' position ; and Thirty stands fronting Thirty, each with a
' gun in his hand. Straightway the word "Fire !" is given :
and they blow the souls out of one another ; and in place of
' sixty brisk useful craftsmen, the world has sixty dead car-
' casses, which it must bury, and anew shed tears for. Had
' these men any quarrel? Busy as the Devil is, not the small-
' est ! They lived far enough apart ; were the entirest stran-
' gers ; nay, in so wide a Universe, there was even, uncon-
' sciously, by Commerce, some mutual helpfulness between
' them. How then? Simpleton ! their Governors had fallen
' out ; and, instead of shooting one another, had the cunning
' to make these poor blockheads shoot.—Alas, so is it in
' Deutschland, and hitherto in all other lands ; still as of old,
' "what devilry soever Kings do, the Greeks must pay the
' piper !"—In that fiction of the English Smollett, it is true,
' the final Cessation of War is perhaps prophetically shadowed
' forth ; where the two Natural Enemies, in person, take each

' a Tobacco-pipe, filled with Brimstone ; light the same, and
' smoke in one another's faces till the weaker gives in : but
' from such predicted Peace-Era, what blood-filled trenches,
' and contentious centuries, may still divide us ! '

Thus can the Professor, at least in lucid intervals, look
away from his own sorrows, over the many-coloured world,
and pertinently enough note what is passing there. We may
remark, indeed, that for the matter of spiritual culture, if for
nothing else, perhaps few periods of his life were richer than
this. Internally, there is the most momentous instructive
Course of Practical Philosophy, with Experiments, going on ;
towards the right comprehension of which his Peripatetic
habits, favourable to Meditation, might help him rather than
hinder. Externally, again, as he wanders to and fro, there
are, if for the longing heart little substance, yet for the seeing
eye sights enough : in these so boundless Travels of his,
granting that the Satanic School was even partially kept
down, what an incredible Knowledge of our Planet, and its
Inhabitants and their Works, that is to say, of all knowable
things, might not Teufelsdröckh acquire !

'I have read in most Public Libraries,' says he, ' including
' those of Constantinople and Samarcand : in most Colleges,
' except the Chinese Mandarin ones, I have studied, or seen
' that there was no studying. Unknown Languages have I
' oftenest gathered from their natural repertory, the Air, by
' my organ of Hearing ; Statistics, Geographies, Topographies
' came, through the Eye, almost of their own accord. The
' ways of Man, how he seeks food, and warmth, and pro-
' tection for himself, in most regions, are ocularly known to
' me. Like the great Hadrian, I meted out much of the ter-
' raqueous Globe with a pair of Compasses that belonged to
' myself only.

' Of great Scenes, why speak ? Three summer days, I lin-
' gered reflecting, and even composing (*dichtete*), by the
' Pine-chasms of Vaucluse ; and in that clear Lakelet mois-
' tened my bread. I have sat under the palm-trees of Tad-
' mor ; smoked a pipe among the ruins of Babylon. The
' great Wall of China I have seen ; and can testify that it is of

'grey brick, coped and covered with granite, and shews only
' second-rate masonry.—Great events, also, have I not wit-
' nessed ?   Kings sweated down (*ausgemergelt*) into Berlin-
' and-Milan Custom-house-officers; the World well won, and
' the world well lost ; oftener than once a hundred thousand
' individuals shot (by each other) in one day.   All kindreds
' and peoples and nations dashed together, and shifted and
' shovelled into heaps, that they might ferment there, and in
' time unite.   The birth-pangs of Democracy, wherewith con-
' vulsed Europe was groaning in cries that reached Heaven,
' could not escape me.

' For great Men I have ever had the warmest predilection ;
' and can perhaps boast that few such in this era have wholly
' escaped me.   Great Men are the inspired (speaking and act-
' ing) Texts of that divine BOOK OF REVELATIONS, whereof a
' Chapter is completed from epoch to epoch, and by some
' named HISTORY ; to which inspired Texts your numerous
' talented men, and your innumerable untalented men, are
' the better or worse exegetic Commentaries, and wagonload
' of too-stupid, heretical or orthodox, weekly Sermons.   For
' my study, the inspired Texts themselves !   Thus did I not,
' in very early days, having disguised me as tavern-waiter,
' stand behind the field-chairs, under that shady Tree at Treis-
' nitz by the Jena Highway ; waiting upon the great Schiller
' and greater Goethe ; and hearing what I have not forgotten.
' For——'

——But at this point the Editor recalls his principle of
caution, some time ago laid down, and must suppress much.
Let not the sacredness of Laurelled, still more, of Crowned
Heads, be tampered with.   Should we, at a future day, find
circumstances altered, and the time come for Publication,
then may these glimpses into the privacy of the Illustrious be
conceded ; which for the present were little better than
treacherous, perhaps traitorous Eavesdroppings.   Of Lord
Byron, therefore, of Pope Pius, Emperor Tarakwang, the
' White Water-roses' (Chinese Carbonari) with their mysteries,
no notice here !   Of Napoleon himself we shall only, glancing
from afar, remark that Teufelsdröckh's relation to him seems

to have been of very varied character. At first we find our poor Professor on the point of being shot as a spy; then taken into private conversation, even pinched on the ear, yet presented with no money; at last indignantly dismissed, almost thrown out of doors as an 'Ideologist.' 'He himself,' says the Professor, 'was among the completest Ideologists, at 'least Ideopraxists: in the Idea (*in der Idee*) he lived, moved, 'and fought. The man was a Divine Missionary, though un- 'conscious of it; and preached, through the cannon's throat, 'that great doctrine, *La carrière ouverte aux talens* (The Tools 'to him that can handle them), which is our ultimate Politi- 'cal Evangel, wherein alone can Liberty lie. Madly enough 'he preached, it is true, as Enthusiasts and first Missionaries 'are wont, with imperfect utterance, amid much frothy rant; 'yet as articulately perhaps as the case admitted. Or call 'him, if you will, an American Backwoodsman, who had to 'fell unpenetrated forests, and battle with innumerable wolves, 'and did not entirely forbear strong liquor, rioting, and even 'theft; whom, notwithstanding, the peaceful Sower will fol- 'low, and, as he cuts the boundless harvest, bless.'

More legitimate and decisively authentic is Teufelsdröckh's appearance and emergence (we know not well whence) in the solitude of the North Cape, on that June Midnight. He has a 'light-blue Spanish cloak' hanging round him, as his 'most commodious, principal, indeed sole upper-garment;' and stands there, on the World-promontory, looking over the infinite Brine, like a little blue Belfry (as we figure), now motionless indeed, yet ready, if stirred to ring quaintest changes.

'Silence as of death,' writes he; 'for midnight, even in the 'Arctic latitudes, has its character: nothing but the granite 'cliffs ruddy-tinged, the peaceable gurgle of that slow-heaving 'Polar Ocean, over which in the utmost North the great Sun 'hangs low and lazy, as if he too were slumbering. Yet is 'his cloud-couch wrought of crimson and cloth-of-gold; yet 'does his light stream over the mirror of waters, like a trem- 'ulous fire-pillar, shooting downwards to the abyss, and hide 'itself under my feet. In such moments, Solitude also is in- 'valuable; for who would speak, or be looked on, when behind

10

'him lies all Europe and Africa, fast asleep, except the watch-
'men; and before him the silent Immensity, and Palace of
'the Eternal, whereof our Sun is but a porch-lamp.

'Nevertheless, in this solemn moment, comes a man, or mon-
'ster, scrambling from among the rock-hollows; and, shaggy,
'huge as the Hyperborean Bear, hails me in Russian speech:
'most probably, therefore, a Russian Smuggler.   With cour-
'teous brevity, I signify my indifference to contraband trade,
'my humane intentions, yet strong wish to be private.   In
'vain: the monster, counting doubtless on his superior
'stature, and minded to make sport for himself, or perhaps
'profit, were it with murder, continues to advance; ever assail-
'ing me with his importunate train-oil breath; and now has
'advanced, till we stand both on the verge of the rock, the
'deep Sea rippling greedily down below.   What argument
'will avail?   On the thick Hyperborean, cherubic reasoning,
'seraphic eloquence were lost.   Prepared for such extremity,
'I, deftly enough, whisk aside one step; draw out, from my
'interior reservoirs, a sufficient Birmingham Horse-pistol, and
'say, "Be so obliging as retire, Friend (*Er ziehe sich zurück,
'Freund*), and with promptitude!"   This logic even the Hy-
'perborean understands: fast enough, with apologetic peti-
'tionary growl, he sidles off; and, except for suicidal as well
'as homicidal purposes, need not return.

'Such I hold to be the genuine use of Gunpowder: that it
'makes all men alike tall.   Nay, if thou be cooler, cleverer
'than I, if thou have more *Mind*, though all but no *Body*
'whatever, then canst thou kill me first, and art the taller.
'Hereby, at last, is the Goliath powerless, and the David re-
'sistless; savage Animalism is nothing, inventive Spiritualism
'is all.

'With respect to Duels, indeed, I have my own ideas.   Few
'things, in this so surprising world, strike me with more sur-
'prise.   Too little visual Spectra of men, hovering with insecure
'enough cohesion in the midst of the UNFATHOMABLE, and to
'dissolve therein, at any rate, very soon,—make pause at the
'distance of twelve paces asunder; whirl round; and, sim-
'ultaneously by the cunningest mechanism, explode one

'another into Dissolution ; and off-hand become Air, and Non-
'extant! Deuse on it (*verdammt*), the little spitfires!—Nay,
'I think with old Hugo von Trimberg: "God must needs
'laugh outright, could such a thing be, to see his wondrous
'Manikins here below." '

But amid these specialities, let us not forget the great gen-
erality, which is our chief quest here : How prospered the
inner man of Teufelsdröckh under so much outward shifting?
Does Legion still lurk in him, though repressed ; or has he
exorcised that Devil's Brood ? We can answer that the symptoms continue promising. Experience is the grand spiritual
Doctor ; and with him Teufelsdröckh has now been long a
patient, swallowing many a bitter bolus. Unless our poor
Friend belong to the numerous class of Incurables, which
seems not likely, some cure will doubtless be effected. We
should rather say that Legion, or the Satanic School, was now
pretty well extirpated and cast out, but next to nothing introduced in its room ; whereby the heart remains, for the
while, in a quiet but no comfortable state.

'At length, after so much roasting,' thus writes our Autobiographer, 'I was what you might name calcined. Pray only
'that it be not rather, as is the more frequent issue, reduced
'to a *caput-mortuum !* But in any case, by mere dint of
'practice, I had grown familiar with many things. Wretch-
'edness was still wretched ; but I could now partly see
'through it, and despise it. Which highest mortal, in this
'inane Existence, had I not found a Shadow-hunter, or
'Shadow-hunted ; and, when I looked through his brave gar-
'nitures, miserable enough ? Thy wishes have all been sniff-
'ed aside, thought I: but what, had they even been all
'granted ! Did not the Boy Alexander weep because he had
'not two Planets to conquer ; or a whole Solar System ; or
'after that, a whole Universe ? *Ach Gott*, when I gazed into
'these Stars, have they not looked down on me as if with
'pity, from their serene spaces ; like Eyes glistening with
'heavenly tears over the little lot of man ! Thousands of hu-
'man generations, all as noisy as our own, have been swal-

'lowed up of Time, and there remains no wreck of them any
'more ; and Arcturus and Orion and Sirius and the Pleiades
'are still shining in their courses, clear and young, as when
'the Shepherd first noted them in the plain of Shinar. Pshaw !
'what is this paltry little Dog-cage of an Earth ; what art
'thou that sittest whining there ? Thou art still Nothing,
'Nobody : true ; but who then is Something, Somebody ? For
'thee the Family of Man has no use ; it rejects thee ; thou art
'wholly as a dissevered limb : so be it ; perhaps it is better
'so !'

Too heavy-laden Teufelsdröckh ! Yet surely his bands are
loosening ; one day he will hurl the burden far from him, and
bound forth free, and with a second youth.

'This,' says our Professor, 'was the CENTRE OF INDIFFERENCE
'I had now reached ; through which whoso travels from the
'Negative Pole to the Positive must necessarily pass.'

CHAPTER IX.

THE EVERLASTING YEA.

'Temptations in the Wilderness !' exclaims Teufelsdröckh :
'Have we not all to be tried with such ? Not so easily can the
'old Adam, lodged in us by birth, be dispossessed. Our Life
'is compassed round with Necessity ; yet is the meaning of
'Life itself no other than Freedom, than Voluntary Force ;
'thus have we a warfare ; in the beginning, especially, a hard-
'fought battle. For the God-given mandate, *Work thou in*
'*Welldoing,* lies mysteriously written, in Promethean Prophetic
'Characters, in our hearts ; and leaves us no rest, night or
'day, till it be deciphered and obeyed ; till it burn forth,
'in our conduct, a visible, acted Gospel of Freedom. And as
'the clay-given mandate, *Eat thou and be filled,* at the same
'time persuasively proclaims itself through every nerve,—
'must there not be a confusion, a contest, before the better
'Influence can become the upper ?

'To me nothing seems more natural than that the Son of
'Man, when such God-given mandate first prophetically stirs

'within him, and the Clay must now be vanquished or van-
' quish,—should be carried of the spirit into grim Solitudes,
' and there fronting the Tempter do grimmest battle with
' him; defiantly setting him at naught, till he yield and fly.
' Name it as we choose : with or without visible Devil, whether
' in the natural Desert of rocks and sands, or in the populous
' moral Desert of selfishness and baseness,—to such Tempta-
' tion are we all called. Unhappy if we are not. Unhappy if
' we are but Half-men, in whom that divine handwriting has
' never blazed forth, all-subduing, in true sun-splendour ; but
' quivers dubiously amid meaner lights : or smoulders, in dull
' pain, in darkness, under earthly vapours !—Our Wilderness
' is the wide World in an Atheistic Century ; our Forty Days
' are long years of suffering and fasting : nevertheless, to these
' also comes an end. Yes, to me also was given, if not Vic-
' tory, yet the consciousness of Battle, and the resolve to per-
' severe therein while life or faculty is left. To me also, entangled
' in the enchanted forests, demon-peopled, doleful of sight and
' of sound, it was given, after weariest wanderings, to work
' out my way into the higher sunlit slopes—of that Mountain
' which has no summit, or whose summit is in Heaven only ! '

He says elsewhere, under a less ambitious figure ; as figures
are, once for all, natural to him : ' Has not thy Life been that
' of most sufficient men (*tüchtigen Männer*) thou hast known
' in this generation ? An outflush of foolish young Enthusi-
' asm, like the first fallow-crop, wherein are as many weeds
' as valuable herbs : this all parched away, under the Droughts
' of practical and spiritual Unbelief; as Disappointment, in
' thought and act, often-repeated gave rise to Doubt, and
' Doubt gradually settled into Denial ! If I have had a second-
' crop, and now see the perennial greensward, and sit under
' unbrageous cedars, which defy all Drought (and Doubt) ;
' herein too, be the Heavens praised, I am not without ex-
' amples, and even exemplars.'

So that, for Teufelsdröckh also, there has been a ' glorious
revolution : ' these mad shadow-hunting and shadow-hunted
Pilgrimings of his were but some purifying ' Temptation in
the Wilderness,' before his apostolic work (such as it was)

could begin ; which Temptation is now happily over, a nd the
Devil once more worsted ! Was 'that high moment in the
Rue de l'Enfer,' then, properly the turning point of the battle ;
when the Fiend said, *Worship me, or be torn in shreds,* and
was answered valiantly with an *Apage Satana ?*—Singular Teufelsdröckh, would thou hadst told thy singular story in plain
words ! But it is fruitless to look there, in those Paper-bags,
for such. Nothing but inuendoes, figurative crotchets : a
typical Shadow, fitfully wavering, prophetico-satiric ; no clear
logical Picture. 'How paint to the sensual eye,' asks he once,
' what passes in the Holy-of-Holies of Man's Soul ; in what
' words, known to these profane times, speak even afar off of
' the unspeakable ?' We ask in turn : Why perplex these
times, profane as they are, with needless obscurity, by omis-
sion and by commission ? Not mystical only is our Professor,
but whimsical ; and involves himself, now more than ever, in
eye-bewildering *chiaroscuro.* Successive glimpses, here faith-
fully imparted, our more gifted readers must endeavour to
combine for their own behoof.

He says : 'The hot Harmattan-wind had raged itself out :
' its howl went silent within me ; and the long-deafened soul
' could now hear. I paused in my wild wanderings ; and sat
' me down to wait, and consider ; for it was as if the hour of
' change drew nigh. I seemed to surrender, to renounce ut-
' terly, and say : Fly, then, false shadows of Hope ; I will
' chase you no more, I will believe you no more. And ye too
' haggard spectres of Fear, I care not for you ; ye too are all
' shadows and a lie. Let me rest here : for I am way-weary
' and life weary ; I will rest here, were it but to die : to die
' or to live is alike to me ; alike insignificant.'—And again :
'Here, then, as I lay in that CENTRE OF INDIFFERENCE ; cast,
' doubtless by benignant upper Influence, into a healing sleep,
' the heavy dreams rolled gradually away, and I awoke to a
' new Heaven and a new Earth. The first preliminary moral
' Act, Annihilation of Self (*Sebst-tödtung*), had been happily ac-
' complished ; and my minds' eyes were now unsealed, and its
' hands ungyved.'

Might we not also conjecture that the following passage refers to his Locality, during this same 'healing sleep;' that his Pilgrim-staff lies cast aside here on 'the high table-land;' and indeed that the repose is already taking wholesome effect on him? If it were not that the tone, in some parts, has more of riancy, even of levity, than we could have expected! However, in Teufelsdröckh, there is always the strangest Dualism: light dancing, with guitar-music, will be going on in the fore-court, while by fits from within comes the faint whimpering of woe and wail. We transcribe the piece entire:

' Beautiful it was to sit there, as in my skyey Tent, musing
' and meditating; on the high table-land, in front of the
' Mountains; over me, as roof, the azure Dome, and around
' me, for walls, four azure flowing curtains,—namely, the Four
' azure Winds, on whose bottom-fringes also I have seen gild-
' ing. And then to fancy the fair Castles, that stood sheltered
' in these Mountain hollows; with their green flower lawns,
' and white dames and damosels, lovely enough: or better
' still, the straw-roofed Cottages, wherein stood many a Mother
' baking bread, with her children round her:—all hidden and
' protectingly folded up in the valley-folds; yet there and
' alive, as sure as if I beheld them. Or to see, as well as
' fancy, the nine Towns and Villages, that lay round my moun-
' tain-seat, which in still weather, were wont to speak to me
' (by their steeple-bells) with metal tongue; and, in almost all
' weather, proclaimed their vitality by repeated Smoke-clouds;
' whereon, as on a culinary horologe, I might read the hour
' of the day. For it was the smoke of cookery, as kind house-
' wives at morning, midday, eventide, were boiling their hus-
' bands' kettles; and ever a blue pillar rose up into the air,
' successively or simultaneously, from each of the nine, say-
' ing, as plainly as smoke could say: Such and such a meal is
' getting ready here. Not uninteresting! For you have the
' whole Borough, with all its love-makings and scandal-mon-
' geries, contentions and contentments, as in miniature, and
' could cover it all with your hat.—If, in my wide Wayfarings,
' I had learned to look into the business of the World in its
' details, here perhaps was the place for combining it into
' general propositions, and deducing inferences therefrom.

' Often also could I see the black Tempest marching in an-
' ger through the Distance : around some Schreckhorn, as yet
' grim-blue, would the eddying vapour gather, and there tumul-
' tuously eddy, and flow down like a mad witch's hair; till,
' after a space, it vanished, and, in the clear sunbeam, your
' Schreckhorn stood smiling grim-white, for the vapour had
' held snow. How thou fermentest and elaboratest in thy
' great fermenting-vat and laboratory of an Atmosphere, of a
' World, O Nature! Or what is nature? Ha! why do I not
' name thee GOD? Art thou not the "Living Garment of
' God?" O Heavens, is it, in very deed, HE then that ever
' speaks through thee ; that lives and loves in thee, that lives
' and loves in me ?

' Fore-shadows, call them rather fore-splendours, of that
' Truth, and Beginning of Truths, fell mysteriously over my
' soul. Sweeter than Dayspring to the Shipwrecked in Nova
' Zembla; ah! like the mother's voice to her little child that
' strays bewildered, weeping, in unknown tumults; like soft
' streamings of celestial music to my too exasperated heart,
' came that Evangel. The Universe is not dead and demon-
' iacal, a charnel-house with spectres : but godlike, and my
' Father's !

' With other eyes, too, could I now look upon my fellow man ;
' with an infinite Love, an infinite Pity. Poor, wandering,
' wayward man ! Art thou not tried, and beaten with stripes,
' even as I am ? Ever, whether thou bear the royal mantle
' or the beggar's gabardine, art thou not so weary, so heavy-
' laden ; and thy Bed of Rest is but a grave. O my Brother,
' my Brother, why cannot I shelter thee in my bosom, and
' wipe away all tears from thy eyes !—Truly, the din of many-
' voiced Life, which in this solitude, with the mind's organ, I
' could hear, was no longer a maddening discord, but a melt-
' ing one : like inarticulate cries, and sobbings of a dumb
' creature, which in the ear of Heaven are prayers. The poor
' Earth, with her poor joys, was now my needy Mother, not
' my cruel Stepdame ; Man, with his so mad Wants and so
' mean Endeavours, had become the dearer to me ; and even
' for his sufferings and his sins, I now first named him brother

' Thus was I standing in the porch of that " *Sanctuary of Sor-*
' *row ;*" by strange, steep ways, had I too been guided thither ;
' and ere long its sacred gates would open, and the " *Divine*
' *Depth of Sorrow* " lie disclosed to me.'

The Professor says, he here first got eye on the Knot that
had been strangling him, and straightway could unfasten it,
and was free. ' A vain interminable controversy,' writes he,
' touching what is at present called Origin of Evil, or some
' such thing, arises in every soul, since the beginning of the
' world ; and in every soul, that would pass from idle Suffer-
' ing into actual Endeavouring, must first be put an end to.
' The most, in our time, have to go content with a simple, in-
' complete enough Suppression of this controversy ; to a few,
' some Solution of it is indispensable. In every new era, too,
' such Solution comes out in different terms ; and ever the So-
' lution of the last era has become obsolete, and is found un-
' serviceable. For it is man's nature to change his Dialect
' from century to century ; he cannot help it though he would.
' The authentic *Church-Catechism* of our present century has
' not yet fallen into my hands : meanwhile, for my own private
' behoof, I attempt to elucidate the matter so. Man's Unhap-
' piness, as I construe, comes of his Greatness ; it is because
' there is an Infinite in him, which with all his cunning he
' cannot quite bury under the Finite. Will the whole Finance
' Ministers and Upholsterers and Confectioners of modern
' Europe undertake, in joint-stock company, to make one
' Shoeblack HAPPY ? They cannot accomplish it, above an
' hour or two ; for the Shoeblack also has a Soul quite other
' than his Stomach : and would require, if you consider it,
' for his permanent satisfaction and saturation, simply this al-
' lotment, no more, and no less : *God's infinite Universe alto-*
' *gether to himself*, therein to enjoy infinitely, and fill every
' wish as fast as it rose. Oceans of Hochheimer, a Throat
' like that of Ophiuchus : speak not of them ; to the infinite
' Shoeblack they are as nothing. No sooner is your ocean
' filled, than he grumbles that it might have been of better
' vintage. Try him with half of a Universe, of an Omnipotence,
' he sets to quarrelling with the proprietor of the other half,

' and declares himself the most maltreated of men.—Always
' there is a black spot in our sunshine : it is even, as I said, the
' *Shadow of Ourselves.*

'But the whim we have of Happiness is somewhat thus.
' By certain valuations, and averages, of our own striking, we
' we come upon some sort of average terrestrial lot ; this we
' fancy belongs to us by nature, and of indefeasible right.   It
' is simple payment of our wages, of our deserts ; requires
' neither thanks nor complaint : only such *overplus* as there
' may be do we account Happiness ; any *deficit* again is Misery.
' Now consider that we have the valuation of our own deserts
' ourselves, and what a fund of Self-conceit there is in each of
' us,—do you wonder that the balance should so often dip the
' wrong way, and many a Blockhead cry : See there, what a
' payment ; was ever worthy gentleman so used !—I tell thee,
' Blockhead, it all comes of thy Vanity ; of what thou *fanciest*
' those same deserts of thine to be.   Fancy that thou deserv-
' est to be hanged (as is most likely), thou wilt feel it happi-
' ness to be only shot : fancy that thou deservest to be hanged
' in a hair-halter, it will be a luxury to die in hemp.

' So true it is, what I then said, that *the Fraction of Life can
' be increased in value not so much by increasing your Numera-
' tor as by lessening your Denominator.*   Nay, unless my Al-
' gebra deceive me, *Unity* itself divided by *Zero* will give *In-
' finity.*   Make thy claim of wages a zero, then ; thou hast the
' world under thy feet.   Well did the Wisest of our time
' write : "It is only with Renunciation (*Entsagen*) that Life,
' properly speaking, can be said to begin."

' I asked myself : What is this that, ever since earliest years,
' thou hast been fretting and fuming, and lamenting and self-
' tormenting, on account of ?   Say it in a word : is it not be-
' cause thou art not HAPPY ?   Because the THOU (sweet gentle-
' man) is not sufficiently honoured, nourished, soft-bedded,
' and lovingly cared for ?   Foolish soul !   What Act of Leg-
' islature was there that *thou* shouldst be Happy ?   A little
' while ago thou hadst no right to *be* at all.   What if thou
' wert born and predestined not to be Happy, but to be Un-
' happy !   Art thou nothing other than a Vulture, then, that

'fliest through the Universe seeking after somewhat to *eat*;
'and shrieking dolefully because carrion enough is not given
'thee? Close thy *Byron;* open thy *Goethe.*'

'*Es leuchtet mir ein*, I see a glimpse of it!' cries he elsewhere: 'there is in man a HIGHER than Love of Happiness:
'he can do without Happiness, and instead thereof find Bless-
'edness! Was it not to preach forth this same HIGHER that
'sages and martyrs, the Poet and the Priest, in all times,
'have spoken and suffered; bearing testimony, through life
'and through death, of the Godlike that is in Man, and how
'in the Godlike only has he Strength and Freedom? Which
'God-inspired Doctrine art thou also honoured to be taught;
'O Heavens! and broken with manifold merciful Afflictions,
'even till thou become contrite, and learn it! O thank thy
'Destiny for these; thankfully bear what yet remain: thou
'hadst need of them; the Self in thee needed to be annihi-
'lated. By benignant fever-paroxysms is Life rooting out the
'deep-seated chronic Disease, and triumphs over Death. On
'the roaring billows of Time, thou art not engulphed, but
'borne aloft into the azure of Eternity. Love not Pleasure;
'love God. This is the EVERLASTING YEA, wherein all contra-
'diction is solved; wherein whoso walks and works, it is well
'with him.'

And again: 'Small is it that thou canst trample the Earth
'with its injuries under thy feet, as old Greek Zeno trained
'thee: thou canst love the Earth while it injures thee, and
'even because it injures thee; for this a Greater than Zeno
'was needed, and he too was sent. Knowest thou that "*Wor-
'ship of Sorrow?*" The Temple thereof, founded some eigh-
'teen centuries ago, now lies in ruins, overgrown with jungle,
'the habitation of doleful creatures: nevertheless, venture for-
'ward; in a low crypt, arched out of falling fragments, thou
'findest the Altar still there, and its sacred Lamp perennially
'burning.'

Without pretending to comment on which strange utterances, the Editor will only remark, that there lies beside them
much of a still more questionable character; unsuited to the
general apprehension; nay wherein he himself does not see

his way. Nebulous disquisitions on Religion, yet not without bursts of splendour; on the 'perennial continuance of Inspiration;' on Prophecy; that there are 'true Priests, as well as Baal-Priests, in our own day:' with more of the like sort. We select some fractions by way of finish to this farrago.

'Cease, my much-respected Herr von Voltaire,' thus apostrophises the Professor: 'shut thy sweet voice; for the 'task appointed thee seems finished. Sufficiently hast thou 'demonstrated this proposition, considerable or otherwise: 'That the Mythus of the Christian Religion looks not in the 'eighteenth century as it did in the eighth. Alas, were thy 'six-and-thirty quartos, and the six-and-thirty thousand other 'quartos and folios, and flying sheets or reams, printed be- 'fore and since on the same subject, all needed to convince 'us of so little! But what next? Wilt thou help us to em- 'body the divine Spirit of that Religion in a new Mythus, in 'a new vehicle and vesture, that our Souls, otherwise too 'like perishing, may live? What! thou hast no faculty in 'that kind? Only a torch for burning, no hammer for build- 'ing? Take our thanks, then, and——thyself away.

'Meanwhile what are antiquated Mythuses to me? Or is 'the God present, felt in my own heart, a thing which Herr 'von Voltaire will dispute out of me; or dispute into me? 'To the "Worship of Sorrow" ascribe what origin and genesis 'thou pleasest, has not that Worship originated, and been 'generated; is it not here? Feel it in thy heart, and then 'say whether it is of God! This is Belief; all else is Opin- 'ion,—for which latter whoso will let him worry and be wor- 'ried.'

'Neither,' observes he elsewhere, 'shall ye tear out one an- 'other's eyes, struggling over "Plenary Inspiration," and such 'like: try rather to get a little even Partial Inspiration, each 'of you for himself. One BIBLE I know, of whose Plenary 'Inspiration doubt is not so much as possible; nay with my 'own eyes I saw the God's-Hand writing it: thereof all other 'Bibles are but Leaves,—say, in Picture-Writing to assist the 'weaker faculty.'

Or to give the wearied reader relief, and, bring it to an end, let him take the following perhaps more intelligible passage:

' To me, in this our Life,' says the Professor, ' which is an
' internecine warfare with the Time-spirit, other warfare seems
' questionable. Hast thou in any way a Contention with thy
' brother, I advise thee, think well what the meaning thereof is.
' If thou gauge it to the bottom, it is simply this : "Fellow,
' see ? thou art taking more than thy share of Happiness in the
' world, something from *my* share : which, by the Heavens,
' thou shalt not ; nay I will fight thee rather."—Alas ! and the
' whole lot to be divided in such a beggarly matter, truly a
' " feast of shells," for the substance has been spilled out :
' not enough to quench one Appetite ; and the collective hu-
' man species clutching at them !—Can we not, in all such
' cases, rather say : "Take it, thou too-ravenous individual ;
' take that pitiful additional fraction of a share, which I reck-
' oned mine, but which thou so wantest : take it with a
' blessing : would to Heaven I had enough for thee ! "—If
' Fichte's *Wissenschaftslehre* be, " to a certain extent, Applied
' Christianity," surely to a still greater extent, so is this.   We
' have here not a Whole Duty of Man, yet a Half Duty, namely
' the Passive half : could we but do it, as we can demonstrate
' it !

' But indeed Conviction, were it never so excellent, is worth-
' less till it convert itself into Conduct. Nay properly Convic-
' tion is not possible till then ; inasmuch as all Speculation
' is by nature endless, formless, a vortex amid vortices : only
' by a felt indubitable certainty of Experience does it find
' any centre to revolve round, and so fashion itself into a sys-
' tem.   Most true is it, as a wise man teaches us, that " Doubt
' of any sort cannot be removed except by Action." On which
' ground too let him who gropes painfully in darkness or un-
' certain light, and prays vehemently that the dawn may
' ripen into day, lay this other precept well to heart, which to
' me was of invaluable service : " *Do the Duty which lies near-
' est thee*," which thou knowest to be a Duty ! Thy second
' Duty will already have become clearer.

' May we not say, however, that the hour of Spiritual En-

' franchisement is even this : When your Ideal World, wherein
' the whole man has been dimly struggling and inexpressibly
' languishing to work, becomes revealed and thrown open ;
' and you discover, with amazement enough, like the Lotha-
' rio in *Wilhelm Meister*, that your "America is here or no-
' where ?" The Situation that has not its Duty, its Ideal,
' was never yet occupied by man. Yes here, in this poor,
' miserable, hampered, despicable Actual, wherein thou even
' now standest, here or nowhere is thy Ideal : work it out
' therefrom ; and working, believe, live, be free. Fool ! the
' Ideal is in thyself, the Impediment too is in thyself : thy
' Condition is but the stuff thou art to shape that same Ideal
' out of ; what matters whether such stuff be of this sort or
' that, so the Form thou give it be heroic, be poetic ? O thou
' that pinest in the imprisonment of the Actual, and criest
' bitterly to the gods for a kingdom wherein to rule and
' create, know this of a truth : the thing thou seekest is al-
' ready with thee, "here or nowhere," couldst thou only see !

' But it is with man's Soul as it was with Nature : the be-
' ginning of Creation is—Light. Till the eye have vision, the
' whole members are in bonds. Divine moment, when over
' the tempest-tost Soul, as once over the wild-weltering Chaos,
' it is spoken : Let there be light ? Ever to the greatest that
' has felt such moment, is it not miraculous and God-announc-
' ing ; even as, under simpler figures, to the simplest and
' least. The mad primeval Discord is hushed ; the rudely-
' jumbled conflicting elements bind themselves into separate
' Firmaments : deep silent rock-foundations are built beneath ;
' and the skyey vault with its everlasting Luminaries above :
' instead of a dark wasteful Chaos, we have a blooming, fer-
' tile, Heaven-encompassed World.

' I too could now say to myself : Be no longer a Chaos, but
' a World, or even Worldkin. Produce ! Produce ! Were it
' but the pitifulest infinitesimal fraction of a Product, produce
' it in God's name ! 'Tis the utmost thou hast in thee ; out
' with it then. Up, up ! Whatsoever thy hand findeth to do,
' do it with thy whole might. Work while it is called To-day,
' for the Night cometh wherein no man can work.'

CHAPTER X.

PAUSE.

Thus have we, as closely and perhaps satisfactorily as, in such circumstances, might be, followed Teufelsdröckh through the various successive states and stages of Growth, Entanglement, Unbelief, and almost Reprobation, into a certain clearer state of what he himself seems to consider as Conversion. ' Blame not the word,' says he ; ' rejoice rather that such a ' word, signifying such a thing, has come to light in our ' Modern Era, though hidden from the wisest Ancients. The ' Old World knew nothing of Conversion : instead of an *Ecce* ' *Homo*, they had only some *Choice of Hercules*. It was a ' new-attained progress in the Moral Development of Man : ' hereby has the Highest come home to the bosoms of the ' most Limited ; what to Plato was but a hallucination, and ' to Socrates a chimera, is now clear and certain to your Zin- ' zendorfs, your Wesleys, and the poorest of their Pietists and ' Methodists.'

It is here then that the spiritual majority of Teufelsdröckh commences : we are henceforth to see him ' work in well-doing,' with the spirit and clear aims of a Man. He has discovered that the Ideal Workshop he so panted for, is even this same Actual ill-furnished Workshop he has so long been stumbling in. He can say to himself : ' Tools ? Thou hast ' no Tools ? Why, there is not a Man, or a Thing, now alive ' but has tools. The basest of created animalcules, the Spider ' itself has a spinning-jenny, and warping-mill, and power- ' loom, within its head ; the stupidest of Oysters has a Papin's- ' Digester, with stone-and-lime house to hold it in : every ' being that can live can do something ; this let him *do*. ' Tools ? Hast thou not a Brain, furnished, furnishable with ' some glimmerings of Light ; and three fingers to hold a ' Pen withal ? Never since Aaron's Rod went out of practice, ' or even before it, was there such a wonder-working Tool : ' greater than all recorded miracles have been performed by

'Pens. For strangely in this so solid-seeming World, which
'nevertheless is in continual restless flux, it is appointed that
'*Sound*, to appearance the most fleeting, should be the most
'continuing of all things. The WORD is well said to be om-
'nipotent in this world ; man, thereby divine, can create as
'by a *Fiat*. Awake, arise! Speak forth what is in thee ;
'what God has given thee, what the Devil shall not take
'away. Higher task than that of Priesthood was allotted to
'no man : wert thou but the meanest in that sacred Hier-
'archy, is it not honour enough therein to spend and be
'spent ?

'By this Art, which whoso will may sacrilegiously degrade
'into a handicraft,' adds Teufelsdröckh, 'have I thenceforth
'abidden. Writings of mine, not indeed known as mine (for
'what am *I?*), have fallen, perhaps not altogether void, into
'the mighty seed-field of Opinion ; fruits of my unseen sow-
'ing gratifyingly meet me here and there. I thank the
'Heavens that I have now found my Calling ; wherein, with
'or without perceptible result, I am minded diligently to
'persevere.

'Nay how knowest thou,' cries he, 'but this and the other
'pregnant Device, now grown to be a world-renowned far-
'working Institution ; like a grain of right mustard-seed once
'cast into the right soil, and now stretching out strong
'boughs to the four winds, for the birds of the air to lodge
'in,—may have been properly my doing ? Some one's doing
'it without doubt was ; from some Idea, in some single
'Head, it did first of all take beginning : why not from some
'Idea in mine ?' Does Teufelsdröckh here glance at that
'SOCIETY FOR THE CONSERVATION OF PROPERTY (*Eigenthums-con-*
'*servirende Gesellschaft*),' of which so many ambiguous notices
glide spectre-like through these inexpressible Paperbags?
'An Institution,' hints he, 'not unsuitable to the wants of the
'time ; as indeed such sudden extension proves ; for already
'can the Society number, among its office-bearers or corre-
'sponding members, the highest Names, if not the highest
'Persons, in Germany, England, France ; and contributions,
'both of money and of meditation, pour in from all quarters ;

' to, if possible, enlist the remaining Integrity of the world,
' and, defensively and with forethought, marshal it round this
' Palladium.' Does Teufelsdröckh mean, then, to give him
self out as the originator of that so notable *Eigenthums-*
conservirende ('Owndom-conserving') *Gesellschaft;* and, if so,
what, in the Devil's name, is it? He again hints : ' At a time
' when the divine Commandment, *Thou shalt not steal*, where-
' in truly, if well understood, is comprised the whole Hebrew
' Decalogue, with Solon's and Lycurgus's Constitutions, Jus-
' tinian's Pandects, the Code Napoleon, and all Codes, Cate-
' chisms, Divinities, Moralities whatsoever, that man has hith-
' erto devised (and enforced with Altar-fire and Gallows-ropes)
' for his social guidance : at a time, I say, when this divine
' Commandment has all but faded away from the general re-
' membrance ; and, with little disguise, a new opposite Com-
' mandment, *Thou shalt steal*, is everywhere promulgated,—it
' perhaps behoved in this universal dotage and deliration the
' sound portion of mankind to bestir themselves and rally.
' When the widest and wildest violations of that divine right
' of Property, the only divine right now extant or conceiva-
' ble, are sanctioned and recommended by a vicious Press,
' and the world has lived to hear it asserted that *we have no*
' *Property in our very Bodies but only an accidental Possession,*
' *and Life-rent*, what is the issue to be looked for? Hangmen
' and Catchpoles may, by their noose-gins and baited fall-
' traps, keep down the smaller sort of vermin : but what, ex-
' cept perhaps some such Universal Association, can protect
' us against whole meat-devouring and man-devouring hosts
' of Boa-constrictors? If, therefore, the more sequestered
' Thinker have wondered, in his privacy, from what hand that
' perhaps not ill-written *Program* in the Public Journals, with
' its high *Prize-Questions* and so liberal *Prizes*, could have
' proceeded,—let him now cease such wonder ; and, with un-
' divided faculty, betake himself to the *Concurrenz* (Compe-
' tition).'

We ask : Has this same ' perhaps not ill-written *Program*,'
or any other authentic Transaction of that Property-conserv-
ing Society, fallen under the eye of the British Reader, in any

11

Journal, foreign or domestic? If so, what are those *Prize Questions;* what are the terms of Competition, and when and where? No printed Newspaper leaf, no farther light of any sort, to be met with in these Paperbags! Or is the whole business one other of those whimsicalities, and perverse inex-plicabilities, whereby Herr Teufelsdröckh, meaning much or nothing, is pleased so often to play fast and loose with us?

Here, indeed, at length, must the Editor give utterance to a painful suspicion which, through late Chapters, has begun to haunt him; paralysing any little enthusiasm, that might still have rendered his thorny Biographical task a labour of love. It is a suspicion grounded perhaps on trifles, yet con-firmed almost into certainty by the more and more discernible humoristico-satirical tendency of Teufelsdröckh, in whom un-derground humours, and intricate sardonic rogueries, wheel within wheel, defy all reckoning: a suspicion in one word, that these Autobiographical Documents are partly a mystifica-tion! What if many a so-called Fact were little better than a Fiction; if here we had no direct Camera-obscura Picture of the Professor's History; but only some more or less fantastic Adumbration, symbolically, perhaps significantly enough, shadowing forth the same! Our theory begins to be that, in receiving as literally authentic what was but hieroglyphically so, Hofrath Heuschrecke, whom in that case we scruple not to name Hofrath Nose-of-Wax, was made a fool of, and set adrift to make fools of others. Could it be expected, indeed, that a man so known for impenetrable reticence as Teufelsdröckh, would all at once frankly unlock his private citadel to an English Editor and a German Hofrath; and not rather decep-tively *in*lock both Editor and Hofrath, in the labyrinthic tor-tuosities and covered ways of said citadel (having enticed them thither), to see, in his half-devilish way, how the fools would look?

Of one fool, however, the Herr Professor will perhaps find himself short. On a small slip formerly thrown aside as blank, the ink being all but invisible, we lately notice, and with effort decipher, the following: 'What are your historical

'Facts ; still more your biographical? Wilt thou know a
'Man, above all, a Mankind, by stringing together beadrolls
'of what thou namest Facts? The man is the spirit he
'worked in ; not what he did, but what he became. Facts
'are engraved Hierograms, for which the fewest have the key.
'And then how your Blockhead (*Dummkopf*) studies not their
'Meaning ; but simply whether they are well or ill cut, what
'he calls Moral or Immoral! Still worse is it with your
'Bungler (*Pfüscher*): such I have seen reading some Rous-
'seau, with pretences of interpretation ; and mistaking the ill-
'cut Serpent-of-Eternity for a common poisonous Reptile.'
Was the Professor apprehensive lest an Editor, selected as the
present boasts himself, might mistake the Teufelsdröckh Serpent-of-Eternity in like manner? For which reason it was
to be altered, not without underhand satire, into a plainer
Symbol? Or is this merely one of his half-sophisms, half-
truisms, which if he can but set on the back of a Figure, he
cares not whither it gallop? We say not with certainty ; and
indeed, so strange is the Professor, can never say. If our
Suspicion be wholly unfounded let his own questionable ways,
not our necessary circumspectness, bear the blame.

But be this as it will, the somewhat exasperated and indeed
exhausted Editor determines here to shut these Paperbags,
for the present. Let it suffice that we know of Teufelsdröckh,
so far, if 'not what he did, yet what he became :' the rather,
as his character has now taken its ultimate bent, and no new
revolution of importance is to be looked for. The imprisoned
Chrysalis is now a winged Psyche : and such, wheresoever be
its flight, it will continue. To trace by what complex gyra-
tions (flights or involuntary waftings) through the mere external Life-element, Teufelsdröckh reaches his University
Professorship, and the Psyche clothes himself in civic Titles,
without altering her now fixed nature,—would be comparatively an unproductive task, were we even unsuspicious of its
being, for us at least, a false and impossible one. His outward Biography, therefore, which, at the Blumine Lover's-
Leap, we saw churned utterly into spray-vapour, may hover
in that condition, for aught that concerns us here. Enough

that, by survey of certain 'pools and plashes,' we have ascertained its general direction : do we not already know that, by one way and other, it *has* long since rained down again into a stream ; and even now, at Weissnichtwo, flows deep and still, fraught with the *Philosophy of Clothes*, and visible to whoso will cast eye thereon ? Over much invaluable matter that lies scattered, like jewels among quarry-rubbish, in those Paper catacombs, we may have occasion to glance back, and, somewhat will demand insertion at the right place : meanwhile, be our tiresome diggings therein suspended.

If now, before reopening the great *Clothes-Volume,* we ask what our degree of progress, during these Ten Chapters, has been, towards right understanding of the *Clothes-Philosophy,* let not our discouragement become total. To speak in that old figure of the Hell-gate Bridge over Chaos, a few flying pontoons have perhaps been added, though as yet they drift straggling on the Flood ; how far they will reach, when once the chains are straightened and fastened, can, at present, only be matter of conjecture.

So much we already calculate : Through many a little loophole, we have had glimpses into the internal world of Teufelsdröckh ; his strange mystic, almost magic Diagram of the Universe, and how it was gradually drawn, is not henceforth altogether dark to us. Those mysterious ideas on TIME, which merit consideration, and are not wholly unintelligible with such, may by and by prove significant. Still more may his somewhat peculiar view of Nature ; the decisive Oneness he ascribes to Nature. How all Nature and Life are but one *Garment,* a 'Living Garment,' woven and ever a-weaving in the 'Loom of Time ;' is not here, indeed, the outline of a whole *Clothes-Philosophy ;* at least the arena it is to work in ? Remark too that the Character of the man, nowise without meaning in such a matter, becomes less enigmatic : amid so much tumultuous obscurity almost like diluted madness, do not a certain indomitable Defiance and yet a boundless Reverence seem to loom forth, as the two mountain-summits, on whose rock-strata all the rest were based and built ?

Nay, further, may we not say that Teufelsdröckh's Biography, allowing it even, as suspected, only a hieroglyphical truth, exhibits a man as it were preappointed for Clothes-Philosophy? To look through the Shows of things into Things themselves he is led and compelled. The 'Passivity' given him by birth is fostered by all turns of his fortune. Everywhere cast out, like oil out of water, from mingling in any Employment, in any public Communion, he has no portion but Solitude and a life of Meditation. The whole energy of his existence is directed, through long years, on one task; that of enduring pain, if he cannot cure it. Thus everywhere do the Shows of things oppress him, withstand him, threaten him with fearfulest destruction; only by victoriously penetrating into Things themselves, can he find peace and a stronghold. But is not this same looking through the Shows, or Vestures, into the Things, even the first preliminary to a *Philosophy of Clothes?* Do we not, in all this, discern some beckonings towards the true higher purport of such a Philosophy; and what shape it must assume with such a man, in such an era?

Perhaps in entering on Book Third, the courteous Reader is not utterly without guess whither he is bound: nor, let us hope, for all the fantastic Dream-Grottoes through which, as is our lot with Teufelsdröckh, he must wander, will there be wanting between whiles some twinkling of a steady Polar Star.

BOOK III.

CHAPTER I.

INCIDENT IN MODERN HISTORY.

As a wonder-loving and wonder-seeking man, Teufelsdröckh, from an early part of his Clothes-Volume, has more and more exhibited himself. Striking it was, amid all his perverse cloudiness, with what force of vision and of heart he pierced into the mystery of the World; recognising in the highest sensible phenomena, so far as Sense went, only fresh or faded Raiment; yet ever, under this, a celestial Essence thereby rendered visible; and while, on the one hand, he trod the old rags of Matter, with their tinsels, into the mire, he on the other everywhere exalted Spirit above all earthly principalities and powers, and worshipped it, though under the meanest shapes, with a true Platonic Mysticism. What the man ultimately purposed by thus casting his Greek-fire into the general Wardrobe of the Universe; what such, more or less complete, rending and burning of Garments throughout the whole compass of Civilized Life and Speculation, should lead to: the rather as he was no Adamite, in any sense, and could not, like Rousseau, recommend either bodily or intellectual Nudity, and a return to the savago state: all this our readers are now bent to discover; this is, in fact, properly the gist and purport of Professor Teufelsdröckh's Philosophy of Clothes.

Be it remembered, however, that such purport is here not so much evolved as detected to lie ready for evolving. We are to guide our British Friends into the new Gold-country, and shew them the mines; nowise to dig out and exhaust its wealth, which indeed remains for all time inexhaustible.

Once there, let each dig for his own behoof, and enrich him‹ self.

Neither, in so capricious inexpressible a Work as this of the Professor's, can our course now more than formerly be straight forward, step by step, but at best leap by leap. Significant Indications stand out here and there ; which for the critical eye, that looks both widely and narrowly, shape them‹ selves into some ground-scheme of a Whole : to select these with judgment, so that a leap from one to the other be pos- sible, and (in our old figure) by chaining them together, a passable Bridge be effected : this, as heretofore, continues our only method. Among such light-spots, the following, floating in much wild matter about *Perfectibility*, has seemed worth clutching at :

' Perhaps the most remarkable incident in Modern History,' says Teufelsdröckh, ' is not the Diet of Worms, still less the ' Battle of Austerlitz, Waterloo, Peterloo, or any other Battle ; ' but an incident passed carelessly over by most Historians, ' and treated with some degree of ridicule by others : namely, ' George Fox's making to himself a suit of Leather. This ' man, the first of the Quakers, and by trade a Shoemaker, ' was one of those, to whom, under ruder or purer form, the ' Divine Idea of the Universe is pleased to manifest itself ; ' and, across all the hulls of Ignorance and earthly Degrada- ' tion, shine through, in unspeakable Awfulness, unspeakable ' Beauty, on their souls ; who therefore are rightly accounted ' Prophets, God-possessed ; or even Gods, as in some periods ' it has chanced. Sitting in his stall ; working on tanned ' hides, amid pincers, paste-horns, rosin, swine-bristles, and a ' nameless flood of rubbish, this youth had nevertheless a ' Living Spirit belonging to him ; also an antique Inspired ' Volume, through which, as through a window, it could look ' upwards, and discern its celestial Home. The task of a ' daily pair of shoes, coupled even with some prospect of vic‹ ' tuals, and an honourable Mastership in Cordwainery, and per- haps the post of Thirdborough in his Hundred, as the crown ' of long faithful sewing,—was nowise satisfaction enough ' to such a mind : but ever amid the boring and hammering

' came tones from that far country, came Splendours and
' Terrors ; for this poor Cordwainer, as we said, was a Man ;
' and the Temple of Immensity, wherein as Man he had been
' sent to minister, was full of holy mystery to him.

' The Clergy of the neighbourhood, the ordained Watchers
' and Interpreters of that same holy mystery, listened with
' unaffected tedium to his consultations, and advised him, as
' the solution of such doubts, to " drink beer, and dance with
' the girls." Blind leaders of the blind ! For what end were
' their tithes levied and eaten ; for what were their shovel-hats
' scooped out, and their surplices and cassock-aprons girt on ;
' and such a church-repairing, and chaffering, and organing,
' and other racketing, held over that spot of God's Earth,—if
' Man were but a Patent Digester, and the Belly with its ad-
' juncts the grand Reality? Fox turned from them, with
' tears and a sacred scorn, back to his Leather-parings and
' his Bible. Mountains of encumbrance, higher than Ætna,
' had been heaped over that Spirit : but it was a Spirit, and
' would not lie buried there. Through long days and nights
' of silent agony, it struggled and wrestled, with a man's
' force, to be free : how its prison-mountains heaved and
' swayed tumultuously, as the giant spirit shook them to this
' hand and that, and emerged into the light of Heaven ! That
' Leicester shoe-shop, had men known it, was a holier place
' than any Vatican or Loretto-shrine.—" So bandaged, and
' hampered, and hemmed in," groaned he, " with thousand
' requisitions, obligations, straps, tatters, and tagrags, I can
' neither see nor move : not my own am I, but the World's ;
' and Time flies fast, and Heaven is high, and Hell is deep :
' Man ! bethink thee, if thou hast power of Thought ! Why
' not ; what binds me here ? Want, want !—Ha, of what ?
' Will all the shoe-wages under the Moon ferry me across into
' that far Land of Light? Only Meditation can, and devout
' Prayer to God. I will to the woods : the hollow of a tree
' will lodge me, wild berries feed me ; and for Clothes, cannot
' I stitch myself one perennial suit of Leather ?"

' Historical Oil-painting,' continues Teufelsdröckh, ' is one
' of the Arts I never practised ; therefore shall I not decide

' whether this subject were easy of execution on the canvas.
' Yet often has it seemed to me as if such first outflashing of
' man's Freewill, to lighten, more and more into Day, the
' Chaotic Night that threatened to engulph him in its hin-
' drances and its horrors, were properly the only grandeur
' there is in History. Let some living Angelo or Rosa, with
' seeing eye and understanding heart, picture George Fox on
' that morning, when he spreads out his cutting-board for the
' last time, and cuts cow-hides by unwonted patterns, and
' stitches them together into one continuous all-including Case,
' the farewell service of his awl! Stitch away, thou noble
' Fox: every prick of that little instrument is pricking into
' the heart of Slavery, and World-worship, and the Mammon-
' god. Thy elbows jerk, as in strong swimmer-strokes, and
' every stroke is bearing thee across the Prison-ditch, within
' which Vanity holds her Workhouse and Ragfair, into lands
' of true liberty ; were the work done, there is in broad Eu-
' rope one Free Man, and thou art he !

  ' Thus from the lowest depth there is a path to the loftiest
' height ; and for the Poor also a Gospel has been published.
' Surely, if, as D'Alembert asserts, my illustrious namesake,
' Diogenes, was the greatest man of Antiquity, only that he
' wanted Decency, then by stronger reason is George Fox the
' greatest of the Moderns ; and greater than Diogenes him-
' self : for he too stands on the adamantine basis of his Man-
' hood, casting aside all props and shoars ; yet not, in half-
' savage Pride, undervaluing the Earth ; valuing it rather, as
' a place to yield him warmth and food, he looks Heavenward
' from his Earth, and dwells in an element of Mercy and Wor-
' ship, with a still Strength, such as the Cynic's Tub did no-
' wise witness. Great, truly, was that Tub ; a temple from
' which man's dignity and divinity was scornfully preached
' abroad ; but greater is the Leather Hull, for the same ser-
' mon was preached there, and not in Scorn but in Love.'

George Fox's 'perennial suit,' with all that it held, has been
worn quite into ashes for nigh two centuries : why, in a dis-
cussion on the *Perfectibility of Society*, reproduce it now?

Not out of blind sectarian partisanship : Teufelsdröckh him-self is no Quaker ; with all his pacific tendencies, did we not see him, in that scene at the North Cape, with the Archangel Smuggler, exhibit fire-arms?

For us, aware of his deep Sansculottism, there is more meant in this passage than meets the ear. At the same time, who can avoid smiling at the earnestness and Bœotian sim-plicity (if indeed there be not an underhand satire in it), with which that 'Incident' is here brought forward ; and, in the Professor's ambiguous way, as clearly perhaps as he durst in Weissnichtwo, recommended to imitation! Does Teufels-dröckh anticipate that, in this age of refinement, any consid-erable class of the community, by way of testifying against the 'Mammon-god,' and escaping from what he calls 'Vanity's Workhouse and Ragfair,' where doubtless some of them are toiled and whipped and hoodwinked sufficiently,—will sheathe themselves in close-fitting cases of Leather? The idea is ridiculous in the extreme. Will Majesty lay aside its robes of state, and Beauty its frills and train-gowns, for a second-skin of tanned hide? By which change Huddersfield and Manchester, and Coventry and Paisley, and the Fancy-Bazaar, were reduced to hungry solitudes ; and only Day and Martin could profit. For neither would Teufelsdröckh's mad day-dream, here as we presume covertly intended, of levelling Society (*levelling* it indeed with a vengeance, into one huge drowned marsh!), and so attaining the political effects of Nudity without its frigorific or other consequences,—be there-by realised. Would not the rich man purchase a waterproof suit of Russia Leather ; and the high-born Belle step forth in red or azure morocco, lined with shamoy ; the black cowhide being left to the Drudges and Gibeonites of the world ; and so all the old Distinctions be re-established?

Or has the Professor his own deeper intention ; and laughs in his sleeve at our strictures and glosses, which indeed are but a part thereof?

CHAPTER II.

CHURCH-CLOTHES.

Not less questionable is his Chapter on *Church-Clothes*, which has the farther distinction of being the shortest in the Volume.   We here translate it entire :

' By Church Clothes, it need not be premised, that I mean
' infinitely more than Cassocks and Surplices ; and do not at
' all mean the mere haberdasher Sunday Clothes that men go
' to Church in.   Far from it !   Church-Clothes are, in our
' vocabulary, the Forms, the *Vestures*, under which men have
' at various periods embodied and represented for themselves
' the Religious Principle ; that is to say, invested the Divine
' Idea of the World with a sensible and practically active Body,
' so that it might dwell among them as a living and life-giving
' WORD.

' These are unspeakably the most important of all the ves-
' tures and garnitures of Human Existence.   They are first
' spun and woven, I may say, by that wonder of wonders,
' SOCIETY ; for it is still only when " two or three are gathered
' together " that Religion, spiritually existent, and indeed in-
' destructible however latent, in each, first outwardly manifests
' itself (as with " cloven tongues of fire "), and seeks to be em-
' bodied in a visible Communion, and Church Militant.   Mysti-
' cal, more than magical, is that Communing of Soul with Soul,
' both looking heavenward ; here properly Soul first speaks
' with Soul ; for only in looking heavenward, take it in what
' sense you may, not in looking earthward, does what we can
' call Union, mutual Love, Society, begin to be possible.
' How true is that of Novalis ; "It is certain, my Belief gains
' quite *infinitely* the moment I can convince another mind
' thereof ! "   Gaze thou in the face of thy Brother, in those
' eyes where plays the lambent fire of Kindness, or in those
' where rages the lurid conflagration of Anger ; feel how thy
' own so quiet Soul is straightway involuntarily kindled with
' the like, and ye blaze and reverberate on each other, till it

' is all one limitless confluent flame (of embracing Love, or of
' deadly-grappling Hate) ; and then say what miraculous virtue
' goes out of man into man. But if so, through all the thick-
' plied hull of our Earthly Life ; how much more when it is
' of the Divine Life we speak, and inmost ME is, as it were,
' brought into contact with inmost ME !

' Thus was it that I said, the Church-Clothes are first spun
' and woven by Society ; outward Religion originates by So-
' ciety, Society becomes possible by Religion. Nay, perhaps
' every conceivable Society, past and present, may well be fig-
' ured as properly and wholly a Church, in one or other of
' these three predicaments : an audibly preaching and prophe-
' sying Church, which is the best ; second, a Church that strug-
' gles to preach and prophesy, but cannot as yet, till its Pen-
' tecost come ; and third and worst, a Church gone dumb with
' old age, or which only mumbles delirium prior to dissolution.
' Whoso fancies that by Church is here meant Chapterhouses
' and Cathedrals, or by preaching and prophesying, mere
' speech and chaunting, let him,' says the oracular Professor,
' read on, light of heart (*getrosten Muthes*).

' But with regard to your Church proper, and the Church-
' Clothes specially recognised as Church-Clothes, I remark,
' fearlessly enough, that without such Vestures and sacred Tis-
' sues Society has not existed, and will not exist. For if Gov-
' ernment is, so to speak, the outward SKIN of the Body Politic,
' holding the whole together and protecting it ; and all your
' Craft-Guilds, and Associations for Industry, of hand or of
' head, are the Fleshly Clothes, the muscular and osseous Tis-
' sues, (lying *under* such SKIN), whereby Society stands and
' works ;—then is Religion the inmost Pericardial and
' Nervous Tissue, which ministers Life and warm Circulation
' to the whole. Without which Pericardial Tissue the Bones
and Muscles (of Industry) were inert, or animated only by a
' Galvanic vitality : the SKIN would become a shrivelled pelt, or
: fast-rotting raw-hide ; and Society itself a dead carcass,—
' deserving to be buried. Men were no longer Social, but
' Gregarious ; which latter state also could not continue, but
' must gradually issue in universal selfish discord, hatred,

'savage isolation, and dispersion ;—whereby, as we might
'continue to say, the very dust and dead body of Society
'would have evaporated and become abolished. Such, and so
'all-important, all-sustaining, are the Church-Clothes, to civi-
'lised or even to rational man.

'Meanwhile, in our era of the World, those same Church-
'Clothes have gone sorrowfully out at elbows : nay, far worse,
'many of them have become mere hollow Shapes, or Masks,
'under which no living Figure or Spirit any longer dwells ;
'but only spiders and unclean beetles, in horrid accumulation,
'drive their trade ; and the Mask still glares on you with its
'glass-eyes, in ghastly affectation of Life,—some generation
'and half after Religion has quite withdrawn from it, and in
'unnoticed nooks is weaving for herself new Vestures, where-
'with to reappear, and bless us, or our sons or grandsons. As
'a Priest, or Interpreter of the Holy, is the noblest and high-
'est of all men, so is a Shampriest (*Schein-priester*) the falsest
'and basest : neither is it doubtful that his Canonicals, were
'they Popes' Tiaras, will one day be torn from him, to make
'bandages for the wounds of mankind ; or even to burn into
'tinder, for general scientific or culinary purposes.

'All which, as out of place here, falls to be handled in my
'Second Volume, *On the Palingenesia, or Newbirth of Society ;*
'which volume, as treating practically of the Wear, Destruc-
'tion, and Re-texture of Spiritual Tissues, or Garments, forms,
'properly speaking, the Transcendental or ultimate Portion
'of this my Work *on Clothes,* and is already in a state of for-
'wardness.'

And herewith, no farther exposition, note, or commentary
being added, does Teufelsdröckh, and must his Editor now,
terminate the singular chapter on Church-Clothes !

CHAPTER III.

SYMBOLS.

Probably it will elucidate the drift of these foregoing obscure utterances, if we here insert somewhat of our Professor's speculations on *Symbols.* To state his whole doctrine, indeed, were beyond our compass : nowhere is he more mysterious, impalpable, than in this of 'Fantasy being the organ of 'the Godlike ;' and how 'Man thereby, though based, to all 'seeming, on the small Visible, does nevertheless extend down 'into the infinite deeps of the Invisible, of which Invisible, 'indeed, his Life is properly the bodying forth.' Let us, omitting these high transcendental aspects of the matter, study to glean (whether from the Paperbags or the Printed Volume) what little seems logical and practical, and cunningly arrange it into such degree of coherence as it will assume. By way of proem, take the following not injudicious remarks :

'The benignant efficacies of Concealment,' cries our Professor, 'who shall speak or sing? Silence and Secrecy! Al-
'tars might still be raised to them (were this an altar-build-
'ing time) for universal worship. Silence is the element in
'which great things fashion themselves together ; that at
'length they may emerge, full-formed and majestic, into the
'daylight of Life, which they are thenceforth to rule. Not
'William the Silent only, but all the considerable men I have
'known, and the most undiplomatic and unstrategic of these,
'forbore to babble of what they were creating and projecting.
'Nay, in thy own mean perplexities, do thou thyself but *hold*
'*thy tongue for one day* : on the morrow, how much clearer
'are thy purposes, and duties ; what wreck and rubbish have
'those mute workmen within thee swept away, when intru-
'sive noises were shut out! Speech is too often not as the
'Frenchman defined it, the art of concealing Thought; but
'of quite stifling and suspending Thought, so that there is
'none to conceal. Speech too is great, but not the greatest.
'As the Swiss Inscription says : *Sprechen ist silbern, Schweigen*

'*ist golden* (Speech is silvern, Silence is golden); or as I
'might rather express it : Speech is of Time, Silence is of
'Eternity.

'Bees will not work except in darkness; Thought will not
'work except in Silence; neither will Virtue work except in
'Secrecy. Let not thy right hand know what thy left hand
'doeth! Neither shalt thou prate even to thy own heart of
'"those secrets known to all." Is not Shame the soil of all
'Virtue, of all good manners, and good morals? Like other
'plants, Virtue will not grow unless its root be hidden,
'buried from the eye of the sun. Let the sun shine on it,
'nay, do but look at it privily thyself, the root withers, and
'no flower will glad thee. O my Friends, when we view the
'fair clustering flowers that over-wreathe, for example, the
'Marriage-bower, and encircle man's life with the fragrance
'and hues of Heaven, what hand will not smite the foul
'plunderer that grubs them up by the roots, and, with grin-
'ning, grunting satisfaction, shews us the dung they flourish
'in! Men speak much of the Printing Press with its News-
'papers : *du Himmel!* what are these to Clothes and the
'Tailor's Goose?'

'Of kin to the so incalculable influences of Concealment,
'and connected with still greater things, is the wondrous
'agency of *Symbols.* In a Symbol there is concealment and
'yet revelation: here, therefore, by Silence and by Speech
'acting together, comes a doubled significance. And if both
'the Speech be itself high, and the Silence fit and noble, how
'expressive will their union be! Thus in many a painted
'Device, or simple Seal-emblem, the commonest Truth stands
'out to us proclaimed with quite new emphasis.

'For it is here that Fantasy with her mystic wonderland
'plays into the small prose domain of Sense, and becomes in-
'corporated therewith. In the Symbol proper, what we can
'call a Symbol, there is ever, more or less distinctly and di-
'rectly, some embodiment and revelation of the Infinite; the
'Infinite is made to blend itself with the Finite, to stand vis-
'ible, and as it were, attainable there. By Symbols, accord-
'ingly, is man guided and commanded, made happy, made

'wretched. He everywhere finds himself encompassed with
'Symbols, recognised as such or not recognised : the Uni-
'verse is but one vast Symbol of God ; nay, if thou wilt have
'it, what is man himself but a Symbol of God ; is not all that
'he does symbolical ; a revelation to Sense of the mystic god-
'given Force that is in him ; a " Gospel of Freedom," which
'he, the "Messias of Nature," preaches, as he can, by act and
'word ? Not a Hut he builds but is the visible embodiment
'of a Thought ; but bears visible record of invisible things ;
'but is, in the transcendental sense, symbolical as well as
'real.'

'Man,' says the Professor elsewhere, in quite antipodal contrast with these high-soaring delineations, which we have
here cut short on the verge of the inane, 'man is by birth
'somewhat of an owl. Perhaps, too, of all the owleries that
'ever possessed him, the most owlish, if we consider it, is
'that of your actually existing Motive-Millwrights. Fantas-
'tic tricks enough has man played, in his time ; has fancied
'himself to be most things, down even to an animated heap
'of Glass : but to fancy himself a dead Iron-Balance for
'weighing Pains and Pleasures on, was reserved for this his
'latter era. There stands he, his Universe one huge Manger,
'filled with hay and thistles to be weighed against each other ;
'and looks long-eared enough. Alas, poor devil ! spectres
'are appointed to haunt him : one age, he is hagridden, be-
'witched ; the next, priestridden, befooled ; in all ages, be-
'devilled. And now the Genius of Mechanism smothers him
'worse than any Nightmare did ; till the Soul is nigh choked
'out of him, and only a kind of Digestive, Mechanic life re-
'mains. In Earth and in Heaven he can see nothing but
'Mechanism ; has fear for nothing else, hope in nothing else :
'the world would indeed grind him to pieces ; but cannot he
'fathom the Doctrine of Motives, and cunningly compute
'these, and mechanise them to grind the other way ?

'Were he not, as has been said, purblinded by enchant-
'ment, you had but to bid him open his eyes and look. In
'which country, in which time, was it hitherto that man's his-
'tory, or the history of any man, went on by calculated or

12

'calculable "Motives?" What make ye of your Christiani-
'ties, and Chivalries, and Reformations, and Marseillese
'Hymns, and Reigns of Terror? Nay, has not perhaps, the
'Motive-grinder himself been *in Love?* Did he never stand
'so much as a contested Election? Leave him to Time, and
'the medicating virtue of Nature.'

'Yes, Friends,' elsewhere observes the Professor, 'not our
'Logical, Mensurative faculty, but our Imaginative one is
'King over us; I might say, Priest and Prophet to lead us
'heavenward; or Magician and Wizard to lead us hellward.
'Nay, even for the basest Sensualist, what is Sense but the
'implement of Fantasy; the vessel it drinks out of? Ever in
'the dullest existence, there is a sheen either of Inspiration
'or of Madness (thou partly hast it in thy choice, which of
'the two) that gleams in from the circumambient Eternity,
'and colours with its own hues our little islet of Time. The
'Understanding is indeed thy window, too clear thou canst
'not make it; but Fantasy is thy eye, with its colour-giving
'retina, healthy or diseased. Have not I myself known five
'hundred living soldiers sabred into crows' meat, for a piece
'of glazed cotton, which they called their Flag; which, had
'you sold it at any market-cross, would not have brought
'above three groschen? Did not the whole Hungarian Na-
'tion rise, like some tumultuous moon-stirred Atlantic, when
'Kaiser Joseph pocketed their Iron Crown; an implement, as
'was sagaciously observed, in size and commercial value, little
'differing from a horse-shoe? It is in and through *Symbols*
'that man, consciously or unconsciously, lives, works, and has
'his being: those ages, moreover, are accounted the noblest
'which can the best recognise symbolical worth, and prize it
'the highest. For is not a Symbol ever, to him who has eyes
'for it, some dimmer or clearer revelation of the Godlike?

'Of Symbols, however, I remark farther, that they have
'both an extrinsic and intrinsic value; oftenest the former
'only. What, for instance, was in that clouted Shoe, which
'the peasants bore aloft with them as ensign in their *Bauern-*
'*krieg* (Peasants' War)? Or in the Wallet-and-staff round
'which the Netherland *Gueux*, glorying in that nickname of

' Beggars, heroically rallied and prevailed, though against
' King Philip himself? Intrinsic significance these had none :
' only extrinsic ; as the accidental Standards of multitudes
' more or less sacredly uniting together ; in which union it-
' self, as above noted, there is ever something mystical and
' borrowing of the Godlike. Under a like category too,
' stand, or stood, the stupidest heraldic Coats-of-arms ; mili-
' tary Banners everywhere ; and generally all national or
' other sectarian Costumes and Customs : they have no in-
' trinsic, necessary divineness, or even worth ; but have
' acquired an extrinsic one. Nevertheless through all these
' there glimmers something of a Divine Idea ; as through
' military Banners themselves, the Divine Idea of Duty, of
' heroic Daring ; in some instances of Freedom, of Right.
' Nay, the highest ensign that men ever met and embraced
' under, the Cross itself, had no meaning save an accidental
' extrinsic one.

' Another matter it is, however, when your Symbol has
' intrinsic meaning, and is of itself *fit* that men should unite
' round it. Let but the Godlike manifest itself to Sense ; let
' but Eternity look, more or less visibly, through the Time-
' figure (*Zeitbild*) ! Then is it fit that men unite there ; and
' worship together before such Symbol ; and so from day to
' day, and from age to age, superadd to it new divineness.

' Of this latter sort are all true Works of Art : in them (if
' thou know a Work of Art from a Daub of Artifice) wilt
' thou discern Eternity looking through Time ; the Godlike
' rendered visible. Here too may an extrinsic value grad-
' ually superadd itself : thus certain *Iliads*, and the like, have,
' in three thousand years, attained quite new significance.
' But nobler than all in this kind are the Lives of heroic god-
' inspired Men ; for what other Work of Art is so divine ? In
' Death too, in the Death of the Just, as the last perfection of
' a Work of Art, may we not discern symbolic meaning ? In
' that divinely transfigured Sleep, as of Victory, resting over
' the beloved face which now knows thee no more, read (if
' thou canst for tears) the confluence of Time with Eternity,
' and some gleam of the latter peering through.

'Highest of all Symbols are those wherein the Artist or 'Poet has risen into Prophet, and all men can recognise a 'present God, and worship the same : I mean religious Sym-'bols. Various enough have been such religious Symbols, 'what we call *Religions ;* as men stood in this stage of culture 'or the other, and could worse or better body forth the God-'like ; some Symbols with a transient intrinsic worth ; many 'with only an extrinsic. If thou ask to what height man has 'carried it in this manner look on our divinest Symbol : on 'Jesus of Nazareth, and his Life, and his Biography, and what 'followed therefrom. Higher has the human Thought not 'yet reached : this is Christianity, and Christendom ; a Sym-'bol of quite perennial, infinite character ; whose significance 'will ever demand to be anew inquired into, and anew made 'manifest.

'But, on the whole, as Time adds much to the sacredness 'of Symbols, so likewise in his progress he at length defaces, 'or even desecrates them ; and Symbols, like all terrestrial 'Garments, wax old. Homer's Epos has not ceased to be 'true ; yet it is no longer *our* Epos, but shines in the dis-'tance, if clearer and clearer, yet also smaller and smaller, 'like a receding Star. It needs a scientific telescope, it needs 'to be reinterpreted and artificially brought near us, before 'we can so much as know that it *was* a Sun. So likewise a 'day comes when the Runic Thor, with his Eddas, must with-'draw into dimness ; and many an African Mumbo-Jumbo, 'and Indian Pawaw be utterly abolished. For all things, even 'Celestial Luminaries, much more atmospheric meteors, have 'their rise, their culmination, their decline.'

'Small is this which thou tellest me, that the Royal Sceptre 'is but a piece of gilt wood ; that the Pyx has become a most 'foolish box, and truly, as Ancient Pistol thought, " of little 'price." A right Conjuror might I name thee, couldst thou 'conjure back into these wooden tools the divine virtue they 'once held.'

'Of this thing, however, be certain : wouldst thou plant for 'Eternity, then plant into the deep infinite faculties of man, 'his Fantasy and Heart : wouldst thou plant for Year and

' Day, then plant into his shallow superficial faculties, his
' Self-love and Arithmetical Understanding, what will grow
' there A Hierarch, therefore, and Pontiff of the World will
' we call him, the Poet and inspired Maker ; who, Prome-
' theus-like, can shape new Symbols, and bring new Fire from
' Heaven to fix it there. Such too will not always be want-
' ing ; neither perhaps now are. Meanwhile, as the average
' of matter goes, we account him Legislator and wise who can
' so much as tell when a Symbol has grown old, and gently
' remove it.

' When, as the last English Coronation * was preparing,'
concludes this wonderful Professor, ' I read in their News-
' papers that the " Champion of England," he who has to offer
' battle to the Universe for his new King, had brought it so
' far that he could now " mount his horse with little assist-
' ance," I said to myself : Here also we have a Symbol well
' nigh superannuated. Alas, move whithersoever you may, are
' not the tatters and rags of superannuated worn-out Symbols
' (in this Ragfair of a World) dropping off everywhere, to hood-
' wink, to halter, to tether you ; nay, if you shake them not
' aside, threatening to accumulate, and perhaps produce suffo-
' cation.'

CHAPTER IV.

HELOTAGE.

At this point we determine on adverting shortly, or rather
reverting, to a certain Tract of Hofrath Heuschrecke's, entitled
Institute for the Repression of Population ; which lies, dishon-
ourably enough (with torn leaves, and a perceptible smell of
aloetic drugs), stuffed into the Bag *Pisces.* Not indeed for
the sake of the Tract itself, which we admire little ; but of the
marginal Notes, evidently in Teufelsdröckh's hand, which
rather copiously fringe it. A few of these may be in the right
place here.

Into the Hofrath's *Institute,* with its extraordinary schemes,
and machinery of Corresponding Boards and the like, we shall

* That of George IV.—ED.

not so much as glance. Enough for us to understand that Heu-schrecke is a disciple of Malthus ; and so zealous for the doc-trine, that his zeal almost literally eats him up. A deadly fear of Population possesses the Hofrath ; something like a fixed-idea ; undoubtedly akin to the more diluted forms of Madness. Nowhere, in that quarter of his intellectual world, is there light ; nothing but a grim shadow of Hunger ; open mouths opening wider and wider ; a world to terminate by the fright-fulest consummation ; by its too dense inhabitants, famished into delirium, universally eating one another. To make air for himself in which strangulation, choking enough to a be-nevolent heart, the Hofrath founds, or proposes to found, this *Institute* of his, as the best he can do. It is only with our Professor's comments thereon that we concern ourselves.

First, then, remark that Teufelsdröckh, as a speculative Radical, has his own notions about human dignity ; that the Zähdarm palaces and courtesies have not made him forgetful of the Futteral cottages. On the blank cover of Heuschrecke's Tract, we find the following indistinctly engrossed :

' Two men I honour, and no third. First, the toilworn
' Craftsman that with earth-made Implement laboriously con-
' quers the Earth, and makes her man's. Venerable to me is
' the hard Hand ; crooked, coarse ; wherein notwithstanding
' lies a cunning virtue, indefeasibly royal, as of the Sceptre of
' this Planet. Venerable too is the rugged face, all weather-
' tanned, besoiled, with its rude intelligence ; for it is the
' face of a Man living manlike. Oh, but the more venerable
' for thy rudeness, and even because we must pity as well as
' love thee ! Hardly-entreated Brother ! For us was thy
' back so bent, for us were thy straight limbs and fingers so
' deformed : thou wert our Conscript, on whom the lot fell,
' and fighting our battles wert so marred. For in thee too
' lay a god-created Form, but it was not to be unfolded ; en-
' crusted must it stand with the thick adhesions and deface-
' ments of Labour ; and thy body, like thy soul, was not to
' know freedom. Yet toil on, toil on : *thou* art in thy duty,
' be out of it who may ; thou toilest for the altogether indis-
' pensable, for daily bread.

' A second man I honour, and still more highly : Him who
' is seen toiling for the spiritually indispensable ; not daily
' bread, but the Bread of Life. Is not he too in his duty ;
' endeavouring towards inward Harmony ; revealing this by
' act, or by word, through all his outward endeavours, be
' they high or low ? Highest of all, when his outward and
' his inward endeavour are one : when we can name him
' Artist ; not earthly Craftsman only, but inspired Thinker,
' who with heaven-made Implement conquers Heaven for us !
' If the poor and humble toil that we have Food, must not
' the high and glorious toil for him in return, that he have
' Light, have Guidance, Freedom, Immortality ?—These two,
' in all their degrees, I honour : all else is chaff and dust,
' which let the wind blow whither it listeth.

' Unspeakably touching is it, however, when I find both
' dignities united ; and he that must toil outwardly for the
' lowest of man's wants, is also toiling inwardly for the high-
' est. Sublimer in this world know I nothing than a Peasant
' Saint, could such now any where be met with. Such a one
' will take thee back to Nazareth itself ; thou wilt see the
' splendour of Heaven spring forth from the humblest depths
' of Earth, like a light shining in great darkness.'

And again : 'It is not because of his toils that I lament for
' the poor : we must all toil, or steal (howsoever we name our
' stealing), which is worse ; no faithful workman finds his task
' a pastime. The poor is hungry and athirst ; but for him
' also there is food and drink : he is heavy-laden and weary ;
' but for him also the Heavens send Sleep, and of the deep-
' est ; in his smoky cribs, a clear dewy heaven of Rest envel-
' opes him, and fitful glitterings of cloud-skirted Dreams.
' But what I do mourn over is, that the lamp of his soul
' should go out ; that no ray of heavenly, or even of earthly
' knowledge, should visit him ; but only, in the haggard
' darkness, like two spectres, Fear and Indignation bear him
' company. Alas, while the Body stands so broad and
' brawny, must the Soul lie blinded, dwarfed, stupified, al-
' most annihilated ! Alas, was this too a Breath of God ; be-
' stowed in Heaven, but on earth never to be unfolded !—

'That there should one Man die Ignorant who had capacity
'for Knowledge, this I call a tragedy, were it to happen more
'than twenty times in the minute, as by some computations
'it does. The miserable fraction of Science which our united
'Mankind, in a wide Universe of Nescience, has acquired,
'why is not this, with all diligence, imparted to all?'

Quite in an opposite strain is the following: 'The old
'Spartans had a wiser method; and went out and hunted
'down their Helots, and speared and spitted them, when
'they grew too numerous. With our improved fashions of
'hunting, Herr Hofrath, now after the invention of fire-arms.
'and standing armies, how much easier were such a hunt!
'Perhaps in the most thickly-peopled country, some three
'days annually might suffice to shoot all the able-bodied
'Paupers that had accumulated within the year. Let Gov-
'ernments think of this. The expense were trifling: nay,
'the very carcasses would pay it. Have them salted and bar-
'relled; could not you victual therewith, if not Army and
'Navy, yet richly such infirm Paupers, in workhouses and
'elsewhere, as enlightened Charity, dreading no evil of them,
'might see good to keep alive?'

'And yet,' writes he farther on, 'there must be something
'wrong. A full-formed Horse will, in any market, bring
'from twenty to as high as two hundred Friedrichs d'or:
'such is his worth to the world. A full-formed Man is not
'only worth nothing to the world, but the world could afford
'him a round sum would he simply engage to go and hang
'himself. Nevertheless, which of the two was the more cun-
'ningly-devised article, even as an Engine? Good Heavens!
'A white European man, standing on his two Legs, with his
'two five-fingered Hands at his shackle-bones, and miraculous
'Head on his shoulders, is worth, I should say, from fifty to
'a hundred Horses!'

'True, thou Gold-Hofrath,' cries the Professor elsewhere:
'too crowded indeed! Meanwhile, what portion of this in-
'considerable terraqueous Globe have ye actually tilled and
'delved, till it will grow no more? How thick stands your
'Population in the Pampas and Savannas of America; round

' ancient Carthage, and in the interior of Africa ; on both
' slopes of the Altaic chain, in the central Platform of Asia ;
' in Spain, Greece, Turkey, Crim Tartary, the Curragh of Kil-
' dare ? One man, in one year, as I have understood it, if you
' lend him Earth, will feed himself and nine others. Alas,
' where now are the Hengsts and Alarics of our still glowing,
' still expanding Europe ; who, when their home is grown too
' narrow, will enlist and, like Fire-pillars, guide onwards those
' superfluous masses of indomitable living Valour ; equipped,
' not now with the battle-axe and war-chariot, but with the
' steam-engine and ploughshare ? Where are they ?—Pre-
' serving their Game ! '

CHAPTER V.

THE PHŒNIX.

Putting which four singular Chapters together, and along-
side of them numerous hints, and even direct utterances,
scattered over these Writings of his, we come upon the start-
ling, yet not quite unlooked-for conclusion, that Teufelsdröckh
is one of those who consider Society, properly so called, to
be as good as extinct ; and that only the Gregarious feelings,
and old inherited habitudes, at this juncture, hold us from
Dispersion, and universal national, civil, domestic and personal war ! He says expressly : ' For the last three centuries,
' above all, for the last three quarters of a century, that same
' Pericardial Nervous Tissue (as we named it) of Religion,
' where lies the Life-essence of Society, has been smote at and
' perforated, needfully and needlessly ; till now it is quite rent
' into shreds ; and Society, long pining, diabetic, consump-
' tive, can be regarded as defunct ; for those spasmodic, gal-
' vanic sprawlings are not life ; neither indeed will they en-
' dure, galvanise as you may, beyond two days.'

' Call ye that a Society,' cries he again, ' where there is no
' longer any Social Idea extant ; not so much as the Idea of a
' common Home, but only of a common, over-crowded Lodg-
' ing-house ? Where each, isolated, regardless of his neigh-
' bour, turned against his neighbour, clutches what he can

' get, and cries " Mine!" and calls it Peace, because, in the
' cut-purse and cut-throat Scramble, no steel knives, but only
' a far cunninger sort, can be employed ? Where Friendship,
' Communion, has become an incredible tradition ; and your
' holiest Sacramental Supper is a smoking Tavern Dinner,
' with Cook for Evangelist ? Where your Priest has no
' tongue but for plate-licking: and your high Guides and
' Governors cannot guide ; but on all hands hear it passion-
' ately proclaimed : *Laissez faire ;* Leave us alone of *your*
' guidance, such light is darker than darkness ; eat you your
' wages, and sleep!

' Thus, too,' continues he, ' does an observant eye discern
' everywhere that saddest spectacle : The Poor perishing, like
' neglected, foundered Draught-Cattle, of Hunger and Over-
' work ; the Rich, still more wretchedly, of Idleness, Satiety,
' and Overgrowth. The Highest in rank, at length, without
' honour from the Lowest ; scarcely, with a little mouth-
' honour, as from tavern-waiters who expect to put it in the
' bill. Once sacred Symbols fluttering as empty Pageants,
' whereof men grudge even the expense ; a World becoming
' dismantled : in one word, the CHURCH fallen speechless, from
' obesity and apoplexy ; the STATE shrunken into a Police-
' Office, straitened to get its pay !"

We might ask, are there many ' observant eyes,' belonging
to Practical men, in England or elsewhere, which have descried
these phenomena ; or is it only from the mystic elevation of a
German *Wahngasse* that such wonders are visible ? Teufelsdröckh contends that the aspect of a ' deceased or expiring
Society ' fronts us everywhere, so that whoso runs may read.
' What, for example,' says he, ' is the universally-arrogated
' Virtue, almost the sole remaining Catholic Virtue, of these
' days ? For some half century, it has been the thing you
' name, "Independence." Suspicion of "Servility," of rever-
' ence for Superiors the very dogleech is anxious to disavow.
' Fools ! Were your Superiors worthy to govern, and you
' worthy to obey, reverence for them were even your only pos-
' sible freedom. Independence, in all kinds, is rebellion ; if
' unjust rebellion, why parade it, and everywhere prescribe ?'

But what then? Are we returning, as Rousseau prayed, to the state of Nature? 'The Soul Politic having departed,' says Teufelsdröckh, 'what can follow but that the Body Pol-'itic be decently interred, to avoid putrescence? Liberals, 'Economists, Utilitarians enough I see marching with its 'bier, and chaunting loud pæans, towards the funeral-pile, 'where, amid wailings from some, and saturnalian revelries 'from the most, the venerable Corpse is to be burnt. Or, in 'plain words, that these men, Liberals, Utilitarians, or what-'soever they are called, will ultimately carry their point, and 'dissever and destroy most existing Institutions of Society, 'seems a thing which has some time ago ceased to be doubtful.

'Do we not see a little subdivision of the grand Utilitarian 'Armament come to light even in insulated England? A 'living nucleus, that will attract and grow, does at length 'appear there also; and under curious phasis; properly as 'the inconsiderable fag-end, and so far in the rear of the 'others as to fancy itself the van. Our European Mechanis-'ers are a sect of boundless diffusion, activity, and coöpera-'tive spirit: has not Utilitarianism flourished in high places of 'Thought, here among ourselves, and in every European coun-'try, at some time or other, within the last fifty years? If now 'in all countries, except perhaps England, it has ceased to 'flourish, or indeed to exist, among Thinkers, and sunk to 'Journalists and the popular mass,—who sees not that, as 'hereby it no longer preaches, so the reason is, it now needs 'no Preaching, but is in full universal Action, the doctrine 'everywhere known, and enthusiastically laid to heart? The 'fit pabulum, in these times, for a certain rugged workshop-'intellect and heart, nowise without their corresponding 'workshop-strength and ferocity, it requires but to be stated 'in such scenes to make proselytes enough.—Admirably cal-'culated for destroying, only not for rebuilding! It spreads 'like a sort of Dog-madness; till the whole World-kennel 'will be rabid: then woe to the Huntsmen, with or without 'their whips! They should have given the quadrupeds water,' adds he; 'the water, namely, of Knowledge and of Life, 'while it was yet time.'

Thus, if Professor Teufelsdröckh can be relied on, we are at this hour in a most critical condition; beleaguered by that boundless 'Armament of Mechanisers' and Unbelievers, threatening to strip us bare! 'The World,' says he, 'as it 'needs must, is under a process of devastation and waste, 'which, whether by silent assiduous corrosion, or open quick-'er combustion, as the case chances, will effectually enough 'annihilate the past Forms of Society; replace them with 'what it may. For the present, it is contemplated that when 'man's whole Spiritual Interests are once *divested*, these in-'numerable stript-off Garments shall mostly be burnt; but 'the sounder Rags among them be quilted together into one 'huge Irish watch-coat for the defence of the Body only!'—This, we think, is but Job's news to the humane reader.

'Nevertheless,' cries Teufelsdröckh, 'who can hinder it; 'who is there that can clutch into the wheel-spokes of Destiny, 'and say to the Spirit of the Time : Turn back, I command 'thee?—Wiser were it that we yielded to the Inevitable and 'Inexorable, and accounted even this the best.'

Nay, might not an attentive Editor, drawing his own inferences from what stands written, conjecture that Teufelsdröckh individually had yielded to this same 'Inevitable and Inexorable' heartily enough; and now sat waiting the issue, with his natural diabolico-angelical Indifference, if not even Placidity? Did we not hear him complain that the World was a 'huge Ragfair,' and the 'rags and tatters of old Symbols' were raining down everywhere, like to drift him in, and suffocate him? What with those 'unhunted Helots' of his; and the uneven *sic-vos-non-vobis* pressure, and hard-crashing collision he is pleased to discern in existing things; what with the so hateful 'empty Masks,' full of beetles and spiders, yet glaring out on him, from their glass-eyes, 'with a ghastly affecta-tion of life,'—we feel entitled to conclude him even willing that much should be thrown to the Devil, so it were but done gently! Safe himself in that 'Pinnacle of Weissnichtwo,' he would consent, with a tragic solemnity, that the monster UTILITARIA, held back, indeed, and moderated by nose-rings, halters, foot-shackles, and every conceivable modification of rope, should go forth to do her work ;—to tread down old ruinous Palaces and Temples, with her broad hoof, till the whole were trodden down, that new and better might be built! Remarkable in this point of view are the following sentences.

'Society,' says he, 'is not dead : that Carcass, which you call 'dead Society, is but her mortal coil which she has shuffled 'off, to assume a nobler; she herself, through perpetual 'metamorphoses, in fairer and fairer development, has to live 'till Time also merge in Eternity. Wheresoever two or three 'Living Men are gathered together, there is Society; or there 'it will be, with its cunning mechanisms and stupendous 'structures, overspreading this little Globe, and reaching up- 'wards to Heaven and downwards to Gehenna : for always, 'under one or the other figure it has two authentic Revela- 'tions, of a God and of a Devil ; the Pulpit, namely, and the 'Gallows.'

Indeed, we already heard him speak of 'Religion, in un- noticed nooks, weaving for herself new Vestures ;'—Teufels- dröckh himself being one of the loom-treadles? Elsewhere he quotes without censure that strange aphorism of Saint-Simon's, concerning which and whom so much were to be said : '*L'age 'd'or, qu'une aveugle tradition a placé jusqu'ici dans le passé, est 'devant nous ;* The golden age, which a blind tradition has 'hitherto placed in the Past, is Before us.'—But listen again :

'When the Phœnix is fanning her funeral pyre, will there 'not be sparks flying! Alas, some millions of men, and among 'them such as a Napoleon, have already been licked into that 'high-eddying Flame, and like moths consumed there. Still 'also have we to fear that incautious beards will get singed.

'For the rest, in what year of grace such Phœnix-cremation 'will be completed, you need not ask. The law of Persever- 'ance is among the deepest in man : by nature he hates 'change ; seldom will he quit his old house till it has actually 'fallen about his ears. Thus have I seen Solemnities linger 'as Ceremonies, sacred Symbols as idle Pageants, to the ex- 'tent of three hundred years and more after all life and sacred- 'ness had evaporated out of them. And then, finally, what

'time the Phœnix Death-Birth itself will require, depends on
'unseen contingencies.—Meanwhile, would Destiny offer Man-
'kind that after, say two centuries of convulsion and confla-
'gration, more or less vivid, the fire-creation should be accom-
'plished, and we find ourselves again in a Living Society, and
'no longer fighting but working,—were it not perhaps prudent
'in Mankind to strike the bargain?'

Thus is Teufelsdröckh content that old sick Society should
be deliberately burnt (alas! with quite other fuel than spice-
wood); in the faith that she is a Phœnix; and that a new
heavenborn young one will rise out of her ashes! We ourselves, restricted to the duty of Indicator shall forbear commentary. Meanwhile, will not the judicious reader shake his
head, and reproachfully, yet more in sorrow than in anger, say
or think: From a *Doctor utriusque Juris*, titular Professor in
a University, and man to whom hitherto, for his services, Society, bad as she is, has given not only food and raiment (of a
kind) but books, tobacco and gukguk, we expected more
gratitude to his benefactress; and less of a blind trust in the
future, which resembles that rather of a philosophical Fatalist
and Enthusiast, than of a solid householder paying scot and
lot in a Christian country.

CHAPTER VI.

OLD CLOTHES.

As mentioned above, Teufelsdröckh, though a Sansculott-
ist, is in practice probably the politest man extant: his whole
heart and life are penetrated and informed with the spirit of
Politeness: a noble natural Courtesy shines through him,
beautifying his vagaries: like sunlight, making a rosy-fingered,
rainbow-dyed Aurora out of mere aqueous clouds; nay,
brightening London-smoke itself into gold vapour, as from
the crucible of an alchemist. Hear in what earnest though
fantastic wise he expresses himself on this head:

' Shall Courtesy be done only to the rich, and only by the
' rich? In Good-breeding, which differs, if at all, from High-

'breeding, only as it gracefully remembers the rights of others,
'rather than gracefully insists on its own rights, I discern no
'special connexion with wealth or birth: but rather that it lies in
'human nature itself, and is due from all men towards all
'men. Of a truth, were your Schoolmaster at his post, and
'worth any thing when there, this, with so much else, would be
'reformed. Nay, each man were then also his neighbour's
'schoolmaster; till at length a rude-visaged, unmannered
'Peasant could no more be met with, than a Peasant unac-
'quainted with botanical Physiology, or who felt not that the
'clod he broke was created in Heaven.

'For whether thou bear a sceptre or a sledge-hammer, art
'thou not ALIVE; is not this thy brother ALIVE? "There is
'but one Temple in the world," says Novalis, "and that Tem-
'ple is the Body of Man. Nothing is holier than this high
'Form. Bending before men is a reverence done to this Rev-
'elation in the Flesh. We touch Heaven, when we lay our
'hands on a human Body."

'On which ground, I would fain carry it farther than most
'do; and whereas the English Johnson only bowed to every
'Clergyman, or man with a shovel-hat, I would bow to every
'Man with any sort of hat, or with no hat whatever. Is he
'not a Temple, then; the visible Manifestation and Imper-
'sonation of the Divinity? And yet, alas, such indiscrimi-
'nate bowing serves not. For there is a Devil dwells in man,
'as well as a Divinity; and too often the bow is but pocketed
'by the *former*. It would go to the pocket of Vanity (which
'is your clearest phasis of the Devil, in these times); therefore
'must we withhold it.

'The gladder am I, on the other hand, to do reverence to
'those Shells and outer Husks of the Body, wherein no devil-
'ish passion any longer lodges, but only the pure emblem and
'effigies of Man: I mean, to Empty, or even to Cast Clothes.
'Nay, is it not to Clothes that most men do reverence: to the
'fine frogged broad-cloth, nowise to the "straddling animal
'with bandy legs" which it holds, and makes a Dignitary of?
'Who ever saw any Lord my-lorded in tattered blanket, fast-
'ened with wooden skewer? Nevertheless, I say, there is in such

'worship a shade of hypocrisy, a practical deception : for
'how often does the Body appropriate what was meant for the
'Cloth only ! Whoso would avoid Falsehood, which is the
'essence of all Sin, will perhaps see good to take a different
'course. That reverence which cannot act without obstruc-
'tion and perversion when the Clothes are full, may have free
'course when they are empty. Even as, for Hindoo Worship-
'pers, the Pagoda is not less sacred than the God ; so do I
'too worship the hollow cloth Garment with equal fervour, as
'when it contained the Man ; nay, with more, for I now fear
'no deception, of myself or of others.

'Did not King *Toomtabard*, or, in other words, John Balliol,
'reign long over Scotland ; the man John Balliol being quite
'gone, and only the "Toom Tabard" (Empty Gown) remain-
'ing? What still dignity dwells in a suit of Cast Clothes !
'How meekly it bears its honours ! No haughty looks, no
'scornful gesture : silent and serene, it fronts the world ;
'neither demanding worship, nor afraid to miss it. The Hat
'still carries the physiognomy of its Head : but the vanity
'and the stupidity, and goose-speech which was the sign of
'these two, are gone. The Coat-arm is stretched out, but
'not to strike ; the Breeches, in modest simplicity, depend at
'ease, and now at last have a graceful flow ; the Waistcoat
'hides no evil passion, no riotous desire ; hunger or thirst now
'dwells not in it. Thus all is purged from the grossness of
'sense, from the carking cares and foul vices of the World ;
'and rides there, on its Clothes-horse ; as, on a Pegasus,
'might some skyey Messenger, or purified Apparition, visit-
'ing our low Earth.

'Often, while I sojourned in that monstrous tuberosity of
'Civilized Life, the Capital of England ; and meditated and
'questioned Destiny, under that ink-sea of vapour, black,
'thick, and multifarious as Spartan broth ; and was one lone
'Soul amid those grinding millions ;—often have I turned in-
'to their Old-Clothes Market to worship. With awe-struck
'heart I walk through that Monmouth Street, with its empty
'Suits, as through a Sanhedrim of stainless Ghosts. Silent
'are they, but expressive in their silence : the past witnesses

'and instruments of Woe and Joy, of Passions, Virtues,
'Crimes, and all the fathomless tumult of Good and Evil in
'"the Prison men call Life." Friends! trust not the heart of
'that man for whom old Clothes are not venerable. Watch,
'too, with reverence, that bearded Jewish Highpriest, who
'with hoarse voice, like some Angel of Doom, summons them
'from the four winds! On his head, like the Pope, he has
'three Hats,—a real triple tiara; on either hand, are the
'similitude of wings, whereon the summoned Garments come
'to alight; and ever, as he slowly cleaves the air, sounds forth
'his deep fearful note, as if through a trumpet he were pro-
'claiming: "Ghosts of Life, come to Judgment!" Reck not,
'ye fluttering Ghosts he will purify you in his Purgatory,
'with fire and with water; and, one day, new-created ye shall
'reappear. Oh! let him in whom the flame of Devotion is
'ready to go out, who has never worshipped, and knows not
'what to worship, pace and repace, with austerest thought, the
'pavement of Monmouth Street, and say whether his heart
'and his eyes still continue dry. If Field Lane, with its long
'fluttering rows of yellow handkerchiefs, be a Dionysius' Ear,
'where, in stifled jarring hubbub, we hear the Indictment
'which Poverty and Vice bring against lazy Wealth, that it
'has left them there cast out and trodden under foot of Want,
'Darkness, and the Devil,—then is Monmouth Street a Mirza's
'Hill, where, in motley vision, the whole Pageant of Exist-
'ence passes awfully before us; with its wail and jubilee, mad
'loves and mad hatreds, church-bells and gallows-ropes, farce-
'tragedy, beast-godhood,—the Bedlam of Creation!'

To most men, as it does to ourselves, all this will seem over-
charged. We too have walked through Monmouth Street;
but with little feeling of 'Devotion:' probably in part because the contemplative process is so fatally broken in upon
by the brood of money-changers, who nestle in that Church,
and importune the worshipper with merely secular proposals.
Whereas Teufelsdröckh might be in that happy middle-state,
which leaves to the Clothes-broker no hope either of sale or
of purchase, and so be allowed to linger there without moles-

tation.—Something we would have given to see the little phil
osophical figure, with its steeple-hat and loose flowing skirts,
and eyes in a fine frenzy, 'pacing and repacing in austerest
thought' that foolish Street; which to him was a true Del-
phic avenue, and supernatural Whispering-gallery, where the
'Ghost of Life' rounded strange secrets in his ear. O thou
philosophic Teufelsdröckh, that listenest while others only
gabble, and with thy quick tympanum hearest the grass
grow!

At the same time is it not strange that, in Paperbag Documents destined for an English Work, there exists nothing like
an authentic diary of this his sojourn in London; and of his
Meditations among the Clothes-shops only the obscurest emblematic shadows? Neither, in conversation (for, indeed, he
was not a man to pester you with his Travels), have we heard
him more than allude to the subject.

For the rest, however, it cannot be uninteresting that we
here find how early the significance of Clothes had dawned on
the now so distinguished Clothes-Professor. Might we but
fancy it to have been even in Monmouth Street, at the bottom
of our own English 'ink-sea,' that this remarkable Volume
first took being, and shot forth its salient point in his soul,—
as in Chaos did the Egg of Eros, one day to be hatched into
a Universe!

CHAPTER VII.

ORGANIC FILAMENTS.

For us, who happen to live while the World-Phœnix is
burning herself, and burning so slowly that, as Teufelsdröckh
calculates, it were a handsome bargain would she engage to
have done 'within two centuries,' there seems to lie but an
ashy prospect. Not altogether so, however, does the Professor figure it. 'In the living subject,' says he, 'change is wont
' to be gradual: thus, while the serpent sheds its old skin,
' the new is already formed beneath. Little knowest thou of
' the burning of a World-Phœnix, who fanciest that she must
' first burn out, and lie as a dead cinereous heap; and there-

' from the young one start up by miracle, and fly heavenward.
' Far otherwise! In that Fire-whirlwind, Creation and De-
' struction proceed together; ever as the ashes of the Old are
' blown about, do organic filaments of the New mysteriously
' spin themselves: and amid the rushing and the waving of
' the Whirlwind-Element, come tones of a melodious Death-
' song, which end not but in tones of a more melodious Birth-
' song. Nay, look into the Fire-whirlwind with thy own eyes,
' and thou wilt see.' Let us actually look, then: to poor individuals, who cannot expect to live two centuries, those same
organic filaments, mysteriously spinning themselves, will be
the best part of the spectacle. First, therefore, this of Mankind in general:

' In vain thou deniest it,' says the Professor; ' thou *art* my
' Brother. Thy very Hatred, thy very Envy, those foolish
' Lies thou tellest of me in thy splenetic humour: what is all
' this but an inverted Sympathy? Were I a Steam-engine,
' wouldst thou take the trouble to tell Lies of me? Not thou!
' I should grind all unheeded, whether badly or well.

' Wondrous truly are the bonds that unite us one and all;
' whether by the soft binding of Love, or the iron chaining of
' Necessity, as we like to choose it. More than once have I
' said to myself of some perhaps whimsically strutting Figure,
' such as provokes whimsical thoughts: "Wert thou, my
' little Brotherkin, suddenly covered up within the largest
' imaginable Glass-bell,—what a thing it were, not for thyself
' only but for the world! Post Letters, more or fewer, from
' all the four winds, impinge against thy Glass walls, but have
' to drop unread: neither from within comes there question
' or response into any Postbag; thy Thoughts fall into no
' friendly ear or heart, thy Manufacture into no purchasing
' hand; thou art no longer a circulating venous-arterial Heart,
' that, taking and giving, circulatest through all Space and all
' Time: there has a Hole fallen out in the immeasurable, uni-
' versal World-tissue, which must be darned up again!"

' Such venous-arterial circulation, of Letters, verbal Mes-
' sages, paper and other Packages, going out from him and
' coming in, are a blood-circulation, visible to the eye; but

'the finer nervous circulation, by which all things, the mi-
'nutest that he does, minutely influence all men, and the
'very look of his face blesses or curses whomso it lights on,
'and so generates ever new blessing or new cursing : all this
'you cannot see, but only imagine. I say, there is not a
'red Indian, hunting by Lake Winnipic, can quarrel with his
'squaw, but the whole world must smart for it : will not the
'price of beaver rise ?   It is a mathematical fact that the cast-
'ing of this pebble from my hand alters the centre-of-gravity
'of the Universe.

   'If now an existing generation of men stand so woven to-
'gether, not less indissolubly does generation with genera-
'tion.   Hast thou ever meditated on that word, Tradition :
'how we inherit not Life only, but all the garniture and form
'of Life ; and work, and speak, and even think and feel, as
'our Fathers, and primeval grandfathers, from the beginning,
'have given it us ?—Who printed thee, for example, this un-
'pretending Volume on the Philosophy of Clothes ?   Not the
'Herren Stillschweigen and Company : but Cadmus of
'Thebes, Faust of Mentz, and innumerable others whom thou
'knowest not.   Had there been no Mœsogothic Ulfila, there
'had been no English Shakspeare, or a different one.   Sim-
'pleton ! it was Tubalcain that made thy very Tailor's needle,
'and sewed that court suit of thine.

   'Yes, truly, if Nature is one, and a living indivisible whole,
'much more is Mankind, the Image that reflects and creates
'Nature, without which Nature were not.   As palpable life-
'streams in that wondrous Individual Mankind, among so
'many life-streams that are not palpable, flow-on those main-
'currents of what we call Opinion ; as preserved in Institu-
'tions, Politics, Churches, above all in Books.   Beautiful it is
'to understand and know that a Thought did never yet die ;
'that as thou, the originator thereof, hast gathered it and
'created it from the whole Past, so thou wilt transmit it to
'the whole Future.   It is thus that the heroic Heart, the see-
'ing Eye of the first times, still feels and sees in us of the
'latest ; that the Wise Man stands ever encompassed, and
'spiritually embraced, by a cloud of witnesses and brothers ;

and there is a living, literal *Communion of Saints*, wide as
" the World itself, and as the History of the World.

' Noteworthy also, and serviceable for the progress of this
' same Individual, wilt thou find his subdivision into Genera-
' tions. Generations are as the Days of toilsome Mankind ;
' Death and Birth are the vesper and the matin bells, that
' summon Mankind to sleep, and to rise refreshed for new
' advancement. What the Father has made, the Son can
' make and enjoy ; but has also work of his own appointed
' him. Thus all things wax, and roll onwards ; Arts, Estab-
' lishments, Opinions, nothing is completed, but ever com-
' pleting. Newton has learned to see what Kepler saw ; but
' there is also a fresh heaven-derived force in Newton ; he
' must mount to still higher points of vision. So to the He-
' brew Lawgiver is, in due time, followed by an Apostle of the
' Gentiles. In the business of Destruction, as this also is
' from time to time a necessary work, thou findest a like
' sequence and perseverance : for Luther it was as yet hot
' enough to stand by that burning of the Pope's Bull ; Vol-
' taire could not warm himself at the glimmering ashes, but
' required quite other fuel. Thus likewise, I note, the Eng-
' lish Whig has, in the second generation, become an English
' Radical ; who, in the third again, it is to be hoped, will be-
' come an English Rebuilder. Find mankind where thou
' wilt, thou findest it in living movement, in progress faster or
' slower : the Phœnix soars aloft, hovers with outstretched
' wings, filling Earth with her music ; or, as now, she sinks,
' and with spheral swan-song immolates herself in flame, that
' she may soar the higher and sing the clearer.'

Let the friends of social order, in such a disastrous period,
lay this to heart, and derive from it any little comfort they
can. We subjoin another passage, concerning Titles :

' Remark, not without surprise,' says Teufelsdröckh, ' how
' all high Titles of Honour come hitherto from Fighting. Your
' *Herzog* (Duke, *Dux*) is Leader of Armies ; your Earl (*Jarl*) is
' Strong Man ; your Marshal cavalry Horse-shoer. A Millen-
' nium, or reign of Peace and Wisdom, having from of old
' been prophesied, and becoming now daily more and more

' indubitable, may it not be apprehended that such **Fighting-**
' titles will cease to be palatable, and new and higher need to
' be devised ?

' The only Title wherein I, with confidence, trace eternity,
' is that of King. *König* (King), anciently *Könning* means
' Kenning (Cunning), or which is the same thing, Can-ning.
' Ever must the Sovereign of Mankind be fitly entitled
' King.'

' Well, also,' says he elsewhere, ' was it written by Theolo-
' gians : a King rules by divine right. He carries in him an
' authority from God, or man will never give it him. Can I
' choose my own King ? I can choose my own King Popinjay,
' and play what farce or tragedy I may with him : but he who
' is to be my Ruler, whose will is to be higher than my will,
' was chosen for me in Heaven. Neither except in such Obe-
' dience to the Heaven-chosen is Freedom so much as con-
' ceivable.'

The Editor will here admit that, among all the wondrous
provinces of Teufelsdröckh's spiritual world, there is none he
walks in with such astonishment, hesitation, and even pain, as
in the Political. How, with our English love of Ministry and
Opposition, and that generous conflict of Parties, mind warm-
ing itself against mind in their mutual wrestle for the Public
Good, by which wrestle, indeed, is our invaluable Constitution
kept warm and alive ; how shall we domesticate ourselves in
this spectral Necropolis, or rather City both of the Dead and
of the Unborn, where the Present seems little other than an
inconsiderable Film dividing the Past and the Future ? In
those dim longdrawn expanses, all is so immeasurable ; much
so disastrous, ghastly ; your very radiances, and straggling
light-beams, have a supernatural character. And then with
such an indifference, such a prophetic peacefulness (accounting the inevitably-coming as already here, to him all one
whether it be distant by centuries or only by days), does he
sit ;—and live, you would say, rather in any other age than
his own ! It is our painful duty to announce, or repeat, that,
looking into this man, we discern a deep, silent, slow-burning,

inextinguishable Radicalism, such as fills us with shuddering admiration.

Thus, for example, he appears to make little even of the Elective Franchise ; at least so we interpret the following : ' Sat-' isfy yourselves,' he says, ' by universal, indubitable experi-' ment, even as ye are now doing or will do, whether FREEDOM, ' heavenborn and leading heavenward, and so vitally essential ' for us all, cannot peradventure be mechanically hatched and ' brought to light in that same Ballot-Box of yours ; or at worst ' in some other discoverable or devisable Box, Edifice, or Steam-' mechanism. It were a mighty convenience ; and beyond all ' feats of manufacture witnessed hitherto.' Is Teufelsdröckh acquainted with the British Constitution, even slightly ?—He says, under another figure : ' But after all, were the problem, ' as indeed it now everywhere is, To rebuild your old House ' from the top downwards (since you must live in it the while), ' what better, what other, than the Representative Machine ' will serve your turn ? Meanwhile, however, mock me not ' with the name of Free, "when you have but knit up my ' chains into ornamental festoons." '—Or what will any member of the Peace Society make of such an assertion as this : ' The lower people everywhere desire War. Not so unwisely ; ' there is then a demand for lower people—to be shot ! '

Gladly, therefore, do we emerge form those soul-confusing labyrinths of speculative Radicalism, into somewhat clearer regions. Here, looking round, as was our hest, for ' organic filaments,' we ask, may not this, touching ' Hero-Worship,' be of the number? It seems of a cheerful character ; yet so quaint, so mystical, one knows not what, or how little, may lie under it. Our readers shall look with their own eyes :

' True is it that, in these days, man can do almost all things, ' only not obey. True likewise that whoso cannot obey can-' not be free, still less bear rule ; he that is the inferior of ' nothing, can be superior of nothing, the equal of nothing. ' Nevertheless, believe not that man has lost his faculty of Rev-' erence ; that if it slumber in him, it has gone dead. Pain-' ful for man is that same rebellious Independence, when it has ' become inevitable ; only in loving companionship with his

' fellows does he feel safe ; only in reverently bowing down
' before the Higher does he feel himself exalted.

' Or what if the character of our so troublous Era lay even in
' this : that man had forever cast away Fear, which is the
' lower ; but not yet risen into perennial Reverence, which is
' the higher and highest ?

' Meanwhile, observe with joy, so cunningly has Nature
' ordered it, that whatsoever man ought to obey he cannot but
' obey. Before no faintest revelation of the Godlike did he
' ever stand irreverent ; least of all, when the Godlike shewed
' itself revealed in his fellow-man. Thus is there a true relig-
' ious Loyalty forever rooted in his heart ; nay, in all ages,
' even in ours, it manifests itself as a more or less orthodox
' *Hero-worship.* In which fact, that Hero-worship exists, has
' existed, and will for ever exist, universally among Mankind,
' mayest thou discern the corner-stone of living-rock, whereon
' all Polities for the remotest time may stand secure.'

Do our readers discern any such corner-stone, or even so
much as what Teufelsdröckh is looking at ? He exclaims,
' Or hast thou forgotten Paris and Voltaire ? How the aged,
' withered man, though but a Sceptic, Mocker, and millinery
' Court-poet, yet because even he seemed the Wisest, Best,
' could drag mankind at his chariot-wheels, so that princes
' coveted a smile from him, and the loveliest of France would
' have laid their hair beneath his feet ! All Paris was one vast
' Temple of Hero-worship ; though their Divinity, moreover,
' was of feature too apish.

' But if such things,' continues he, ' were done in the dry
' tree, what will be done in the green ? If, in the most parched
' season of Man's History, in the most parched spot of Europe,
' when Parisian life was at best but a scientific *Hortus Siccus,*
' bedizened with some Italian Gumflowers, such virtue could
' come out of it ; what is to be looked for when Life again
' waves leafy and bloomy, and your Hero-Divinity shall have
' nothing apelike, but be wholly human ? Know that there is
' in man a quite indestructible Reverence for whatsoever holds
' of Heaven, or even plausibly counterfeits such holding.
' Shew the dullest clodpole, shew the haughtiest featherhead,

' that a soul Higher than himself is actually here ; were his
' knees stiffened into brass, he must down and worship.'

Organic filaments, of a more authentic sort, mysteriously
spinning themselves, some will perhaps discover in the following passage :

' There is no Church, sayest thou ?   The voice of Prophecy
' has gone dumb ?   This is even what I dispute : but, in any
' case, hast thou not still Preaching enough ?   A Preaching
' Friar settles himself in every village ; and builds a pulpit,
' which he calls Newspaper.   Therefrom he • preaches what
' most momentous doctrine is in him, for man's salvation ;
' and dost not thou listen, and believe ?   Look well, thou seest
' everywhere a new Clergy of the Mendicant Orders, some
' bare-footed, some almost bare-backed, fashion itself into
' shape, and teach and preach, zealously enough, for copper
' alms and the love of God.   These break in pieces the ancient
' idols ; and, though themselves too often reprobate, as idol-
' breakers are wont to be, mark out the sites of new Churches,
' where the true God-ordained, that are to follow, may find
' audience, and minister.   Said I not, Before the old skin was
' shed, the new had formed itself beneath it ? '

Perhaps, also, in the following ; wherewith we now hasten
to knit up this ravelled sleeve :

' But there is no Religion ? ' reiterates the Professor.
' Fool !   I tell thee, there is.   Hast thou well considered all
' that lies in this immeasurable froth-ocean we name LITERA-
' TURE ?   Fragments of a genuine Church-*Homiletic* lie scat-
' tered there, which Time will assort : nay fractions even of a
' *Liturgy* could I point out.   And knowest thou no Prophet,
' even in the vesture, environment, and dialect of this age ?
' None to whom the Godlike had revealed itself, through all
' meanest and highest forms of the Common ; and by him
' been again prophetically revealed : in whose inspired melody,
' even in these rag-gathering and rag-burning days, Man's
' Life again begins, were it but afar off, to be divine ?   Know-
' est thou none such ?   I know him, and name him—Goethe.

' But thou as yet standest in no Temple ; joinest in no
' Psalm-worship ; feelest well that, where there is no minister-

' ing Priest, the people perish ? Be of comfort ! Thou art
' not alone, if thou have Faith. Spake we not of a Commun-
' ion of Saints, unseen, yet not unreal, accompanying and
' brother-like embracing thee, so thou be worthy ? Their
' heroic Sufferings rise up melodiously together to Heaven,
' out of all lands, and out of all times, as a sacred *Miserere ;*
' their heroic Actions also, as a boundless, everlasting Psalm
' of Triumph. Neither say that thou hast now no Symbol of
' the Godlike. Is not God's Universe a Symbol of the God-
' like ; is not Immensity a Temple ; is not Man's History, and
' Men's History, a perpetual Evangel ? Listen, and for organ-
' music thou wilt ever, as of old, hear the Morning Stars sing
' together.'

CHAPTER VIII.

NATURAL SUPERNATURALISM.

It is in his stupendous Section, headed *Natural Supernaturalism*, that the Professor first becomes a Seer ; and, after
long effort, such as we have witnessed, finally subdues under
his feet this refractory Clothes-Philosophy, and takes victori-
ous possession thereof. Phantasms enough he has had
to struggle with ; ' Cloth-webs and Cob-webs,' of Imperial
Mantles, Superannuated Symbols, and what not : yet still did
he courageously pierce through. Nay, worst of all, two quite
mysterious, world-embracing Phantasms, TIME and SPACE, have
ever hovered round him, perplexing and bewildering : but
with these also he now resolutely grapples, these also he victoriously rends asunder. In a word, he has looked fixedly on
Existence, till, one after the other, its earthly hulls and garnitures have all melted away ; and now, to his rapt vision, the
interior celestial Holy of Holies lies disclosed.

Here therefore properly it is that the Philosophy of Clothes
attains to Transcendentalism ; this last leap, can we but clear
it, takes us safe into the promised land, where *Palingenesia*, in
all senses, may be considered as beginning. ' Courage, then !'
may our Diogenes exclaim, with better right than Diogenes
the First once did. This stupendous Section we, after long

painful meditation, have found not to be unintelligible ; but
on the contrary to grow clear, nay radiant, and all-illuminat-
ing. Let the reader, turning on it what utmost force of speculative intellect is in him, do his part; as we, by judicious
selection and adjustment, shall study to do ours :

'Deep has been, and is, the significance of Miracles,' thus
quietly begins the Professor ; 'far deeper perhaps than we
' imagine. Meanwhile, the question of questions were : What
' specially is a Miracle? To that Dutch King of Siam, an
' icicle had been a miracle ; whoso had carried with him an
' air-pump, and vial of vitriolic ether, might have worked a
' a miracle. To my horse again, who unhappily is still more
' unscientific, do not I work a miracle, and magical " *Open*
' *sesame !* " every time I please to pay twopence, and open for
' him an impassable *Schlagbaum,* or shut Turnpike ?

' "But is not a real Miracle simply a violation of the Laws
' of Nature?" ask several. Whom I answer by this new ques-
' tion : What are the Laws of Nature? To me perhaps the
' rising of one from the dead were no violation of these Laws,
' but a confirmation ; were some far deeper Law, now first
' penetrated into, and by Spiritual Force, even as the rest
' have all been, brought to bear on us with its Material
' Force.

' Here too may some inquire, not without astonishment :
' On what ground shall one, that can make Iron swim, come
' and declare that therefore he can teach Religion? To us,
' truly, of the Nineteenth Century, such declaration were inept
' enough; which nevertheless to our fathers, of the First Cen-
' tury, was full of meaning.

' "But is it not the deepest Law of Nature that she be con-
' stant?" cries an illuminated class : "Is not the Machine of
' the Universe fixed to move by unalterable rules?" Probable
' enough, good friends : nay, I too must believe that the God,
' whom ancient inspired men assert to be " without variable-
' ness or shadow of turning," does indeed never change ; that
' Nature, that the Universe, which no one whom it so pleases
' can be prevented from calling a Machine, does move by the
' most unalterable rules. And now of you too I make the old

'inquiry : What those same unalterable rules, forming the
' complete Statute-Book of Nature, may possibly be ?

'They stand written in our Works of Science, say you ; in
' the accumulated records of man's Experience ?—Was Man
' with his Experience present at the Creation, then, to see how
' it all went on ? Have any deepest scientific individuals yet
' dived down to the foundations of the Universe, and gauged
' every thing there ? Did the Maker take them into His
' counsel ; that they read His ground-plan of the incompre-
' hensible All ; and can say, This stands marked therein, and
' no more than this ? Alas ! not in anywise ! These scientific
' individuals have been nowhere but where we also are ; have
' seen some handbreadths deeper than we see into the Deep
' that is infinite, without bottom as without shore.

'Laplace's Book on the Stars, wherein he exhibits that cer-
' tain Planets, with their Satellites, gyrate round our worthy
' Sun, at a rate and in a course, which, by greatest good for-
' tune, he and the like of him have succeeded in detecting,—
' is to me as precious as to another. But is this what thou
' namest "Mechanism of the Heavens," and "System of the
' World ;" this, wherein Sirius and the Pleiades, and all Her-
' schel's Fifteen thousand Suns per minute, being left out,
' some paltry handful of Moons, and inert Balls, had been—
' looked at, nicknamed, and marked in the Zodiacal Waybill ;
' so that we can now prate of their Whereabout ; their How,
' their Why, their What, being hid from us as in the signless
' Inane ?

'System of Nature ! To the wisest man, wide as is his
' vision, Nature remains of quite *infinite* depth, of quite infinite
' expansion ; and all Experience thereof limits itself to some
' few computed centuries, and measured square miles. The
' course of Nature's phases, on this our little fraction of a
' Planet, is partially known to us : but who knows what deeper
' courses these depend on ; what infinitely larger Cycle (of
' causes) our little Epicycle revolves on ? To the Minnow
' every cranny and pebble, and quality and accident, of its
' little native Creek may have become familiar : but does the
' Minnow understand the Ocean Tides and periodic Currents,

'the Trade-winds, and Monsoons, and Moon's Eclipses; by all
'which the condition of its little Creek is regulated, and may,
'from time to time (*un*miraculously enough), be quite overset
'and reversed? Such a minnow is man; his Creek this
'Planet Earth; his Ocean the immeasurable All; his Mon-
'soons and periodic Currents the mysterious Course of Provi-
'dence through Æons of Æons.

'We speak of the Volume of Nature: and truly a Volume
'it is,—whose Author and Writer is God. To read it! Dost
'thou, does man, so much as well know the Alphabet thereof?
'With its Words, Sentences, and grand descriptive Pages,
'poetical and philosophical, spread out through Solar Systems,
'and Thousand's of Years, we shall not try thee. It is a Vol-
'ume written in celestial hieroglyphs, in the true Sacred-writ-
'ing; of which even Prophets are happy that they can read
'here a line and there a line. As for your Institutes, and
'Academies of Science, they strive bravely; and, from amid
'the thick-crowded, inextricably intertwisted hieroglyphic
'writing, pick out, by dexterous combination, some Letters
'in the vulgar Character, and therefrom put together this and
'the other economic Recipe, of high avail in Practice. That
'Nature is more than some boundless Volume of such Recipes,
'or huge, well-nigh inexhaustible Domestic Cookery Book, of
'which the whole secret will in this manner one day evolve it-
'self, the fewest dream.

'Custom,' continues the Professor, 'doth make dotards of
'us all. Consider well, thou wilt find that Custom is the
'greatest of Weavers; and weaves airy raiment for all the
'Spirits of the Universe; whereby indeed these dwell with
'us visibly, as ministering servants, in our houses and work-
'shops; but their spiritual nature becomes, to the most, for-
'ever hidden. Philosophy complains that Custom has hood-
'winked us, from the first; that we do every thing by
'Custom, even Believe by it; that our very Axioms, let us
'boast of Free-thinking as we may, are oftenest simply such
'Beliefs as we have never heard questioned. Nay, what is
'Philosophy throughout but a continual battle against Cus-

'tom; an ever-renewed effort to *transcend* the sphere of blind 'Custom, and so become Transcendental?

'Innumerable are the illusions and legerdemain tricks of 'Custom: but of all these perhaps the cleverest is her knack 'of persuading us that the Miraculous, by simple repetition, 'ceases to be Miraculous. True, it is by this means we live; 'for man must work as well as wonder: and herein is Cus- 'tom so far a kind nurse, guiding him to his true benefit. 'But she is a fond foolish nurse, or rather we are false foolish 'nurslings, when in our resting and reflecting hours, we pro- 'long the same deception. Am I to view the Stupendous 'with stupid indifference, because I have seen it twice, or two 'hundred, or two million times? There is no reason in Na- 'ture or in Art why I should: unless indeed, I am a mere 'Work-Machine, for whom the divine gift of Thought were no 'other than the terrestrial gift of Steam is to the Steam-en- 'gine; a power whereby Cotton might be spun, and money 'and money's worth realised.

'Notable enough too, here as elsewhere, wilt thou find the 'potency of Names; which indeed are but one kind of such 'Custom-woven, wonder-hiding Garments. Witchcraft, and 'all manner of Spectre-work, and Demonology, we have now 'named Madness, and Diseases of the Nerves. Seldom re- 'flecting that still the new question comes upon us: What is 'Madness, what are Nerves? Ever, as before, does Madness 'remain a mysterious-terrific, altogether *infernal* boiling up 'of the Nether Chaotic Deep, through this fair-painted Vision 'of Creation, which swims thereon, which we name the Real. 'Was Luther's Picture of the Devil less a Reality, whether it 'were formed within the bodily eye, or without it? In every 'the wisest soul lies a whole world of internal Madness, an 'authentic Demon-Empire; out of which, indeed, his world 'of Wisdom has been creatively built together, and now rests 'there, as on its dark foundations does a habitable flowery 'Earth-rind.

'But deepest of all illusory Appearances, for hiding Won- 'der, as for many other ends, are your two grand fundamen-

' tal world-enveloping Appearances, SPACE and TIME. These,
' as spun and woven for us from before Birth itself, to clothe
' our celestial ME for dwelling here, and yet to blind it,—lie
' all-embracing, as the universal canvas, or warp and woof,
' whereby all minor Illusions, in this Phantasm Existence,
' weave and paint themselves. In vain, while here on Earth,
' shall you endeavour to strip them off; you can, at best, but
' rend them asunder for moments, and look through.

' Fortunatus had a wishing Hat, which when he put on, and
' wished himself Anywhere, behold he was there. By this
' means had Fortunatus triumphed over Space, he had anni-
' hilated Space; for him there was no Where, but all was
' Here. Were a Hatter to establish himself, in the Wahn-
' gasse of Weissnichtwo, and make felts of this sort for all
' mankind, what a world we should have of it! Still stranger,
' should, on the opposite side of the street, another Hatter
' establish himself; and, as his fellow-craftsman made Space-
' annihilating Hats, make Time annihilating! Of both would
' I purchase, were it with my last groschen; but chiefly of this
' latter. To clap on your felt, and, simply by wishing that
' you were Any*where*, straightway to be *There!* Next to clap
' on your other felt, and simply by wishing that you were Any-
' *when*, and straightway to be *Then!* This were indeed the
' grander: shooting at will from the Fire-Creation of the
' World to its Fire-Consummation; here historically present
' in the First Century, conversing face to face with Paul and
' Seneca; there prophetically in the Thirty-first, conversing
' also face to face with other Pauls and Senecas, who as yet
' stand hidden in the depth of that late Time!

' Or thinkest thou, it were impossible, unimaginable? Is
' the Past annihilated, then, or only past; is the Future non-
' extant or only future? Those mystic faculties of thine,
' Memory and Hope, already answer: already through those
' mystic avenues, thou the Earth-blinded summonest both
' Past and Future, and communest with them, though as yet
' darkly, and with mute beckonings. The curtains of Yester-
' day drop down, the curtains of To-morrow roll up; but
' Yesterday and To-morrow both *are*. Pierce through the

' Time-Element, glance into the Eternal.   Believe what thou
' findest written in the sanctuaries of Man's Soul, even as all
' Thinkers, in all ages, have devoutly read it there : that Time
' and Space are not God, but creations of God ; that with God
' as it is a universal HERE, so it is an everlasting Now.

   ' And seest thou therein any glimpse of IMMORTALITY ?—O
' Heaven !   Is the white Tomb of our Loved One, who died
' from our arms, and had to be left behind us there, which
' rises in the distance, like a pale, mournfully receding Mile
' stone, to tell how many toilsome uncheered miles we have
' journeyed on alone,—but a pale spectral Illusion !   Is the
' lost Friend still mysteriously Here, even as we are Here mys-
' teriously, with God !—Know of a truth that only the Time-
' shadows have perished, or are perishable ; that the real
' Being of whatever was, and whatever is, and whatever will
' be, *is* even now and forever.   This, should it unhappily seem
' new, thou mayst ponder at thy leisure ; for the next twenty
' years, or the next twenty centuries : believe it thou must ;
' understand it thou canst not.

   ' That the Thought-forms, Space and Time, wherein, once
' for all, we are sent into this Earth to live, should condition
' and determine our whole Practical reasonings, conceptions,
' and imagings or imaginings,—seems altogether fit just, and
' unavoidable.   But that they should, furthermore, usurp such
' sway over pure spiritual Meditation, and blind us to the
' wonder everywhere lying close on us, seems nowise so.
' Admit Space and Time to their due rank as Forms of
' Thought ; nay, even, if thou wilt, to their quite undue rank of
' Realities : and consider, then, with thyself how their thin dis-
' guises hide from us the brightest God-effulgences !   Thus,
' were it not miraculous, could I stretch forth my hand, and
' clutch the Sun ?   Yet thou seest me daily stretch forth my
' hand, and therewith clutch many a thing, and swing it hither
' and thither.   Art thou a grown baby, then, to fancy that the
' Miracle lies in miles of distance, or in pounds avoirdupois of
' weight ; and not to see that the true inexplicable God-reveal-
' ing Miracle lies in this, that I can stretch forth my hand at
' all ; that I have free Force to clutch aught therewith ?   In-

' numerable other of this sort are the deceptions, and wonder
' hiding stupefactions, which Space practices on us.

' Still worse is it with regard to Time. Your grand anti-ma-
' gician, and universal wonder-hider, is this same lying Time.
' Had we but the Time-annihilating Hat, to put on for once
' only, we should see ourselves in a World of Miracles, where-
' in all fabled or authentic Thaumaturgy, and feats of Magic,
' were outdone. But unhappily we have not such a Hat; and
' man, poor fool that he is, can seldom and scantily help him
' self without one.

' Were it not wonderful, for instance, had Orpheus, or Am-
' phion, built the walls of Thebes by the mere sound of his
' Lyre? Yet tell me, Who built these walls of Weissnichtwo;
' summoning out all the sandstone rocks, to dance along from
' the *Stein-bruch* (now a huge Troglodyte Chasm, with fright-
' ful green-mantled pools); and shape themselves into Doric
' and Ionic pillars, squared ashlar houses, and noble streets?
' Was it not the still higher Orpheus, or Orpheuses, who, in
' past centuries, by the divine Music of Wisdom, succeeded
' in civilising man? Our highest Orpheus walked in Judea,
' eighteen hundred years ago: his sphere-melody, flowing in
' wild native tones, took captive the ravished souls of men;
' and, being of a truth sphere-melody, still flows and sounds,
' though now with thousandfold Accompaniments, and rich
' symphonies, through all our hearts; and modulates, and
' divinely leads them. Is that a wonder, which happens in
' two hours; and does it cease to be wonderful if happening
' in two million? Not only was Thebes built by the music of
' an Orpheus; but without the music of some inspired Or-
' pheus was no city ever built, no work that man glories in
' ever done.

'Sweep away the Illusion of Time; glance, if thou have
' eyes, from the near moving-cause, to its far distant Mover;
'The stroke that came transmitted through a whole galaxy of
' elastic balls, was it less a stroke than if the last ball only
' had been struck, and sent flying? Oh, could I (with the
' Time-annihilating Hat) transport thee direct from the Begin-
' nings to the Endings, how were thy eyesight unsealed. and

14

'thy heart set flaming in the Light-sea of celestial wonder!
'Then sawest thou that this fair Universe, were it in the
'meanest province thereof, is in very deed the star-domed
'City of God; that through every star, through every grass-
'blade, and most through every Living Soul, the glory of a
'present God still beams. But Nature, which is the Time-
'vesture of God, and reveals Him to the wise, hides Him from
'the foolish.

'Again, could anything be more miraculous than an actual
'authentic Ghost? The English Johnson longed, all his life
'to see one ; but could not, though he went to Cock Lane,
'and thence to the church-vaults, and tapped on coffins.
'Foolish Doctor! Did he never, with the mind's eye as well
'as with the body's, look round him into that full tide
'of human Life he so loved; did he never so much as look
'into Himself? The good Doctor was a Ghost, as actual and
'authentic as heart could wish; well nigh a million of Ghosts
'were travelling the streets by his side. Once more I say,
'sweep away the illusion of Time ; compress the threescore
'years into three minutes : what else was he, what else are
'we? Are we not Spirits, that are shaped into a body, into
'an Appearance ; and that fade away again into air, and In-
'visibility? This is no metaphor, it is a simple scientific *fact ;*
'we start out of Nothingness, take figure, and are Apparitions;
'round us, as round the veriest spectre, is Eternity ; and to
'Eternity minutes are as years and æons. Come there not
'tones of Love and Faith, as from celestial harp-strings, like
'the Song of beatified Souls? And again, do we not squeak and
'gibber (in our discordant, screech-owlish debatings and re-
'criminatings); and glide bodeful and feeble, and fearful ; or
'uproar (*poltern*), and revel in our mad Dance of the Dead,—
'till the scent of the morning-air summons us to our still
'Home ; and dreamy Night becomes awake and Day? Where
'now is Alexander of Macedon : does the steel Host, that
'yelled in fierce battle-shouts, at Issus and Arbela, remain
'behind him ; or have they all vanished utterly, even as per-
'turbed Goblins must? Napoleon too, and his Moscow Re-
'treats and Austerlitz Campaigns! Was it all other than the

'veriest Spectre-hunt; which has now, with its howling tumult
'that made night hideous, flitted away?—Ghosts! There
'are nigh a thousand million walking the Earth openly at
'noontide; some half-hundred have vanished from it, some
'half-hundred have arisen in it, ere thy watch ticks once.

'O Heaven, it is mysterious, it is awful to consider that we
'not only carry each a future Ghost within him; but are, in
'very deed, Ghosts! These Limbs, whence had we them; this
'stormy Force; this life-blood with its burning passion? They
'are dust and shadow; a Shadow-system gathered round our
'ME; wherein through some moments or years, the Divine
'Essence is to be revealed in the Flesh. That warrior on his
'strong war-horse, fire flashes through his eyes; force dwells
'in his arm and heart; but warrior and war-horse are a vision;
'a revealed Force, nothing more. Stately they tread the
'Earth, as if it were a firm substance: fool! the Earth is but
'a film; it cracks in twain, and warrior and war-horse sink
'beyond plummet's sounding. Plummet's? Fantasy herself
'will not follow them. A little while ago they were not; a
'little while and they are not, their very ashes are not.

'So has it been from the beginning, so will it be to the
'end. Generation after generation takes to itself the Form
'of a Body; and forth-issuing from Cimmerian Night, on
'Heaven's mission APPEARS. What Force and Fire is in each
'he expends: one grinding in the mill of Industry; one
'hunter-like climbing the giddy Alpine heights of Science;
'one madly dashed in pieces on the rocks of Strife, in war
'with his fellow:—and then the Heaven-sent is recalled; his
'earthly Vesture falls away, and soon even to Sense becomes
'a Vanished Shadow. Thus, like some wild-flaming, wild-
'thundering train of Heaven's Artillery, does this mysterious
'MANKIND thunder and flame, in long-drawn, quick-succeeding
'grandeur, through the unknown Deep. Thus, like a God-
'created, fire-breathing Spirit-host, we emerge from the
'Inane; haste stormfully across the astonished Earth; then
'plunge again into the Inane. Earth's mountains are levelled,
'and her seas filled up, in our passage: can the Earth, which
'is but dead and a vision, resist Spirits which have reality

'and are alive ?   On the hardest adamant some foot-print of
'us is stamped in ; the last Rear of the host will read traces
'of the earliest Van.   But whence?—O Heaven, whither?
'Sense knows not ; Faith knows not ; only that it is through
'Mystery to Mystery, from God and to God.

> ' "We *are such stuff*
> 'As Dreams are made of, and our little Life
> 'Is rounded with a sleep !" '

CHAPTER IX.

CIRCUMSPECTIVE.

Here then arises the so momentous question : Have many
British Readers actually arrived with us at the new promised
country ; is the Philosophy of Clothes now at last opening
around them ?   Long and adventurous has the journey been :
from those outmost vulgar, palpable Woollen Hulls of Man ;
through his wondrous Flesh-Garments, and his wondrous
Social Garnitures ; inwards to the Garments of his very Soul's
Soul, to Time and Space themselves !   And now does the
Spiritual, eternal Essence of Man, and of Mankind, bared of
such wrappages, begin in any measure to reveal itself?   Can
many readers discern, as through a glass darkly, in huge wavering outlines, some primeval rudiments of Man's Being, what
is changeable divided from what is unchangeable ?   Does
that Earth-Spirit's speech in *Faust :*

> '' Tis thus at the roaring Loom of Time I ply,
> 'And weave for God the Garment thou see'st him by ;'

or that other thousand-times repeated speech of the Magician,
Shakspeare :

> 'And like the baseless fabric of this vision,
> 'The cloudcapt Towers, the gorgeous Palaces,
> 'The solemn Temples, the great Globe itself,
> 'And all which it inherit shall dissolve ;
> 'And like this unsubstantial pageant faded,
> 'Leave not a wrack behind :'

begin to have some meaning for us? In a word, do we at length stand safe in the far region of Poetic Creation and Palingenesia, where that Phœnix Death-Birth of Human Society, and of all Human Things, appears possible, is seen to be inevitable?

Along this most insufficient, unheard-of Bridge, which the Editor, by Heaven's blessing, has now seen himself enabled to conclude if not complete, it cannot be his sober calculation, but only his fond hope, that many have travelled without accident. No firm arch, overspanning the Impassable with paved highway, could the Editor construct; only, as was said, some zigzag series of rafts floating tumultuously thereon. Alas, and the leaps from raft to raft were too often of a breakneck character; the darkness, the nature of the element, all was against us!

Nevertheless, may not here and there one of a thousand, provided with a discursiveness of intellect rare in our day, have cleared the passage, in spite of all? Happy few! little band of Friends! be welcome, be of courage. By degrees, the eye grows accustomed to its new Whereabout; the hand can stretch itself forth to work there: it is in this grand and indeed highest work of Palingenesia that ye shall labour, each according to ability. New labourers will arrive; new Bridges will be built; nay, may not our own poor rope-and-raft Bridge, in your passings and repassings be mended in many a point, till it grow quite firm, passable even for the halt?

Meanwhile, of the innumerable multitude that started with us, joyous and full of hope, where now is the innumerable remainder, whom we see no longer by our side? The most have recoiled, and stand gazing afar off, in unsympathetic astonishment, at our career: not a few, pressing forward with more courage, have missed footing, or leaped short; and now swim weltering in the Chaos-flood, some towards this shore, some towards that. To these also a helping hand should be held out; at least some word of encouragement be said.

Or, to speak without metaphor, with which mode of utterance Teufelsdröckh unhappily has somewhat infected us,— can it be hidden from the Editor that many a British Reader sits reading quite bewildered in head, and afflicted rather than instructed by the present Work? Yes, long ago has many a British Reader been, as now, demanding, with something like a snarl : Whereto does all this lead ; or what use is in it ?

In the way of replenishing thy purse, or otherwise aiding thy digestive faculty, O British Reader, it leads to nothing, and there is no use in it ; but rather the reverse, for it costs thee somewhat. Nevertheless, if through this unpromising Horngate, Teufelsdröckh, and we by means of him, have led thee into the true Land of Dreams; and through the Clothes-Screen, as through a magical *Pierre-Pertuis,* thou lookest, even for moments, into the region of the Wonderful, and seest and feelest that thy daily life is girt with Wonder, and based on Wonder, and thy very blankets and breeches are Miracles,— then art thou profited beyond money's worth ; and hast a thankfulness towards our Professor ; nay, perhaps in many a literary Tea-circle, wilt open thy kind lips, and audibly express that same.

Nay, farther, art not thou too perhaps by this time made aware that all Symbols are properly Clothes ; that all Forms whereby Spirit manifests itself to Sense, whether outwardly or in the imagination, are Clothes ; and thus not only the parchment Magna Charta, which a Tailor was nigh cutting into measures, but the Pomp and Authority of Law, the sacredness of Majesty, and all inferior Worships (Worthships) are properly a Vesture and Raiment ; and the Thirtynine Articles themselves are articles of wearing apparel (for the Religious Idea)? In which case, must it not also be admitted that this Science of Clothes is a high one, and may with infinitely deeper study on thy part yield richer fruit : that it takes scientific rank beside Codification, and Political Economy, and the Theory of the British Constitution ; nay, rather, from its prophetic height looks down on all these, as on so many weaving-shops and spinning-mills, where the Vestures which *it* has to fashion, and consecrate, and distribute, are, too often by haggard hungry operatives who see no farther than their nose, mechanically woven and spun ?

But omitting all this, much more all that concerns Natural

Supernaturalism, and indeed whatever has reference to the Ulterior or Transcendental Portion of the Science, or bears never so remotely on that promised Volume of the *Palingenesie der menschlichen Gesellschaft* (Newbirth of Society),—we humbly suggest that no province of Clothes-Philosophy, even the lowest, is without its direct value, but that innumerable inferences of a practical nature may be drawn therefrom. To say nothing of those pregnant considerations, ethical, political, symbolical, which crowd on the Clothes-Philosopher from the very threshold of his Science; nothing even of those 'architectural ideas' which, as we have seen, lurk at the bottom of all Modes, and will one day, better unfolding themselves, lead to important revolutions,—let us glance for a moment, and with the faintest light of Clothes-Philosophy, on what may be called the Habilatory Class of our fellow-men. Here too overloooking, where so much were to be looked on, the million spinners, weavers, fullers, dyers, washers, and wringers, that puddle and muddle in their dark recesses, to make us Clothes, and die that we may live,—let us but turn the reader's attention upon two small divisions of mankind, who, like moths, may be regarded as Cloth-animals, creatures that live, move and have their being in Cloth: we mean, Dandies and Tailors.

In regard to both which small divisions it may be asserted, without scruple, that the public feeling, unenlightened by Philosophy, is at fault; and even that the dictates of humanity are violated. As will perhaps abundantly appear to readers of the two following Chapters.

CHAPTER X.

THE DANDIACAL BODY.

First, touching Dandies, let us consider, with some scientific strictness, what a Dandy specially is. A Dandy is a Clothes-wearing man, a Man whose trade, office, and existence consists in the wearing of Clothes. Every faculty of his soul, spirit, purse, and person is heroically consecrated to this one object, the wearing of Clothes wisely and well: so that as others dress to live, he lives to dress. The all-importance of Clothes, which a German Professor, of unequalled learning and acumen, writes his enormous Volume to demonstrate, has sprung up in the intellect of the Dandy, without effort, like an instinct of genius ; he is inspired with Cloth, a Poet of Cloth. What Teufelsdröckh would call a ' Divine Idea of Cloth ' is born with him ; and this, like other such Ideas, will express itself outwardly, or wring his heart asunder with un-utterable throes.

But, like a generous, creative enthusiast, he fearlessly makes his Idea an Action ; shews himself, in peculiar guise, to mankind ; walks forth, a witness and living Martyr to the eternal Worth of Clothes. We call him a Poet : is not his body the (stuffed) parchment-skin whereon he writes, with cunning Huddersfield dyes, a Sonnet to his mistress' eyebrow ? Say, rather, an Epos, and *Clotha Virumque cano*, to the whole world, in Macaronic verses, which he that runs may read. Nay, if you grant, what seems to be admissible, that the Dandy has a thinking-principle in him, and some notions of Time and Space, is there not in this Life-devotedness to Cloth, in this so willing sacrifice of the Immortal to the Perishable, something (though in reverse order) of that blending and iden-tification of Eternity with Time, which, as we have seen, con-stitutes the Prophetic character ?

And now, for all this perennial Martyrdom, and Poesy, and even Prophecy, what is it that the Dandy asks in return ? Solely, we may say, that you would recognise his existence ; would admit him to be a living object ; or even failing this, a visual object, or thing that will reflect rays of light. Your silver or your gold (beyond what the niggardly Law has al-ready secured him) he solicits not ; simply the glance of your eyes. Understand his mystic significance, or altogether miss and misinterpret it ; do but look at him, and he is contented. May we not well cry shame on an ungrateful world, which refuses even this poor boon ; which will waste its optic faculty on dried Crocodiles, and Siamese Twins : and over the domestic wonderful wonder of wonders, a live Dandy, glance with hasty indifference, and a scarcely concealed contempt ! Him no

Zoologist classes among the Mammalia, no Anatomist dissects with care : when did we see any injected Preparation of the Dandy, in our Museums ; any specimen of him preserved in spirits? Lord Herringbone may dress himself in a snuff-brown suit, with snuff-brown shirt and shoes : it skills not ; the undiscerning public, occupied with grosser wants, passes by regardless on the other side.

The age of Curiosity, like that of Chivalry, is indeed, properly speaking, gone. Yet perhaps only gone to sleep : for here arises the Clothes-Philosophy to resuscitate, strangely enough, both the one and the other ! Should sound views of this Science come to prevail, the essential nature of the British Dandy, and the mystic significance that lies in him, cannot always remain hidden under laughable and lamentable hallucination. The following long Extract from Professor Teufelsdröckh may set the matter, if not in its true light, yet in the way towards such. It is to be regretted however that here, as so often elsewhere, the Professor's keen philosphic perspicacity is somewhat marred by a certain mixture of almost owlish purblindness, or else of some perverse, ineffectual, ironic tendency ; our readers shall judge which :

' In these distracted times,' writes he, ' when the Religious ' Principle, driven out of most Churches, either lies unseen ' in the hearts of good men, looking and longing, and silently ' working there towards some new Revelation ; or else wan- ' ders homeless over the world, like a disembodied soul seek- ' ing its terrestrial organisation,—into how many strange ' shapes, of Superstition and Fanaticism, does it not tentatively ' and errantly cast itself ! The higher Enthusiasm of man's ' nature is for the while without Exponent ; yet does it con- ' tinue indestructible, unweariedly active, and work blindly in ' the great chaotic deep : thus Sect after Sect, and Church ' after Church, bodies itself forth, and melts again into new ' metamorphosis.

' Chiefly is this observable in England, which, as the ' wealthiest and worst-instructed of European nations, offers ' precisely the elements (of Heat, namely, and of Darkness),

' in which such moon-calves and monstrosities are best gen-
' erated.   Among the newer Sects of that country, one of the
' most notable, and closely connected with our present sub-
' ject, is that of the *Dandies ;* concerning which, what little
' information I have been able to procure may fitly stand here.

   ' It is true, certain of the English Journalists, men generally
' without sense for the Religious Principle, or judgment for
' its manifestations, speak, in their brief enigmatic notices, as
' if this were perhaps rather a Secular Sect, and not a Re-
' ligious one : nevertheless, to the psychologic eye its devotional
' and even sacrificial character plainly enough reveals itself.
' Whether it belongs to the class of Fetish-worships, or of
' Hero-worships or Polytheisms, or to what other class, may
' in the present state of our intelligence remain undecided
' (*schweben*).   A certain touch of Manicheism, not indeed in
' the Gnostic shape, is discernible enough : also (for human
' Error walks in a cycle, and reappears at intervals) a not in-
' considerable resemblance to that Superstition of the Athos
' Monks, who by fasting from all nourishment, and looking
' intensely for a length of time into their own navels, came to
' discern therein the true Apocalypse of Nature, and Heaven
' Unveiled.   To my own surmise, it appears as if this Dan-
' diacal Sect were but a new modification, adapted to the new
' time, of that primeval Superstition, *Self-Worship ;* which
' Zerdusht, Quangfoutchee, Mohamed, and others, strove rather
' to subordinate and restrain than to eradicate ; and which
' only in the purer forms of Religion has been altogether re-
' jected.   Wherefore, if any one chooses to name it revived
' Ahrimanism, or a new figure of Demon-Worship, I have, so
' far as is yet visible, no objection.

   ' For the rest, these people, animated with the zeal of a new
' Sect, display courage and perseverance, and what force there
' is in man's nature, though never so enslaved.   They affect
' great purity and separatism ; distinguish themselves by a
' particular costume (whereof some notices were given in the
' earlier part of this Volume) ; likewise, so far as possible, by
' a particular speech (apparently some broken *Lingua-franca,*
' or English-French) ; and, on the whole, strive to maintain a

true Nazarene deportment, and keep themselves unspotted
' from the world.

' They have their Temples, whereof the chief, as the Jewish
'Temple did, stands in their metropolis ; and is named *Al-*
' *mack's,* a word of uncertain etymology. They worship prin-
' cipally by night ; and have their Highpriests and Highpriest-
' esses, who, however, do not continue for life. The rites, by
' some supposed to be of the Menadic sort, or perhaps with
' an Eleusinian or Cabiric character, are held strictly secret.
' Nor are Sacred Books wanting to the Sect ; these they call
' *Fashionable Novels :* however, the Canon is not completed,
' and some are canonical and others not.

' Of such Sacred Books I, not without expense, procured
' myself some samples ; and in hope of true insight, and with
' the zeal which beseems an Inquirer into Clothes, set to in-
' terpret and study them. But wholly to no purpose : that
' tough faculty of reading, for which the world will not refuse
' me credit, was here for the first time foiled and set at naught.
' In vain that I summoned my whole energies (*mich weidlich*
' *anstrengte*), and did my very utmost ; at the end of some
' short space, I was uniformly seized with not so much what I
' can call a drumming in my ears, as a kind of infinite, unsuf-
' ferable Jew's-harping and scrannel-piping there ; to which the
' frightfulest species of Magnetic Sleep soon supervened. And
' if I strove to shake this away, and absolutely would not yield,
' came a hitherto unfelt sensation, as of *Delirium Tremens,*
' and a melting into total deliquium : till at last, by order of
' the Doctor, dreading ruin to my whole intellectual and bodily
' faculties, and a general breaking-up of the constitution, I re-
' luctantly but determinedly forbore. Was there some miracle
' at work here ; like those Fire-balls, and supernal and infernal
' prodigies, which, in the case of the Jewish Mysteries, have
' also more than once scared back the Alien ? Be this as it
' may, such failure on my part, after best efforts, must excuse
' the imperfection of this sketch ; altogether incomplete, yet the
' completest I could give of a Sect too singular to be omitted.

' Loving my own life and senses as I do, no power shall in-
' duce me, as a private individual, to open another *Fashionable*

' *Novel.* But luckily, in this dilemma, comes a hand from the
' clouds ; whereby if not victory, deliverance is held out to
' me. Round one of those Book-packages, which the *Stillschwei-*
' *gen'sche Buchhandlung* is in the habit of importing from
' England, come, as is usual, various waste printed-sheets
' (*macalatur-blätter*), by way of interior wrappage : into these
' the Clothes-Philosopher, with a certain Mohamedan reverence
' even for waste paper, where curious knowledge will some-
' times hover, disdains not to cast his eye. Readers may judge
' of his astonishment when on such a defaced stray, sheet,
' probably the outcast fraction of some English Periodical,
' such as they name *Magazine,* appears something like a Dis-
' sertation on this very subject of *Fashionable Novels!* It sets
' out, indeed, chiefly from the Secular point of view ; directing
' itself, not without asperity, against some to me unknown in-
' dividual, named *Pelham,* who seems to be a Mystagogue, and
' leading Teacher and Preacher of the Sect ; so that, what in-
' deed otherwise was not to be expected in such a fugitive
' fragmentary sheet, the true secret, the Religious physiognomy
' and physiology of the Dandiacal Body, is nowise laid fully
' open there. Nevertheless, scattered lights do from time to
' time sparkle out, whereby I have endeavoured to profit.
' Nay, in one passage selected from the Prophecies, or Mythic
' Theogonies, or whatever they are (for the style seems very
' mixed) of this Mystagogue, I find what appears to be a Con-
' fession of Faith, or Whole Duty of Man, according to the
' tenets of that Sect. Which Confession or Whole Duty, there-
' fore, as proceeding from a source so authentic, I shall here
' arrange under Seven distinct Articles, and in very abridged
' shape lay before the German world ; therewith taking leave
' of this matter. Observe, also, that to avoid possibility of
' error, I, as far as may be, quote literally from the Original.'

' ARTICLES OF FAITH.

"1. Coats should have nothing of the triangle about them ;
' at the same time, wrinkles behind should be carefully avoided.

"2. The collar is a very important point · it should be low
' behind, and slightly rolled.

" 3. No license of fashion can allow a man of delicate taste
' to adopt the posterial luxuriance of a Hottentot.

" 4. There is safety in a swallow-tail.

" 5. The good sense of a gentleman is nowhere more finely
' developed than in his rings.

" 6. It is permitted to mankind, under certain restrictions,
' to wear white waistcoats.

" 7. The trowsers must be exceedingly tight across the
' hips."

' All which Propositions I, for the present, content myself
with modestly but peremptorily and irrevocably denying.

' In strange contrast with this Dandiacal Body stands
' another British Sect, originally, as I understand, of Ireland,
' where its chief seat still is ; but known also in the main
' Island, and indeed everywhere rapidly spreading. As this
' Sect has hitherto emitted no Canonical Books, it remains to
' me in the same state of obscurity as the Dandiacal, which
' has published Books that the unassisted human faculties are
' inadequate to read. The members appear to be designated
' by a considerable diversity of names, according to their
' various places of establishment : in England they are gener-
' ally called the *Drudge* Sect ; also, unphilosophically enough,
' the *White Negroes ;* and, chiefly in scorn by those of other
' communions, the *Ragged-Beggar* Sect. In Scotland, again,
' I find them entitled *Hallanshakers*, or the *Stook-of-Duds*
' Sect ; any individual communicant is named *Stook-of-Duds*
' (that is, Shock of Rags), in allusion, doubtless, to their pro-
' fessional Costume. While in Ireland, which, as mentioned,
' is their grand parent hive, they go by a perplexing multi-
' plicity of designations, such as *Bogtrotters, Redshanks, Ribbon-*
' *men, Cottiers, Peep-of-Day Boys, Babes in the Wood, Rockites,*
' *Poor-Slaves :* which last, however, seems to be the primary
' and generic name ; whereto, probably enough, the others
' are only subsidiary species, or slight varieties ; or, at most,
' propagated offsets from the parent stem, whose minute sub-
' divisions, and shades of difference, it were here loss of time
' to dwell on. Enough for us to understand, what seems in-

' dubitable, that the original Sect is that of the *Poor-Slaves* ;
' whose doctrines, practices, and fundamental characteristics
' pervade and animate the whole Body, howsoever denomi-
' nated or outwardly diversified.

'The precise speculative tenets of this Brotherhood : how the
' Universe, and the Man, and Man's Life, picture themselves
' to the mind of an Irish Poor-Slave ; with what feelings and
' opinions he looks forward on the Future, round on the
' Present, back on the Past, it were extremely difficult to
' specify. Something Monastic there appears to be in their
' Constitution : we find them bound by the two Monastic
' Vows of Poverty and Obedience ; which Vows, especially the
' former, it is said, they observe with great strictness ; nay, as
' I have understood it, they are pledged, and be it by any
' solemn Nazarene ordination or not, irrevocably consecrated
' thereto, even *before* birth. That the third Monastic Vow, of
' Chastity, is rigidly enforced among them, I find no ground
' to conjecture.

' Furthermore, they appear to imitate the Dandiacal Sect
' in their grand Principle of wearing a peculiar Costume. Of
' which Irish Poor-Slave Costume no description will indeed
' be found in the present Volume ; for this reason, that by
' the imperfect organ of Language it did not seem describable.
' Their raiment consists of innumerable skirts, lappets, and
' irregular wings, of all cloths and of all colours ; through the
' labyrinthic intricacies of which their bodies are introduced
' by some unknown process. If is fastened together by a
' multiplex combination of buttons, thrums, and skewers ; to
' which frequently is added a girdle of leather, of hempen or
' even of straw rope, round the loins. To straw rope, indeed,
' they seem partial, and often wear it by way of sandals. In
' head-dress they affect a certain freedom ; hats with partial
' brim, without crown, or with only a loose, hinged, or valve
' crown ; in the former case, they sometimes invert the hat,
' and wear it brim uppermost, like a University cap, with
' what view is unknown.

' The name Poor-Slaves, seems to indicate a Slavonic, Polish,
' or Russian origin : not so, however, the interior essence and

' spirit of their Superstition, which rather displays a Teutonic
' or Druidical character. One might fancy them worshippers
' of Hertha, or the Earth: for they dig and affectionately work
' continually in her bosom ; or else, shut up in private Ora-
' tories, meditate and manipulate the substances derived from
' her ; seldom looking up towards the Heavenly Luminaries,
' and then with comparative indifference. Like the Druids,
' on the other hand, they live in dark dwellings ; often even
' breaking their glass-windows, where they find such, and
' stuffing them up with pieces of raiment, or other opaque
' substances, till the fit obscurity is restored. Again, like all
' followers of Nature-Worship, they are liable to outbreakings
' of an enthusiasm rising to ferocity ; and burn men, if not in
' wicker idols, yet in sod cottages.

    'In respect of diet, they have also their observances. All
' Poor-Slaves are Rhizophagous (or Root-eaters) ; a few are
' Ichthyophagous, and use Salted Herrings: other animal food
' they abstain from ; except indeed, with perhaps some strange
' inverted fragment of a Brahminical feeling, such animals as
' die a natural death. Their universal sustenance is the root
' named Potato, cooked by fire alone ; and generally without
' condiment or relish of any kind, save an unknown condiment
' named *Point*, into the meaning of which I have vainly in-
' quired ; the victual *Potatoes-and-Point* not appearing, at least
' not with specific accuracy of description, in any European
' Cookery-Book whatever. For drink they use, with an almost
' epigrammatic counterpoise of taste, Milk, which is the mild-
' est of liquors, and *Potheen*, which is the fiercest. This latter
' I have tasted, as well as the English *Blue-Ruin*, and the Scotch
' *Whisky*, analogous fluids used by the Sect in those countries:
' it evidently contains some form of alcohol, in the highest state
' of concentration, though disguised with acrid oils : and is, on
' the whole, the most pungent substance known to me,—in-
' deed, a perfect liquid fire. In all their Religious Solemnities,
' Potheen is said to be an indispensable requisite, and largely
' consumed.

    ' An Irish Traveller, of perhaps common veracity, who pre-
' sents himself under the to me unmeaning title of *The late*

' *John Bernard,* offers the following sketch of a domestic estab-
' lishment, the inmates whereof, though such is not stated ex-
' pressly, appear to have been of that Faith.   Thereby shall
' my German readers now behold an Irish Poor-Slave, as it
' were with their own eyes ; and even see him at meat.   More-
' over, in the so precious waste-paper sheet, above mentioned,
' I have found some corresponding picture of a Dandiacal
' Household, painted by that same Dandiacal Mystagogue, or
' Theogonist: this also, by way of counterpart and contrast,
' the world shall look into.

    ' First, therefore, of the Poor-Slave, who appears likewise to
' have been a species of Innkeeper.   I quote from the original:
' " The furniture of this Caravansera consisted of a large iron
' Pot, two oaken Tables, two Benches, two Chairs, and a Pot-
' heen Noggin.   There was a Loft above (attainable by a lad-
' der), upon which the inmates slept ; and the space below was
' divided by a hurdle into two Apartments ; the one for their
' cow and pig, the other for themselves and guests.   On enter-
' ing the house we discovered the family, eleven in number,
' at dinner ; the father sitting at the top, the mother at bot-
' tom, the children on each side of a large oaken Board which
' was scooped out in the middle, like a Trough, to receive the
' contents of their Pot of Potatoes.   Little holes were cut at
' equal distance to contain Salt ; and a bowl of Milk stood on
' the table : all the luxuries of meat and beer, bread, knives,
' and dishes were dispensed with."   The Poor-Slave himself
' our Traveller found, as he says, broad-backed, black-browed,
' of great personal strength, and mouth from ear to ear.   His
' Wife was a sun-browned but well-featured woman ; and his
' young ones, bare and chubby, had the appetite of ravens.
' Of their Philosophical, or Religious tenets or observances,
' no notice or hint.

    ' But now, secondly, of the Dandiacal Household ; in which,
' truly, that often-mentioned Mystagogue and inspired Pen-
' man himself has his abode : " A Dressing-room splendidly
' furnished ; violet-coloured curtains, chairs and ottomans of
' the same hue.   Two full-length Mirrors are placed, one on
each side of a table, which supports the luxuries of the Toi-

'let. Several Bottles of Perfumes, arranged in a peculiar
'fashion, stand upon a smaller table of mother-of-pearl: op-
'posite to these are placed the appurtenances of Lavation
'richly wrought in frosted silver. A Wardrobe of Buhl is on
'the left; the doors of which being partly open discover a
'profusion of Clothes; Shoes of a singularly small size monop-
'olise the lower shelves. Fronting the wardrobe a door ajar
'gives some slight glimpse of a Bath-room. Folding-doors
'in the back-ground.—Enter the Author," our Theogonist in
'person, "obsequiously preceded by a French Valet, in white
'silk Jacket and cambric Apron."

'Such are the two Sects which, at this moment, divide the
'more unsettled portion of the British People; and agitate,
'that ever-vexed country. To the eye of the political Seer,
'their mutual relation, pregnant with the elements of discord
'and hostility, is far from consoling. These two principles of
'Dandiacal Self-worship or Demon-worship, and Poor-Slavish
'or Drudgical Earth-worship, or whatever that same Drudgism
'may be, do as yet indeed manifest themselves under distant
'and nowise considerable shapes: nevertheless, in their roots
'and subterranean ramifications, they extend through the en-
'tire structure of Society, and work unweariedly in the secret
'depths of English national Existence; striving to separate and
'isolate it into two contradictory, uncommunicating masses.

'In numbers, and even individual strength, the Poor-Slaves
'or Drudges, it would seem, are hourly increasing. The
'Dandiacal, again, is by nature no proselytising Sect; but it
'boasts of great hereditary resources, and is strong by union;
'whereas the Drudges, split into parties, have as yet no
'rallying-point; or at best, only co-operate by means of par-
'tial secret affiliations. If, indeed, there were to arise a *Com-*
'*munion of Drudges,* as there is already a Communion of
'Saints, what strangest effects would follow therefrom!
'Dandyism as yet affects to looks down on Drudgism: but
'perhaps the hour of trial, when it will be practically seen
'which ought to look down, and which up, is not so distant.

'To me it seems probable that the two Sects will one day

15

' part England between them ; each recruiting itself from the
' intermediate ranks, till there be none left to enlist on
' either side.   Those Dandiacal Manicheans, with the host of
' Dandyising Christians, will form one body : the Drudges,
' gathering round them whosoever is Drudgical, be he Chris-
' tian or Infidel Pagan ; sweeping up likewise all manner of
' Utilitarians, Radicals, refractory Potwalloppers, and so forth,
' into their general mass, will form another.   I could liken
' Dandyism and Drudgism to two bottomless boiling Whirl-
' pools that had broken out on opposite quarters of the firm
' land : as yet they appear only disquieted, foolishly bubbling
' wells, which man's art might cover in ; yet mark them, their
' diameter is daily widening ; they are hollow Cones that boil
' up from the infinite Deep, over which your firm land is but
' a thin crust or rind !   Thus daily is the intermediate land
' crumbling in, daily the empire of the two Buchan-Bullers
' extending ; till now there is but a foot-plank, a mere film of
' Land between them ; this too is washed away ; and then—
' we have the true Hell of Waters, and Noah's Deluge is out-
' deluged !

    ' Or better, I might call them two boundless, and indeed
' unexampled Electric Machines (turned by the "Machinery
' of Society"), with batteries of opposite quality; Drudgism
' the Negative, Dandyism the Positive : one attracts hourly
' towards it and appropriates all the Positive Electricity of the
' Nation (namely, the Money thereof) ; the other is equally
' busy with the Negative (that is to say the Hunger), which is
' equally potent.   Hitherto you see only partial transient
' sparkles and sputters ; but wait a little, till the entire nation
' is in an electric state ; till your whole vital Electricity, no
' longer healthfully Neutral, is cut into two isolated portions
' of Positive and Negative (of Money and of Hunger) ; and
' stands there bottled up in two World-Batteries !   The stir-
' ring of a child's finger brings the two together ; and then—
' What then ?   The Earth is but shivered into impalpable
' smoke by that Doom's-thunderpeal ; the Sun misses one of
' his Planets in Space, and thenceforth there are no eclipses of
' the Moon.—Or better still, I might liken'——

Oh! enough, enough of likenings and similitudes; in excess of which, truly, it is hard to say whether Teufelsdröckh or ourselves sin the more.

We have often blamed him for a habit of wire-drawing and over-refining ; from of old we have been familiar with his tendency to Mysticism and Religiosity, whereby in every thing he was still scenting out Religion : but never perhaps did these amaurosis-suffusions so cloud and distort his otherwise most piercing vision, as in this of the *Dandiacal Body!* Or was there something of intended satire ; is the Professor and Seer not quite the blinkard he affects to be? Of an ordinary mortal we should have decisively answered in the affirmative ; but with a Tuefelsdröckh there ever hovers some shade of doubt. In the meanwhile, if satire were actually intended, the case is little better. There are not wanting men who will answer : Does your Professor take us for simpletons? His irony has overshot itself ; we see through it, and perhaps through him.

CHAPTER XI.

TAILORS.

Thus, however, has our first Practical Inference from the Clothes-Philosophy, that which respects Dandies, been sufficiently drawn ; and we come now to the second, concerning Tailors. On this latter our opinion happily quite coincides with that of Teufelsdröckh himself, as expressed in the concluding page of his Volume ; to whom therefore we willingly give place. Let him speak his own last words, in his own way :

'Upwards of a century,' says he, 'must elapse, and still the 'bleeding fight of Freedom be fought, whoso is noblest per- 'ishing in the van, and thrones be hurled on altars like Pelion 'on Ossa, and the Moloch of Iniquity have his victims, and 'the Michael of Justice his martyrs, before Tailors can be ad- 'mitted to their true prerogatives of manhood, and this last 'wound of suffering Humanity be closed.

'If aught in the history of the world's blindness could sur
'prise us, here might we indeed pause and wonder. An idea
'has gone abroad, and fixed itself down into a wide-spreading
'rooted error, that Tailors are a distinct species in Physiology,
'not Men, but fractional Parts of a Man. Call any one a
'*Schneider* (Cutter, Tailor), is it not, in our dislocated, hood-
'winked, and indeed delirious condition of Society, equivalent
'to defying his perpetual fellest enmity? The epithet
'*Schneidermässig* (Tailor-like) betokens an otherwise unap-
'proachable degree of pusillanimity: we introduce a *Tailor's*
'*Melancholy*, more opprobrious than any Leprosy, into our
'Books of Medicine; and fable I know not what of his genera-
'ting it by living on Cabbage. Why should I speak of Hans
'Sachs (himself a Shoemaker, or kind of Leather Tailor), with
'his *Schneider mit dem Panier?* Why of Shakspeare, in his
'*Taming of the Shrew*, and elsewhere? Does it not stand on
'record that the English Queen Elizabeth, receiving a depu-
'tation of Eighteen Tailors, addressed them with a "Good
'morning, gentlemen both!" Did not the same virago boast
'that she had a Cavalry Regiment, whereof neither horse nor
'man could be injured: her Regiment, namely, of Tailors on
'Mares? Thus everywhere is the falsehood taken for granted,
'and acted on as an indisputable fact.

'Nevertheless, need I put the question to any Physiologist,
'whether it is disputable or not? Seems it not at least pre-
'sumable, that, under his Clothes, the Tailor has bones, and
'viscera, and other muscles than the sartorius? Which
'function of manhood is the Tailor not conjectured to per-
'form? Can he not arrest for debt? Is he not in most
'countries a tax-paying animal?

'To no reader of this Volume can it be doubtful which
'conviction is mine. Nay, if the fruit of these long vigils,
'and almost preternatural Inquiries is not to perish utterly,
'the world will have approximated towards a higher Truth;
'and the doctrine, which Swift, with the keen forecast of
'genius, dimly anticipated, will stand revealed in clear light:
'that the Tailor is not only a Man, but something of a Crea-
'tor or Divinity. Of Franklin it was said, that "he snatched

' the Thunder from Heaven and the Sceptre from Kings:"
' but which is greater, I would ask, he that lends, or he that
' snatches? For, looking away from individual cases, and
' how a Man is by the Tailor new-created into a Nobleman,
' and clothed not only with Wool but with Dignity and
' a Mystic Dominion,—is not the fair fabric of Society it-
' self, with all its royal mantles and pontifical stoles, whereby,
' from nakedness and dismemberment, we are organised into
' Polities, into nations, and a whole co-operating Mankind,
' the creation, as has here been often irrefragably evinced,
' of the Tailor alone?—What too are all Poets, and moral
' Teachers, but a species of Metaphorical Tailors? Touching
' which high Guild the greatest living Guild-brother has tri-
' umphantly asked us : " Nay, if thou wilt have it, who but
' the Poet first made Gods for men ; brought them down to
' us ; and raised us up to them ?"

' And this is he, whom sitting downcast, on the hard basis
' of his Shopboard, the world treats with contumely, as the
' ninth part of a man! Look up, thou much-injured one,
' look up with the kindling eye of hope, and prophetic bod-
' ings of a nobler better time. Too long hast thou sat there,
' on crossed legs, wearing thy ancle-joints to horn ; like some
' sacred Anchorite, or Catholic Fakir, doing penance, drawing
' down Heaven's richest blessings, for a world that scoffed at
' thee. Be of hope ! Already streaks of blue peer through
' our clouds; the thick gloom of Ignorance is rolling asunder,
' and it will be day. Mankind will repay with interest their
' long-accumulated debt : the Anchorite that was scoffed at
' will be worshipped ; the Fraction will become not an In-
' teger only, but a Square and Cube. With astonishment the
' world will recognise that the Tailor is its Hierophant, and
' Hierarch, or even its God.

' As I stood in the Mosque of St. Sophia, and looked upon
' these Four-and-Twenty Tailors, sewing and embroidering
' that rich Cloth, which the Sultan sends yearly for the Caaba
' of Mecca, I thought within myself : How many other Un-
' holies has your covering Art made holy, besides this Arabian
' Whinstone !

' Still more touching was it when, turning the corner of a
' lane, in the Scottish Town of Edinburgh, I came upon a
' Signpost, whereon stood written that such and such a one
' was " Breeches-Maker to his Majesty ; " and stood painted
' the Effigies of a Pair of Leather Breeches, and between the
' knees these memorable words, Sɪᴄ ɪᴛᴜʀ ᴀᴅ ᴀsᴛʀᴀ. Was not
' this the martyr prison-speech of a Tailor sighing indeed in
' bonds, yet sighing towards deliverance ; and prophetically
' appealing to a better day ? A day of justice, when the
' worth of Breeches would be revealed to man, and the
' Scissors become for ever venerable.

' Neither, perhaps, may I now say, has his appeal been alto-
' gether in vain. It was in this high moment, when the soul,
' rent as it were, and shed asunder, is open to inspiring in-
' fluence, that I first conceived this Work on Clothes : the
' greatest I can ever hope to do ; which has already, after
' long retardations, occupied, and will yet occupy, so large a
' section of my Life ; and of which the Primary and simpler
' Portion may here find its conclusion.'

CHAPTER XII.

FAREWELL.

So have we endeavoured, from the enormous, amorphous
Plum-pudding, more like a Scottish Haggis, which Herr Teufelsdröckh had kneaded for his fellow mortals, to pick out the
choicest Plums, and present them separately on a cover of
our own. A laborious, perhaps a thankless enterprise ; in
which, however, something of hope has occasionally cheered
us, and of which we can now wash our hands not altogether
without satisfaction. If hereby, though in barbaric wise,
some morsel of spiritual nourishment have been added to the
scanty ration of our beloved British world, what nobler recom-
pense could the Editor desire? If it prove otherwise, why
should he murmur ? Was not this a Task which Destiny, in
any case, had appointed him ; which having now done with,
he sees his general Day's-work so much the lighter, so much
the shorter ?

Of Professor Teufelsdröckh it seems impossible to take leave without a mingled feeling of astonishment, gratitude and disapproval. Who will not regret that talents, which might have profited in the higher walks of Philosophy, or in Art itself, have been so much devoted to a rummaging among lumber-rooms ; nay, too often to a scraping in kennels, where lost rings and diamond-necklaces are nowise the sole con-quests? Regret is unavoidable ; yet censure were loss of time. To cure him of his mad humours British Criticism would essay in vain : enough for her if she can, by vigilance, prevent the spreading of such among ourselves. What a re-sult, should this piebald, entangled, hyper-metaphorical style of writing, not to say of thinking, become general among our Literary men ! As it might so easily do. Thus has not the Editor himself, working over Teufelsdröckh's German, lost much of his own English purity ? Even as the smaller whirl-pool is sucked into the larger, and made to whirl along with it, so has the lesser mind, in this instance, been forced to be-come portion of the greater, and, like it, see all things figura-tively : which habit time and assiduous effort will be needed to eradicate.

Nevertheless, wayward as our Professor shews himself, is there any reader that can part with him in declared enmity? Let us confess, there is that in the wild, much-suffering, much-inflicting man, which almost attaches us. His attitude, we will hope and believe, is that of a man who had said to Cant, Begone ; and to Dilettantism, Here thou canst not be : and to Truth, Be thou in place of all to me : a man who had manfully defied the 'Time-Prince,' or Devil, to his face ; nay, perhaps, Hannibal-like, was mysteriously consecrated from birth to that warfare, and now stood minded to wage the same, by all weapons, in all places, at all times. In such a cause, any soldier, were he but a Polack Scytheman, shall be welcome.

Still the question returns on us : How could a man occa-sionally of keen insight, not without keen sense of propriety, who had real Thoughts to communicate, resolve to emit them in a shape bordering so closely on the absurd? Which ques-tion he were wiser than the present Editor who should satis factorily answer. Our conjecture has sometimes been, that perhaps Necessity as well as Choice was concerned in it. Seems it not conceivable that, in a Life like our Professor's, where so much bountifully given by Nature had in Practice failed and misgone, Literature also would never rightly prosper : that striving with his characteristic vehemence to paint this and the other Picture, and ever without success, he at last desperately dashes his sponge, full of all colours, against the canvass, to try whether it will paint Foam ? With all his stillness, there were perhaps in Teufelsdröckh desperation enough for this.

A second conjecture we hazard with even less warranty. It is that Teufelsdröckh is not without some touch of the universal feeling, a wish to proselytise. How often already have we paused, uncertain whether the basis of this so enigmatic nature were really Stoicism and Despair, or Love and Hope only seared into the figure of these ! Remarkable, moreover, is this saying of his : 'How were Friendship possible ? In ' mutual devotedness to the Good and True : otherwise im-' possible ; except as Armed Neutrality, or hollow Commercial ' League. A man, be the Heavens ever praised, is sufficient ' for himself ; yet were ten men, united in Love, capable of ' being and of doing what ten thousand singly would fail in. ' Infinite is the help man can yield to man.' And now in conjunction therewith consider this other : ' It is the Night of ' the World, and still long till it be Day : we wander amid the ' glimmer of smoking ruins, and the Sun and the Stars of ' Heaven are as if blotted out for a season ; and two immeas-' urable Fantoms, HYPOCRISY and ATHEISM, with the Gowle, ' SENSUALITY, stalk abroad over the Earth, and call it theirs : ' well at ease are the Sleepers for whom Existence is a shallow ' Dream.'

But what of the awestruck Wakeful who find it a Reality ? Should not these unite ; since even an authentic Spectre is not visible to Two ?—In which case were this enormous Clothes-Volume properly an enormous Pitchpan, which our Teufelsdröckh in his lone watchtower had kindled, that it might flame far and wide through the Night, and many a disconsolately wandering spirit be guided thither to a Brother's bosom !—We say as before, with all his malign Indifference, who knows what mad Hopes this man may harbour ?

Meanwhile there is one fact to be stated here, which harmonises ill with such conjecture ; and, indeed, were Teufelsdröckh made like other men, might as good as altogether subvert it. Namely, that while the Beacon-fire blazed its brightest, the Watchman had quitted it ; that no pilgrim could now ask him : Watchman, what of the Night? Professor Teufelsdröckh, be it known, is no longer visibly present at Weissnichtwo, but again to all appearance lost in Space ! Some time ago, the Hofrath Heuschrecke was pleased to favor us with another copious Epistle ; wherein much is said about the 'Population-Institute ;' much repeated in praise of the Paperbag Documents, the hieroglyphic nature of which our Hofrath still seems not to have surmised ; and, lastly, the strangest occurrence communicated, to us for the first time, in the following paragraph :

'*Ew. Wohlgebohren* will have seen, from the public Prints, 'with what affectionate and hitherto fruitless solicitude Weiss- 'nichtwo regards the disappearance of her Sage. Might 'but the united voice of Germany prevail on him to return ; 'nay, could we but so much as elucidate for ourselves by 'what mystery he went away ! But, alas, old Leischen ex- 'periences or affects the profoundest deafness, the profound- 'est ignorance : in the Wahngasse all lies swept, silent, sealed 'up ; the Privy Council itself can hitherto elicit no answer.

'It had been remarked that while the agitating news of 'those Parisian Three Days flew from mouth to mouth, and 'dinned every ear in Weissnichtwo, Herr Teufelsdröckh was 'not known, at the *Ganse* or elsewhere, to have spoken, for a 'whole week, any syllable except once these three : *Es geht an* '(It is beginning). Shortly after, as *Ew. Wohlgebohren* knows, 'was the public tranquillity here, as in Berlin, threatened by 'a Sedition of the Tailors. For did there want Evil-wishers, 'or perhaps mere desperate Alarmist, who asserted that the 'closing Chapter of the Clothes-Volume was to blame. In 'this appalling crisis, the serenity of our Philosopher was

' indescribable : nay, perhaps, through one humble índí
' vidual, something thereof might pass into the *Rath* (Council}
' itself, and so contribute to the country's deliverance. The
' Tailors are now entirely pacificated.—To neither of these
' two incidents can I attribute our loss : yet still comes there
' the shadow of a suspicion out of Paris and its Politics. For
' example, when the *Saint-Simonian Society* transmitted its
' Propositions hither, and the whole *Ganse* was one vast cackle
' of laughter, lamentation, and astonishment, our Sage sat
' mute ; and at the end of the third evening, said merely :
' "Here also are men who have discovered, not without
' amazement, that Man is still Man ; of which high, long-for-
' gotten Truth you already see them make a false application."
' Since then, as has been ascertained by examination of the
' Post-Director, there passed at least one Letter with its
' Answer between the Messieurs Bazard-Enfantin and our
' Professor himself ; of what tenor can now only be con-
' jectured. On the fifth night following, he was seen for the
' last time !

  ' Has this invaluable man, so obnoxious to most of the
' hostile Sects that convulse our Era, been spirited away by
' certain of their emissaries ; or did he go forth voluntarily to
' their headquarters to confer with them, and confront them ?
' Reason we have, at least of a negative sort, to believe the
' Lost still living : our widowed heart also whispers that ere
' long he will himself give a sign. Otherwise, indeed, must
' his archives, one day, be opened by Authority ; where much,
' perhaps the *Palingenesie* itself, is thought to be reposited.'

Thus far the Hofrath ; who vanishes, as is his wont, too like
an Ignis Fatuus, leaving the dark still darker.

So that Teufelsdröckh's public History were not done, then,
or reduced to an even, unromantic tenor ; nay, perhaps, the
better part thereof were only beginning? We stand in a
region of conjectures, where substance has melted into
shadow, and one cannot be distinguished from the other.
May Time, which solves or suppresses all problems, throw
glad light on this also ! Our own private conjecture, now

amounting almost to certainty, is that, safe-moored in some stillest obscurity, not to lie always still, Teufelsdröckh is actually in London !

Here, however, can the present Editor, with an ambrosial joy as of over-weariness falling into sleep, lay down his pen. Well does he know, if human testimony be worth aught, that to innumerable British readers likewise, this is a satisfying consummation ; that innumerable British readers consider him, during these current months, but as an uneasy interruption to their ways of thought and digestion ; and indicate so much, not without a certain irritancy and even spoken invective. For which, as for other mercies, ought he not to thank the Upper Powers? To one and all of you, O irritated readers, he, with outstretched arms and open heart, will wave a kind farewell. Thou too, miraculous Entity, who namest thyself YORKE and OLIVER, and with thy vivacities and genialities, with thy all too Irish mirth and madness, and odour of palled punch, makest such strange work, farewell ; long as thou canst, fare-*well !* Have we not, in the course of Eternity, travelled some months of our Life-journey in partial sight of one another ; have we not existed together, though in a state of quarrel ?